The Bride Stands Alone

by

Jackie Ullerich

Brighton Publishing LLC
501 W. Ray Road
Suite 4
Chandler, AZ 85225
www.BrightonPublishing.com

The Bride Stands Alone

by

Jackie Ullerich

Brighton Publishing LLC
501 W. Ray Road, Suite 4
Chandler, AZ 85225
www.BrightonPublishing.com

Copyright © 2012

ISBN13: 978-1-936587-69-8
ISBN10: 1-936-58769-6

First Edition

Printed in the United States of America
Cover Design by Tom Rodriquez

All rights reserved. No part of this publication may be reproduced or transmitted in any form or by any means, electronic or mechanical, including photocopy, recording, or any information storage retrieval system, without permission in writing from the copyright owner.

◈ *Prologue* ◈

Acapulco, Mexico
February 23, 2005

*K*elly awakened to the glare of sunlight through closed lids. The brightness jarred, an assault on the senses, but she couldn't bring herself to turn on her side or even to avert her face. It wasn't worth the effort.

Through the fog of semi consciousness, she reached for Larry, but he wasn't beside her. This small exertion cost her, bringing on a wave of nausea, a throbbing at her temples.

Kelly opened her eyes, quickly shut them, and then peered with one eye. A man stood with his back to her at the window. He was a blur, but she could tell he wasn't Larry because he wasn't tall enough to be her husband.

She blinked several times, and then sat up, her vision clearing as awareness flooded over her. "Steve?" Her voice came out a croak.

He hurried to her side. *He looks terrible,* she thought, *spent, with reddened eyes, a grayish tinge to his skin.*

Kelly pressed her stepfather's hand. "I'm glad you're here." She looked beyond him. "Mom? Is she with you?"

"Honey, your mother wanted to come, but rightly or wrongly, I persuaded Nadine to wait for you at home."

Kelly nodded. It was the right decision. "Steve, is there any news?"

"Nothing yet; however another search is under way."

She took a shaky breath. "I remember now, the doctor arriving, giving me a shot."

"I thought it best to let you sleep, but as soon as we hear something, we can be on our way. Don't you think that's best?"

"Yes, oh yes." She broke into sobs. "Why would I stay? This was our honeymoon, for God's sake."

He sat on the bed next to her and cradled her in his arms. "Kelly, dear one, I'm so sorry. You can't imagine how your mother and I grieve for you. We want you back with us at the Victorian for however long you want to stay."

She had come full circle. Now it was back to Pacific Heights, San Francisco's haven for the crème de la crème, and to the Victorian where she and Larry had met.

Full circle.

She clenched her fists and closed her eyes against the stream of tears. She didn't want endings; she wanted beginnings. She wanted to go back to the beginning.

✍ *Chapter One* ❧

San Francisco
August 2004

The encounter at the breakfast table between mother and daughter began when Nadine Hanson thrust aside the society pages of the *San Francisco Chronicle*.

"Not one word about tonight's fundraiser. Steve will be furious."

Kelly stifled a giggle. "*Who* are we calling furious?"

"With Steve's banking and political connections, you'd think that opening our home to honor Senator Lewis would garner a mention at the very least. The man is running for governor, for God's sake."

"Steve doesn't need affirmation from some sycophantic social hotshot." Kelly pushed her plate aside. "I don't understand how you can be upset over something so trivial."

Nadine started to respond, and then waited as Kwon, the houseboy, removed their plates. When he was out of earshot she said, "Listen, Miss Smarty Pants, I can tell you Vanessa would leap to my side to support me on this issue."

"Too bad you're stuck with me."

"Only for this week, and it's gone by way too fast. As for your sister, how she can live in that godforsaken place is beyond me."

"Vanessa says she loves Turkey. You've read her letters."

"It's not the country she loves; it's Gordon she's gaga about. Leave it to the military to send her husband to the Middle East, of all places. But back to Gordon, he's simply too handsome for his own good. I predict trouble ahead."

"Why are you so negative? Mom, be happy for Vanessa."

Nadine shrugged, started to reach for her cigarettes, and then held back. "On a happier note, let's talk about this evening. What do you plan to wear? Remember, it's a dressy affair."

"I know the proper attire for a cocktail party. Living in Los Angeles hasn't turned me into a rustic rube. However . . ."

"What?" Nadine frowned. "Do I want to hear this?"

"I'm afraid I'm going to have to pass on tonight."

Nadine, eyes widened, mouth agape, sat mute.

The silence was more intimidating than a burst of invective. Now Kelly waited as her mother, her movements deliberate, reached for her cigarettes, lit up, inhaled deeply, and then followed the trail of expelled smoke with her gaze.

She turned to Kelly. "I can understand your wanting to get back at me because of some perceived injustice on my part, but why punish Steve? Think of how hurt he would be if you failed to show."

"Mother, this isn't about you or Steve. It's about me. I detest fundraisers—the phoniness, smiling 'til your jaw hurts, having to dance attendance on prospective donors, yet not resort to pandering. It's all a sham."

"But think of the challenge to your acting skills." Steve Hanson had quietly moved into the room.

Nadine stubbed out her cigarette in a display of frustration. "Steve, talk to her."

"Sorry," Kelly said. "I guess I came on a bit strong. I don't mean to impose my views"—she turned to Nadine—"but it does seem to run in the family."

Steve glanced at his watch. "I'll have to make this brief, but let me assure you, Kelly, I won't be the least bit offended if you want to skip tonight. But having said that, I'd be mighty proud to show you off."

"Let me think a minute?" Oh, shoot, it might be fun to assume a role in what should be the theater of the absurd, her stage the Victorian great room.

She could picture herself posed beneath the huge crystal chandelier, the centerpiece for a setting where Persian rugs competed

4

with Italian marble floors, where antique Turkish brass and glass sculptures provided texture for contemporary furnishings.

As for her role amid all this opulence and glitter? Who knows? She'd simply have to wing it. If she attended.

"Thank you for being so understanding," she said to Steve. "I'm still not sure. The debate rages on."

"Take all the time you need."

After Steve left the room, Nadine turned to her daughter. "For heaven's sake, Kelly, this isn't a decision that's going to affect the rest of your life. Come and enjoy the party." She smiled. "You may be surprised at what a great time you'll have."

Kelly had made her way toward the center of the great room, staying long enough to accept a glass of champagne from a passing waiter before retreating from clusters of elegantly attired guests to a corner of the room. She stood now before the Gauguin that lorded over ferns and ficus. The painting, with its bold strokes and intense colors, was a provocative rendering of South Seas island life. It also provided an oasis among party pandemonium.

Her game plan was a fizzle, the 'great time' concept yet to materialize. She was pondering her next move when the fragrance of Joy perfume and a mellow, "There you are," brought her out of her reverie and face to face with Nadine.

Mother looks smashing, Kelly thought, svelte in a black faille cocktail suit, set off by small diamond drop earrings and a diamond and emerald broach.

"I sneaked out for a cigarette," Nadine said, her rings flashing as she gestured toward the back hallway. "Now tell me. Why were you hiding behind a potted plant?"

Kelly shrugged. "I was taking a short timeout."

"From what? Working to make yourself invisible? Kelly, I have eyes. The young men out there would be falling all over you if you gave them a chance. You do look lovely."

"Thank you. So do you." As Nadine's large violet eyes swept over her, Kelly waited for the inevitable *but.*

"As becoming as your dress is, I do think the color is a bit stark for you. Mind you, black can be stunning with auburn hair, but with your pale complexion, pastels or neutral shades would be far more suitable."

"Gosh, Mother, as if it mattered. These earnest young guys are much too busy making points with all the Powerful, Political Potentates to have eyes for me. Furthermore . . ." She paused, her attention drawn to a man talking to her stepfather. "Wow."

"Wow? What are you looking at?"

"The man standing with Steve. Who is that tall blond?"

Nadine glanced over her shoulder, and then turned, facing in the direction Kelly had indicated. "Larry somebody. Thompson? No, Townsend. I think they connected in L.A. at a Young Democrats meeting where Steve was guest speaker. I know Steve's spoken favorably of him."

"You're saying he's from L.A.?"

"Why don't you check him out? He is attractive, isn't he? If you like the rugged type. Oops. I see Steve signaling me."

Kelly followed her mother's progress as she made her way across the room to join her husband.

They formed a threesome: Steve, Nadine, and Larry Townsend. Kelly raised her glass to her lips. *It was time,* she decided, *to make it a foursome.*

After introductions and small talk about Larry and Kelly being fellow Angelinos, Kelly noted that the party, though still lively, was winding down. She wondered if Larry Townsend was booked on an evening flight back to L.A. Whatever his plans, she sensed they would meet again, that it was okay for her to take the initiative.

So. An invitation was in order. Perhaps he would like to drop by the Hollywood Playhouse?

"Your playhouse?" he asked, his eyes widening, a smile playing at the corners of his mouth.

"Not my playhouse," she said, sharing his amusement. "The

6

Hollywood Playhouse."

"Oh. Now I get it. You're an actress."

She was nodding slowly. "I am. I really am." She paused to take a sip of her drink, staring at him over the rim of her glass, enjoying his puzzled expression. "If I sound a little spooked, it's because I'm still not used to calling the theater my work place. Up until seven months ago, I reported daily to the classroom."

"Teacher or student?"

"I should have said in front of the classroom. High school English and drama."

Larry started to speak, but stopped and rolled his eyes in the direction of the piano. The music had escalated in volume, keeping pace with voices now raised in proportion to the number of cocktails consumed.

Kelly gestured toward the terrace doors. "Shall we?"

"By all means. Lead the way."

As they stepped outside, Kelly took in her breath, dazzled by the panoply of brilliance. She wondered at Larry's reaction. As much as a visitor might express admiration for the room they'd left, it was the view from the terrace that inspired an outpouring of eloquence or a hushed reverence. Straight ahead was San Francisco Bay, while to the left was the Golden Gate Bridge, and beyond that, the hills of Marin County.

"It's almost wickedly ostentatious, isn't it?" Kelly said. "However, we'd better enjoy the show while we can, because I think the fog is rolling in."

"It's truly a spectacular sight. I'm awed." He turned to her. "Did you grow up here?"

"No such luck. My mother didn't meet Steve until I was in my first year of college. Vanessa, my sister, was already married, so this wasn't exactly home. But I must say it's been a great place to visit."

"I think you're right," he said, "about the fog, I mean." He looked at his watch. "Tell you what. Let me check with Steve. I think I've pressed hands with all the right people, including Senator Lewis, so I see no reason to stay on." He placed his hand lightly on her shoulder.

"May I take you to dinner?"

"I'd like that."

"You can tell me about your playhouse." He smiled at her. "The Hollywood Playhouse?"

Returning his smile, she took his arm, leading them back to the terrace doors. "You may be sorry. According to my mother, I'm becoming a bit of a bore on that subject."

"I'll take my chances," he said.

Perhaps in heeding her mother's advice, Kelly was overly conscientious in her efforts to steer the conversation away from herself and the stage. It was Larry who guided them back to theater talk. Moreover, before the evening was over, he had confessed that he, too, shared her fascination for the theater, both as a spectator and as an occasional performer in local productions back in Phoenix.

She had to mask her surprise. Did he also write poetry and attend the symphony?

She wouldn't push her luck. One out of three was good enough for her.

Breakfast the next morning had been pleasant. Perhaps because of Steve's presence, Kelly's mother refrained from an all-out interrogation about her date with Larry, asking only if she had a good time, her smile just edging into smugness.

Now in the late afternoon, Kelly took stock of clothes, shoes, and bags strewn about her room and on top of the bed. Preparing for her return to Los Angeles had been preempted by reflecting on the events of the previous evening.

She recalled her mother's comment that a decision to attend the fundraiser wouldn't affect the rest of her life. But had it? What if she had stayed away? Then Kelly Myers wouldn't have met Larry Townsend. She felt a shiver of anticipation, a strong sense that something could ignite between them. *If* he called or even emailed her.

Kelly moved to the dresser to empty another drawer, and then was sidetracked as she looked into the mirror. She wondered if the old saying that opposites attract held any validity. Not that she was delicate, for she was stronger than she looked. But with her slender build, she presented a somewhat fragile appearance, while Larry, with his rugged good looks, could pose for the Marlboro Man, except that he was blond and blue-eyed and vastly more articulate than what she imagined to be the prototype for Big Country Man.

One thing was certain: She hadn't stopped thinking about Larry all day. He would be home by now. They might have shared the flight to L.A., but Kelly had promised her mother a full week in San Francisco.

A knock on the door erased her frown and she called out, "Come in."

"Hi, sweetheart." Steve Hanson hesitated in the doorway. "Maybe this isn't a good time?"

Kelly moved quickly to give her stepfather a hug. "Ignore the mess," she said, leading him to one of the wing chairs positioned alongside the fireplace. Removing her jewelry case from the companion chair, she plopped down and forged a smile. "With all that's in store for tomorrow, I thought I'd better get my act together before cocktails, dinner, and the theater."

He laughed. "Sounds like a heavy evening when you put it that way. Incidentally, I'm going to have to part from all of you after cocktails. I need to get together with Senator Lewis one last time before he leaves for Sacramento, so we'll probably have to make do with room service."

"I guess that's not so bad when you consider he's at the Fairmont. But I'm disappointed."

"There'll be other times."

"I would hope so." She paused. "There's something I've wanted to say for some time."

He raised his hand in a go-ahead gesture. "I'm listening."

"Well. Your stature in the world of banking and politics can't be questioned. But Steve, you're also a caring and considerate man and the best thing ever to have happened to my mother."

Head bowed, he sat quietly for a moment, and then met her gaze, his eyes glistening. "And you, your mother, and Vanessa have touched me in ways I've never dreamed possible."

"Oh, Steve, we've all benefitted. But, we'd better not say more, or we'll be reaching for our hankies."

"How true. Now, on a less emotional note, I must say you made a great impression last evening."

"Really?"

"You sound doubtful."

"Let's just say I wasn't part of the mission. But I had fun—well, some fun—as an observer." She paused. "Actually, the evening turned out better than I expected."

"Is that so?" Steve's gray eyes widened in a semblance of innocence.

"All right, you know Larry Townsend and I went to dinner. I understand you two met at a Young Democrats meeting in Los Angeles."

Steve nodded. "I'm always on the lookout for intelligent, energetic young people. Larry met those qualifications. What's more, he's physically impressive. I've found prospective donors are drawn to attractive men and women."

"So you obviously approve of him."

"Yes, I have the highest regard for Larry."

"For bringing in the money. What do you know about him personally?"

He looked pensive, even troubled, and he didn't answer right away.

"Steve, is something wrong?"

"You mean about Larry? No. At least not to my knowledge. If I seem a little hesitant, it's because I sense you may have a serious interest in the man. Which is fine."

"So?"

"Take your time. Get to know him, that's all. Just don't rush into things." Steve paused as if he had more to add about Larry, but then had second thoughts. He said simply, "Well, I'm going to move on so you can finish your packing."

She walked him to the door.

"Come back soon, Kelly."

They hugged, and she threw him a kiss as he headed for the master suite down the hall. She watched him for a moment before shutting her door. Was he really close to sixty? True, he was quite gray, but he moved like a young man, and if there were any bulges, only his tailor and Nadine knew for sure. For a moment she felt envious of her mother. It was a twinge of a thought that quickly passed.

With renewed energy, Kelly tore into her packing. She wished she could delete tonight and tomorrow and simply head on home. She ached to start the fall production. Also, Larry Townsend had said he would be in touch.

The thought of seeing Larry again gave her pause. She had been instantly attracted to him and captivated by his easy charm. Now she questioned if there was a downside. She also wondered how he felt about her.

Dusk had filled the room, settling over her like wisps of doubt. She brushed them aside with the flip of a switch, the glow from her bedside lamp banishing gloom and uncertainty.

Beginnings. She loved beginnings, the thrill of the unknown, with its element of risk.

She smiled. Better make that an acceptable risk.

Chapter Two

t the end of a long day, Larry Townsend looked forward to returning to his small home in the Hollywood Hills, but not, as it turned out, to late afternoon heat that had turned muggy and oppressive. Worse, his house was uncomfortably close and stuffy.

Correction. His house was hot, as in miserably hot, making it imperative he open windows and create a cross-draft with an open door. It was simply one of those days where even a hillside location dotted with shade trees provided scant relief.

After retiring his traveling clothes for shorts and a tank top, Larry carried a beer from his kitchen to his deck and settled into a lounge chair.

He gazed at the horizon, enjoying incredibly brilliant orange-red streaks slashed across a canvas of muted day tones. Light would prevail for a while, but already he could detect tentative glimmerings of neon and street lights. Hollywood Boulevard and the Sunset Strip beyond were gearing up for the nightly razzle-dazzle.

He tasted his beer and thought how good it was to be home.

The past few days of meetings, committee conferences and working dinners, culminating with the cocktail party for State Senator John Lewis, had proved a stimulating and interesting diversion from his usual routine, but now it was time to direct his full attention to Townsend Construction.

Beer in hand, Larry moved to the railing that defined the perimeters of his property. He had been intrigued by the variance in his surroundings, rustic cottages sharing space with more pretentious properties, all enhanced by eucalyptus and fruit bearing trees. The view was what sold him on the house. But he was beginning to recognize a downside as well: that his place was small, that it would be stark for a woman.

Whoa. Back up. One beer and he was thinking domestic bliss? He shook his head. No way. Not in the cards for him. Or so he had always believed.

His thoughts turned to Kelly. She'd seemed a little quiet for him at first, not really his type, which ran more to curvy and cute. But she had beautiful dark hair—maybe more of an auburn shade—framing a flawless creamy complexion, and her large hazel eyes had focused on him, not on a space beyond his ear. He thought it refreshing to be around a woman who was somewhat reserved, a break from the high-voltage types he often fancied.

He thought back to their conversation about the theater. When he'd mentioned his stage experience, Kelly reacted with great interest, suggesting he try out for a role in their fall production. A role, she insisted, that could have been written expressly for him.

In the waning light, Larry shivered a little as a night breeze tickled his bare shoulders. He questioned if he had the time or energy to take on another project. He wasn't sure about auditioning, but he was positive he was going to show up at the Hollywood Playhouse.

With that, he finished his drink and started toward the kitchen, hurrying now as he realized his phone was ringing.

Too late, Larry stared at the now-silent wall phone. How long had the darn thing been ringing? He shrugged and turned away, his mind more on food than missed calls.

The lineup of packaged dinners that crowded the freezer compartment of his refrigerator invited comparison with meals he'd enjoyed the past week, and for a moment he wished he were back in San Francisco. Pursing his lips as he tried to decide, he figured one was as unappetizing as the other. Ah. He nudged the door shut as the phone rang again.

"Hello."

"Larry. Did you just come in? I tried you a couple of minutes ago. Didn't know if I'd missed you or misdialed."

Voice recognition brought about a momentary queasiness, borderline panic, and then a resolution: Whatever the tenor of this conversation, he wouldn't be suckered into working for them again. "You missed me by a minute or two," he said. "I was enjoying a brew on my deck. What can I do for you?"

"You sound in a good mood."

"Why not?"

"Why not, indeed? I'd say neither of us has anything to complain about. Not with a new project in the works."

"We need to talk."

"I can't discuss the particulars right now."

"That's not what I meant."

"Larry! I was wondering if you received the check."

"Oh, the check. Yes, it arrived." Larry ran his tongue over his lips. "I can't accept it."

"I didn't catch that. Can you speak a little louder?"

"I said I can't accept it. I'm returning it."

"Returning it? Why should you?"

"We've had this conversation before."

"Oh, come now. You know you weren't serious. I wasn't at all convinced."

Larry sighed. "That doesn't come as a surprise. I tiptoed around the subject; or maybe I wasn't completely sure."

"You're saying you're sure now? You want out?"

"Yes. Absolutely."

There was a short silence, followed by the metallic sound of rapid tapping against a hard surface. The words came out slowly. "What makes you think we would even consider such a request?"

"For God's sake, you know I can be trusted. I certainly don't have to explain why. Besides, how could I possibly expose you without ruining myself?"

"Yes, Larry, we covered that. But you must understand that while I believe you, others might take a dim view of your defection. It's not only you and me, my friend."

"Oh, for Christ's sake, I know that."

"Then what? You think you don't count because you're a minor player? In our line of business everyone counts."

"Yeah, had I known more about your line of business, as you call it."

"I see. You were misled, an innocent, corrupted by forces beyond your control. Bullshit. It's a little late to be spouting, 'What a good boy am I'."

"I don't deny I've benefited."

"There you are, and you'll continue to benefit. The new project I mentioned?"

"Don't bother wasting your breath."

"Oh, I think you'll come around. It could be fall or later before we make our move. By then, I'm sure you'll have come to your senses."

Jesus, man, I have come to my senses! He wanted to shout into the phone; instead, he said, "Look, we could bounce this back and forth all night, but I really have to get going."

"Yes, I think enough has been said. For now. Goodnight, Larry. Oh, and take care."

There was a click as the caller broke the connection, but in the interval before the line went dead, Larry heard something. Another click, he thought. Had someone been listening in on an extension or could it be his line was bugged? The last words, *Oh, and take care,* echoed in his mind, coming across as vaguely menacing. He ran his hand across his forehead, aware he was perspiring. He placed the receiver back on the hook. The house. The house had been a hot box.

He walked swiftly out of the kitchen and into his dining area. The glass doors that opened onto the deck had been secure when he arrived home. He was sure of that. The transom above the doors, however, had been shut, which was odd now that he thought about it, because he usually left it open for ventilation. Even when he was away.

He forced himself to concentrate, to trace his actions the morning he'd left for San Francisco. He hadn't overslept, and had moved along at a normal pace, but he'd been preoccupied, his mind on business matters. Would he have neglected to open the transom? The answer was it wouldn't have been closed in the first place, not with August's unforgiving heat.

Slowly, thoughtfully, Larry moved into the smaller of the two bedrooms that served as his office and sat down at his desk. Earlier, when he'd collected the mail, he'd held out hope that one small clasp envelope would be conspicuously missing from the pile. But there it was, hidden under a full page ad for patio furniture. His check. It had been sent after all.

He stared now at the neatly typed name—Lawrence C. Townsend. Great name. Tack on *Esquire* and the clients would be flocking to him. If he'd finished law school. Instead, he'd elected to change course to explore other avenues. When he'd decided to enter the construction business, his family, usually so supportive of his efforts, had been disappointed.

"Larry, for Christ's sake," his father had said, "you want to quit law school, that's up to you. But you're telling me that after four years at Arizona State and a degree in business administration, you want to start vocational school?"

He did not and had not. He worked in the field, getting on-the-job experience until he was operating his own business. At the age of thirty-three, he was Mr. Contractor, running a successful construction firm with an eye toward expansion, perhaps into real estate development.

His success came about a little too easily, a little too quickly. He fingered the envelope and thought about its contents, a generous check made out to Lawrence Townsend for services rendered. How sad that it also served as a symbol of his shame, a reminder of his transgressions. Roughly, he shoved it aside. *That's it,* he decided. He didn't want or need the fucking check. He wanted out. Period.

He looked down at his clenched hands, and then slowly stretched out his fingers. It would all work out. Once he made his position clear, once they realized he was no longer vacillating, they would leave him alone. Better yet, why not negotiate a deal to pay back some, or even all, of the money? It made sense. He nodded, feeling a lessening of the tightness across his shoulders and through the midsection of his body.

He would have to be assertive, present his side forcefully and

16

convincingly. He drummed his fingers on the desk. It would take planning, the words, the timing, the approach. He would have to think it out very carefully. But not tonight.

Once again, Larry thought about his homecoming. His neighbor, Gus Struthers, a retired stuntman, had been faithful in collecting his newspapers while he was away. Larry reached for the phone. Possibly Gus could be of further assistance.

Gus's deep voice was warm. "How was San Francisco?"

"Fantastic, as always. Say, thanks for picking up my papers. I meant to cancel delivery, but I guess my brain went on vacation when I was getting ready to leave."

"Glad to help out, though like I said when you called from Frisco, I didn't even know you were gone."

"Because of the car. You mentioned there was a car parked in front of the house. Uh, Gus, I'm curious. Did you see anyone approach or leave my place?"

"Not a soul."

"Would you happen to remember anything about the car? The make, the color?"

"I'm not sure, but I think it could have been a Dodge or Chrysler. I know it was definitely a white four-door."

"You saw the car in the morning or afternoon?"

"It was there when I drove by your house around two in the afternoon, and it was still there when I returned about an hour later."

"Oh. So it couldn't have been someone coming to see me."

His neighbor responded with a chuckle. "What do you bet Jo Ellen was entertaining again. She probably told the guy to park a block away, to be on the safe side. Her old man has a habit of cruising by the house now and then to check up on her."

Jo Ellen, a former starlet who lived nearby, had graduated from the casting couch to engage in her own form of private enterprise, or so it was rumored. Larry acknowledged that what Gus had suggested was a likely scenario and brought the conversation to a close.

He remained at his desk, sorting out his thoughts, telling himself he was acting like a suspicious old lady. *Next thing you know, I'll be checking under the bed and opening closets,* he thought. If he needed an outlet for an overactive imagination, he could try the Hollywood Playhouse. He smiled at the thought, and then pushed back his chair. Food. That was what he needed. Suddenly, he was ravenous. It was time to head for the kitchen.

Later, in bed, but still wide awake, Larry reached into the top shelf of his nightstand for a book he'd started on stock market investments. The book was there, but something, an object, rested on top of it.

What he drew out was a small glass ashtray. In it were ashes and the remains of a half-smoked cigarette. Larry didn't smoke, no recent visitor to his home had smoked, and the ashtray belonged in the living room.

As if mesmerized, he held onto the ashtray as he swung his legs over the side of the bed. Then, wrinkling his nose in disgust, he shoved it onto his nightstand. Someone had been in this room, had come uninvited into his home!

He jumped up, rounded the foot of the bed and strode to the companion nightstand. Flinging open the drawers, he examined their contents and ran his hand over the shelf. Nothing. The same with his bureau drawers. His closet had revealed nothing missing nor askew, but he looked again, taking care to examine the top shelf.

He traipsed into the living room and turned on the light. Except for a little dust on the coffee table and TV, everything looked the same. He turned to the bookcase, but stood apart from it, fixing his gaze on the rows of books. His library appeared intact, but something was out of kilter.

Puzzled, Larry moved in for a closer look. Arranged according to size, he had placed his collection of biographies and a smattering of fiction in the center of the bookcase, filling the other shelves with a variety of non-fiction and how-to books. What confronted him now was entirely different. All his books, whatever their category or size, were neatly stacked, lined up alphabetically by author. Jesus. Was this someone's idea of a joke?

He turned out the light and walked slowly back into his bedroom. He stood in front of his nightstand, staring at the squashed butt, and then lowering himself onto his bed, he sat motionless, eyes narrowed in concentration as he grasped for answers. Aside from weird and crazy, particularly the setup with the ashtray and bookcase, there was clear proof someone had entered his home.

Why? They weren't searching for something or they'd have trashed the place. Another thought. If the intruder or intruders had broken in to tap his phone or bug his office, they had been brazen, stupid, or both, for calling attention to an uninvited presence. Unless, and the thought made his stomach churn, it was a deliberate and not-so-subtle attempt to convey a message: *See how easily we can slip into your home. We want you to know we've invaded your premises, that you're being watched, because it would concern us if you decided to defect.*

Sick. The whole thing was sick. Brusquely he swung his legs under the covers, and then reached to turn off the light. He wasn't about to be intimidated by anyone, nor would he put up with this nonsense.

He lay there, listening to his heart pounding, willing himself to take deep, slow breaths, to shut out distressing thoughts. It was just that he was furious—with them, with himself.

He turned restlessly, his mind going in a thousand directions. A moment later, much to his own surprise, he was sitting up, his breathing quiet and regular. He knew what he had to do, and it couldn't wait until morning.

He switched on his bedside lamp, and then was out of bed, reaching for his robe.

Marching through his living room to his office, he ignored the feel of cold wood against bare feet. He could imagine the reaction. *Do you know what time it is? I thought we agreed to defer this discussion.* But therein lay his advantage. There would be no hesitating, no equivocating, no agonizing over approaches. He would tell them where to get off, get graphic, if he had to.

He was through with them. It was that simple.

✍ *Chapter Three* ❧

*K*elly kept sneaking glances at her watch. It wasn't like her to break concentration, even for a blocking rehearsal. Larry Townsend should have arrived forty-five minutes ago. She glanced at the door, and then into the darkened auditorium, wondering what possibly could have delayed him.

He had responded enthusiastically to her invitation to attend this evening's rehearsal; additionally, he'd come up with an invitation of his own: that she join him for a late supper at Enrico's on the Strip; now she stood out like Mrs. Rich Bitch at a rummage sale. No less a fashion statement among jeans-clad cast members, she was attired in a sleeveless black cotton form fitting dress that had elicited whistles and comments. The thought of having to beg a ride home with one of the cast or crew members did not sit well.

Much less did the idea of public transportation. She thought about the trip into Hollywood. The bus driver had glared at her for not having the right change. Mr. Sleaze himself had chosen her for a seatmate, his whiskey breath overpowering, the lurching bus providing unavoidable contact.

It was the thundering silence that caused Kelly to look up from her script. Rick stood on the apron of the stage, staring at her, waiting. Waiting for what? She glanced down at her script. Oh shoot, she was supposed to be out of there. She shot Rick a pained look and made a hurried exit, only to stop as he called out, "Kelly, what the hell are you doing?"

"I'm supposed to exit."

"Not like that. Show some hesitation, look back. These people," he pointed to the actors seated stage center, "only pretend to be your friends. They're jerks and you know it."

Of course, she knew that, and deciding Larry Townsend had

earned another demerit, she promptly performed her exit to Rick's satisfaction and found a seat in the auditorium, determined now to concentrate fully on what was taking place on stage. Actually, it was Rick she enjoyed watching, whether he was acting, directing or simply being himself.

It hadn't always been so. She had first come upon Richard O'Hara at UCLA in Drama I, a beginning acting class. The son of the popular character actor, Evan O'Hara, Richard, as he insisted on being called in those days, had an attitude problem and could out-sneer the most formidable member of the theater arts faculty. He also made himself unpopular with the students, and it was with some satisfaction that Kelly and others noted his failure to be cast in major productions.

Maybe he finally tired of the game. For whatever reasons, in their junior year Rick became a fixture backstage, performing skillfully in building sets, working the lighting booth and even showing up on production Sundays to sew snaps and buttons on costumes. He was less argumentative and no longer appeared disdainful of his peers or superiors. Whether his newly found humility was genuine or calculated, it must have been this change in attitude that opened doors hitherto barred. He was cast in a major production, his performance deemed electric, incredible. From then on, he was the department's fair-haired boy.

Kelly reserved judgment. She remembered the cynical and sullen Richard of times past. Could the tiger change his stripes?

Her question was answered the following year when she was cast opposite Rick, each in a lead role. If he sensed she had reservations about working with him, it wasn't obvious to Kelly. Moreover, there were no tantrums, no crushing come-downs to rupture one's self-esteem. They clicked; they were a team, each drawing strength from the other in the creative process of building their characters. What flourished on stage carried over into their personal lives, as well, and they formed a friendship shaped by mutual respect and affection.

Kelly smiled to herself as she watched Rick demonstrate a bit of stage business to one of the actors. Not everyone was comfortable with this man. He could be cocky and temperamental, his face turning almost as red as his hair; he also could be a true friend, generous with his time, and accepting and forgiving. More than a few girls, taken in by his

21

mischievous smile and warm brown eyes, sought more than friendship, for when he was at his charming best it hardly mattered that he wasn't movie star handsome.

He could also be a pain in the rear end, like today when she'd approached him with the suggestion he audition Larry Townsend.

He had stared at her. "So who's this Larry person? Some jock you've been dating?"

Put off by his tone, she had given him a look of exasperation. "I've seen him once, in San Francisco, but he's from L.A., and he happened to express an interest in our theater."

"Can he act?"

"That remains to be seen. He says he's done some acting in Phoenix, in community theater. Rick, come on. Larry is a big, good-looking man. He'd make a perfect John Sawyer."

"I think I have my John Sawyer."

"The kid who read yesterday?"

"Maybe."

"Maybe, huh? I didn't think you were that impressed."

He shrugged and turned away, but when he avoided eye contact, she couldn't resist a small smile. It would appear Rick was jealous. The soft tap on her shoulder startled her. She turned, surprised but relieved to see Larry seated directly behind her.

"Hi," he said. Then in a whisper, he added, "Sorry to be so late. There was a last minute text message from a client, an accident on Hollywood Boulevard . . ." He trailed off, raising his hands in a what-can-you-do gesture.

"I had no idea you were sitting there. You were so quiet."

"Comes with practice. Sometimes I sneak up on the guys at a construction site to be sure they're not goofing off."

She nodded and gestured toward the stage. "We're almost ready to break. I want you to meet Rick." Her voice low, she continued, "I told him I thought you'd be perfect for the role of the FBI agent."

He looked beyond her at the stage, and then back at Kelly. "I

22

need to talk to you about that. At the break."

"Okay, fine." She turned away from him, her attention diverted to the stage as she heard her name.

"Kelly, I said we'll start Act III in ten minutes." It sounded like an order or a complaint—Kelly wasn't exactly sure which—but Rick scowled at her as others in the cast headed for the coffee pot or stared curiously at Larry.

Kelly beckoned to Larry. "Come on, I'll introduce you to Richard the Wretched."

Larry stood now, but he placed a restraining hand on her arm. "Look. I appreciate your efforts on my behalf, but I'm going to have to pass. Something came up today, a rush job. Plus, I'm losing one of my best workers to jury duty, for crying out loud."

Her tone was sympathetic as she commiserated with him. A good actress, she managed to hide her disappointment.

They moved quickly through Act III and Kelly, for once, was glad to be whisked out of the theater. Though Rick had been cordial to her for the remainder of the rehearsal, she sensed his antagonism toward Larry, no doubt blaming him for her preoccupation throughout much of the evening.

However, now that they were on their way, headed for the Sunset Strip, Kelly was beginning to wonder if her elation over seeing Larry again was as misguided as her attempts to keep a conversation going. Though he had been talkative, complimenting her on her appearance, and he had taken her arm in a proprietary manner as they left the Hollywood Playhouse, once he was behind the wheel of his red Mustang, Larry had turned distant and self-absorbed.

Maybe he can't drive and talk at the same time, she theorized, taking in his set jaw and the hands clenched on the steering wheel. Or possibly he hadn't adjusted to driving in California. Whatever the problem, she decided to relax; the ball was in his court.

After a silence of several minutes, Larry said, "You're so quiet. Is everything all right?"

She opened her mouth and then closed it, biting her tongue to stifle a comeback that might be misinterpreted. He wasn't being nasty or sarcastic; his tone, she was sure, conveyed genuine concern. The man probably had a lot on his mind and was unaware he was being uncommunicative. She assured him all was well. He definitely was worth another try, in light of their instant rapport in San Francisco. And there was another reason: her weakness for tall, good-looking blond men.

Enrico's on the Sunset Strip was a favorite meeting place for the Hollywood A-list, or so it was reported in the columns. If the hottie-of-the-moment plus entourage weren't in attendance, it still was a good place to hang out, at least in the bar, which was as friendly and lively as any neighborhood pub. In contrast, the dining room, with its thick carpeting, soft lighting and cozy booths nestled against crimson tapestried walls, was designed to encourage intimacy. Flaming entrees and desserts created theatrical moments for the diners.

Larry hadn't selected Enrico's for the camaraderie of the bar or for its status among celebrities. Rather, he had judged it an attractive after-hours place where he and Kelly could better get to know each other.

They waited at the maître d's station, expecting to be seated momentarily, when someone called out Larry's name. The man who approached them had broken away from a group of six who were about to exit the restaurant. In his early fifties, he matched Larry in height and build. *Still a good looking guy,* was Larry's thought, *except for the tight smile.*

The men shook hands. "Kelly, I'd like you to meet Ben Forbes. Ben, this is Kelly Meyers." Introductions completed, no one seemed to have anything to say. It was Larry who broke the silence to announce the maître d' was signaling them.

"Well." Ben nodded to Kelly, and then addressed Larry. "Nice to see you. Let's keep in touch." He was gone before Larry could muster a response.

Larry caught Kelly's puzzled expression as they were led to their table. He was sure she had sensed the awkwardness of the meeting but was too polite to comment or question.

Larry waited until they were settled into their booth and had given the waiter their drink order. Addressing his menu, he said, "Hell of a nice guy. We used to work together, Ben and I." He cleared his throat, and then turned his gaze on Kelly. "Actually, Ben taught me most of what I know about the construction business. I guess you could say he was my mentor; when I set up my own shop, though, he had a lot to say on the subject." He dropped his gaze. "He wasn't willing to let go."

"A shame. Now you're estranged?"

"Oh, no. We talked just the other day. He still calls." He grew pensive as he thought about their last conversation, and then decided it was time to lighten up. "So how do you get along with your mentor?"

She raised her eyebrows. "You mean Rick?"

He started to respond, and then cut himself off as their waiter appeared with drinks and to take their dinner order. When they had gone through the ceremony of toasting and tasting, Larry said, "Tell me about Rick. Does he direct all your shows? I mean, is he a permanent fixture?"

"I'm afraid so." She raised her hand. "Only kidding. To be fair, Larry, he's multi-talented, a modern Renaissance man. Oh, he can be a pill, but he's a superb actor, and an inspired director. I've seen him build a set or light a scene with as much expertise as any qualified technician. But don't tell him I said that."

Larry had no intention of giving the man his due, even if he was as deserving as Kelly maintained. Besides, he didn't much care for Mr. O'Hara. While he might be worthy of a dozen or more accolades, Larry had a hunch that Rick O'Hara could also be an arrogant SOB. He took a sip of his scotch, and then, careful to phrase his question without offending, said, "Not to take away from the Hollywood Playhouse, but didn't you mention on the way over here that Rick is the son of the famous character actor Evan O'Hara?"

"I did. I suppose you're wondering why this paragon isn't making millions in the movies or huddling with Zanuck in the Polo Lounge?"

"Something like that."

She was silent for a moment. "The O'Hara name has opened some doors. Rick's been in a couple of movies and has played some featured roles on TV, but I think I understand him well enough to say that right now he's doing what he loves. Besides, he's pretty much had to prove himself."

"Not much support from the old man?"

"With the father, it's on-again, off-again. Maybe they're too much alike, or maybe it's Evan's drinking problem. They're on the outs much of the time. However, during a benign period, Evan agreed to help finance Rick's venture into community theater, and it seems they worked out a good arrangement. As far as I know, they've managed to remain on good business terms."

"Where do you fit into all of this?"

"In more ways than I can count."

"I'm willing to bet you're a match for The Great One."

She gave a short laugh. "Thanks. Someday, I may be. For now I'm a salaried production assistant, which means I work with casting, publicity, write up the program, and sell space, among other things. I'll also be acting in most of the productions."

Their salads had arrived, and Larry picked up his fork, only to set it down. "You know, I'd say we're both mavericks."

"You mean by changing course in midstream?"

He nodded, starting on his salad. "I had to buck my father because it gave him fits when I dropped out of law school. Fortunately, before he died, I'd started up my business and he gave his blessing, though grudgingly."

"There we differ. When I decided to take a personal leave from teaching to pursue the theater, it was with Nadine's encouragement. She never approved of my going into teaching. *It's so pedestrian and unglamorous, Kelly. How can you meet an attractive man?*"

"That's a switch."

"I know. My mother, unlike most mothers, doesn't favor security over pursuit of the impossible dream."

"On the other hand, your mother pretty much locked herself into a secure position."

"True, but she had to go after Steve. And give her credit. My stepfather's a lovely man."

He nodded. "She picked the best. Or maybe I have it backwards.

Anyway, you had the courage to bust out of safe and solid into what? Precarious but exciting?"

"Yes, on both counts, but you left out hard, hard work. That hasn't changed. Nor," she added, "has my monopolizing the conversation."

"That's not so. At dinner in San Francisco I practically recited my life history. I'm sure you remember all the exciting details, like growing up in Phoenix, father in the stationery supply business, mother a housewife, a sister named Fern. Now that's an exotic name. It's no wonder I'm writing my autobiography. Trouble is, I can't seem to get past chapter two."

"Ha! You think the studios are clamoring to option my life story?"

"Who knows?" he said. "Someday they might. I'm serious. You've got the looks, the talent, the dedication . . . the looks." He grinned. "Have I left anything out?" He noted her mock-grave expression. "Well?"

"You know you made a dreadful mistake by going into the construction business."

"I did? Do you know something I don't?"

"I've decided you'd make a terrific press agent."

"I'll give that serious consideration for my second career." He covered her hand with his, and then removed it. Their dinners had arrived.

On the way home Kelly sat close to Larry, comfortable now with their occasional silences. The evening had been extraordinary, fulfilling the promise of their first encounter. Only this time more than laughter and get-acquainted chit-chat had nourished the conversation. As the evening progressed, they spoke earnestly of their aspirations, of their capabilities and frailties. She had amazed herself as to the extent she'd opened up to reveal her vulnerabilities, to confess her fear of failure.

Kelly gave him a sidelong look, lingering over his profile, her gaze traveling to his hands. They were strong masculine hands; she could imagine them touching her, exploring her body. The thought excited her, and she felt her breathing quicken as she pictured him taking her into his arms, of their pressing close in an intimate embrace.

Shutting out the image, she leaned back to rest her head against the seat. She didn't want to think beyond tonight. It was enough to savor the moment.

Larry noted Kelly's closed eyes, her lips curved into a half smile. He was becoming aroused, excited by her nearness. He wanted to place his lips against hers, to cover her throat with kisses, caress her breasts and feel her warmth. He stopped himself. *In time, in time.*

When he glanced at her again, her eyes were open, and he answered her smile with his. *The evening,* he reflected, *had turned out to be about as perfect as one could ask for.*

Then Larry remembered. Their evening almost had been doomed before it started.

Chapter Four

The white Chrysler sedan had appeared in Larry's rearview mirror only minutes after he and Kelly left the Hollywood Playhouse. It was the image of the car crowding them, staying on his tail that had encroached upon his concept of the perfect evening.

Larry thought about the incident as he walked to his car from Kelly's apartment. At first he'd been tolerant, figuring the guy would opt for a lane change over wearing out his brakes, but when the idiot persisted, Larry longed to convey by gesture specific instructions as to what the clown could do with himself.

The driver, a heavyset man, oddly wearing what appeared to be dark glasses, had seemed intent in his quest to play bumper cars, creating in Larry a perverse desire to hold his ground.

Meanwhile, Kelly had been chatting about the play, relating an anecdote about one of the actors, or possibly the stage manager. Distracted, Larry pretty much tuned Kelly out. He had, however, become aware of her silence, of his chance to share his aggravation over the jerk riding his tail. What stopped him was the sudden intrusion of an appalling thought: He was being followed.

He had decided to switch lanes after all and did so, while managing to keep an eye on the Chrysler. *Come on,* he'd coaxed, *tag your next victim. Show me you're just a good old boy out for a little Friday night fun.*

What he'd seen in his rearview mirror had made his mouth go dry. It was the Chrysler signaling to move into Larry's lane, the driver able in seconds to squeeze behind the Ford Explorer that now separated the two cars.

Larry had checked his mirror again. *Oh, shit.* The Explorer had sprinted into the next lane, allowing the Chrysler to close in. They were back where they had started.

He'd felt himself choke up, eyes tearing out of a sense of helplessness. Fighting his panic, he'd permitted his anger to take control, to override his fears. When he'd looked again, the Chrysler was no longer behind him. It didn't take long to discover he had company in the lane to the right, the pudgy profile of his tormentor silhouetted against the dazzling neon of a famous eatery. Then, unexpectedly, the driver, brakes squealing, had turned off, hightailing it down a side street.

His relief had been tempered with disgust for allowing himself to conjure up a scenario of sinister proportions. It was an all-too-common event, the Mr. Nice Guy who becomes a monster behind the wheel of a car, the compliant tub of lard who turns into an ogre on the road. The creep in the Chrysler hadn't been following him.

Such had been his conclusions.

Now as he settled himself behind the wheel of his car, he was having second thoughts. What came to mind, as he left the side street to swing into traffic, was his conversation with Gus, a nagging reminder of the white sedan parked in front of his house. Possibly a Chrysler. If this was the same car, if the same people were involved, then tonight's escapade had been staged to further intimidate him.

Now he was shooting down his milquetoast-to-monster theory. Big deal. Either it was part of the plot or it wasn't. At this moment he really didn't care.

Larry rolled down his window, inhaled the night, and let the cool, crisp air wash over him like a bracing tonic. Upping the volume on the late-night music station, he began to sing along, recognizing the tune but not the singer. The euphoria of the evening, like a potent drug, was in his system, permeating his senses, blocking out all negatives. He was on a high, caught up in the rapture of the present. This night, these hours with Kelly were all that mattered.

When they had arrived at her apartment, Kelly didn't invite Larry in. It was too soon for that, and besides, he hadn't seemed to want to linger. A soft kiss on the lips, a promise to call, and he was gone.

After locking up, she stood by the door, viewing her living room as it would appear to a stranger. (Okay. Through Larry's eyes.)

Small but functional, it was a place to work and take her meals and, on occasion, to watch TV. Other than two framed, faded impressionistic prints provided by the management, and a collection of African violets inherited from a teacher friend who'd fled L.A. to return to her Midwestern roots, the room stood bare of ornamentation. Nothing about it reflected the personality or tastes of the occupant of apartment 104.

Her bedroom, however, was intensely personal. Creamy and peachy tones predominated, contrasting with accent shades of deep coral and burnished mahogany. The room served as a retreat where she indulged her passions for music and reading. Inspired by the structured rhythms of a Bach Brandenburg Concerto or the intricate jazz meanderings of a Dave Brubeck composition, she might create a poem or, more prosaically, take pause to record in her journal the trials and triumphs of the day. It was her sanctuary, and as she entered it now, she carried her shoes, enjoying as always, the feel of deep pile under her feet.

Passing her bed on the way to the closet, Kelly bit down on her lip as she noted its rumpled appearance, the satin coverlet trailing over one side, a pair of pantyhose and a half slip draping the foot of the bed.

Though three years had passed since they'd broken up, Kelly could hear Mark's lazy baritone, all mumbles, yet heavy on the sarcasm.

"Jeez, Meyers, I gotta tell you, ladies' lingerie doesn't exactly turn me on." The grand finale to a disastrous four-month live-in arrangement hadn't come about in the heat of acrimonious exchange, but in the aftermath of a tedious discussion of their incompatibilities, including her slovenly housekeeping habits and his constant harping on this issue.

It had been a relief to live alone, to keep her own hours, to eat or not to eat, to put off tidying up if she so desired. She even worked to achieve several grades above slob status and had succeeded for the most part, despite today's lapse. But this life of independence with its silent rooms and bed for one had worn thin. At twenty-eight, she was ready to commit to one person, to find her mate.

Kelly dropped her shoes to the floor of her closet, and as she began to undress she thought about her family. Her mother, widowed when Kelly was five, was now happily married. She hoped the same was true for her sister, Vanessa.

When Vanessa's husband Gordon Stuart, a major in the Air Force, was assigned to Ankara Turkey, Kelly had been excited for the couple, yet apprehensive. How would they—especially Vanessa—adjust to living so far from home in a culture so foreign from their own? As for Gordon, yes, he was handsome. Very. Kelly had danced with him at her sister's wedding and remembered how he'd looked into her eyes and how close he'd held her. She had scoffed at Nadine's comments regarding trouble ahead for Vanessa. But what if her mother were right? Then there'd be hell to pay.

Her bedside phone was purposely set on soft. Even so, she could hear its summons above the running water. Quickly, she grabbed a small towel to pat her face and wipe her hands.

To her relief, it was no panting pervert; to her surprise, it was her mother.

"Darling, I know it's late, but with Steve away on business I can't seem to get to sleep. Besides, we hardly got in a chat, the two of us. Oh, I'm not thinking. Are you alone?"

"Yes, Mother, I'm alone. Why wouldn't I be?"

"Now, Kelly, don't take that defensive tone."

"Mom, I'm sorry. I've had a very full day. And evening. I arrived home only twenty minutes ago. Look, is everything okay?"

"Of course. Can't I call my own daughter? And incidentally, my dear, I don't think my question was out of line. After all, you're a grown woman."

Kelly laughed. "Do I detect a tinge of disappointment in your voice?"

"Only a tinge."

"Have faith. I'm sure I'll find someone one of these days."

"I don't doubt that one bit. Though I do think you go overboard in finding fault with the men you date. I can't help thinking about Dave Edwards. What was wrong with him? Oh, now I remember. He was too ambitious, you said."

"Overly ambitious, bigoted, and a hypocrite. And don't bring up Ray what's-his-name."

"I don't know why not. He was certainly handsome."

"You were the one who pointed out he was too predictable and less intelligent than I. As for Andy Warner—"

"His face was too round, and he wore brown trousers with a blue jacket. We don't need to get into all that. Tell me about the new production. Tell me about the part you play."

Good. They were out of the minefield and on safe ground. Kelly plunged ahead with a vivid account of her work, both on stage and off. Finally, though, she had to beg off, citing her need for sleep.

"I know I shouldn't have called at this hour," Nadine said, "but I was feeling restless and out of sorts." She had trailed off with a deep sigh.

Kelly thought her mother sounded depressed and wondered if trouble loomed on the domestic front, but stifled her curiosity, reluctant to pry.

Apparently not so Nadine. Her tone much brighter, her manner direct, she said, "So you went out this evening. Could it be you're seeing Larry Townsend?"

"I don't know if 'seeing' is the correct word, but yes, Mother, Larry and I went out on a date."

After a short silence, Nadine said, "You know, Kelly, that brittle quality in your voice isn't the least bit attractive."

Kelly answered with silence.

Nadine finally continued, "I know you're tired, and I apologize for keeping you up. One question, and then I'll let you go: Did you have a good time?"

"I had a wonderful time."

"I'm delighted."

"You are?"

"Don't sound so surprised. You certainly deserve the best; Larry's not only good looking and personable, but Steve says he's a fine young man. When we have time, I'll want to hear all about him."

"It's a deal."

"There's one more thing." Nadine hesitated, but only for a moment. "Of course, this may not bother you," she said, "but I'm wondering if you're aware blond men usually become bald by middle age. I can see where Larry's hairline is beginning to recede the tiniest bit."

"Goodnight, Mother."

"All right. I've kept you too long as it is. Goodnight, Kelly. Give me a call in a few days." She broke the connection.

Kelly sat for a moment, staring at the receiver before slowly placing it in its cradle. At once she felt her anger dissipate, felt her mouth quiver into a smile. Her mother would enter a flaming building, an earthquake-flattened shell to rescue her girls, all the while casting a critical eye on hairstyles, makeup, and clothing. As for the men in Kelly's life, that was a sore spot. Face it, she was as bad as her mother, always assessing, analyzing, and being picky. For once, she wanted to go with her feelings.

She remembered to set her alarm before slipping into bed. She was due at the Playhouse for a nine a.m. staff meeting and wanted to be up in time to review her notes. She yawned and turned on her side. Why bother with notes? It was all in her head, the matters to be resolved, like casting the role of the FBI agent and the write-up for the Sunday Times. And properties. Rick wanted to discuss props for Act III. She tried to visualize the set, but already she was drifting. No clutter, no junk. That was it. They wanted—What was it they wanted? Still drifting, edging into darkness, stage lights flickering, dimming, she tried to focus on an unadorned table positioned downstage right. What came to mind was Larry's blue tie that matched his eyes, wine in a crystal decanter, a kiss goodnight. No, the table. She should concentrate on the table, but the image slowly receded, as did the rest of the set, all of it vanishing into total darkness.

She dreamed she was seated in a crowded auditorium among men and women resplendent in evening attire, brocades and satins embellished by fiery opals and a kaleidoscope of blazing gems, their brilliance set off by the simplicity of black tie elegance. Surely such opulence was *de rigueur* for an event of historic or artistic significance. Missing, however, were the smiles, the laughter, the brightly anticipatory pre-curtain chatter. Oddly enough, the attendees were a strangely quiet group, given only to an occasional whisper or murmur. Kelly wondered what it was behind the curtain that could inspire such solemnity.

At last the houselights dimmed and, as the curtains parted, the audience drew a collective breath. In place at center stage was the larger-than-life presence of a handsome blond man. It was Larry. To one side stood an attractive older woman. Kelly strained to see. Was it Nadine? The woman was smiling at Larry and nodding approvingly. Then in a sudden shift, the stage had become a giant TV screen, granting a close-up of the woman. The smile remained, but her mother's eyes now reflected doubt and uncertainty.

Despite his earlier exuberance, his delight in being caught up in the joy of the here and now, Larry's euphoria began to wane as he entered his home. True, it had been months since he'd been so taken with a woman; moreover, it appeared Kelly's interest in him was as genuine and intense as his feelings for her, or what he perceived at this time to be his feelings, her feelings. Because things change. *Oh, baby, do things ever change. What seems fresh and vibrant, like in the beginning of a relationship, can turn, and become jaded and dull. Just,* he thought gloomily, *as a cozy retreat can become an open zone, subject to trespass.*

He stood in the middle of his living room, his mood now as dark as the room. Seeking reassurance, he turned on the lamp by the sofa, fighting off what was becoming a recurring sense of uneasiness, a feeling of foreboding each time he stepped through his front door.

He couldn't shake off these feelings, even though no evidence of surveillance equipment had surfaced. And, God knows, he'd searched every room twice over, his only reward the discovery of a small paper airplane, the kind he'd made as a kid, stuck behind the TV.

He walked slowly into his bedroom and switched on the overhead light. Nothing was out of place, at least nothing obvious. He stopped himself. Jesus! He threw his keys on the bed. He was becoming paranoid, acting like a little kid ready to wet his pants over the bogeyman.

He shrugged out of his jacket, marched over to the closet and flung open the door. *See, Larry? Clothes and shoes and a pair of dirty socks you forgot to put into the hamper. That's it.*

Later in bed, when sleep wouldn't come, he thought back to the night he'd left his bed for his office, propelled by fury and indignation, determined to have it out, to sound tough, at all costs.

It hadn't been a productive exchange. Despite his efforts, the element of surprise, the forceful approach carried on the wave of spontaneity, the outcome had been almost a blow-by-blow recap of the earlier exchange. *We need to be reasonable. What's the hurry? Let's give it time.* As for Larry's accusation of a conspiracy to frighten him into submission, there was outright denial.

What now? What was the next step? Common sense dictated he set up a powwow with Jason Underwood, but he wasn't sure he was ready to confide in his attorney.

He turned on his back and kicked the covers down to his ankles, shutting his eyes, the better to concentrate. If only he could look at his situation objectively, put some distance between himself and his predicament. Predicament? He almost laughed. Try *mess,* as in goddamned mess, and all because of a need to prove himself, to appear worthy in his father's eyes. He stared into the dark. No, that was all wrong. Lofty goals notwithstanding, for financial gain he had consorted with the devil; for financial gain he had chosen to become an accomplice in an activity that was devious, unlawful, stupid. He had made a mistake, and no amount of rationalizing would make it go away. Immaturity, lack of judgment, and greed. That pretty much summed it up. But he had changed.

Not that he had become mature, responsible, and repentant overnight. Hardly. The transformation had been gradual, had come about as he began to take pride in his accomplishments, to recognize his strengths. Now he couldn't wait to disassociate himself from these people and their enterprises.

Repentant but flawed. He would be punished, and deserved to be punished.

Larry sighed and turned on his side. Maybe his situation wasn't all that bleak. If the friendship was now tenuous at best, there was, he suspected, respect and understanding, if not yet acceptance, for his decision to stand firm.

God knows, everything else in my life is positive, he thought. A major contract he had been laboring over was practically a shoo-in, and he was profiting from contacts made through fund-raising projects.

Then there was Kelly. Whether she was a complication or the key to his survival remained to be seen. He didn't want to think too far into the future. The present was exciting enough.

At last, he felt drowsy. He allowed his mind to roam, and as bits of the evening floated past, he concentrated on Kelly, his inner eye lingering over lush auburn locks. A sudden switch and auburn turned red, with Kelly's lovely smile dissolving into Rick O'Hara's perpetual frown. He thought back, replaying their encounter at the theater. This man, this *wunderkind,* didn't like him. Maybe resent was the better word. So okay. No big deal.

He flopped onto his other side. The guy resented him all right, and it looked as if he had competition. Serious competition.

The apartment house where Rick lived on San Vicente Boulevard was close enough to the ocean that in a matter of minutes he could drive to his favorite spot overlooking the water or shoot over to Santa Monica Pier to the Fisherman's Grotto for a quick supper, or nightcap when he was too wound up to sleep, like tonight.

He wasn't much of a drinker, coming from a household where Evan's excessive boozing had destroyed three marriages and poisoned a number of friendships. He figured it was in his genes—that he could end up like his father—so he'd opted for moderation.

He chose a back booth in the nearly empty lounge and sipped a Cutty Sark and water. He had come to the Grotto not only to unwind but to think. The theater—no, *his* theater—was his *raison d'être,* the center of his existence. It was as if he had given birth to this fabulous creature, a free spirit with potential to soar into greatness. To expand the metaphor, he pictured himself as the strict but benevolent parent entrusted to nurture and oversee its growth to eventual ascendancy.

As a born strategist, Rick rarely failed in his quest to acquire whatever it was he needed or desired. He was shrewd enough to refrain from coveting the impossible, thereby conserving his energy to pursue goals that were challenging but within reach. One of those goals was to make the Hollywood Playhouse into a flourishing, prosperous enterprise, worthy of critical acclaim.

"What noble aspirations," Evan had sneered. "Richard's Will Be Done and hallelujah, it is ordained?"

He'd replied that ordination had nothing to do with it. He would go with hard work, dedication and perseverance, not to mention a talented staff and a little blind luck. So far he was on track. To remain so required a single mindedness of purpose, and total self-absorption in his projects.

In the last few days he had discovered cracks in the carefully designed mosaic of his present and future game plan. While that raised risks and uncertainties, there remained also the probability of a new and richer dimension to his life, in the person of Kelly Meyers.

His feelings toward her had changed dramatically. His good friend—this lovely, talented, remarkable lady—was about to slip away from him into the arms of a tall, blond Adonis. What was so funny, so ridiculous, was that like in some corny sitcom, it had taken another man on the scene to awaken feelings he had been harboring for months. He was in love with Kelly.

He drained his glass and reached for his check, and as he brought out his wallet, he smiled. Barry, Larry, whatever his name, wouldn't be appearing in their current production, nor in any other production in his theater. With Kelly at his side day and night, he had more than a fighting chance to woo and win his love.

Minutes later, as he walked to his car, Rick felt a sense of buoyancy, and despite the late hour, a warm, tingling sensation coursed through his body. Failure was out of the question. His theater, his woman; it was simply a matter of time. He was back on track.

His next thought caused him to slow his pace as he approached his car. An image had popped into his mind. It was of Kelly in a long, white, flowing gown with a train. It was of Kelly in her wedding dress. Missing was a clear image of the groom.

ᴄᴧ *Chapter Five* ᴄᴧ

Wayfarers Chapel, Portuguese Bend, CA
February 15, 2005

 ix months after Kelly Myers and Larry Townsend first met, guests gathered to see them united in marriage.

Jason Underwood sat toward the back of the wedding chapel, the better to enjoy the late afternoon sun filtering through evergreens framed by towering glass panels that formed the sides of the church. Overhead the sky provided a pale blue canopy to match the serene waters of the Pacific below. *Winter wonderland, Southern California style,* was Jason's wry observation as the image of swirling masses of snow supplanted woodsy tranquility. He had grown up in a small town in northeastern New York—a negative, if enlightening experience that taught him a better place existed, a city or town that combined beauty with liveliness, that offered cultural diversity, as well. Blizzards he could do without.

Of the many places he had explored, San Francisco not only surpassed his expectations, it offered unlimited opportunities to a young man with a law degree. It had been home for many years, and he missed his city. He missed its charm, the bright, breezy days that so invigorated him. He even missed the fog that often veiled the city, quieting the senses, fostering meditation or mystery.

The move five years ago to Los Angeles, at his wife's insistence, had paid off after all, for in record time he'd achieved a partnership with a prestigious law firm on Sunset Boulevard. He had also acquired a change in marital status, with the collapse of his second marriage.

Jason studied the mother of the bride. Nadine was a little old for him, but he liked her style. Not that she was available, and not that he was looking for wife number three.

The sound of chimes caused him to shift his attention to the altar, to Kelly in a cloud of white, her auburn tresses flecked with sunlight, Larry at her side. With the service now in progress, Jason concentrated on the attendees, seeking out a familiar profile in the crowded chapel. Other than the families of the bride and groom, people he'd met for the first time at the engagement party, most of those assembled were strangers, yet familiar in that he could identify with people who dressed tastefully, whose behavior was genteel.

Now, as the bride and groom exchanged rings, Jason locked eyes with a man seated across the aisle from him. He'd come in late, just seconds before the service began, and seemed an oddity in this homogenous group. Certainly his appearance left something to be desired. His suit was funereal black, his belly protruded, and his neck, constricted by a tight-fitting collar, bore an ugly blush. Strangely, something seemed familiar about the man.

Jason broke eye contact, distracted by the muffled sound of a door opening and closing. Someone entering this late? Containing his curiosity, he kept his eyes front. The bride and groom were kissing, marking the end of the ceremony.

As if on cue, the man across from Jason, eyes now concealed by dark glasses, hunched out of his seat. With head down, he lumbered up the aisle toward the exit.

Now the bridal couple had broken their embrace to pose for the photographer as the first triumphal notes of the recessional filled the chapel.

Jason glanced backward. But it wasn't the flash of disappearing black that drew his attention; it was another man—youngish, well dressed and presumably the latecomer. Though his presence was unremarkable in this stylish gathering, Jason noted his rigid posture, his lack of expression in this assemblage of smiling faces. Were there tears in his eyes? *Oh my, how very sad. A mourner among the celebrants. But he'll survive—we all do,* Jason concluded.

Once again he turned his attention to the wedding couple, a slight frown indenting his brow as he observed the smiling bridegroom. One week before his wedding, Larry Townsend had sought his services, putting in a call to Jason through his private line. Larry hadn't detailed the problem, whether it was business related or of a personal nature, but every indication pointed to a man in distress. Imperative. He had said it was imperative he see his attorney.

Larry had failed to keep the appointment, hadn't even called to cancel. Nor had he, thus far, offered any explanation for his nonappearance.

Jason exchanged his frown for a broad smile in response to the approaching newlyweds, and as they swept past him, he caught something in Larry's expression and the formation of a word. *Later.*

They would talk later? His smile faded. Somehow it wasn't a comforting thought.

Palos Verdes Country Club

Kelly straightened her veil, and then felt at her throat, her fingers sliding over diamonds and pearls. A wedding gift from Nadine and Steve, the jewels were the focal point of an exquisitely crafted white gold pendant that dramatically set off the portrait neckline of her dress. She'd been told how breathtaking she looked in her gown, how moving the ceremony, how unique the setting. The comments and compliments continued as Kelly, resplendent in her wedding finery, the pearl-encrusted lace bodice giving way to graceful folds of silk shantung, pressed hands or lent her cheek to guests inching their way through the receiving line.

She had fussed at her mother, deploring the idea of a catered country club extravaganza, but Nadine had been right; it was a time for celebration, this prelude to Act I of Wedded Life. Here within the traditional wedding milieu, with velvety pink orchids nestled among pristine white roses, and wedding bell mobiles cascading over tables adorned with stephanotis and lily of the valley, she was thrilled to convey her happiness, to share her joy over becoming Mrs. Larry Townsend.

She glanced at her husband, in conversation with his best man, Brad Garrett, a close friend from Phoenix, and then over at Steve. Both men, attired in dark formal suits, looked as if they'd stepped out of a bridal magazine except, as she'd noted earlier, Steve seemed distracted, on edge.

Her mother, in contrast, had zeroed in on the task at hand, relishing her role of stylish mother of the bride. Nadine was stunning in

41

emerald green silk, her dress harmonizing with the pale green chiffon cocktail length gowns Kelly had chosen for her two attendants.

Larry's mother, Audrey Townsend, presented a pastel portrait, her frock embellished by flounces and frills, a look her mother would declare as déclassé. On the other hand, Larry's sister would undoubtedly receive Nadine's fashion stamp of approval. Fern Champion, voguishly turned out in a teal-blue chinchilla-trimmed designer suit, had breezed in from Arizona about an hour before the wedding, sans husband and four children. A tall, willowy strawberry-blond, with Larry's blue eyes, she had been cordial, if somewhat reserved, upon meeting her sister-in-law. Neither Fern nor her family had been available over the Christmas holidays when Larry had taken Kelly to Phoenix to meet his mother. Audrey mumbled something about the Champions being out of town, and Larry had been equally uncommunicative. Kelly did wonder at the absence today of Tom Champion and Larry's nieces and nephews.

At least Fern had made it to the wedding. However she was a poor substitute for Vanessa. Kelly missed her energetic, outgoing older sister.

Not that they'd always been comfortable with one another. The four-year age difference had cheated them of a closeness in their younger years; moreover, they had been labeled as personality opposites, with little in common. Later, they'd delighted in their dissimilarities, and then seized upon their likenesses. Each had a playful side but was no pushover. Each could hang in tough in support of people or projects she valued.

Kelly smiled to herself. If Vanessa weren't a world away, she'd be in the receiving line, brandishing her great smile, charming the pants off one and all, and perhaps even upstaging the bride. Instead, her sister would receive pictures and write-ups of the wedding.

The setting alone was worth writing about, Kelly mused, envisioning glass and greenery mounted high on a bluff overlooking the ocean. Rain was predicted, but the afternoon turned out to be perfectly lovely, with gentle breezes carrying the scent of attar from the rose gardens, the slanting rays of the sun softening the sentry-like evergreens.

The service had been wonderful, as well, a flawless production with one exception. A supporting player who should have remained off stage had entered late and positioned himself within touching distance of the leading lady. She hadn't expected Rick O'Hara to show up at the chapel. Though his presence hadn't marred her wedding, it was a shock, nonetheless, to meet his gaze, to read the hurt in his eyes.

Apparently, he had elected to skip the reception—pray God he had, for no love existed between Larry and Rick. She sighed, remembering these past difficult weeks at the Playhouse and reached for her husband's hand, only to make contact with air. Larry had stepped aside and was talking with a man who looked vaguely familiar. She watched from the corner of her eye, while carrying on with her duties. Then it came to her. It was Ben Forbes, he of the rigid bearing, with whom they had engaged in a non-conversation at Enrico's. Thankfully, the men appeared to be conversing peaceably enough, though she was unable to hear what was being said. Only one voice stood out in the crowd. It was Nadine's. She caught her mother's eye and gave her a small wink.

Nadine acknowledged her daughter's wink with a quick smile, all the while remaining attentive to Jason Underwood. She really did like the man. Not only did he breathe charm, he was tall, tanned (or was his complexion a bit swarthy?), and about her age, mid-fifties, she guessed. He was, perhaps, a little frayed around the edges and a shade too heavy, but his thick dark hair, touched with silver at the sides, outweighed any imperfections.

Mainly, though, it was his warmth that was so appealing, his large dark eyes signaling something beyond flirtation. It was a seductive look that invited intimacy, a look, she sensed, that had appropriated many a female heart. Was he attracted to her? She thought so, could feel the chemistry between them. However it wasn't her intention to join ranks with the Jason camp. She checked her watch. Time to break up the line.

With the bridal party dispersing, Larry, as he turned away from Ben, gave a small sigh of relief. Now he could relax, be himself—he tugged at his collar—except for the formal attire. He dodged a waiter carrying a tray of drinks and almost collided with his mother-in-law. Nadine barely acknowledged him and, as she moved on, seemed to be searching for someone. He watched as Steve joined his wife. Now both of them looked at their watches, and Nadine shook her head. Maybe the band was late or a VIP had failed to show. Their actions aroused his curiosity, but didn't concern him. Besides, it was time to claim his bride. Or was it? It appeared several guests had similar intentions, with Kelly now surrounded by well-wishers. He could join them, of course, or he could find Jason. He decided to seek out his attorney.

Larry noted that despite Jason's broad smile of greeting, his eyes showed a hint of puzzlement. Or was it reproach? He caught himself. Whatever the nature of his attorney's thoughts, this wasn't the time to give in to his paranoia. Raising his arms in a supplicating gesture, he said, "Jeez, I'm sorry. I really owe you an explanation."

"For failure to appear? Well, I think we can overlook—"

Larry cut him off by taking the attorney's arm and steering him out of earshot of the mingling guests. "I know this is going to sound crazy, but I didn't show for my appointment because of a last minute hitch. It seems I was being followed. And not for the first time," he added, responding to Jason's startled look.

"But why on earth—"

He held up his hand. "I can't go into that. Look, I can imagine what you're thinking. 'What's with this clown if he can't even confide in his attorney?'"

"Larry, I would never presume to judge you."

"I know. I know." He shook his head. "I just wish it weren't all so complicated." He studied the carpet for a moment, and then met the attorney's gaze. "You're going to receive a letter from me when we return from our honeymoon."

"A letter, you say." Jason's eyes took on a spark of curiosity.

"But not to be opened"—he had lowered his voice to a near whisper—"unless something should happen to me." He paused, but Jason, for once, was speechless. "I know this sounds off-the-wall."

"No, just so unexpected and . . . alarming," Jason said, recovering. "Good lord, man, you're obviously in a great deal of trouble, but we can't leave it like this, for God's sake." He kept his voice low, but there was no mistaking the urgency in his tone. "Let me help you.

Whatever this is about, surely there's something I can do."

"Jason, believe me, I'm not in any danger." He fell silent, reading the attorney's expression of disbelief. "All right. This much I can tell you." He thought a moment, considering what to divulge, what to omit. "I became involved with some people in"—he hesitated—"in an undertaking I shouldn't have committed to in the first place. Dumb move on my part. Anyway, I want out; they have other ideas."

"Mmm, I don't like the sound of this at all. Now you say you're in no danger. But what about this letter?"

"Insurance, that's all it is." Larry paused to gather his thoughts. "You see, if I can wait this out, convince these people I have no intention of capitulating, they'll back off, the harassment will stop, and—all's well that ends well," he finished lamely.

"I'm more interested in this letter. Shouldn't it be in my safekeeping now, at this very moment?"

"Don't I wish? Unfortunately, there's one small problem. I need to show proof of the allegations I make, and my data is incomplete." He paused. "The truth is I only started to compose the damn thing yesterday."

"Larry, I can't tell you how concerned I am. I really wish you had confided in me."

"So do I. Now." His smile, he hoped, masked his concern. Then he remembered something. "Jason, you didn't happen to notice a short, heavyset man at the wedding? He was wearing a black suit—"

"And bulged in all the wrong places? Yes, I did; he sat across the aisle from me. You, uh, know this man?"

"No, but I'd swear he's the guy who's been following me. Of course, I only caught a glimpse of him in the courtyard as we left the chapel."

"I have to admit, he looked familiar." Jason shook his head. "I can't place him; however—" He stopped, apparently distracted by noise coming from the club entrance.

Larry followed Jason's gaze. Sounds of greetings and laughter erupted, followed by more commotion as a pretty young woman, flanked by Steve and Nadine, made her way into the main reception area. "Well,

I'll be damned," Larry whispered.

Kelly had broken away from her group, and now laughter was eclipsed by whoops of delight as the two women fell into each other's arms.

"Vanessa! Oh, I can't believe this." Kelly, tears forming, stared at her sister.

Vanessa wiped away a tear. "Would you look at us! They'll have to bring in the bucket brigade. Now where is this husband of yours? I'm dying to meet this fantastic man."

"I don't think I was supposed to hear that." Larry, smiling broadly, had joined Kelly who brought him forward to meet his sister-in-law, Vanessa Stuart.

As the two made small talk, Kelly read approval in Vanessa's expression, observed that flirtatious tilt of the chin that men found endearing. *My sister, the extrovert,* Kelly thought, watching Vanessa's green eyes light up over something Larry said.

Determined to quash surfacing pangs of jealousy, Kelly turned to her parents, both of whom were grinning like Cheshire cats. "I'm flabbergasted! I'm pinching myself, this is so unreal," she said.

"What can I say?" Steve snapped his fingers. "Your wish, our command. Oh, honey, we're as thrilled as you are. Actually, it was your mother's idea to have Vanessa with us; then, between us, we did our best to make this day as special as possible."

"Well, I, for one, was beside myself when Vanessa didn't show for the wedding." Nadine, for the first time in the long day, exhibited signs of weariness as she explained that she had almost given up on Vanessa. "God knows, it had been difficult enough to convince her to make the trip in the first place, particularly with Gordon not able to get away." But, with all due credit to Nadine's powers of persuasion, Vanessa had finally realized her place was here with Kelly.

"Mom was right." Vanessa had come to her sister's side, and then, in an undertone, said to Kelly, "I'm sorry I missed the wedding, but blame it on delays en route and other problems I'll tell you about later."

"You'll be here when we get back? I mean, you've come all this way," Kelly said.

Steve gave Vanessa a warm smile. "She's coming home with us while you're on your honeymoon."

Vanessa nodded, but she looked worried. "Oh, I'll still be around," she said to Kelly.

"Why don't you plan a week or two with Larry and me?"

"Better make that a weekend," Vanessa said, her expression veiled.

"Now girls, we'll work this out later." Nadine, with renewed energy, was all business. It was imperative that they take their places at the head table, though not just yet, as the newlyweds were expected to take the lead on the dance floor.

As the strains of the *Anniversary Waltz* filled the room, Larry offered his arm. "We'll have to fake it," he whispered, "I never learned to waltz."

"Now he tells me," Kelly said, pretending shock. "What else haven't you told me about yourself?"

Larry's smile was a mere flicker. "No comment," he said.

Later, when Kelly was ready to slip away from the table to change into street clothes, she motioned for Vanessa to follow. Though she felt guilty bypassing her matron of honor, Kelly wanted some time alone with her sister; it would be the only opportunity until their return, because she and Larry would soon depart for a nearby hotel, and in the morning, they would join the family for brunch before flying off to Acapulco.

The dressing room, an accommodation for special parties, was set apart from the ladies' lounge, thus affording them privacy.

Kelly, in her bra and half-slip, sat at the dressing table, touching up her makeup; her sister had turned to the task of packing away part of the wedding paraphernalia that she now folded in tissue paper. Just moments before, while helping Kelly out of her gown, Vanessa, preoccupied and quiet throughout much of the dinner, suddenly had sprung to life, bubbling on about Larry and Kelly as a couple and pronouncing them a perfect match. "It's obvious," she had added, "he's head over heels about you. Just the way he looks at you gives me palpitations." Then her expression had turned mischievous. "I'll bet he's good in bed, right?"

Kelly had looked at her sister in surprise. Feeling the warmth in her cheeks, she said, "Now how would I know that?" The truth? After weeks of dating, of practicing restraint, of repressing feelings of intense, overwhelming sexual desire, on one cold, silent November night, they had surrendered to their urges and deserted the living room sofa for her bedroom, shedding clothes in their wake. Once in bed, they'd made love with frantic haste, their need overpowering. The experience was unsettling, over too soon, leaving them both shaken and somewhat bemused.

At her door, however, Larry held her close in a long, tender embrace. Stepping back, his hands grasping hers, his gaze lingering over her lips and her eyes, as if to memorize her features, he whispered, "I love you, Kelly. I adore you."

She had moved through the next week in something of a daze, preoccupied and self-absorbed. Mostly, though, she felt at sixes and sevens, one moment longing to be with Larry, the next apprehensive over where the relationship was headed. Everything had changed. They couldn't possibly resume within the framework of casual dating.

By the same token, they couldn't have continued in that ridiculous state of celibacy. But now they were vulnerable, subject to hurt and disillusionment. Well, wasn't that what love was all about, taking chances? Besides, *vulnerable* sounded like a disease, with no relevance to people in love.

In love for how long? A lasting love or a flash in the pan? A Cole Porter kind of love, *too hot not to cool down?* Maybe they needed to back off, view one another more objectively and address their differences. Her inner dialogue was to continue, and continue. Her conclusions? Mixed, contradictory, befuddled.

On the following Monday when the theater was dark, they had driven to Santa Barbara. There, on the wharf, in a restaurant overlooking the harbor, with all the fanciful trappings of birds swooping gracefully over waters burnished with sunset colors, of a meal enhanced by a premium Chardonnay and the flicker of candlelight, Larry had proposed. Forget a week of exhaustive analytical probing into the depths of one's psyche, of contemplation designed to arrive at Truth. Without hesitating, Kelly had accepted Larry's proposal, her answer an unqualified *yes*. Was he good in bed? Oh, my, yes, but she wasn't about to broadcast this bit of news. Not to Vanessa, not to anyone.

Kelly put down her mascara brush but continued to look into the mirror, watching her sister flit about the room, poking and prodding, obviously in search of something. It had been on the tip of her tongue to come back with a ribald remark regarding her sister's sex life; instead, she said, "Vanessa, for heaven's sake, what are you doing? Looking for hidden treasure?"

"That's about it. Try to find an ashtray in this place."

"I didn't know you smoked. That is, until dinner this evening."

Vanessa drew up a stool to place herself beside Kelly. "There are a lot of things you don't know."

Kelly studied her sister. She had always thought of her as almost beautiful. Taller than Kelly, with a wiry build and long blond hair framing a face broad at the cheekbones, she had inherited her father's Germanic features, his pale green eyes. Vanessa, in repose, was just another pretty woman. Animated, she was electric, dazzling, endowed with a radiance Kelly sought to emulate on stage. The glow was missing, had been nonexistent for most of the evening.

"Things I don't know." Kelly looked hard at her sister. "That's a provocative statement."

"I know. It was meant to be." Vanessa gave her sister a playful jab, but her accompanying smile lacked conviction. "Now, you're supposed to ask me whatever it is you want to ask."

Kelly didn't smile in return. "All right. What's wrong?"

Green eyes met hazel eyes in the mirror and then faltered, breaking eye contact. "I don't know this for a fact, but I think Gordon's involved with someone."

Kelly felt a sinking sensation. "Having an affair?"

"Maybe. I don't know. I just suspect—oh, Kelly, this is one hell of a time to bring this up. I'm sorry." She gave her sister a hug. "Let's table this topic. At least until you're back."

"Poor timing all around. Now I understand your reluctance to leave."

"Nonsense. I would have been furious with myself if I'd stayed in Ankara." The attempted smile turned into a grimace. "I have a confession to make. At the last minute I waffled and thought about—No, I inquired about getting a refund on the tickets. Even after a good night's sleep in New York, I couldn't make up my mind whether to continue on into L.A. or to hop on the next flight back to Turkey. Unfortunately, that bit of indecision cost me. I missed your wedding."

Kelly gave Vanessa's hand a squeeze. "Do you suppose Mom suspects?"

"That something's wrong? Probably. She's held her tongue so far, but when we get to San Francisco and have one of our mother-daughter chats, I suppose the shit will hit the fan. Oh, hey. Let's drop this right now. I love my husband, and he loves me. Can I help it if I wound up with the kind of good-looking guy all the ladies drool over?"

"Handsome, Vanessa, handsome."

"He is that, isn't he?" Her smile, this time, was genuine, and Vanessa had turned cheery, from bleak and brooding.

"I think I'd better get some clothes on," Kelly said, relieved that Vanessa had perked up.

"Incidentally," Vanessa said, "I think our mother gets better looking every day. She's a stunner in that emerald green dress." She removed Kelly's suit jacket from its hanger. "Now Larry's mother seems like a sweet person."

"But?"

"Obviously she lacks Nadine's style."

"Audrey is a lovely woman."

"I wasn't commenting on her character."

Kelly stared at her sister. "Do you know who you sounded like just now?"

Vanessa laughed. "Someone near and dear to us both. And you, my love, could be back in the classroom."

Kelly's mouth was quivering. "They loved me in the classroom. I was a saint, a pussycat, most of the time. Furthermore—" She stopped, startled by the sound of a light rapping at the door.

"Kelly? Sweetheart, its Larry."

Vanessa cast her a knowing look. "You know what they say – three's a crowd. See you tomorrow, Sis." She threw a kiss, flung open the door, paused a beat to say hi to Larry, and proceeded down the hallway at a fast clip.

"Now, that lady is in one hell of a hurry," Larry said.

"Don't mind her," Kelly said, her mind switching from Vanessa to her bridegroom. She was more than a little turned on as she viewed her husband, his blond good looks set off by a navy blue blazer and gray trousers. It was a sporty look that matched, at least in spirit, her going-away outfit. She gave a slight tug to the jacket which flared becomingly at the hips. Creamy beige with jade-green trim was a color combination that complemented her coloring and should have garnered a rave review from Larry, or so she'd been certain. Apparently, she'd been mistaken. From his thoughtful expression, she perceived that matters far weightier than her trousseau occupied his mind.

Something had jolted him, perhaps her attitude of expectancy. Stepping forward now to take her hand, he regarded her lovingly. "You look beautiful. I think I'll take you on a honeymoon."

"Don't forget, we have a date at the Hilton. First things first, you know?"

He nodded absently. "Kelly, would you be disappointed if we missed the brunch tomorrow morning? Since we'll be away for only a week, I thought an earlier flight would give us a head start. What do you think?"

"You can change our tickets?"

"I had Brad call the airlines earlier, and it so happens there are two seats available on the eight-thirty flight."

Kelly chewed on her lower lip, "With the time difference, we'd have the whole afternoon for the beach." She grinned. "Or for whatever.

However, our families would be disgruntled, to say the least. Nadine and Steve made all the arrangements for tomorrow, so you know what that means. Hurt feelings. Not to mention guilty feelings." She pointed at herself, and then at him.

Larry nodded. "Not exactly the way to make points with the in-laws." He drew her to him. "Now you know what a selfish SOB I am. Seems I have this fixation about you, about us together. All these pictures come to mind, of the two of us in bed, of romantic dinners, of us in bed, at the beach. Did I mention bed?"

"And you're wondering where, oh where, does brunch fit in?"

He gave a short laugh and released her. But his gaze, serious and intent, held hers. "God, I love you."

"And I love you." Kelly blinked back tears. "You keep this up, and you'll be sorry. A face streaked with mascara is not a pretty sight." She reached for a tissue and dabbed at her eyes. Then, giving the box a little shove, she said, "You know, I've made a career out of trying to please my mother." She turned to him. "If you want to change our tickets, and then why not? Let's do what's best for us—what we want to do."

"No." He leaned down to give her a quick kiss. "It wouldn't be right. I can see that now. Anyway, what's the big deal about a few hours, when we'll be together for the rest of our lives?"

His tone was upbeat, his smile genuine, but she saw in his eyes, a hollow look, a flicker of uncertainty. Kelly dismissed its relevance, burying the moment, as she allowed the sentiment of the day to take hold. A dream had been fulfilled; she had found her mate, the love of her life. The best was yet to come.

Chapter Six

*W*edded bliss—ha! Maybe for some guys. In his case, wedded torment was more like it. It was bad enough he had to show for the wedding; now he was going on the goddamned honeymoon. If, that is, he could unglue himself from the friggin' phone. He removed his glasses and rubbed his eyes. Jesus, how long did it take to connect with Mexico City? He began a rapid tapping with his foot. Come on, come on, cucaracha, we're talking today, not mañana.

With his free hand, he fiddled with the paper glider he had fashioned, gave it a toss, and then watched as it fell limply by his feet. He scooped it up. Games. He liked games, but not tag, you're it, that hide-and-seek crap. Christ, all that futzin' around in Hollywood. It was enough to—Static, now a clicking sound brought him to attention, a sudden quiver invading his gut as he responded to the expressionless, "Yes?" at the other end.

With their identities established, he came directly to the point, lowering his voice as he leaned into the phone. "An accident. He says we gotta make it look like an accident." He waited a beat. A second beat. The silence grated on him. "Hey, you with me?"

"That depends."

"Look, it's been checked out, like always. We're safe, no bugs. Okay? I mean, come on, Joe, we've done business before. Uh, speaking of which, I'm stuck here in San Diego through tomorrow. A dinner coming up with the regional managers."

"I'd forgotten. You do have a day job, don't you? Plumbing, is it?"

"Clothing. Don't I wish, plumbing. Let me tell you, those guys make big bucks. Listen, its okay. I can still meet you in Mexico City."

"Let's make it Acapulco. At your hotel. You can give me the particulars at that time."

"Right. Fuckin' shame, though. I could have taken him out in L.A." With his free hand he thrust the glider into the air, chortling his satisfaction as it remained airborne for seconds before nosing toward the carpet.

"Sorry you were denied that pleasure. On the other hand, this present setup is more of a challenge, which is probably why they brought me in. I'm curious, though, as to why this approach?"

"I'm not exactly privy to what's mushing around in their brains, but it would seem there's a conflict of interests. My man says pop him, he's a lost cause, the weak link, you know. But I guess the guy at the top don't want him blown away."

"What about the woman?"

"His wife? Not on the agenda. Unless there's no other way."

"Tell me, what is she like?"

"Class with a capital C."

"Class, trash, it hardly matters. It will all be over soon. *Honeymoon interruptus.*" He had lingered over the words as if coining a beautiful phrase. "And who will console the bride?"

"Joe, you're nuts."

"I've been called worse. So. Where are they now?"

"Still in L.A. But according to my contact"—he looked at his watch—"they should be hopping aboard the fly-buggy within the hour."

"I'd better be on my way, as well. Enjoy your dinner with the uh, clothiers?"

"No strain there. You should see the spread they put out. And what comes before could knock you under the table. Jeez, all those toasts. I'll hoist one for us, Joe, to our success. Hey"—the sound he made was halfway between a wheeze and laughter—"how about I drink a toast to the bride and groom?"

"You find that funny?"

"Kinda. Actually, it breaks me up."

"Toast Ivan the Terrible, for all I care. Just show up at the appointed time." The line went dead.

Sure, sure, Joe. Whatever you say, Joe. *Asshole.*

The morning was marked by toasts, first at brunch and now as part of a rousing sendoff to the bride and groom at Los Angeles International Airport.

In the bar where they congregated, the guests sipped champagne, with the newlyweds the center of attraction. Now all eyes converged on Kelly and Larry as Steve proposed a final toast. Nadine, raising her glass with the others, found her attention straying from the honorees as she focused upon her husband. Quite unexpectedly, she felt teary-eyed. Perhaps it was the champagne or the sentiment engendered by the occasion, but at this moment, she fought an overpowering urge to proclaim to the assembled guests, to anyone who would listen, that she had been fortunate beyond her dreams to have found Steve Hanson, a man she could love with every fiber of her mind and body.

She smiled inwardly. Venting her emotions, much less telling the world, was hardly her style. But she would reveal her feelings to Steve in a very special, private way. God knows, he deserved to be told and shown how much he was loved and appreciated. Though seldom surrendering to introspection, Nadine recognized she wasn't the easiest person to live with. She could list outspoken, impulsive, and fault-finding in the negative column, for starters. And how many times had she acted the bitch, badgering Steve until she got her way? Especially if a business trip or an unexpected conference took precedence over an activity of her choosing.

But on the flip side of the coin, persistence, ambition, and drive were traits indicative of the doer, the attainer, a person such as herself who, when presented with the opportunity, had seized the moment to finesse her way into the life of this man. That he was a prominent banker, a mover and shaker in the community, had furthered her cause. Whatever his status, whatever her motives, she had fallen deeply in love.

For certain, she was no Dorothy Hanson. Steve's first wife, despite her retiring manner, commanded respect. Her upright carriage, fine patrician features, and understated but costly attire attested to her membership in an upper echelon of society. Nadine knew the type, had immediately spotted old m-o-n-e-y when Dorothy, vacationing in

Southern California, had wandered into Nadine's millinery shop on fashionable Ocean Boulevard.

Santa Monica wasn't star-studded Malibu, nor could it compete in status with Laguna Beach or La Jolla, beachfront cities farther to the south where bougainvillea-draped villas perched over the Pacific. However, an ocean-view penthouse suite atop a luxury hotel, standing side by side with similar properties, was a snug retreat for an ailing woman, a welcome intermission from a demanding social life.

Steve had accompanied his wife to Nadine's establishment on repeat visits, and then on one damp, chilly day in early June when fog drabbed the trees and grayed the ocean, Steve came into the shop alone. His wife had succumbed to cancer; the rest was history.

Eventually Nadine had taken the place of the gentle, unassuming Dorothy. Though the two women differed dramatically, Steve hadn't conferred sainthood on his deceased wife, and despite her own deficiencies, Nadine could take pride in how she had handled the transition from Santa Monica shop owner to San Francisco socialite. Even if some of the old guard regarded her with distaste, the majority of Steve's circle had come to accept her by now, some most affirmatively. She was a good hostess, a creative party-giver, and a lively conversationalist. Moreover, Steve had praised her as an exuberant and loving companion, as well as a zestful sex partner. However. There was always room for improvement, and step number one, she decided, was for her to become familiar with the concept of restraint. Ergo, she would leash her tongue. Also, she would strive for more understanding of the demands placed upon a man of Steve's stature.

Enough soul searching. Her thoughts now returned to the newlyweds, to Kelly as a wife. Would she be doting, sacrificing, compliant? No, hardly. She would be a 'good' wife, whatever that meant, without forfeiting her integrity. She would wield her intelligence in solving domestic skirmishes and exercise caution before running off at the mouth (unlike her mother). However, her daughter could be stubborn, like her father, and uncompromising, as well. Perhaps if she had talked to Kelly before the wedding, had offered counsel?

Nadine almost choked on her champagne. Who was she kidding? She loved her daughter with a passion, but the Independent One would interpret such a move on her part as interference, fault-finding.

Vanessa was another story. Though Nadine's firstborn had inherited her father's looks, she was closer to her mother in temperament, and through the years, they had enjoyed a special camaraderie.

Vanessa, also, had been a radiant bride. Nadine watched as Kelly turned to her sister, as the girls hugged goodbye. *Shit! It all looks so promising in the beginning.* She set her glass down hard, spilling some of her drink, and then rummaged in her purse for her cigarettes. Eyes narrowed as she lighted up, she contemplated the week ahead. Vanessa was hurting. Her baby was stressed-out, torn, and fragmented, and she, Nadine, was determined to get at the truth. But it wouldn't be easy, particularly if what she suspected was correct: that marital problems were at issue. She inhaled deeply and expelled the smoke. Vanessa wouldn't care to admit that her mother had been right after all, that she had detected character flaws in Gordon Stuart from the very onset of their courtship.

She sighed, remembering her vows concerning restraint and tolerance. Well, that was with Steve. With her daughter, she would, of course, show compassion and offer the wisdom of her years. But game-playing was out of the question. If Vanessa chose not to confide in her, she would make it her business to extract the truth. They would go from there.

It was past time to check in at their departure gate, but Kelly wanted to speak with Larry's mother before they boarded. She was becoming increasingly fond of her mother-in-law and regretted that they had spent so little time together. A quiet woman, Audrey could hold her own in turning a phrase; moreover, she was a good listener. Away from her turf, however, she appeared rigid and lacking in spontaneity. Of course, in Phoenix she hadn't had to compete with Nadine.

Audrey and Fern, standing off to the side, had distanced themselves from the others. As Kelly approached, Fern leaned down to her mother. "I'm going to find Larry," she said.

Audrey nodded, but her eyes, a pale imitation of her children's, were on Kelly. What a wonderful girl, so right for Larry. It would be a fine marriage, rich in love and respect. She could sense it and feel it deep down in the core of her body. Their happiness, so evident, might rub off on other family members. *Wouldn't that be a godsend? Lord knows, it's time for a happy marriage in the Townsend family.*

"I didn't have the chance to say this yesterday," Fern was saying to Larry, "but Kelly is one classy lady; the future, I'd say, is definitely looking up for you."

"I'm counting on that," Larry said. He was pleased by his sister's comments, but disturbed, too, as he took note of her brittle tone and the way her gaze darted from him to something beyond. She was like a beautifully tended, sleek feline, brushed, manicured, bejeweled to perfection. But within the glittering cage prowled a trapped and despairing creature.

He wanted to comfort her, to help her, but he didn't know what to say and besides, she seemed caught up in her own thoughts now, a faraway look in her eyes. He cleared his throat and waited. When he had her attention, he said, "Why didn't Tom come? Why didn't you bring the kids?" When she didn't answer, he persisted. "Fern, what the hell is going on with you and Tom?"

She shrugged. "We pretty much lead separate lives. You know that. Oh, Tom's a good provider and cares about the children, when he's around. I'm not even sure there've been other women. I don't know, Larry." A wistful note had crept into her voice. "He's charm personified, all attentiveness when we're in public. At home"—she shook her head—"I'm living with someone who's polite, distant, preoccupied. Maybe we've simply grown apart. As for the kids, we do have a live-in housekeeper, so they're in good hands. Oh, I guess they would have enjoyed the wedding, all of this." She gestured to indicate their surroundings. "However, I felt the need to get away, to be unencumbered, shall we say?" The mask was once again in place, the edge back in her voice.

He gave her arm a squeeze, started to turn away, and then bent down to give her a kiss. "You hang in there." This time his retreat was swift and deliberate. It wouldn't do for her to see the tears that formed in his eyes.

At last they were on their way, in line to board their flight. As they presented tickets and boarding passes, Larry glanced behind them, his gaze sweeping the waiting area. The room was practically empty, and of the few who remained, there was no sign of the short, squat man, his trademark dark glasses concealing his eyes. In his dreams, Larry had seen those eyes. Loathsome and bug-like or aloof and merciless, they characterized the man—defined him. They were the eyes of a killer.

Chapter Seven

Acapulco Honeymoon

*L*arry set down his piña colada, relishing the aftertaste of the cool, sweet liquid. "Ah, that's good," he said to Kelly. "A life saver."

Kelly pushed her hair away from her face. "I guess I'm not going to melt after all."

They sat at their hotel's poolside bar, its thatched roof shielding them from the sun. Squealing children cavorted in the water while the adults chatted over drinks, pausing to fan themselves or request familiar Latin songs from the ever-obliging mariachi musicians. It was a lively scene, though far from jarring, the fiesta flavor kept low key in deference to the sun's benevolence.

The transformation of 'lively' into 'raucous' commenced in a matter of seconds, with the arrival of a party of three couples whose raised voices and excessive laughter suggested an intake of margaritas over main courses.

Larry observed his wife's wary expression upon the entrance of the fun-in-the-sun bunch. He noted her look of incredulity as she watched one of the six-some—a tall, skinny man with thinning brown hair—flap his pasty white arms and bark out walrus-like sounds to the utter delight of his group. To add to the incongruity, the man wore against his bare chest a large pendant-style watch, the face adorned with a smirking Donald Duck, who had traded in his jaunty sailor's hat for a weighty sombrero.

Kelly turned to him, breaking into a soft giggle. Larry thought she had never appeared lovelier. Her pale skin was flushed, and her eyes, which seemed to take on the light of the tropics, glinted green and gold.

"We can remove ourselves," he said, gesturing toward the gardens. Against ever-increasing decibels of noise, the hotel's acreage beyond the pool area offered the solace of tropical foliage and gardens, of exotic creatures and wildlife made up of turtles, parrots, peacocks, and a range of colorful birds. "Care to take a stroll?"

"In this heat? You're not serious," she said, her smile softening her response. "Besides, I'm about strolled out for today."

Within the last hour, they had returned by taxi to their hillside hotel, exhausted after a long walk that had carried them away from the beaches and through an older part of town to the Zocalo. Drawn by the sound of music to the main plaza opposite the waterfront, they'd stayed for a band concert, camera in hand, as they'd snapped dutifully at everything in sight. Later, they had explored the flea market, dodging sidewalk vendors and beggar children. (Give to one and you have an army following you, Larry had insisted.) Finally, they'd ventured down to the docks to watch the arrival of a fishing boat and to view, anchored out on the bay, a cruise ship, stately with its fluttering flags, yet enticing, too, an alluring presence to all who might yearn for adventure in far-off exotic ports.

"We'll sail off someday, maybe book passage on a freighter," Larry had said, pulling Kelly close.

"You're a romantic, a bloody romantic," she had teased back. "I love it! I love you." She'd raised her lips to be kissed.

The day before had been more relaxing. They had signed up for a cruise of Acapulco Bay, which featured a stop at a secluded beach. There, in a party atmosphere, they'd gorged on chapulas—a tortilla-based concoction topped with chicken and beans, chilies, tomatoes, and onions—and on melons and mangos, all the while enjoying the antics of a beer-drinking donkey. The mementos of the day included a photo of themselves at the dock before boarding, as well as one taken of them on board, standing at the rail after departure.

That evening, they had dined on the terrace of El Mirador Hotel, where, cooled by ocean breezes, they watched in awe as divers, some with flaming torches plunged from nearby cliffs into the shallow waters below. It was a dazzling performance, marked by skill and precision, each graceful dive timed to coincide with the incoming tide. Later as the divers moved quietly among the patrons of El Mirador, Larry had tipped ungrudgingly, but he could feel a change come over him, a chill pervade his very being.

As he had become increasingly quiet, Kelly had questioned his mood. Why was he so pensive, so somber? He'd struggled to respond in a rational manner, but in the end, he'd blurted out his feelings. "What we've seen tonight is absolutely insane. Like that!" He'd snapped his fingers. "Like that, those guys could be splattered all over those rocks. It's crazy, it's stupid."

"So is jumping out of an airplane, or running with the bulls in Spain. I can't imagine why you're so upset, so . . . so discombobulated, Larry. You're the one who was all excited about coming here."

"I know. I know. The famous cliff divers of La Quebrada. I'd read about them, couldn't imagine being in Acapulco and not seeing them." He'd paused, looking past her toward the cliffs, his anger diluted by a mixture of sadness and regret. Then he'd shrugged and met her gaze. "Don't mind me. I guess I was thinking life is too short as it is. Why ask for trouble?"

He'd tried to sound offhand, offering a smile as he posed his question, but he could tell from Kelly's demeanor that she'd been rattled by his outburst.

"Some people like living on the edge," she'd said, "need to take chances, gamble, speculate, and play hell with their lives. It's in their blood."

They had dropped the subject, and for the rest of the evening and the ensuing day, he'd remained in good spirits. Now, he was able to view the jolly six-some with tolerance, if not pleasure. "Would you like to have another?" Larry pointed to their empty glasses.

Kelly shook her head and glanced about her. "These people seem to have unlimited energy, which is more than I can say for myself. Would you agree to a little siesta time?"

"I would. Does that mean what I think it means?"

Kelly raised her eyebrows, her eyes wide with the look of innocence. "Why Lawrence Townsend, whatever can you mean?"

They rose from the table, Kelly preceding Larry as they made their way through the narrow aisle that separated the tables. They had to pass by the party people, and as Kelly neared the group, Larry noticed the man who had imitated the walrus follow Kelly with his gaze, a silly grin on his face. Then, suddenly, the man dropped his jaw, his leer replaced by a look of uncertainty.

"I winked at him," Kelly told Larry later. "I gave him a broad, slow wink."

What they didn't see was the man's expression as he focused on Larry. Detached, dispassionate, as if appraising a piece of merchandise, the besotted buffoon had metamorphosed into a sober-minded, no-nonsense type of individual. And indeed, he was a man with a mission.

It was almost ten in the evening before they were seated for dinner. The long, sultry afternoon was now a languid memory, the torpor of the day replaced by an energizing coolness rendered by breezes off the bay.

Kelly, outfitted in a multi-hued sundress of a soft gauzy fabric, pulled a matching stole across her bare shoulders.

"Are you chilly?" Larry asked.

"Just the tiniest bit, but it would probably take a January blizzard to discourage me from dining al fresco."

"I take it you like eating out of doors?"

"Out of doors?" She repressed a giggle. "Sweetheart, you make it sound like munching hot dogs at a backyard barbecue."

"You're right. This place deserves something a little more descriptive," he said, looking around.

The restaurant was an extension of a mountaintop Mediterranean-style villa, the huge terrace providing diners with panoramic views of the bay and city lights in the distance. For closer viewing, a rectangular lighted pool, bordered on one side by palm trees, created a lavish centerpiece. Glass-topped tables reflected decorative lighting artistically displayed in potted plants and in shrubbery that rimmed the terrace.

Larry had given their drink order to the waiter, and now he leaned back in his chair, the picture of contentment. "You have my

permission to serve meals on the deck when we get home"—he bowed—
"al fresco, that is, any time you like." They had decided to live in Larry's
house, for the time being, with Kelly partially moved in.

"Are you talking pre-theater or post-theater?"

He sighed, playacting the martyr. "That's what I get for marrying
into the theater. All those screwy hours."

"Well, not immediately."

"That's right. The current production sports an all-male cast. Pity
I didn't try out."

She laughed. "You're joking, of course." She turned serious.
"Look, it's nobody's fault we fell in love. Rick will get used to the idea
of my being your wife. He's not going to fire me or force me out of the
Playhouse by making my life miserable. He's certainly not going to cut
me out of parts." She stated this emphatically, praying she was right, that
Rick would be fair.

She should have seen it coming, that his interest in her had taken
a romantic turn. The signs had been there, but because of her
involvement with Larry, she'd been insensitive to Rick's growing
devotion. Occasionally, she had joined him for a drink or late supper
after a performance, and on one such evening, he'd professed his love for
her. It hadn't been a great moment for either of them, and Kelly,
struggling with feelings of guilt, had consoled herself that Rick wasn't
blameless either. He could have avoided the humiliation, the awkward
aftermath, had it not been for his gigantic ego, his absolute conviction he
couldn't fail at anything.

But enough about Rick, Kelly thought. Their drinks had arrived
and when they had toasted one another, Larry plucked a small hibiscus
blossom from the flower arrangement that decorated their table. Placing
it in her hair, he studied the effect. "It's perfect," he said. "Adds just the
right touch."

She raised her glass. "My husband, the fashion expert." Then,
half-seriously, she added, "You don't suppose there's a law against
filching flowers?"

He shook his head. "The way I figure it, they wouldn't dare
complain. Not at these prices."

She looked backward, and then over Larry's shoulder. "I don't see the Mexican militia swooping down on us." She caught her breath. "But oh, God, I do see a familiar figure."

"What are you talking about? Who would we know here?" He turned to follow her gaze. Descending the staircase—a long, fluid creation that transported guests from the enclosed entrance—were a man and woman: she of the irritating laugh and he of the walrus imitation. "It couldn't be," Larry said. "People like that don't come to places like this."

"It's hard to tell in this light," Kelly said, squinting into the darkness, "but I'd swear it's the fun couple, and it looks as if they're coming our way."

They were; however the maître d', who was in the lead, was heading to a section far removed from the Townsends, beyond them. Still, it was necessary to pass their table, and as they did so, the man, his expression solemn, favored Kelly with a slight bow, his eye closing in a slow wink.

Later, their passion spent, Kelly lay in Larry's arms, warm, drowsy, and tingling, savoring the lingering aftereffects of love. She was deeply stirred, imbued with a sense of wonder that two people could provide for one another such intense pleasure, achieve an intimacy so profound. "It's not fair to be this happy," she said.

He nuzzled her ear. "I know. I feel like we've been to the moon and back."

"Don't sell yourself short. I feel as if I've just returned from another solar system."

"We'll start all our romantic evenings with dinner under the stars," he said, biting gently at her earlobe.

"And what of our romantic mornings and afternoons?"

"So who needs stars?" He raised himself to place a kiss on her forehead, and then to a sitting position. "Since we don't smoke, I can't very well offer you a cigarette, but if you'd like, I'll sing for you."

"Sing? You sing? Larry,"—she was laughing as she sat up— "since when do I need to be entertained? Look, if you need something to do, how about turning off the air conditioning and opening up the windows?"

"Good idea. About the only song I know is *Home on the Range.*" He was up and then back in bed moments later, tasks accomplished, nestled comfortably next to her, his arm draped lightly over her shoulders. The breeze was slight, but it was cooling and carried the fragrance of gardenias, the sounds of the tropics. "Not exactly a match for the trade winds of Hawaii," he said, "but pleasant."

"Vanessa and Gordon honeymooned in Hawaii. I was happy for her, that two such beautiful people had found one another and were beginning their lives together in such an idyllic place. I was also a bit jealous." She gave a little snort. "Make that wildly jealous."

When she didn't continue, Larry said, "And?"

She sighed. "Now, I feel sorry for Vanessa, because she suspects Gordon is cheating on her. If he is, she'll probably look the other way—she's so loony in love with the guy." She mulled over what she had said. "If the worst happens, if they divorce, at least there are no children."

"That always presents a complication." He shifted position, removing his arm from around her.

She looked sideways at him, hesitant to probe, but too curious to keep still. "Tell me about Fern."

He was silent for a moment, and then as if reciting a laundry list, said, "She's married to a successful businessman. They have four children, a beautiful home in Scottsdale, outside Phoenix; three cars, one a Mercedes convertible; household help; membership in two country clubs . . . I could go on." He turned to her. "She's also unhappy, frustrated"—he raised his hands—"living a 'nothing' existence, I guess."

"I don't understand the problem. I realize being showered with luxuries doesn't necessarily bring the bluebird of happiness, but something can be said for the good life and four children. Does he run around on her or abuse her or the children?"

"She says not, but she also says he ignores her, and that there's no love there. So despite the kids, she's a very lonely woman. I'd judge her self-esteem—say on a scale of one to ten—at about zero."

"Sounds like emotional abuse to me. Why doesn't she get out, start a new life?"

"And give up what she has? I don't mean to sound cynical; deep down Fern's not shallow, but she's a very insecure woman, and more fragile than she appears. I wonder if she isn't at the breaking point."

"I guess I've learned a thing or two about judging from first impressions. How sad for everyone concerned."

"When it comes to happily ever after, we Townsends have a poor track record. Take my father. Opinionated. Set in his ways. He didn't encourage discussion, much less argument. We either caved in, or it was all-out war."

"I can guess who capitulated, and I don't mean you."

"Yeah, right. Fern found it easier not to make waves. As for my mother, she pretty much went along with his demands, at least when we were kids." He smiled. "When Fern was out of the house, and I was in college, I think Audrey staged a quiet rebellion and told the old man where to go, because in their later years, when she stood up to him, he backed off and treated her with respect. At any rate, when I looked at Fern and at my parents, I figured one of us had to avoid the marriage trap." He fell silent for a moment, and then turned to Kelly, gathering her into his arms. "I was wrong," he murmured. "Was I ever wrong."

In the morning Kelly and Larry left their hotel for an outing at the beach—or more specifically, for what their brochure described as being 'transported by air-conditioned bus to a picturesque beach club for swimming and a picnic lunch.' The bus provided air, but of the hot and humid variety, through vents and open windows; the 'club' was a rustic dining facility, partly enclosed, with one side open to the beach.

The setting, however, was lovely, with tables set up on the beach. Their meal was a typical Mexican spread of tamales, refried beans and rice, along with servings of watermelon, cantaloupe and papaya.

The combination of bountiful food, generous drinks, and the unrelenting sun was, Larry observed, enough to produce a lethargy of monumental proportions. His eyes slitted, he stared at the surf, soothed by the rhythmic motion, the sound of the waves lapping onto the shore, as the sun wrapped him in a downy comforter. "I can't move," he murmured. "I will never, ever move from this spot."

"Then we'll stay," Kelly said. "Forever." Her voice dreamy, she continued, "We'll live on starchy Mexican food and down pitchers of margaritas. We'll sit and grow fat. The sun will turn our bulges brown and wrinkle our bodies so when we touch, the feel will be of dried-out snakeskins."

Larry laughed and sat upright. "I've changed my mind. Besides, you haven't forgotten I'm scuba diving this afternoon?"

"I haven't forgotten." She looked thoughtful. "Kelly, the coward. I wish I'd had the guts to take the course and become certified, but the equipment alone boggles the mind."

"All I plan to use is a face mask and fins. In this climate, you can bypass the rubber suit. Of course, there's the paraphernalia that connects to the tank."

"So the tank is strapped to your back?"

"Right. The straps run over my shoulders and around my waist. Perfectly safe, my love."

"It better be," she said. "I've no intention of giving you up to some bulgy eyed piranha."

"Not to worry. I wouldn't miss celebrating our last night in Acapulco."

"Don't show up draped in seaweed."

"Oh, nag, nag, nag." He reached over to give her a kiss. "Come on, let's take a walk so we can get in shape for dinner."

"Food? Is that all you think about? Never mind," she said, laughing. "Catch me if you can!" They were off on a run down the beach.

Dinner, in the open-air rooftop restaurant at their hotel, was designed to be a gala event, a festive finale to a memorable week, but something was a little off, Kelly decided. Larry had seemed preoccupied since his return from the waters off Roquetta Island, and his comments regarding the pleasures of exploring the deep sounded, to her ear, forced and constrained, as if other matters intruded. She debated, briefly, the wisdom of voicing her concern, and then reached across the table to place her hand on his. "What is it? What's wrong?"

He studied the menu, but appeared angry, his mouth a tight line. When he looked up at her, his expression softened, but in his eyes was the disquieting, almost haunted look she thought she had witnessed the night of their wedding reception.

"Why would you think anything is wrong?"

"Larry, I'm not stupid or insensitive, for God's sake." She removed her hand.

"Anything but, my love. Okay. I guess I was jumping the gun a little, mentally tackling a problem or two at work. Oh, nothing I can't solve. A minor business glitch, that's all."

"You're sure that's all it is? That it's not something I've done to upset you?"

"Oh, honey, for heaven's sake, no. I was projecting ahead, thinking about some specifications that may be in error." He looked down for a moment, and then cast his gaze on Kelly. "I've been a jerk, and I apologize. The honeymoon is still on, you know. In fact, as far as I'm concerned, the honeymoon will never end."

"Spoken like a true bridegroom," she said, pleased by his response, if not entirely convinced by his explanation.

They turned to their menus, to topics of mutual interest, their night illuminated by a shower of stars, their senses stirred by gypsy melodies, replete with rippling cadenzas, performed by the strolling violinist who had singled out the Townsends as grist for his inspiration. The evening now progressed beautifully, a fitting tribute to romance, to rekindled desire. Then Kelly saw Larry stiffen and put down his fork. He stared intently at something beyond her shoulder.

He caught her watching him. "They're like a bad penny," he said, "always turning up."

"Who?" She turned to follow his gaze, attracted also by the sound of laughter. Sure enough, it was the tall, skinny, man who had intruded upon them at the pool, and had dined at the terrace restaurant. He was seated with his blond companion and another couple, the women now breaking into giggles. "You're right," Kelly said, "they do seem to follow us around. What do you bet this jolly group will be on the plane tomorrow? Should be fun and frivolity all the way home." She raised her glass of wine to indicate 'party time', but Larry was frowning.

"He was on the island this afternoon."

"Scuba diving?"

"No, just hanging around, as far as I know. We nodded, and that was about it. I didn't see him when it was time to come back."

"It does seem strange. There's no reason for him to be interested in us. Unless he has designs on you?"

Larry, his good humor returning, rejected the notion, adding that in a very short time, he would show Kelly just who had designs on whom.

❧

But once back in the room, Larry was caught up in his own thoughts, with bed the farthest thing from his mind.

Kelly, too, appeared to be occupied with matters other than romance as she deliberated on whether to pack then or wait until morning. "Oh, let's wait until tomorrow," she said. "After all, the plane doesn't leave until late afternoon. Which reminds me, I'd like to get in some shopping in the morning. I'm not happy with those earrings I bought for Vanessa. They're really better suited for Nadine."

Larry only half-listened. "Kelly, where are the pictures taken of us on the boat trip? Could I see them, please?"

"Sure. If I can remember where I stashed them." She crossed to the closet. "Probably up here, next to the camera," she said, indicating the top shelf. She found and brought down the two photos, pausing now to look them over.

Larry was at her side, his impatience growing. "Uh, do you mind if I take them for a minute?"

"No, you can have them." She handed them over.

He carried them into the bathroom, where the light was brightest. "I barely glanced at them the other day. I wanted to take another look before you packed them away."

"You turned out better than I did in the one with us at the rail of the boat. Don't you think?"

He didn't answer. He had already scanned the one she referred to and had found nothing unusual. It was the other photo that most interested him, the shot of the two of them at the dock, before boarding. They were posed next to a life preserver festively adorned with miniature Mexican flags, with the name of the boat inscribed at the top. And in the background?

He held the picture up to the light. Squinting, he focused on the left side of the photo, on a man and woman, their backs to the camera as they approached the gangplank, on a smiling crew member at a distance behind them; and on the right, a tackle shop, though only a portion of it showed. Two men, one short and heavy, the other tall and thin, stood in front of the shop. Though the features of the latter were indistinct, his face in shadow, there was no mistaking the souvenir watch suspended from the man's neck. Clearly identifiable on the short man were dark glasses, glinting in the sunlight.

Larry lowered the picture and stared at his reflection, his gaze fixed on the eyes in the mirror. They were pale blue agates lost in an ashen field. He shut out the image, making himself breathe slowly and deeply as he fought for control. When he opened his eyes, Kelly stood before him, a stricken look on her face. Before she could say anything, he held up his hand, forcing a smile. "I'm afraid I'm not feeling so hot. Probably shouldn't have had the snapper at dinner, or maybe it was the salad."

"Oh, sweetheart, you look so pale." She took his arm, at the same time relieving him of the photos. "Do you want to lie down? Better yet, I have just the remedy for this kind of emergency." Releasing him, she started for her cosmetic case.

"Kelly, no. I think I need fresh air. Let me try to walk this off." He was at the door. *Have to get out of here, need to be alone, need to think this out.*

"Do you think you should be by yourself? Maybe I'd better go with you—"

But he was out the door before she'd finished her sentence.

When thirty minutes had elapsed, Kelly decided to give Larry five more minutes, but it was no good. Her imagination running wild, she pictured him gray with nausea or collapsed and unconscious in a remote area of the grounds.

Her heart pounded in her ears as she grabbed the key and let herself out of the room. She hurried along the road that led to the front of the hotel, to the open lobby that, in daylight, afforded a spectacular view of the bay. There, she could take an elevator down to the pool area, thus avoiding a nighttime hike over winding pathways and uneven steps that led to the lower grounds.

She pushed past a security guard armed with his walkie-talkie, dodged a couple strolling arm in arm, and as she approached the entrance to the lobby, was only marginally aware of the taxi pulling up to the front of the hotel, discharging its passengers. Laughter and voices in animated conversation awoke her to the realization she was not alone, that people were directly behind her as she climbed the steps to the lobby. Obviously they didn't have a care in the world, an aspect which provoked in her, though fleetingly, a feeling of resentment.

The lobby was in shadows, the only illumination coming from the reception desk. The party that followed Kelly into the hotel consisted of two middle-aged couples whose heavy English accents made their conversation almost unintelligible to Kelly. As they turned from the desk, having collected their room keys from the night clerk, a remark from one of the men elicited spasms of laughter, followed by further commentary of an uproarious nature that evoked even more hilarity. Not to notice them, one had to be deaf or deeply self-absorbed.

She had to wonder about the man standing with his back to them at the far side of the lobby, completely oblivious to their actions. In the dim light, he looked like a statue, unmoving, meditative, head bowed. Kelly had spotted him as she neared the elevator and now moved in for a closer inspection. It was with relief, mixed with a degree of trepidation, that she recognized Larry. Though it was impossible to assess his state of health, he didn't appear to be in a worsened condition. She started toward him, and then stopped. If he had wanted her along, he would have said so.

He had straightened up and was rotating his head as if to relieve neck strain. As far as she could tell, he appeared to be okay. Kelly decided to hightail it back to the room.

Larry had been only vaguely aware of voices, laughter, night sounds. *Come on, think, think,* he told himself. *Cut through the whys, what-ifs, if-onlys.*

Okay. The phone call in late November. He could hear the voice—assured, no-nonsense, direct. "You're needed. We're depending on you."

Then his response, brief and to the point: "Thank you, but no thank you." He was through with them, finished. Period.

His caller had made no further attempt to shake his resolve and seemed resigned over his decision to back out of the operation. Still, Larry had felt edgy, off balance, jumping when the phone rang, constantly checking his rear view mirror. Gradually, though, he'd come to believe he was no longer at risk. Until early in February.

That was when the hang-up calls started, when he began to notice the all-too-familiar white Chrysler cruise past him or keep pace with him two lanes over, the driver sitting squat in his seat, chubby arm resting on the open windowsill, eyes obscured by dark glasses.

What did it mean? Were they acting out of sheer vindictiveness, or was it an omen of something more sinister? The questions loomed and then waned, settling into the back of his mind, and then he put them on hold as his wedding day approached.

Now, he had no choice but to meet the consequences of his folly head-on. He knew who had sent these men, and why. It was because he knew too much. High stakes, big money: that's what it was all about. And no matter his argument that he posed no threat, they weren't buying it; he knew he was a marked man.

God help him, but he had the fight of his life ahead. If he should survive, what then? Would he have lost it all anyway? The love and respect of his wife and family? His business?

He shook his head as if to clear his mind. The future, if he had one, was at the end of a long, hazardous road. The present was Kelly. He needed to get back to his wife.

Kelly had been in bed for about five minutes when she heard the key in the lock. He entered quietly, closing the door behind him slowly, reflectively, it seemed. She tensed, a feeling of uneasiness pervading her as she wondered if he'd caught a glimpse of her in the lobby. Half rising, she was about to switch on the light, but in two quick strides he was next to her, reaching for her, cradling her in his arms.

"You're all right? You're feeling all right now?"

"Shh," he said, brushing his lips against hers, once again drawing her to him, this time with greater urgency. Then releasing her, he began to remove his clothes, stopping once to kiss her lips, her throat, her breasts as he helped her to remove her nightgown.

It might have been a repeat of their first time together, a frantic need to couple, to seek immediate gratification. But he retreated, took time as they kissed and caressed to trace with his fingers the outline of her face, her shoulders, and to make small brush-strokes with his fingers down her spine. Kelly could feel herself melting into a mindless expanse of sensate pleasure, intensifying now as he caressed her breasts, as his fingers moved downward to explore her wetness. Overwhelmed, she buried her face in his chest and then sought his lips, involuntarily rubbing against him, rhythmically moving her hips. Again, he held off to extend the excitement of arousal and continued to kiss and touch her in all the secret places until, when he entered her, there was no prolonging the moment, and they moved with increasing frenzy to climax. Kelly, crying out, was swept up in wave after wave of exquisite sensation.

They held each other for a long time, and when their breathing had slowed, when normality was within reach, Kelly, feeling content and drowsy, snuggled closer to press cheeks, to touch his lips in a goodnight kiss.

Unexpectedly, he turned away, but she had felt his face. It was wet with tears.

Chapter Eight

reakfast by the pool at Hotel Palacio was a leisurely affair, with 'leisurely' a euphemism for slow service, Kelly decided. Larry hadn't commented on the delay; he looked tired and seemed unusually quiet. As they waited for their huevos rancheros, Kelly checked her watch. "If this continues, I'm going to storm the kitchen. Maybe crack a few huevos over somebody's head." Then she amended her statement with a soft "whoops" as the serving cart, with its covered dishes, suddenly appeared.

"We're doing fine." Larry reached for a roll and broke it in two, and then spread butter and jam over the larger half.

Kelly dipped her fork into her egg concoction and brought a small portion gingerly to her mouth. "It's okay, but nothing special. I'm sorry I insisted we come all the way down here."

"Honey, for goodness sake, the dinner we had here the other night was terrific. I hoped we'd make it back."

She nodded, but suspected the kind words were an attempt to spare her feelings. The expense alone was a turn-off, she figured, particularly as Larry had insisted on sharing a taxi into town with three guests from the hotel. Kelly had been careful not to object, wondering if they might be running low on funds. In a business like Larry's, one could expect lean periods, but they hadn't talked finances, swept along on the tide of wedding mania. The thought faded as she studied him, wondering if his self-absorption was related to the problems he'd mulled at dinner the night before. Or was it the dinner? In the morning light, he looked drawn, washed out.

"I was thinking," Larry said, "that even if the meal isn't up to snuff, the location couldn't be better."

"For what? Oh, you mean for shopping."

"Yes, that, and—" He paused. "Well, it occurred to me we're

only minutes from Caleta Beach." He ran his tongue over his lips. "If I time it right, I can catch the ferry to Roquetta Island."

"Wait a minute. You're going scuba diving today?"

"I thought while you shopped, I'd try my luck with a spear gun, go after grouper or trunkfish. I can rent the equipment here at the hotel, buy some swim trunks, and stow my clothes in a locker."

"You're kidding! You don't have that much time."

"Sure I do. Honey, it's only ten. What time does our plane leave—at four? I can probably make it back between one and one thirty, two at the latest."

"When does the boat leave? What if you've missed it?"

"Then I'll come back. It's possible I could even rent a power boat." He reached over to take her hand. "Why are you giving me that funny look?"

"Because this doesn't seem like you, to be so impulsive."

"How long have you known me?"

"Oh, now I get it. Will the real Lawrence Townsend step forward?"

They bantered a bit more as they drank their coffee and finished their rolls. Neither, it appeared, had any appetite for the huevos rancheros. Then Kelly reluctantly wished Larry good luck as he was off to go scuba diving on their last morning in Acapulco.

The shops along Costera Miguel Aleman offered a variety of merchandise, from fine jewelry and designer wear to tacky souvenir goods. Kelly had found a pair of silver earrings, sculptured like a Matisse cut-out, that were perfect for Vanessa. She'd discovered them at her first stop, so with time on her hands, she decided to keep going, to browse if not to buy. Her heart wasn't in it. With just hours left in Acapulco, she wanted her husband with her and not underwater, playing spear-the-fish.

She stopped herself. She was being selfish, working up a snit over nothing. Most men, and this obviously included Larry, found shopping a bore. Better to have him indulge in a macho-male thing than trail unhappily after her. If she wanted togetherness, tennis would do. She resolved then and there to brush up on her game.

Kelly had finished packing and was opening and closing bureau drawers in a last minute inspection. With the exception of a few toilet articles, Larry was packed, which was all to the good, she thought, glancing at her watch. She had called the front desk to see if they could extend their stay beyond check-out time and received gracious assurances the room was theirs until two or even three o'clock, without further charge. It was only twelve-thirty, but the thought that dinner on the plane was hours off made her suddenly famished. She counted on her husband to make it back in time for lunch.

At one o'clock, Kelly left a note for Larry and made her way down to the pool restaurant. Seated in the covered area, she ordered a margarita (So there, Larry!) and then debated whether to snack on tacos or order a club sandwich with its accompanying fruit platter. She decided on the latter, reasoning if Larry were to arrive by one thirtyish or so, there would be ample to share.

The mariachis, it seemed, had the day off. Only a few people were seated for lunch, and no one was in the pool. Kelly would have welcomed a crash of revelers, animal impersonators included, anything to take her mind off the waiting.

She looked at her watch. *Damn! A quarter to two. Where is he? He didn't need to cut it this close.* She picked up a section of her sandwich, looked at it, and then set it down. She nibbled at the fruit and sipped her drink.

"Everything okay, señorita? You want another drink?" The waiter, hovering over her, brushed his hand lightly over her shoulder.

Kelly shifted in her chair. She met his look, her manner cool. "Just the check, please."

He responded with a wide grin. *"Tu eres muy bonita, como mango.* Pretty, like a juicy fruit," he repeated.

She stared at him. "I said I'd like my check. *Now,* if you don't mind." (Jesus, where was Larry?)

He shrugged and left, moving slowly toward the bar.

In minutes, she was making her way up to the room, displeasure replaced by anticipation as she pushed the key into the lock. "Larry?" Slowly she closed the door behind her, aware of utter silence. She moved quickly to the bathroom. Just as she had left it, with no evidence of Larry's presence. Damn.

She remembered the note, and as she focused on the table by the door, breathed a sigh of relief. The note was missing. Okay. Larry had decided to meet her by the pool, rather than waiting in the room. Somehow they'd missed each other, which meant he was on his way back. *He'd better be,* she thought, as she took notice of the time, for it was already a little after two. She moved to the door, decided to leave it ajar, and as she looked down, discovered the sheet of note paper stuck behind the leg of the table. Apparently it had drifted to the floor when she'd left the room. Kelly bit down on her lip. If Larry hadn't seen the note, he could be scouring the hotel grounds, wasting precious minutes in an attempt to track her down.

No, that wasn't right. She could disregard that scenario. Larry, for whatever reason, had been delayed. Maybe he'd called in a message to the hotel while she was at lunch. She started for the phone, and then decided to walk over to the lobby.

When she reached the wide driveway below the steps that led to the entrance, she paused to watch the arrival of two taxis, and then a third. Her husband wasn't among the passengers. Disappointed, she moved swiftly up the steps, pushing her hair back from her face, feeling the wetness in her scalp and between her breasts. *God it's humid,* she thought.

The open lobby provided a refreshing oasis from the afternoon heat, but Kelly took little notice as she hurried to the reception desk. Again, disappointment. No messages. She thought for a minute, and then asked the clerk to call their room. No one picked up the phone.

Where could he be? Why isn't he back? Her inner voice verged on hysteria, her frustration a tangible weight inside her, turning her stomach sour. She took a deep breath, expanding her diaphragm, and then slowly exhaled as she centered on the image of her strong, vital man, capable of looking after himself.

Feeling better, Kelly moved to the far corner of the lobby where she'd observed Larry the evening before. A strong breeze swept back from her forehead tendrils of hair that had curled in the humidity. Of all the hotels, their hilltop lodgings offered the best view of Acapulco Bay, and for the moment, Kelly shelved her mounting concerns to fasten her gaze on diamond glints dancing upon a broad expanse of deepest sapphire. Shutting her eyes against the wind, she pictured the bay, watercraft in gentle motion, dazzling in the sunlight . . . Larry at her side.

Voices nearby, a newly arrived couple exclaiming over the view, broke the spell. She moved away from the ledge to find a place to sit. *Think,* she told herself. *Think of an explanation for Larry's delay. Transportation problems? Very possible. Because if the ferry had conked out, Larry would be stuck on the island. Or what about a snafu over the equipment, or even a traffic tie-up? But not an accident involving Larry—dear God, no.* Still, she harbored the thought while disallowing the possibility.

With one swift movement Kelly rose from her chair to scan the lobby, hoping but failing in her quest to recognize a familiar figure.

She made her way to the lobby entrance to view the parade of arriving and departing vehicles. Several parties, perhaps in a hurry to get to the airport, scrambled to fill the taxis parked along the road leading up to the hotel. One man, descending the steps in a rush, looked faintly familiar, even from the back. Apparently he'd prearranged for the cab that now pulled up in front of him. She watched as the driver scurried around to the passenger side to open the door and saw the man start to get in. Then he paused to look up to where she stood, his gaze fastening on hers. For a second, she was thrown by the suit and tie, and then recognition set in as he broke eye contact and ducked into the back seat of the cab. It was the ubiquitous thin man. Minus the loud shirts, junk jewelry, and his noisy retinue, he projected a disquieting presence. Or was it his expression that was unsettling, the odd look on his face, as if he were trying to convey a message?

Now it was three o'clock, and Kelly abandoned any hope of making their flight. She decided to book their room for one more night and returned to the reception desk. But as she talked to the man at the desk about extending their stay, she had to turn from him as she fought tears.

"Señora, can I help you?"

The young man behind the counter had large, melting brown eyes. *Spanish eyes,* she thought distractedly. Drawn by his soft tone and his sympathetic look, she poured out her concerns, describing the events of the day. "We can always arrange for another flight, but"—and again she blinked back tears—"my husband should have arrived back an hour and a half ago."

"You don't think he forgets about the time?"

"Of course not!" Kelly had been twisting her wedding ring, the band sliding easily over moist skin. Now, she clasped her hands in an effort to restore calm. "I'm sorry," she said. "I didn't mean to raise my voice. You have to understand, my husband is not an irresponsible person. He promised to be back before two, and the fact that he hasn't appeared makes me think something is terribly wrong." She choked on the last word.

"Okay." He stole a glance at the wall clock. "In fifteen minutes, I finish here. We go together, okay? To the Hotel Palacio, to Caleta Beach, if necessary. We check it out."

"Oh, no, I can't let you to do that. I appreciate your offer, but I can't impose on your free time."

"Señora, it is no problem. My girlfriend is in Mexico City this week and"—he raised his hands—"I have the time, and I do speak the language, you know?"

She did know and was grateful beyond words, indicating, over his protestations, that he would be rewarded for his efforts.

She made a quick dash to the room—still no Larry—and penned a note before she hurried back to the lobby where the young assistant manager, whose name she learned was Enrique, waited.

She had judged him to be in his mid- to late-twenties, but wondered now if she'd been mistaken. With his slender frame and diffident manner, he appeared to be a much younger man. His features, in an oval face dominated by the soft brown eyes, were refined, almost feminine.

However, Enrique's take-charge attitude was anything but unmanly as he firmly but courteously shepherded her out of the hotel and down the road to a taxi at the end of the line, where a loud rapping on the front window brought the dozing driver to attention.

With Enrique up front with the driver, Jorge, and Kelly in back, they followed, with Kelly's guidance, the morning route that had taken the Townsends to the Hotel Palacio. They also cast an eye for traffic tie-ups or for evidence of an accident, neither of which materialized.

When they arrived at the hotel, Jorge let them out in front, indicating that he would park around the corner and stay with the car. Kelly had felt relatively calm on the way down as she concentrated on their route. Now, as they entered the lobby, she felt her knees go wobbly and her breathing become shallow. While she didn't expect Larry to pop up before her eyes, she scanned the lobby nonetheless, praying for a tall, blond male to be brought forth by the sheer intensity of her desire.

Reality, however, dictated otherwise, and Kelly and Enrique, intent on seeking information, moved along to find the manager, a Mr. Morales. Without a moment's hesitation, he ushered them into his office and in seconds was on the phone to the person in charge of renting sporting equipment, engaging now in a three-way conversation in Spanish and English as he checked with Enrique and Kelly regarding the facts of the situation.

When he was off the phone, he gave Kelly his full attention. "Señora Townsend." He smiled reassuringly. "Your husband did indeed rent scuba diving equipment at about ten-thirty this morning. However, it hasn't been returned. So you see he probably is still on the island."

"Mr. Morales, that can't be. It doesn't make sense. We're supposed to be flying out of Acapulco, on our way home. Now. This very minute!" She looked at Enrique, seeking confirmation.

Enrique nodded. "She speaks the truth, señor." He added something in rapid Spanish, but the manager, it seemed, wasn't convinced. His raised eyebrows, his barely perceptible shrug, said it all to Enrique: that this wasn't a serious matter, that boys will be boys.

With Kelly, however, his demeanor was of the consummate professional. His voice soft, his expression registering concern, he said, "I fully understand your fears, and I suspect Señor Townsend will, uh, be sent to the doghouse." He smiled at his little joke, and then turned serious. "We would be informed if there had been an accident. Please try not to worry, señora. Believe me, he'll turn up." He rose and held out his hand to each of them.

At the door, he smiled warmly at Kelly and extended his hand

81

once again to Enrique, offering as he did so a parting comment in Spanish.

Outside the office, Kelly pounced on Enrique. "What's possible? I heard *'es possible'*."

Enrique nodded. "Yes, he says it is possible your husband will not stop here but will go straight to your hotel since he is late."

"But the equipment?"

"The boys who work on the boat can bring it here. They ask for maybe a couple of American dollars. It happens all the time."

"That seems risky to me. But if I were frantic, absolutely frantic about getting somewhere—Enrique, let's call the hotel!"

They did so. Julio, who had the evening shift, checked for messages and rang their room. There was nothing to report.

"I can't believe this is happening; this cannot be happening to me." Kelly couldn't suppress a sob as she and Enrique rounded the corner of the hotel to join the waiting Jorge in his taxi. Where was Larry? This was their honeymoon, for God's sake, and here she was with two strangers, running all over town looking for a missing husband. And oh, God, what if something terrible had happened? What if she were never to see him again?

These thoughts were like a hot tong at the back of her head, sending a scorching, blistering message, drying her mouth, making her hurt all over. She felt the tears come in a rush, and though some part of her was aware of the stares of passers-by, Kelly was unable to contain herself. She gave way to her fears and frustrations.

Enrique was instantly at her side, murmuring something in Spanish as he quickly assisted her into the car. When she was settled in the back seat, Enrique slid in beside a clearly bewildered Jorge to apprise him, in a low tone, as to what had transpired.

Kelly fought for control, her sobs subsiding as she replayed the interview with the hotel manager, grasping onto his reassurances. No accident had been reported; therefore Larry was perfectly safe, and surely before long the mystery of his nonappearance would be solved.

With calm returning, Kelly leaned forward to address the two men. "I didn't mean to create a scene," she said. "I apologize for my behavior." The formality of expression was at variance with the quaver in her voice.

"Please, we understand. Do not concern yourself." Enrique's expression was grave, his eyes mirroring her distress. "Señora, what do you want to do?"

"I suppose I should return to the hotel. Unless"—she looked at both Enrique and Jorge and took a deep breath—"unless you wouldn't object to another stop?"

"Anywhere, señora. We are at your service."

Presumably Enrique felt no need to consult Jorge, and Kelly was not about to question the compliant driver. The stop she had in mind was the ferry boat dock at Caleta Beach.

Fortunately, the boat was not scheduled to depart for another twenty minutes. With Jorge wandering off to buy a cold drink, Enrique, with Kelly at his side, sought out the ferry's captain. Kelly didn't need instruction in Spanish to pick up on the captain's response; it was apparent that he had no recollection of a tall, blond gringo boarding his boat. But Enrique was welcome to question the crew, which he did. Again, a negative response.

Oh, God, what do we do now? Kelly thought as she struggled for self-control. Finally she said to Enrique, "Maybe he was never on the ferry. He could have missed it. My husband mentioned the possibility of renting a power boat."

Enrique pointed to a kiosk down the beach. "That is where you buy tickets for the ferry. Someone there maybe saw your husband."

On duty were two young men. When Enrique questioned them, one nodded and raised his arm above his head, while using the word *rubia*—which Kelly knew meant blond in Spanish. *Oh, don't let this be a dead end,* she prayed.

It seemed to take forever, the exchange between the two men, but at last Enrique turned to her, his usually soft voice edged with excitement. "Señora, this man remembers your husband. You see, it was a slow day with not many tourists."

"Okay. But what else? Did he say if he bought a ticket for the ferry?"

"No, no. He did not. The ferry had left. He didn't want to wait around, so he asks him about renting a power boat."

"Where? Do you know where—" She stopped herself. "Boat rentals back by the dock. I saw the sign. Let's go."

They found Jorge, who had been looking for them. He brought them to a man who had rented Larry a boat. At their request, he checked his records and told them the boat hadn't yet been returned.

Kelly knew exactly what she had to do. First, though, she had to call their hotel to inquire if by some miracle Larry had returned. Kelly took a shaky breath and turned to Enrique. "I'm going to find somebody, and pay them to take me over to the island in one of those." She gestured to where the power boats were moored. "I want to go along the bay, see if I can find Larry. My husband was sick last night, so it's possible he became ill again. Or it could be he's injured." She swallowed hard. "Enrique, you and Jorge don't need to stick around." She reached inside her purse. "You've been wonderful and so helpful. I can't thank you enough."

"Señora, it is not necessary." Enrique waved away the bills she held out. "Look, I know where there is a public phone. If Señor Townsend has not returned, we can find someone to take us to the island."

Kelly couldn't muster the strength to protest, at least not with any conviction, so they proceeded to the public phone. There, they placed a call which, sadly, yielded no miracle.

While Enrique arranged for the boat, Kelly paid off Jorge for his services. In heavily accented English, he struggled to express his feelings, to convey a word of hope that the señora would soon be reunited with her husband.

Kelly couldn't respond, could only nod and blink back the tears, but when he walked away, she began to whisper a small prayer, asking a benevolent God to bring her to her husband, to produce him alive and whole. They had pledged to spend a lifetime together. Each had spoken the words *'til death us do part,* thinking it to be a time far in the future, decades away.

They had been married but eight days.

Neither Kelly nor Enrique spoke much on the trip to the island,

and now as they cruised the bay, Enrique appeared to Kelly to be caught up in his own thoughts. Was he thinking about his girlfriend in Mexico City? She stifled a sob. Where was *her* love? Where was *her* precious husband?

Kelly broke off her thoughts, her heart giving a leap as Enrique muttered something, and then pointed straight ahead. A power boat bobbed in the water. As they came upon it, they found it unoccupied. Something, however, rested on the bottom of the boat. What they discovered was a carbon copy of the rental agreement, with Larry's signature.

Kelly didn't want to leave. Suppose Larry, hurt, had crawled up on shore, waiting for help? They looked but found nothing, their search futile.

And as Enrique talked about search teams and divers, Kelly entered a world of anguish so deep, she felt her throat closing off as she choked on her own grief.

The details of getting back to Caleta Beach and then on to the hotel were murky, but later Kelly remembered the doctor arriving and something said about her being unresponsive to their questions.

She didn't want to answer questions, and she knew she was babbling. But couldn't they understand? She needed her family. With her. Now.

Most of all, she needed Larry.

✑ *Chapter Nine* ✑

adine had wanted to accompany Steve to Acapulco, to be with her daughter, but Steve had insisted her presence would just complicate matters; that in dealing with the authorities, questioning witnesses, and talking with hotel personnel, she would be in the way. *Or try to interfere,* she later wondered. In any case, she had acceded to Steve's wishes and had volunteered to take on the unwelcome task of notifying Larry's family of his demise.

Audrey and Fern had coordinated their arrival in San Francisco with Nadine and Vanessa to match as closely as possible Kelly's and Steve's late morning arrival from Acapulco. With Tom Champion scheduled to fly in from Phoenix later in the day, it was the four women, subdued and pensive, who assembled in a waiting area at San Francisco International Airport.

The reunion, in funereal contrast to the festive send-off in Los Angeles, was marked by hugs, tears, and whispered words of solace. Kelly, wan and quiet, had held tight to an anguished Audrey, whose eyes were swollen from continuous weeping. She had turned to her mother, clinging to Nadine, and then to her sister, unsuccessful now in her attempt to staunch her tears.

By mutual consent, the families decided to reunite later in the day, after Tom's arrival. Audrey and Fern had booked rooms at a hotel, having turned down Nadine's invitation to stay with the Hanson's. Each needed to deal privately with her loss.

When the Champions and Audrey arrived at the Pacific Heights Victorian, Steve, looking drawn and tired, ushered his guests into his study.

Kelly sat at the hearth, close to the fire, absorbing warmth from the blaze. Next to her, his back to the room, stood Tom Champion, head bowed, the flames illuminating his fine features, highlighting the sculptured cheekbones, the aquiline nose. He was blond, like Larry, and almost as tall, Kelly observed, but there the resemblance ended. What came to mind was Larry's rugged build, his ready smile, his strong, masculine hands. Her throat tightening, tears welling, she bit down hard on her lip, vowing to put a hold on her memories. She couldn't afford the luxury of an emotional breakdown. Not yet. Not when she had overruled her family's concerns, arguing that she owed it to Larry to be present at this gathering.

Kelly watched now as Tom moved away from the fire to accept a drink from his host, and then to an armchair at a right angle from the couch where Fern sat, holding her mother's hand.

Nadine didn't miss the fact that there's room on the sofa for Tom next to his wife, Kelly thought, glancing at her mother.

As if sensing his defection had occasioned some mentally raised eyebrows, Tom smiled at Fern. "I think there's room for me, too," he said, as he traded the armchair for the place next to his wife.

Kelly, watching them, wasn't surprised to see Fern stiffen, to edge slightly away from her husband. What did surprise her was her reaction to a man she thought she would dislike. Whatever his faults, he came across as a warm and pleasant individual. She could perceive her mother's approval as well, and no wonder. Quiet-spoken, Tom Champion conveyed a courtliness, an old world charm that was most attractive. Also, his sadness over Larry was genuine. She could read it in his eyes.

Vanessa, in the meantime, took over the chair Tom had vacated, presumably to keep a watchful eye on Kelly. *She's there for me every inch of the way,* Kelly thought, shooting her sister a grateful glance. If only she could return the favor, provide the support her sister needed. The thought of Vanessa's pain and sorrow overwhelmed her, and for one weary moment, Kelly gave in to her fatigue.

Had she nodded off? If so, Steve's voice roused her.

No longer at the bar, he had joined Nadine on the loveseat across from the sofa where Larry's family was seated. He was talking about Larry, about his accomplishments, his fine character—and now, his voice cracking, about how much Larry would be missed.

Fern, clutching a tissue, dabbed at her eyes, while Audrey, her shoulders bent inward, held a handkerchief to her lips as if to stifle a sob.

Kelly thought she would suffocate. The room was close, tomb-like, with all these people huddled together, united in their misery. She couldn't sit among the mourners, to hear Larry eulogized and buried by meaningless words. She rose, poised to take flight.

What stopped her was the look on Steve's face as he said, "Oh, God, honey, I'm so sorry!" Tears welled. "I've upset you, I've upset everyone. I only meant—" He shook his head.

"Steve," Tom inched forward, as he addressed the older man, "or Kelly," he added softly, "if you can provide some details, fill us in?" He looked apologetically at Audrey.

Nadine turned to Kelly. "Baby, let Steve do the talking. This isn't good for you. Besides, you should be resting."

"Mom, I'm okay now. Really. I'll rest later when . . . when we're finished here." She reclaimed her place by the fire.

"Kelly, are you sure you want to subject yourself to this?" It was Fern who had spoken. With every hair in place, her makeup and attire subdued but tasteful, she was fashion-perfect. Except for her nails. The polish on both hands was chipped, the nail on her right index finger jagged, another nail bitten to the quick. But her voice was firm and her look direct, telegraphing her concern. Kelly could only nod, wondering at the transformation of Fern Champion. The elitist snob was emerging as a real person, capable of compassion.

In a quiet voice, Kelly related the sequence of events that led to the trip to Caleta Beach and then to Roquetta Island where Kelly and Enrique had canvassed the bay, searching for Larry. And where, eventually, they discovered an unoccupied power boat. She described the rental agreement with Larry's signature that confirmed he'd been in the boat.

"I immediately pictured Larry on shore, hurt, waiting for help. We searched and searched, but could find no trace of him. By that time, I was out of my mind, almost hysterical. I didn't want to leave. Had we missed a spot in our search? Wasn't there something more we could do?" She bowed her head.

Steve's voice cut through the silence. "Kelly, if you'd like for me to continue?"

She shook her head. "Enrique," she continued, "was the voice of reason. He insisted we go for help, because it was getting dark, because we'd done all we could do. He talked about police boats, divers—" She looked to Steve for assistance, unable to continue.

"When Kelly called," Steve said, "the authorities had already conducted a search, both on land and in the water." He cleared his throat. "The divers found a face mask, an air tank, the regulator or tube that's attached to the tank. Uh, let's see. The spear gun?" He looked at Kelly for confirmation.

"No," she said. "And since they didn't find Larry"—she looked at Audrey—"I held out hope that somehow . . ." She swallowed and shook her head, eyes now cast downward.

"You poor, dear girl." Audrey spoke haltingly. "I can't even begin to imagine what it must have been like for you. In a foreign country and all alone." Tears filled her eyes. "The horror of it all."

"The whole evening was a blur, waiting for news, fearing the worst. By the time I heard from the police, I was so distraught that Enrique had to bring in a doctor to sedate me." She attempted a smile. "I don't know what I'd have done without my little friend."

"Enrique, bless his soul, was of immeasurable help," Steve said. "He acted as my personal escort for the day, taking me everywhere and arranging for me to meet with the authorities."

"Steve, excuse me," Tom said, "but I was wondering about Larry's sudden decision to go scuba diving." He turned to Kelly. "That seems a little odd to me, especially as he wasn't carrying along swim trunks."

"It was just a spur of the moment thing. As for trunks, that was no problem. You can buy—I guess even rent—trunks at the hotel."

"And he could stow his street clothes in a locker," Steve continued. "We found them there when I went out to the hotel." He paused. "Tom, you still look perplexed. Have I left something out?"

Fern gave her husband a sidelong glance. "Tom missed his calling. He should have been an investigative reporter, instead of going into the brokerage business."

"I suppose I'd find that to be a lot more fun than poring over charts and corporate reports." He gave his wife a quick smile. Then, to Steve, he added, "I was wondering if you were satisfied with the search. Since they didn't find a body, I would question their thoroughness."

Steve nodded. "It took a little persuasion"—he patted his jacket pocket—"but I was able to convince the police to bring in the divers once again." He sighed. "With the same results."

"Steve, if we've covered it all, I think I'd better take Mother back to the hotel." Fern was looking at Audrey, worry lines etching her forehead.

"Of course."

They all rose. Kelly and Audrey turned to one another for a final hug. "We'll stay in touch," Kelly whispered. "And I'll see you in Phoenix. I promise."

"It's in the *Chronicle*." Nadine, seated at the table, sipping coffee, held out the newspaper to Vanessa, who had just entered the breakfast room.

"Married only eight days . . . tragic disappearance . . . presumed drowned . . ." Vanessa skimmed the article, and then sank into a chair opposite her mother. As if disposing of something obscene, she thrust the paper aside but held her tongue as Kwon, the houseboy, approached with coffee and juice.

"I feel as if I've risen from a sickbed," Vanessa said. She took a sip of her juice, made a face and pushed it away. "Do you think we should check on Kelly?"

"I already have." Nadine reached for her cigarettes and lighter. "She'd been crying, and I doubt she slept much last night, but we managed to talk a little." She paused to light her cigarette, took a deep drag, and then expelled the smoke, narrowing her eyes as she thought. "Basically, she's numb, I'd say, still in shock. Not finding the body makes it so unfinished, I suppose, so unfinal, if there's such a word."

"Kelly's strong, she'll recover. But Mom, it's going to take time."

"At least she has Steve and me. We'll do everything in our power to get her through this dreadful period."

"Speaking of Steve, he seems to be taking all of this as hard as Kelly. He looked wiped out yesterday."

"I know." Nadine drew her finger around the rim of her cup, staring into the dark liquid. When she looked back at Vanessa, it was through her tears. "Steve was so fond of Larry, so thrilled about the marriage. As for you girls, he feels as close as if he were your real father. It was a wrenching experience, having to bring Kelly back from Acapulco."

Nadine and Vanessa grew silent, each lost in thought.

Now, Vanessa helped herself to one of Nadine's cigarettes. After she'd lit up and taken her first puff, she said, "I wouldn't trade places with Kelly for anything in the world." She paused. "Why are you giving me that cynical look?"

"Vanessa, for God's sake, you can't be sure you haven't lost Gordon. Widowhood is tragic, yes, but to lose a man to another woman is a double tragedy, particularly if you continue to love your husband, which you've assured me you do. Think of the hurt, anger, the sense of failure."

"Mom, will you stop! My marriage is *not . . . over . . . yet.*" She spaced out the words as if clenching her teeth. "I don't know why I confided in you." She tapped her cigarette against the edge of the ashtray. "I knew you would blow this . . . this situation of mine completely out of proportion." The ash had dropped, but she continued the tapping motion.

"Oh, have I? Well, maybe you're a tad naive, my dear. You'd better steel yourself, because—" She cut herself off, aware of a warning look from Vanessa, her head tilted in the direction of the staircase. Kelly was descending the stairs.

Nadine pushed her chair back, about to rise. "Hi, sweetheart. Come join us. Have some breakfast."

"Mom, sit still." Kelly was upon them, at the table. "I'd like coffee. Nothing more."

"Kelly, you need—never mind," she said, and then stopped,

reaching to give her daughter a hug.

The houseboy appeared once more to pour coffee and serve juice. When he'd departed, Kelly said, "I heard you talking."

Vanessa spoke up. "Now I don't want you worrying about Gordon and me."

"Vanessa, the world hasn't stopped because of my loss. I care very much about both of you."

"And we care about you, Kelly." Nadine studied her daughter. "I don't know how you did it: got through yesterday, I mean, with Larry's family."

Vanessa nodded. "It took guts, Sis. I'm not sure I'd have had the courage."

Kelly's smile was joyless. "I wasn't exactly marvelous, but thanks." She toyed with her juice, swirling the orange liquid. "I want to go back to L.A."

"Of course, dear, when you're ready."

"Tomorrow. After I've talked with Steve about some legal matters. There's Larry's estate and his business to consider."

"Kelly, for heaven's sake, you can deal with all of that later. You need time to rest, to heal."

"Mom, I'll never heal, never get over missing Larry." She began to sob like a child, but then it was suddenly over, the outburst ceasing as abruptly as it began.

Nadine stared at her daughter, shaking her head, but she had the sense to remain silent.

Vanessa shifted in her chair. "Kelly, whenever you leave, I'm going with you."

"Why?"

"Why? Kelly, you shouldn't be alone! At least not for a while."

"And you should be returning to Gordon."

"Gordon who?"

"Girls, I don't believe this." Nadine threw up her hands. "Stay,

92

go, fly to the moon!" Despite sounding annoyed, she was pleased by the display of spunk from both women.

Kelly turned to her mother. "Mom, I love you, and I love all you're doing for me, but I have to go about my life in my own way. Okay?"

Nadine gave her daughter's hand a squeeze, and then busied herself with lighting another cigarette. But she was thinking, *It's not okay—none of this is okay—and dammit, our world will never, ever be the same.*

A transatlantic call from San Francisco to Ankara, Turkey, provided Vanessa with all the necessary assurances.

Gordon, his voice caressingly warm, was transmitted as clearly as if he were standing before her. And for the moment it didn't matter, the question of his faithfulness, because all she could fathom was this profound desire to be with him, to smell his skin, taste his lips, feel his hands on her body. And oh, he breathed into the phone how he missed his Vanessa and how he longed for her return. But of course he understood the urgency of the situation, that Kelly's need for her sister took precedence over his needs. Vanessa should stay in Los Angeles for as long as was necessary.

"Three days tops. Then I want you back with Gordon," Kelly insisted. They were on the Hollywood Freeway, their taxi struggling to make headway against the afternoon traffic.

"Kelly, let's play it by ear. You're going to need help, you know, moving your things back to your apartment. Or is it the other way around? Have you decided if you want to live in Larry's house?"

Kelly didn't answer, mesmerized by the play of light on the circle of diamonds that adorned her ring finger. The gems, in the sunlight, reflected fire and ice, a fitting contrast, as in blond and auburn, large and small. Larry and Kelly.

Together in that house. Each room would evoke memories of their togetherness, of moments both passionate and playful, of statements beginning with, *When we . . . When we are married, return from our honeymoon, build our home, start our family.*

The wave of nausea was a welcome intrusion, dimming the senses, blocking out voices, his and hers. To Vanessa she said, finally, "I can't imagine living in that house."

"So you'll put the house on the market?"

"I suppose so. Oh, I don't know. There are so many things to deal with. So many imponderables. Steve says because Larry's body wasn't found, complications could arise with his estate. He thinks I should take my time, confer with Larry's lawyer."

Vanessa nodded in agreement and the sisters fell silent, each caught up in her own thoughts as they continued the ride.

When they entered the lobby of the apartment house, Kelly remembered to check her mailbox. Because she had failed to complete change-of-address forms, the box was full. *Procrastination,* she wryly observed, *had paid off.* "The usual junk. Nothing of any consequence," she said, responding to Vanessa's questioning look.

However, once inside the apartment, Kelly, after setting her bags down, plucked from the stack of mail the envelope that showed Rick O'Hara's return address. She stared at it for a moment, and then placed it with the rest of the mail on the coffee table. Whatever Rick had to say could wait.

Vanessa, on the other hand, was determined to have her say. "Kelly," she said, using a sing-song tone, "you're not listening. I said, do you want me to move the luggage into your bedroom?"

"Your luggage, Vanessa."

"Oh, okay. You're going to sleep on this sofa, or whatever you call it, while I take up residence in Milady's boudoir. Now you know I don't go with that room. The color scheme alone washes me out, drabs my complexion. As for my eyes, with all that orange—"

"It's coral, and your eyes won't rust, believe me." Kelly smiled briefly, and then shrugged. "Look, do what you want. I don't care. My point is you're going to be here only three or four nights."

"So?"

She couldn't hide her exasperation. "So then you go back to I-can't-imagine-what in Turkey. Enjoy the western world while you can. Bask in civilization."

"Ankara is the capital of Turkey, not a village, for heaven's sake. And we live pretty darn well, I want you to know." Indignation had righted Vanessa's posture, intensified the green of her eyes. But in seconds, she relaxed her stance and softened her expression as she regarded her sister.

Kelly looked away, uncomfortable with her sister's scrutiny. She saw herself through Vanessa's eyes: the clothes that hung a size too large, the fading tan that revealed her pallor, the sadness that dulled her eyes.

"Okay," Vanessa said, her tone suggesting renewed strength of purpose. "I'll take the bedroom for now. Tomorrow night, we trade. Oh, and while I think about it"—she shrugged off her jacket—"let me check the refrigerator and see if I can scare up something for dinner." Briskly, she moved into the kitchen.

Kelly, about to follow, hesitated, her eyes drawn to the coffee table and Rick's letter. She couldn't resist, had to open it now, though she did so warily, as if handling hazardous material. However nothing appeared noxious in the contents of his letter, nor in his declaration of support or his offer to be there for her as a friend, always.

Touched by his words and relieved, too, that their friendship could be restored, Kelly stared at the page. As the words began to blur, she felt an unbearable sadness—and then, to her surprise, anger. She didn't want to be back in this apartment, the bereaved widow. She didn't want to have to face the next day, the next hour, the next minute, wretched in her sorrow. And yes, she was furious with Larry, that he should abandon her, that he should die.

The letter was crumpled but still readable. Carefully she smoothed it out and commenced reading. Her job was waiting, and soon they would cast the new production. Two female roles, one leading, one supporting, were up for grabs, each a plum part. He hoped she would try out; he would be happy to send her a script. She read on, and then looked up, aware of movement at the door of her bedroom, of a funny gasping sound. Vanessa, still holding on to her suitcase, stood in the doorway. Slowly, she set the bag down, and then turned to Kelly, a most peculiar expression on her face.

"Vanessa, what is it?" Kelly advanced toward her.

"I've always known you were a lousy housekeeper, but this—" Her voice cracked as she pointed through the doorway.

Kelly brushed past her sister to enter the room. Clothing spilled out of drawers. Books were toppled from their shelves. The contents of her desk were strewn about the floor, her clothes in a pile on the floor of the closet. The room had been royally trashed. "Oh, my God."

The police detective who responded to their call had questioned the length of Kelly's absence from the apartment. When informed of her recent marriage, followed by her husband's tragic death, he explained that wedding announcements as well as death notices attract the sickos. And since the wedding gifts and Mrs. Townsend's jewelry were stored in the Hollywood home, he suggested the two women accompany him there.

They found Larry's office a disaster, drawers upturned, books and magazines flipped open, with other items scattered about the room. His bedroom hadn't fared much better, nor the living room sofa or the bookcase; both were in disarray. Spared, however, were their wedding gifts and various personal items, including Kelly's jewelry.

The detective, a man up in years, who had seen it all, felt a tingling in his extremities. What appeared to be a routine burglary now suggested something with more sinister implications, warranting further investigation. A man would be out to interview them the next day, he informed the two women. Then he gave them his instructions.

Chapter Ten

olice Detective Robert Cherney lacked . . . Oh what was the word? Charisma, Kelly concluded. Not that he wasn't conscientious and persevering in his pursuit of facts and background information that might produce a lead. His neutrality, the grayness of his personality robbed him of any spark. *Bland, yes; inept, no,* Kelly decided, as she and Vanessa waited patiently for the detective to resume his questioning.

Late morning of the day following the discovery of the break-ins, the three of them, seated in the living room of Kelly's apartment, had worked together for the better part of an hour. Now the detective rose from his chair, having set aside his notes, to head for the bedroom—his third trip there.

"Thorough," Kelly mouthed to Vanessa, whose shrug was at variance with her pained expression. *Too young, too green,* her sister probably was thinking.

Decidedly earnest, Kelly continued in her mind, enjoying her little game of pin the label on the sleuth. *Ah. Add perplexed to the list,* Kelly decided, as the investigator rejoined the two women.

Apparently, Vanessa had reached the same conclusion. "I have to say in our defense," she said, pointing her chin at Cherney, "that we did our darndest in following instructions about the inventory. We also checked emails and cell phone messages. I don't think we missed anything of my sister's, but listing her husband's things involved a little guesswork."

"I do understand." From all appearances, Robert Cherney could have written the book on maintaining one's professional distance, but now, as he turned to Kelly, the solemnity of his expression and demeanor gave credence to his words. "Mrs. Townsend, I'm sure this is very difficult for you, but if I can toss out a couple of ideas?

"By all means." She gave Vanessa an expectant look. Finally they were getting down to the nitty-gritty.

"All right," he said, as if making a final determination, "since nothing appears to be missing, it's possible the intruder was after one thing only: Your pearl and diamond pendant. Obviously, you wouldn't be carrying such valuable jewelry on your honeymoon. So someone who attended your wedding or reception, or who worked at your reception might speculate the pendant was hidden away in either residence. Or that you might own jewelry of comparable value."

As he paused to review his notes, Kelly began to twist her wedding ring. The pendant, placed by a family member in her safe deposit box, was secure, but she would have traded a thousand pendants or a cache of precious gems for a lifetime with Larry.

Detective Cherney was speaking again, and Kelly forced herself to focus on his clear blue eyes, an attractive feature in an otherwise undistinguished face. But her thoughts—*bachelor, not long out of college, degree in criminology*—drowned out his words. She had to concentrate.

"On the other hand," he was saying, "pendant or no pendant, why not take off with the wedding gifts or other valuables? I can't help but wonder if this would-be thief wasn't after something of your husband's. Something that had nothing to do with the wedding."

"But why tear my bedroom apart? Unless they thought Larry had given me whatever it was they were after." She thought for a moment. "Something belonging to Larry. But what?"

He shrugged. "A document of some sort, business papers, an incriminating letter, or"—the detective's smile was apologetic—"even love letters that might reflect on someone in an embarrassing way." Again, the apologetic smile.

"Tell you what," he said. "I'm going to do some snooping, question some of Mr. Townsend's neighbors, the people at his place of business. See what we can come up with. Meanwhile, Mrs. Townsend, if anything occurs to you, anything at all that might shed some light on this case, please give me a call." He reached for his briefcase, slipped the folder inside, and brought out his card, but held onto it. "I was thinking," he said, "we could be dealing with someone out to settle a grudge, someone vindictive enough to want to trash both places."

Kelly was shaking her head. "If Larry had any enemies, it would be news to me."

"What about you? You work in the theater, don't you?"

"If you're trying to conjure up vengeful prima donnas lurking in the wings or emotional flare-ups over who got what part, you're in for a disappointment. We're a pretty solid group of people." *Give or take one temperamental redhead,* she added silently.

He came to his feet. "We'll find the answer, eventually." He handed Kelly his card.

At the door, Cherney extended his hand, executed a firm handshake, a brief smile, and was gone.

When Kelly turned back to Vanessa, her sister was scowling. "All the personality of a wet towel," she said, "and about as much use."

"He's okay. He'll do his best and then some." But she wasn't really mindful of what she was saying. Kelly had picked up the inventory sheets and was reading down the page. She flipped to the second page, studied it, and then looked at Vanessa. "It's not listed."

"What's not listed? Did we forget something?"

Kelly didn't answer but moved purposely to her bedroom, with Vanessa at her heels.

The room, which had been put to rights, still retained a slightly mussed look, with books and records somewhat askew in the built-in shelves that were a step away from her bed. Intent on her mission, Kelly made a vertical, and then horizontal sweep of the shelves, and then moved on to the other side of the room, to her desk. "It's possible," she said, "you dropped it into a drawer." She did a quick survey, and then, on a note of finality, slammed shut the last drawer. "I didn't think I'd find it here."

"Would you mind telling me what you're talking about?"

But Vanessa's words were lost on Kelly, who, with dogged determination, returned to her shelves.

She took her time as she carefully examined each shelf. It wasn't there. What should have occupied a space among works of fiction and poetry, or texts on the theater was a book she had filled with everything from random jottings to eloquent prose, with some entries far too intimate to share.

Her journal was missing.

Before calling Detective Cherney, Kelly and Vanessa combed every inch of the bedroom, checking under the bed, even rummaging through the trash, on the chance the journal had slipped away from them as they cleaned up. Though Kelly felt certain the book wasn't with her possessions at Larry's house, she resolved to make sure. The search for the journal helped to steady her, to dam her emotions. With Vanessa's help, Kelly sifted through Larry's things, and the two of them put his house in order.

That same day, they moved Kelly's belongings back to her apartment. All, that is, but the wedding gifts. Later, Kelly decided, after Vanessa returned to Ankara, she would ready the packages, some as yet unopened, for return shipment.

Nadine and Steve were informed of the break-ins. Their concern heightened as they learned of the theft of Kelly's journal. She was at risk; she should come home, they insisted.

Kelly felt otherwise. The perpetrator of the crime had, for whatever insane reason, snatched her most private possession; however, she thought it highly unlikely he or she would stage a return visit. Ergo, she was perfectly safe. Furthermore, she wanted to stay in close touch with the detective on the case.

She had put her acting skills to use to come across as tough and convincing. In truth, she needed support and was grateful to have Vanessa. Though her sister's loquaciousness and bursts of energy were sometimes intrusive, Vanessa knew when to back off. Her mother, on the other hand, would impinge upon her privacy, pressing her to get on with her life or imploring her to hold off on decisions; in short, her mother would impose her will.

As it turned out, it was Steve who had the last word. Her stepfather thought it essential that Kelly contact Jason Underwood. The attorney had handled Larry's business affairs. Therefore, he might be privy to information that could help the investigation. Also, she needed to deal with the matter of Larry's estate, of whether or not he left a will.

Kelly agreed. What was one more character-building experience among many?

She had scheduled her appointment with Jason Underwood two days hence, on the afternoon of the day Vanessa was to leave for Turkey.

On the evening before Vanessa's departure, Kelly and her sister sat up late, rehashing events from their childhood and college days, each consciously or unconsciously blocking out the present. Finally, though, Kelly had to express what had been in the back of her mind. "I don't know when I'll see you again," she said, "and it makes me sad. The Middle East seems like the other end of the world."

"I wish you'd think seriously about joining us for a while. Turkey is a wildly colorful and intriguing country."

Vanessa had brought up the subject before, but Kelly couldn't conceive of such a journey. "Going primitive," Kelly said, "has its advantages, I suppose. If you like the simple life." She waited, but Vanessa hadn't taken the bait. Instead, she stared into space, a dreamy, far-off expression paling the green of her eyes.

"I'm sorry. What did you say?" Her sister was back from wherever her thoughts had transported her.

"Nothing, really. Look, can we talk about you, for a change?"

"You mean about Gordon and me. Sure, why not?"

They were seated side by side on the sofa and as Vanessa reached for her cigarettes, Kelly thought, *Here it comes: more pain, more heartbreak.*

Vanessa's pacifier (her word) in place, she squinted through the smoke at her sister. "There's a secretary in the general's office."

"Uh huh. Let me guess. Young, unmarried, busty, an eyelash-batting bimbo. And southern, to boot!"

Vanessa laughed. "Everything's a game with you, you nut."

Kelly was silent for a moment. "I take everything that affects you seriously." Her eyes misting, she said, "It's simply that I'd go crazy if I let it all out."

"I know, I know, sweetie. A little levity now and then can stop us from jumping off a roof or going night-night with a bottle of pills." A non-inhaler, she waved the smoke away. "Well," she said, her tone upbeat, "you got it all except for the southern part. Substitute perky Scottish brogue, and add smoky blue eyes and dark curly hair; she and Gordon could pass for brother and sister, except I've . . . I've seen them exchange looks." Her nonchalance was offset by her woebegone expression.

"Is that all?"

"No. I received a call from a captain's wife. She and her husband were about to go PCS—that's permanent change of station. Anyway, she sputtered around, mumbled something about not having the courage to call before, and then she spit it out. She thought I should know about the general's secretary and my husband, that they were having an affair. It seems it started when this same woman and the caller's husband had broken off a relationship."

"How would she know? Did she offer any proof?"

"No, and when I recovered enough to question her, she became evasive and hung up on me."

"Do you suppose she was simply being spiteful, jealous over your looks, your popularity?"

"Oh, aren't you the doll. Nah, I don't think so." Vanessa shrugged. "So, back to this secretary. I did some checking on her, bent the ears of some of the wives. It seems rumors had floated about her and a married captain, but there'd been no mention of her being involved with a married major. At least not to me." Her eyes followed the tendrils of smoke rising into the air. "I know it's all so nebulous, but I have this kind of sick feeling"—her voice had faltered, only to pick up strength as she turned to Kelly—"also a gut feeling she's right about Gordon. That he is having an affair." Her mouth was a tight line.

"But you don't know for sure."

"No." She stubbed out her cigarette as if to annihilate it. "But I sure as hell am going to find out."

"I'd say those words have a certain ring. As in ominous."

"Damn right. We're going to have a talk, my husband and I."

"If it's true?"

Vanessa sagged against the sofa. "I don't know." She gave her sister a tired smile. "Food for thought on the flight back, right?"

"It wouldn't hurt to examine your options, but whatever happens, you don't want to act impulsively. For heaven's sake, don't stage this confrontation until you're over the jet lag."

Vanessa laughed. "Always the practical one." She gave her sister a hug. "No rash decisions, I promise you, and this time we'll stay in touch. Watch your mailbox for the continuing saga of *As the Middle East Turns* or *Upstaged Wife*. You be sure to write, too. I'll want to know how your appointment with the attorney goes."

As if by mutual consent, both women now stood. It was late and time to retire and besides, they had talked themselves out. Almost.

At the door of Kelly's bedroom where she was to spend her last night, Vanessa paused. Turning now to face Kelly, she offered a slight smile. "Don't say anything to Mom," she said, "but I think I'm pregnant."

'Attractive older man' was how Kelly had categorized Jason Underwood in their brief encounters. It had been a fleeting impression, but now, seated across from him in his office, she mentally reaffirmed that assessment. Though too heavy for her taste, his expressive eyes and his dark hair touched with silver were reminiscent of the look of a handsome, aging movie star. Mostly, though, she was impressed with his warmth, with his outpouring of sympathy which, though florid, was also touching.

He hadn't known about the break-ins, and as she described what had occurred, relating also the theft of her journal, she noted his expression become less open, as if he were cataloging her information in some secret place.

"You mentioned the detective who interviewed you advanced several theories as to the motive for the break-ins, including the intruder's quest for something of Larry's. Now we don't know if he failed to find what he was looking for—though why else would this person go on to ransack your place?"

103

"You're assuming Larry's place was hit first?"

"Only an assumption, but you see, my dear, your diary was seized for a reason."

"Oh, I get it. When they give up on Larry's place, they search through my things. Still no luck, so they grab my journal, which should reveal our deepest, darkest secrets."

"I can accept that explanation."

"Mr. Underwood, Larry appeared only recently in those pages. I suppose I alluded to my feelings about him, but most of the entries pertained to events that took place long before I met Larry."

"Did Larry ever mention he had in his possession anything that might be considered damaging to himself or others?"

"You mean like love letters? Not to me. Somehow I can't picture Larry hanging on to packets of passionate prose, if you'll forgive the alliteration."

"Nor can I, Kelly. I suppose I was thinking more along the lines of business."

"I can't help you there at all."

He gave her a warm smile. "Just thought I'd ask." In the pause that followed, his expression turned solemn. "About Larry's estate." He spread apart his hands. "It's a complicated situation, but I'll try to cut through the legalese. Simply put, Larry is missing, and all the evidence points to the fact he drowned. Because no body was found, by law, his estate cannot be probated for seven years."

"Seven years?" *My God, what next?* "But if he left a will?"

"I have no knowledge of a will. However, that wouldn't change things."

"What about the house, his business?"

"I can point out several possibilities. We can file a petition with the court to appoint someone to manage his property or business, in which case you would receive an allowance from the estate. Another possibility is to petition the court to appoint you as conservator. You wouldn't be able to sell his assets, his business or his house, at least for seven years, but you could hire someone to manage his business, and you would be permitted to live in his home or rent it out."

"All so overwhelming," she said softly.

"A lot to absorb. I know." He reached across the desk to pat her hand. "You don't have to decide right now about the house. We can even wait a bit on the business, though I'd want to look into what projects have been started and talk to his foreman."

They were getting down to specifics, something she could relate to. She leaned forward. "Do you know a man by the name of Ben Forbes?"

"Yes, I do. It was Ben who recommended our firm to Larry."

"Ben Forbes was important to Larry at one time. Do you suppose he might be willing to manage the business?"

"If not, surely he could recommend someone." Jason made a notation on his calendar. "We'll set up a meeting for the three of us." He gave her an appraising look. "Do I hear what I think I'm hearing? That you'd consider being appointed conservator?"

"What do you think?"

"I think it would have pleased Larry very much."

She shut her eyes briefly, and then opened wide in an attempt to contain her tears. "Without any warning, I seem to fall apart." She reached in her purse for a tissue.

"You'll be all right, my dear. In time. It takes time." He rolled back his chair. "I think we've covered enough for today. I'll call you when I've reached Mr. Forbes."

They rose and Jason walked Kelly to the door. "Would you like to stay awhile, sit in our reception area?"

"No, I'm fine now. I'll call you soon with my decision, after I've talked with my stepfather."

Jason watched as Kelly made her way through the outer office and into the corridor which led to the street, to Sunset Boulevard. *What a waste. What a rotten ending to such a promising beginning,* he thought as he closed his office door and returned to his desk.

His next client was due in fifteen minutes. He reached for the case folder but left it closed, unable to switch his thoughts from Kelly. His compassion was real; he ached for her, this lovely young woman who had floated down the aisle with sunshine streaking her hair, whose demeanor now reflected a funereal somberness. But more urgent concerns surfaced. Had Kelly any inkling, any idea at all as to Larry's involvement with what Jason suspected were dealings of an illegal nature? Would he have told her he was being followed and otherwise harassed? He thought not. Larry, in all probability, hadn't confided in his wife, hadn't wanted to place her in jeopardy.

He thought about the letter, the one Larry planned to deliver to his lawyer when he returned from his honeymoon. Damn! If only Larry had his proof and hadn't procrastinated.

As for the break-ins, it was obvious to Jason someone was looking for incriminating evidence, something that would identify the group of individuals with whom Larry was involved, or reveal their operation.

Nothing had been found, or they had been interrupted in mid-search. Kelly's apartment had yielded her diary. He believed they thought it first to be a find, and then a crushing disappointment.

So. Here he sat with all this knowledge but with no proof, no evidence of wrongdoing. He sighed, and then looked at his watch. Time to move on to his next client.

He reached for a folder and opened it with the intention of skimming the brief. Nothing made any sense. In place of the printed words, he saw Larry's face, bright with happiness, his wide grin slowly dissolving into the rictus of death.

Someone feared exposure. Someone hadn't trusted Larry when he chose to defect. Therefore, he had been murdered.

And what of Larry's attorney? Where did he fit in? Did these people suspect Larry had confessed his misdeeds to his attorney or had placed in his possession material that was explosive?

He sighed and picked up his phone in response to his secretary's buzz. As he asked her to send in his next appointment, the thought occurred that it was in his own best interests to think this matter through very carefully. Because possibly, just possibly, his life was in jeopardy.

Chapter Eleven

Early March

The short flight from Phoenix to L.A. should have symbolized for Kelly the bridge between the past and the future, the pause between what was and what was yet to be. They had buried her husband, at least symbolically, in a ceremony where friends and family recounted a this-was-his-life type of service. It had been touching, funny, profound . . . and sad.

Now, she was discovering she couldn't turn the page on the past. The service, rather than serving as a catharsis, had stirred up emotions she'd been trying to repress, creating an unsettled, churning feeling.

Part of the problem, she thought, *dealt with uncertainties relating to Larry's estate.* She had vacillated in her decision to be named conservator, and then, before she could change her mind, instructed Jason Underwood to petition the court in her behalf. It would be at least a month before they could expect a ruling, he'd cautioned, but in the meantime, they would benefit from Ben Forbes' counsel when they met with him.

She didn't want to think about meetings or decisions. If only she could suspend thought, block out the past, shut down the future.

She lay back in her seat and closed her eyes, willing herself to abandon consciousness, to be cast adrift into a vast, dark void. For a few seconds her mind obeyed, only to fail her as trickles of light seeped through the blackness, creating images, at first blurred, and then vivid.

She was in the small church. Like in an out-of-body experience, she could look down upon the congregation and zoom in on herself, one mourner among persons who mostly were strangers. Cut to the reception, and she could see herself standing cramped, unable to move in the confines of Audrey's house. (And why hadn't the Champions offered their presumably large home?)

She mulled this for a moment, and then, distracted by the feel of a gentle downward motion, opened her eyes and automatically pushed her seat upright for the descent into Los Angeles.

Once home, she would call her mother, as promised. A previous commitment prevented the Hansons from attending the service, but it was just as well, in Kelly's opinion. She didn't want to be unfair to her mother, but Nadine would have been a jarring presence in Audrey's circle of friends and neighbors.

Her mother-in-law had sought her out before the service to gather her into her arms, and for one emotional moment, Kelly gave way to her heartbreak, blubbering like a child. It was Audrey's comforting words that restored calm, Audrey's dignity and strength that bolstered Kelly to enable her to endure the service and reception. The woman who'd seemed so feeble, so destroyed in San Francisco had rallied to serve as a role model for her daughter-in-law. Audrey, Kelly felt, was learning to live with her loss.

She wasn't so sure about Fern. At the memorial, she had appeared detached from her family and unresponsive to the service. At the reception, Kelly had observed her standing aloof from the others, speaking only when spoken to. Once, she'd caught Fern staring at her, her face taking on expression as if she wanted to convey a message. But then the moment passed, as the mask of indifference slipped into place.

If Fern had been stand-offish and something of an enigma, Tom Champion, at least, had extended himself to engage Kelly in conversation, to inquire as to her future plans, his manner concerned and attentive. Others, too, made a special effort to draw her out. These people meant well, but she felt diminished by their pitying looks, the hushed tones, the soft words of condolence. But she was no better, surrendering to frequent attacks of self-pity and wallowing in her misery—like now, when she felt so despondent.

Kelly turned to the window for distraction. They were dropping out of the clouds, the city suddenly revealed like a huge bas-relief in need of dusting, with glints of sunshine providing a hint of luster, crowning buildings with tarnished gold.

Soon she would be home. Hooray, hooray. So dance a jig for the bride, for the bride stands alone. She nodded. *Oh, that's very good, Kelly, except in the nursery song it's the cheese that stands alone, heigh ho, whatever.* She started to break into a giggle, and then stopped herself, mindful of how close she was to the edge.

It would be easy to retreat into madness or withdraw into depression. *Choices, always choices,* intoned the mocking inner voice.

Shitty choices. For two weeks she had cried herself to sleep and grieved herself skinny. Now this weirdness. It scared her, and it had to stop. It was that simple. It had to stop.

She thought it was time to return to work.

"You're looking good." They sat in Rick's small office at the back of the auditorium.

"You mean, considering?" Kelly hoped her smile came across as sardonic, rather than sad.

"Considering the memorial service was yesterday. Considering you've been through hell and back."

"Rick, I can't sit in that apartment another day. I want to start back to work, put in extra hours if possible."

"Whoa, girl, slow down."

"Rick O'Hara preaching moderation?"

He gave her his mischievous grin. "No sermons, just advice. The last thing you want to do is push yourself too hard. You could burn out or get sick, and if that happens, you're no good to me. Right?"

"I don't get sick. Incidentally, where is that script you promised? Or have all the roles been cast?"

He stared at the ceiling for a moment, and then met her gaze, his expression sheepish. "I have my leading lady. But!" He held up his hand. "Hold on. The supporting role is a knock-out, meaty beyond belief." He reached into a drawer and pulled out a script, handing it to her. "I've scheduled a couple of call-backs, but nothing's been set. In fact, I think you would do handsprings over the competition."

"As long as you mean that figuratively," she said, giving him a real smile.

"When can you read for me? Tomorrow night?"

"You're on."

They spoke of other things, of matters pertaining to production, before Kelly had to leave. The meeting at the attorney's office, originally scheduled for later in the week, had been moved back to this afternoon, and she was due at Jason Underwood's office in thirty minutes.

"Take the rest of the day off," Rick said, as he walked with Kelly through the foyer of the theater. "I want you to put some time in on the script."

"I will devote every waking hour to it." They had reached the doors leading to the street. Kelly stopped and turned to him. "I can't tell you how good it feels to be clutching a script, to be talking about publicity releases and rehearsal schedules. Rick, I want you to know I really appreciate . . . well, everything." Her voice had turned husky.

He stood for a moment, gazing at her. "Come here, you." He drew her close in a tight hug, and then released her. "Welcome back, Kelly. We've all missed you. I've missed you."

If Jason hadn't exactly been watching his back, he had placed himself on alert, careful to lock up securely before departing his office and to carry important papers with him.

His home, an elegantly appointed apartment, was located on Wilshire Boulevard, near Westwood and the campus of UCLA. Tenants represented a variety of professions, including motion picture people, judges, corporate executives, and doctors. *Attorneys made up the roster as well,* was Jason's smug thought as he rearranged items on his office desk. Most important, his building was secure, from the guarded entrance to the parking garage, with a man on duty at all times. *Breaking in,* he thought, *was next to impossible.* Still, he didn't want to be lulled into a false sense of security. He kept up his guard, being particularly watchful when he was in his car. As far as he could tell, the short, heavyset man he'd locked eyes with at the wedding, the same man Larry had identified as his stalker, hadn't made an appearance.

Something, though, about that man set off little exclamation points in Jason's head. What was it about him that seemed so familiar?

He scribbled a note, a reminder to check it out, and then set down his pen as his secretary buzzed in. Ben Forbes and Kelly Townsend were in the waiting area.

The meeting was going well, Kelly thought, conceding she'd felt some apprehension over an encounter with Mr. Forbes, or Ben, as he insisted she call him. Whatever the conflict between her husband and this man, apparently their friendship had been strong at one time. Larry, Ben told Kelly, had been like a son to him, and it seemed to Kelly that Ben Forbes was clearly devastated over Larry's death.

"Before we wrap this up," Jason was saying, "I'd like to clarify one matter." He addressed himself to Ben. "You did say you'd be willing to meet with Larry's foreman to check on projects in progress?" Ben nodded. "But you haven't said if you'd consider managing the business."

Ben raised his eyes to the Cezanne still-life, a costly reproduction that graced a space above Jason's head. He stared at the picture as if memorizing every brush stroke. Finally he turned to Kelly. "When the time comes for you to appoint a manager, I'll give you my answer." Then, his tone softer, he added, "Don't worry, Kelly. If I can't handle it, I'll find you the best in the business."

Though Kelly was grateful for Ben's assurances, it was evident he hadn't resolved his differences with Larry. She decided not to pursue the matter, as the last thing she wanted was to extend this meeting. A script was waiting for her at home, and Rick's confidence in her notwithstanding, she knew she had to deliver.

As Kelly left the office, Jason indicated to Ben that he would like him to remain for a moment.

"I didn't want to bring this up in front of Kelly," he said when they were alone, "but I thought you should be informed about a couple of break-ins at Kelly's apartment and at Larry's house while they were gone."

"I've known about that. A Detective Cherney came to see me. Said he found my name in Larry's book at work."

Jason waited for him to continue, raising his eyebrows in an unspoken *and?*

Ben shifted in his seat. "Afraid I wasn't any help. That is, I couldn't supply any information that would be useful."

"Ben, Larry appeared, uh, troubled, to me. When I questioned him, he brushed my queries aside; however, he did say he was trying to cut his ties with some sort of business enterprise."

"Did he say what this enterprise was?"

"No, only that he wanted out, but that his partners, for want of a better word, refused to release him from his commitment. Now, if Larry were involved in something shady or illegal, that might explain the break-ins. Because what if these people were convinced that Larry had in his possession something that could expose their operation? Of course, this is all speculation."

Again, Jason waited, but the contractor had no comment.

Jason brought his chair in closer to the desk, leaning inward. "Ben, you were close to Larry. Did he ever confide in you as to what he'd gotten himself into?"

"Nope."

"Knowing him as you did, does anything come to mind, regarding his business contacts or his personal life?"

"I haven't a clue."

Really? Then why so uptight, Jason wanted to ask. Instead, he leaned back in his chair, arms spread outward. "I'm not trying to pry, you understand. I merely thought that if anyone could shed some light, it would be you."

Ben had been gripping the sides of his chair as if to push himself to a standing position. Now, he clasped his hands loosely in front of him, elbows resting on the chair arms. His posture suggested a man at ease, but it was his voice that betrayed him. His tone tight, uncompromising, he said, "I told Kelly that Larry was like a son to me, and in that context, I hold a lot of grief over Larry's death. But in the past six months, we had very little to say to each other. I won't go into the reasons, but we'd had a falling-out. So no, I wasn't privy to Larry's business ventures, or anything involving his personal life."

Period, end of discussion, Jason thought as Ben rose from his chair. Jason also stood, but he remained behind his desk. "Thanks, Ben. I appreciate your time."

"Sorry I wasn't any help." He extended his hand for a brief handshake and was out the door, shutting it behind him.

Jason sank back down into his chair. *Oh my, oh my, what have we here? What could Larry possibly have done to alienate himself from Ben?*

Because he could think better when he focused on an object of beauty, Jason swiveled his chair to gaze upon delicate Chinese lace in a brass planter. Sunlight streaming from an open transom tickled the upper leaves, paling their already fragile green.

Substance and shadow came to mind. But he wasn't thinking of gradations of light on leaves. He was thinking of an angry, uptight Ben Forbes. The man, generally so open and forthcoming was hiding something, knew more about Larry than he let on. Could it be Ben was part of the alliance Larry wanted out of? If so, he might be responsible for the harassment, the intimidation Larry had experienced. But murder?

Ben and Larry, Jason recalled, had been cordial toward one another at the wedding reception, but could that have been merely for show?

His head was beginning to ache, and as he swiveled around to search in a side drawer for some aspirin, he began to discount his theories as wildly speculative. Then again, as he'd learned through his law practice, anything was possible.

In any case—the corners of his mouth curved upward—he had been prudent, hadn't divulged all *he* knew. *Shadow and substance. Tit for tat, Mr. Forbes.*

The morning after her appointment at the attorney's office, Kelly, as promised, reported for work, put in a full day, returned in the evening to audition for Rick and joined him afterwards at Fisherman's Grotto for a celebratory drink over having landed the role.

It was all she could talk about: her part, her character. She raised her fingers to her lips. "I could kiss the playwright for inventing that evil little bitch."

"The lead has her moments, too."

She nodded and took a sip of her drink. "It'll be like the old days, won't it? We dig into motivation, improvise to set the tone, argue a little, or a lot."

She had ticked off the agenda in a breezy manner, but her eyes were the giveaway, Rick thought. Clearly, she was worried. "Hey," he gave her a warm look. "You'll be great. Chances are you'll even steal the show."

"Steal, schmeal. Who cares? Rick, what if I can't do it? My concentration isn't so great these days."

"Kelly." He covered her hands with his. "I'd be surprised if you didn't have the jitters. You'll come through. No question."

By mid-March, Rick had cause to rejoice that he didn't have to eat his words. Kelly, with seemingly unlimited energy, worked at production duties during the day and grew into her character at night as they rehearsed. She was, as he'd predicted, superb in her role.

On the night of technical rehearsal, the actors mostly walked through their parts, putting up with frequent interruptions as their director conferred with the light man, experimented with a sound effect, or checked sight lines from various parts of the auditorium.

Rick scurried to the center aisle and then to the left side of the hall. Now he hastened to the front of the theater to stop the action, to yell at the prop man for missing his cue. *What happened to the phone? It was supposed to be ringing, for Christ's sake.* The dress rehearsal, he reminded the prop man, was tomorrow night, and then the opening, he shouted, as if they all didn't know that. *One more chance to get it right, dummy.* That was the message.

They started the scene again, and Rick took a seat halfway up the aisle, settling himself for Kelly's entrance, all the while tending a critical eye to the lighting. He nodded approvingly. *It was all coming together; it would be a good show. No, make that a great show.*

As if doing penance, he had denied himself the pleasure of taking pride in his work and accomplishments, desolate over being rejected by the woman he loved. Besides the disappointment and humiliation, his ego had taken a gigantic blow. How could he have failed? He hadn't failed at anything in years, had excised that word from his vocabulary—only to have it reappear, like a big, blazing neon fixture, lighting up his nights, depriving him of sleep.

Gradually, in the ensuing weeks, he'd eased up on himself, and now, at this moment, he could only extol his talents, his productivity.

He leaned forward, resting his hands on the back of the seat in front of him, as he watched Kelly. He was still in love with her and would gently woo her to him. *Exit the Bridegroom,* he thought almost meditatively. *Enter the Director.*

Kelly, aware of Rick's absorption in her performance, felt a tingle of excitement. They couldn't miss. He knew it; she knew it. The play, an original, had 'success' written into every act, every line. It would wow the audience and perhaps even bowl over the critics.

They stopped for Rick to confer with the lighting technician, and then he announced a ten-minute break. Good. Now, she could re-read Vanessa's email, which she'd printed but only skimmed. She'd been waiting for days to hear from her sister, and from what she could tell so far, the news was all good.

Kelly hurried back to the greenroom to retrieve her purse, declining an offer of coffee from a cast member as she made a swift exit for the back of the house and Rick's office.

The couch she sank onto had seen better days, but the light was good, and she was free of distractions. Quickly, she reviewed her sister's homecoming. It had been joyous beyond Vanessa's expectations. Gordon had demonstrated how much he cared; his ardor, his show of devotion couldn't be pretense, and so on, which was all well and good, Kelly thought. But what about the burning question? Was he or was he not having an affair with the general's secretary? Had Vanessa even broached the subject?

She read on, and then skipped to the next page, where she found her answer.

The timing couldn't have been worse for a confrontation, Vanessa wrote. *There we were, getting back together again, and so happily, when Gordon received orders to go TDY to Germany. He'll be on temporary duty there for an entire month! Of course, I still harbor some doubts, so maybe when he returns I'll bring up this matter.*

Maybe, Kelly questioned? It was a long email, much of it an expression of concern over Kelly's wellbeing. *What of Vanessa's wellbeing?* Kelly asked herself as she flipped through the pages. Surely her sister would follow up on a certain surprise statement that, despite its low key delivery, had knocked her socks off.

It was there on the last page. Vanessa was pregnant! And ecstatic. She'd been tested, seen the doctor, and as of this writing, only Kelly had been informed of her incredible news. However she planned to join her husband in Wiesbaden for a week's visit, and by the time Kelly read these words, Gordon would be sharing in her joy.

Vanessa hadn't mentioned Nadine, but Kelly thought she could predict her mother's reaction. In a word, ambivalent. The joy of sharing in her daughter's impending motherhood would be offset by skepticism over the state of Vanessa's marriage.

For once, Kelly thought she would have to agree with her mother.

A great opening brought rave reviews and sold out houses. Rick had come up with a winner, was the jubilant consensus. In view of ticket demand, they decided to extend the run one week beyond the mid-April closing date.

Evan O'Hara had attended the production twice and had brought with him a top Hollywood agent on his second visit, occasioning some extravagant rumors among actors and staff: Namely, that one or more of the cast was headed for movie stardom, that a prime television network wanted to expand the script into a TV mini-series, or even that Broadway beckoned.

Kelly heard the rumors, most of which she discounted. On a personal level, she felt disinterest, in tune only with the present, her world circumscribed by a self-imposed commitment to her art. Call it tunnel vision, call it survival; she'd thrown herself into her work, consumed by the demands of her job. Get it done by day, and lose herself in the part by night. It was a formula that worked. For the most part.

After the Tuesday night performance, which constituted the opening of that final week, Rick pulled Kelly aside. Would she join him for a nightcap? He had in mind a little club on Beverly Boulevard, not far from where Kelly lived. It was a quiet place, he added, a perfect place for a conversation. Refusal seemed out of the question.

The club was designed to encourage intimacy, or to ensure privacy during difficult moments, Kelly thought as she settled tiredly into her side of the booth. She sensed what this was about. Her performance. She had slipped since Friday and had really been down tonight. She observed Rick as he ordered a gin and tonic for her and a scotch and water for himself. He didn't seem perturbed, much less angry, and now as he studied her, his expression was thoughtful, contemplative.

"You're awfully quiet tonight," he said, finally.

"Tired, I guess. No, it's more than that. I'm upset over my performance. I know it wasn't up to par tonight, and I suppose you want to talk about that." If he did, she allowed no opening, pressing on. "Rick, it will be okay. I promise tomorrow night I'll light up the stage, electrify the audience."

He snorted. "A sound and light show isn't what I had in mind. As for your performance, it wasn't bad; in fact, it was pretty good."

"But?"

"As you said, not up to par. We can talk about that later." Their drinks had arrived and they toasted with more gusto than either was feeling. Rick set down his drink and leaned back in the booth, slouching a bit. "Let's relax, for now. Tell me what's been going on in your life."

"You don't know? As if I don't spend all my waking hours within yelling distance of you?"

He laughed. "That's my girl. I was wondering, though, about a couple of things—the, uh, disposition of your husband's estate, for one. I can imagine his business becoming a burden for you. Also, you haven't mentioned if the police have come up with a solution to the break-ins."

In the beginning, she had confided her concerns over both issues and thought his questioning was transparent. Obviously, he thought personal problems were making unwelcome inroads into her professional life. This wasn't so. In the last six weeks she had proved herself equal to any task, and had tabled her grief for the duration, except in private moments when she reran in her head a tape of her courtship with Larry, their honeymoon, or when she looked at their wedding pictures, and at those taken in Acapulco.

"I'm not trying to pry," Rick said, breaking into her thoughts.

"Oh, I know. Actually, there's not much to tell. The detective on the case thought he had a lead. It seems that when Larry returned from a business trip, his neighbor mentioned there'd been a car parked for several hours in front of the house. This neighbor told Detective Cherney that Larry had acted concerned and had questioned him about the car. So the detective checked with others in the neighborhood, but no one he spoke with remembered the car or anything suspicious." She sighed and raised her glass to her lips.

"What happens now?"

"I don't know." She smiled. "My journal hasn't turned up in one of the racy tabloids. As for the investigation, I suppose they'll keep the file open for a while. The detective said he'd remain in touch, whatever that means." She paused. "I guess you know I've been appointed conservator of Larry's estate?"

Rick shook his head.

"The business is in capable hands, thank God. A former business associate of Larry's has taken over the management, at least for the time being. Ben has his own business to run, so he may have to pull out eventually, but I know he'd find someone good as a replacement." She toyed with her cocktail napkin, and then looked Rick in the eyes. "I don't think these situations have any bearing on my acting. Maybe I'm simply beat. I could be pushing myself too hard."

"What did I tell you about overdoing?"

"I'll take a break in May. Unless you need an off-key second soprano, I obviously won't be performing in the May musical."

"No, you won't. But if you're up to it, I could use a production assistant during rehearsals. You have my promise I'll go easy on you."

"Sure, you will." She smiled, and then turned serious. "And you have my promise that my next five performances will do us both proud."

Kelly was as good as her word.

It was during the curtain call on closing night that everything fell apart. Smiling, bowing to enthusiastic applause, she stepped forward, breaking rank, feeling that fluttering of excitement as the clapping intensified. It was as she stepped back that she saw him, third row center. Conservatively dressed, the solemn expression unaltered by the slow wink in concert with the slight bow, it was the thin man.

Like a bad penny, as Larry had said, he turned up everywhere.

✑ *Chapter Twelve* ❧

he crush of well-wishers descending upon the actors backstage impeded Kelly's exit from the area, so by the time she reached the auditorium, most of the audience had left, with the exception of a few stragglers. The man she was after wasn't among them.

Had he tried the side exit? She rushed to the door and stepped outside, but in the dark, it was impossible to sort out one individual from another. Back in the theater, she considered checking the lobby, and then swallowed her frustration. Appearing in the lobby in full makeup was a no-no. Besides, it was unlikely he would still be around.

Later she questioned her actions. What had she hoped to accomplish in confronting this person? Why would she even want to talk to him when she found him repulsive? And yet, in some crazy, inexplicable way, she was drawn to him, albeit in a negative sense. She was curious, too, unable to ascribe to him a profession, a family, a home. He was a tourist and a theater-goer. Beyond that, he didn't exist.

The matter of identity, however, was subordinate to the question of why. Why would he turn up at the Hollywood Playhouse?

At the cast party, Kelly tried, without success, to free her mind from the incident. The fact of the thin man's appearance this night persisted, to permeate her thoughts and ruin what should have been a gala celebration. It didn't help that the noise level was an assault on her ears or that she felt suffocated by the presence of too many people squeezed into this cottage-size home. Fortunately, there was a terrace.

The hillside house, volunteered by a cast member, was perched at the apex of a winding road in the Hollywood Hills, its terrace providing a vista of raffish splendor in a panorama of city lights and winking neon. *The view as it would appear from Larry's deck* was her bleak thought. Except that Larry's house was now occupied by a New York writer on temporary assignment at Paramount Studios.

She knew she should return to the party, that Rick undoubtedly had his antenna raised and pointed in her direction, picking up on her preoccupation.

She was right.

She recognized his step, felt his hand on her shoulder.

"You're not having much fun, are you?" he said softly.

She started to answer, and then made a gulping sound. Oh, God, she was losing it, was going to break down.

Gently, Rick began to massage Kelly's shoulders. "Post production letdown? Isn't it a little soon for that? I mean, here are all these guys inside having a hell of a good time, getting drunk, and making out. Even old Red, here, fighting off the girls. You should get a load of Wanda. The way she's following me around, I figure she's either out to seduce me or plotting for the perfect moment to burst into song."

Kelly suppressed a giggle over the picture of the amply endowed costume mistress, the star performer of her church choir, serenading Rick as they engaged in a sexually explicit encounter. "Obviously, she wants to be in the May musical. Though I wouldn't rule out seduction," Kelly said with a short laugh.

"Hey, that's better." He bent down to give her a peck on the cheek. "I think you're ready to come to the party."

She turned to face him, her mood once again somber. "Rick, something happened tonight during the curtain call." She paused to consider where to begin. "I guess I should explain. On our honeymoon, a man at our hotel seemed to turn up everywhere we did—at restaurants, around the pool, at the island where Larry went scuba diving, even down by the docks." She had recognized him in the picture taken of Larry and herself in front of the boat.

"You said something happened tonight during curtain call."

"This man was in the audience."

"And that bothers you."

"Why on earth would he turn up here? It doesn't add up. Besides, he's weird. Oh, at first I pegged him as the ugly American. You know, a loud-mouthed lout, almost too tacky to be real. But the day I lost

Larry I saw him as he left the hotel. He was conservatively dressed." She paused, struggling to find the right words. "I can't explain it," she continued, "but something was different about him, as if he had metamorphosed into another person."

"Nothing unusual about that. Playtime was over, so it was back to the real world." He paused. "I agree, it's strange the guy should turn up, but maybe he overheard you mention the Hollywood Playhouse. Let's say he's from this area, so he checks out the theater, sees you're in the cast, and shows up because he has this monstrous crush on you."

"It wasn't like that. There's something sinister about this man, something about him that gives me the willies." When Rick didn't respond, she gave him a small poke. "What are you thinking? Come on now, look at me."

"Kelly, don't take offense at what I'm going to say, but isn't it possible you were mistaken, that the man in the audience merely resembled the guy in Acapulco?"

"I'd like to believe that." *But what about the wink, the nod?* Slowly, thoughtfully, she turned away from him, gripping the hand railing as she focused on the distant array of lights, on two broad beams of intersecting lights flooding the night.

Rick was saying something, and she started to turn to him, and then stopped, distracted by a sudden glimmer of light in a house at the bottom of the hill. Squinting a little, she could see a man framed in the window; then, in seconds, he was a shadow behind a lowered shade, joined by a smaller figure. The two stood face to face, drawing closer until they formed one silhouette. Abruptly, Kelly turned her back on them. "Rick, I'm not in the mood for this." She gestured toward the sound of laughter and music. "I'm going home."

"This man in the audience really stirred things up, didn't he?"

She shrugged, and then gave him a faint smile. "It had to happen tonight, huh? Don't look so worried. A good night's sleep and I'll put this behind me."

He smiled at her. "Sure you will." He took her by the hand. "Come on, kiddo, I'll walk you to your car."

Rick called in the morning, and it didn't take much persuasion on his part to convince Kelly to take Monday off. Not that she wasn't perfectly fine, she assured him, but she could use the time for shopping and for catching up on household tasks.

She did none of the above. For most of the day she lay in bed, drifting in and out of sleep, too lethargic to dress or even to prepare a meal. The entire night, she replayed each step of her honeymoon, the ubiquitous thin man a constant image she was unable to expunge. Now he was in her dreams, a stick figure devoid of expression, a gigolo with sideburns, leading her onto the dance floor, a puppet come to life, bowing, winking, and clapping.

Stupid! Totally stupid, she decided, as she struggled out of bed. What she needed was to unburden herself, to talk to someone besides Rick. She thought of Jason Underwood or Steve, because they were wise, warm and caring men.

On the other hand—and it was a chilling thought—could she be a step away from a breakdown? At the end of the run, she'd begun to falter in her performances, to feel her energy ebb away. Now, last night, had she ascribed to a stranger the demeanor and mannerisms of the man who had been their shadow?

Behind the footlights, she had scaled the heights in response to a wildly enthusiastic audience, only to plummet into a state of confusion, fear, and depression. It was a long, terrifying drop. "And no, Rick," she whispered, "I'm not having much fun."

Neither was Jason Underwood having much fun. He hadn't slept well the past few nights and at this moment, a desktop away from Robert Cherney, he brooded over his dilemma: Whether to tell this man what he knew about Larry, and what he had learned about the uninvited wedding guest, or to withhold his information. He decided to hedge.

"I've felt all along that I wouldn't be doing my job," Detective Cherney was saying, "if I neglected to speak with you in person."

Jason took in the detective's polite demeanor and earnest expression. *Nothing menacing or smart alecky about this young man.* He relaxed a bit. "I apologize for putting you off when you called. Just so much going on." He gestured vaguely in the direction of folders piled on his desk. "However, I must say I'm surprised you're here. I thought the investigation had been closed."

The detective shrugged. "I'm still on the case."

"Do you mind if I ask why?"

"If by that you want to know if we've uncovered any evidence, the answer is no." He looked Jason straight in the eye. "Between you and me, Mr. Underwood, we may have reached a dead end. Even my superior who instigated the investigation thinks we should close the file."

"You don't?"

The grimace was almost a grin. "I can get as frustrated as the next man, but maybe I'm also more bullheaded, which probably explains why I'm here." Tiny frown lines now invaded the smooth surface of his brow. "I can't help but wonder if you've overlooked something about your former client that could be of help to us. I'm thinking about business agreements that might have gone sour, people he associated with, that sort of thing."

And your tenacity might bring results, Jason was thinking. He cleared his throat. "I guess if you hadn't called me, I'd have gotten in touch with you."

"Oh?" Cherney shifted in his chair, leaning in toward Jason.

"Something has come to mind. I, uh, hadn't mentioned this previously when we talked because it was only a hunch on my part." Jason rose to approach his file cabinet. He withdrew an envelope from one of the drawers and returned to his desk.

"At Kelly's and Larry's wedding," Jason began, "a short, heavyset man sat across from me at the back of the chapel. Not to be snobbish, but he looked exceedingly out of place. More to the point, something about the man struck a chord. However, I didn't give it a lot of thought until the wedding reception, when Larry asked if I'd noticed this person. Seems he'd caught a glimpse of him in the courtyard of the church. This concerned him, I might add, because he thought this man had been following him."

"Did he say why?"

"No." Jason didn't meet the detective's gaze as he opened the envelope and then removed the contents. "It finally came to me: I'd seen this man in a San Francisco courtroom about eight years ago, when I was with the district attorney's office. He was on trial, charged with extortion. Of course, he had been younger then, more pudgy than fat, as I recalled, but the fleshy neck, the prominent ears, his addiction to dark glasses . . . it all suggested this was one and the same man."

"You're sure about this?"

"At first I wasn't positive, no. Then I remembered the notoriety surrounding his trial because of his alleged association with a wheeler-dealer politico type. Also, this punk was represented by a prominent name in criminal defense who, I regret to say, got him off. So it was inevitable that a photo of him and his attorney appeared in the papers on the day he was acquitted of charges."

"You keep a scrapbook, Mr. Underwood?"

Jason laughed. *A police detective with a sense of humor?* "No," he answered, "but I spent a couple of hours in the library going over archives of newspapers published during that time period. I found what I was looking for, and from the picture, there's no doubt in my mind it was the same man."

"You wouldn't happen to have a name?"

Jason grinned. "Several, which brings me to the next step. I contacted a friend of mine who used to practice law but now heads a private investigation firm. Very discreet, works for names in the news, if you get my drift. I've sent clients to him—those willing to pay exorbitant fees. Anyway, in return, my friend, Jack, rewarded me by providing the information I sought.

"So. Shall we pick a name? I can give you Myron Stubbs who became Mickey Schultz, who now goes by the name of Max Scully. If he hasn't acquired a new alias. I can also give you a brief run-down on Scully, or you can see for yourself." He handed Cherney the rap sheet on Scully.

Jason hadn't found it surprising that Myron Stubbs, a small-time hood from New Jersey, had ventured west to establish residency in Las Vegas, where he consorted with various mob figures. Less understandable was his switch to California, in general, and San Francisco, in particular. However, that wasn't a matter worth investigating.

Cherney looked up from his reading. "Apparently, he kept a low profile after the San Francisco acquittal."

"The trail becomes blurred indeed, but read on." Jason waited, curious as to how the detective would react. Surely the stolid features would reflect an inner surge of excitement? It was in his eyes, pale blue intensifying, narrowing in concentration.

"A hired gun?"

"Jack has his informants, some reliable, some not. But as I recall"—Jason nodded in the direction of the report—"Scully has been linked with the murder of several underworld mobsters. This states that he was seen leaving the scene of the crime in one bloodletting, had allegedly set up another victim as they were leaving a restaurant, and so on."

Cherney looked up at Jason. "You say your client told you this man had been following him, but that he offered no explanation?"

"Well, you have to understand, Detective Cherney, a wedding reception is hardly the place to air one's problems."

"Serious, though they may be," Cherney said, half under his breath. "Okay." He reached for his case. "I can take this copy with me?"

"Of course." Jason pushed back his chair in anticipation of seeing Robert Cherney out, but the detective remained seated.

"Mr. Underwood, when Larry Townsend told you he was being followed, what was your impression of him? Did he seem upset, fearful, puzzled?"

Persistent little prick, Jason thought as he mulled his answer. "As I recall, Larry seemed almost off-hand about it. I was certainly startled by his statement, but as I said, under the circumstances, he really had no chance to elaborate."

"He didn't seem distressed?"

"What can I tell you? He was a happy man, very much in love with his bride." Jason got to his feet, Cherney following suit. "This information may or may not provide a tie-in with your investigation, but I thought you'd want to check it out," Jason said, as he came around his desk to see the detective out.

"I'll not only check it out—I'll get back to you if anything develops. Thanks, Mr. Underwood, you've made my day."

Wish I could say the same, was Jason's worried thought as he fixed his gaze on the retreating figure.

Slowly he made his way back to his desk, and as he seated himself, he reflected on what had taken place. He wasn't sure he had acted wisely in bringing Max Scully into the picture. However, if Cherney were able to dig up information as to Scully's recent contacts or to establish he was in Mexico at the time of Larry's drowning, and then Jason would consider stepping forward to reveal all he knew.

He bowed his head. He could be opening Pandora's Box, and it wasn't a happy thought. But if, as he suspected, a murder had taken place, then justice would be served. He straightened with the thought. He would be doing it for Larry. He owed him that much.

The shower helped, food even more so, and as light faded into dusk, Kelly began to feel less like an invalid and more like herself. Even the curtain call episode began to take on a less daunting aspect, though she still couldn't let go of the incident. *A puzzle, for sure,* she thought as she pulled on a sweatshirt to wear over jeans.

At her mirror, she smoothed her hair, applied a little lipstick, and reached for her blush, only to set it down as the nagging question persisted: Had she been fantasizing the presence of this man, inventing him out of memory? She turned from the mirror, as if by avoiding her reflection, the daze of uncertainty in her eyes, she could make it all go away.

In a sudden mood swing, the spread of warmth through her cheeks signaled the onset of a more powerful emotion: anger. At herself. After hours of playing *Victim,* it was time to bury bewilderment, along with self-pity. Action, not introspection, would deliver her from herself, she hoped, as well as spur her on to the supermarket, if only she could find her car keys. After a frantic search through her purse, she found the keys on the kitchen table, in plain sight. As she whipped out the door, the image of bright lights and crowded aisles, of nothing more arduous than concentrating on food selection, seemed heaven-sent distractions.

But once in the lobby, Kelly slowed her pace as she detected a glimmer of white through her mailbox. She hadn't bothered to check earlier, but now she hesitated, wondering if there might be a letter from Vanessa. She decided to stop. Her box was full, mostly with junk items, which she disregarded as she searched for an envelope with red, white, and blue trim and an APO return address. It was there!

The grocery shopping could wait, Kelly determined as she re-entered her apartment, pleased that something good, after all, had come of the day. Her sister was a terrible correspondent, and Kelly had received no emails from her since Vanessa's news of her pregnancy and impending trip to Wiesbaden.

Settling on the sofa, Kelly set her purse and the rest of the mail on the coffee table. Then careful not to disturb its contents, she pried open the envelope.

Her first reaction was disappointment. A single sheet? She moved closer to the light.

Dear Sis,

I'm thrilled your play is such a success and know you are a stunner in the part. Someday I'll be in the audience, your adoring fan. I'm not only proud, but happy for you, as well, because obviously you've found your niche.

I'm sure you're waiting to hear about the trip to Wiesbaden. Sorry to say, I didn't go, as I wasn't feeling up to it. I won't recite the gory details, but morning sickness isn't a thrill-a-minute. The second trimester is supposed to be a smoother ride, however, so maybe we'll plan then for a trip somewhere.

There was a little more, relative to life among the Turks, and then Vanessa's closing paragraph.

You mention a change of pace in May, since you won't be performing in the next show. How about a real change of pace? What better time to come to Ankara? Spring here is brief but delightful, and you would be wonderful company for me, especially if Gordon has to go TDY again.

128

Please consider. The food is fabulous, the bazaars exotic, and Istanbul is but a day trip away. If I haven't enticed you, then I give up.

Write me.

Love ya,
Vanessa

Kelly smiled as she re-read the final paragraph. It had a romantic sound, conjuring up images of mosques, glittering harem rings, and delicacies fit for a sultan. But to journey so far was impossible. She not only had her daytime work, but had promised to assist Rick during rehearsals. Besides, Audrey planned a trip to L.A. in May and had promised to stay with Kelly for part of her visit.

She set the letter aside, only to retrieve it. Something about the tone of the letter bothered her. She fastened her gaze once again on what Vanessa had written—or to be more exact, what she hadn't written. Why had she left out Gordon's reaction to becoming a father? Was he proud, elated, or overwhelmed by the idea? Surely he knew by now. Kelly looked over the paragraph about the failed trip to Germany. She thought for a moment, and then picked up her cell phone, punching in her mother's number, muttering, "Be there, be there."

Nadine answered on the third ring.

"Are you home?" Kelly asked.

"Yes, Steve's at a meeting, so I'm rearranging a closet."

"I'm so glad I caught you."

"Kelly, you sound perturbed. Is something wrong?"

"I'm okay. But I'm wondering if Vanessa is all right."

"You've heard from her?"

"Got a letter today. Well, it really isn't much of a letter. In fact, something's strange about it, as if she'd left out a page or two. Maybe that's what disturbs me."

"What does she have to say?"

"Let's see. She's thrilled over the success of our play, still wants me to come visit in Turkey, and aside from a brief description of her activities, that's it. Nothing at all about Gordon. In fact, I'm beginning to wonder if he's giving her a hard time about the baby." When Nadine didn't respond, Kelly said, "I assume you've heard from Vanessa?"

"I received an email a couple of weeks ago."

"Then you know she didn't get over to Wiesbaden, that she wasn't feeling up to it?"

"Is that what she said?

"That she was suffering from morning sickness and heaven knows what else."

"Yes, to 'heaven knows what else.'"

"What is that supposed to mean?"

There was a sigh at the San Francisco end of the line. "Oh, Kelly, Vanessa didn't want to put you through any more anguish, so she made up the story about morning sickness keeping her away from Wiesbaden."

"I knew something was wrong."

"Unfortunately, you're correct, and since her letter aroused your suspicions, I'm going to tell you the truth. Gordon had a woman with him in Germany."

"Oh, my God."

"It seems someone at an Officers' Wives' Club luncheon asked Vanessa how she had enjoyed Wiesbaden."

"I think I know what's coming."

"The woman's husband, it seems, had been staying at the hotel that houses officers and their dependents. And obviously on the same floor as Gordon, because he'd caught a glimpse of Major Stuart and his wife departing their room for the elevators. Also, he'd seen them together outside the hotel."

"If it's the woman Sis told me about, she doesn't look anything like Vanessa."

"As I understand it, the man who saw them hasn't met Vanessa, because he and his wife are recent arrivals in Ankara. But he knows Gordon. Anyway, Vanessa paid a visit to the general's office on the pretext of consulting with his secretary on some matter of protocol, but it turned out she was on vacation."

"In Germany."

"In Wiesbaden, yes. I am so upset and disgusted with Gordon Stuart, I could strangle him."

"So now Gordon knows that Vanessa knows, and so forth?"

"She talked to him by phone, called him every name in the book, I suppose. He didn't deny the affair."

"Did she tell him about the baby?"

"She decided to wait until he was back in Ankara, so he certainly does know by now. Of course, I wrote her to come home, to up and leave that SOB. Not that she's rushed her response."

"I guess she plans to stay awhile, since she's still after me to come to Turkey."

"If that's the case, your going over there wouldn't be such a bad idea."

"I've never seriously considered doing that, but I feel so awful for Vanessa. My problems certainly pale in comparison."

"Sweetie, I shouldn't have told you about Vanessa. You've had so much to contend with."

"I wasn't referring to losing Larry. Something happened last night that . . . that upset me very much." Kelly was suddenly blurting out her shock at encountering over the footlights the man from Acapulco, relating, as well, his baffling personality change.

"How totally bizarre. Kelly, I don't know what to say. It doesn't make any sense at all. You don't mind if I share this with Steve?"

"No, of course not. It's a relief to get it out." She didn't add that it was Steve, rather than Nadine, in whom she had thought to confide.

They concluded the conversation, with Kelly citing her need to get to the store. Only when she was off the phone did she realize they hadn't returned to the subject of Vanessa and of her probable need to have Kelly at her side.

That her sister's wellbeing was unfinished business became

evident later when Kelly walked into her apartment to the sound of a ringing phone. It was Steve.

After an exchange of pleasantries, Steve disclosed that Nadine had filled him in about the theater incident, adding that he understood Kelly's consternation. "On the other hand, how easy can it be to identify a person in a darkened auditorium?"

"What I saw was a tall, thin man with straight brown hair and expressive eyes. I know that description could fit any number of men. But Steve, I didn't imagine the slow wink, the slight bow."

"Isn't it possible that the man in the audience bore a strong resemblance to this other person?" When she didn't respond, he continued, "Consider, too, how a quirk of lighting or body movement might enhance that impression."

"Does Mom feel as you do?"

"No other explanation seems possible."

"You don't think I'm . . . I'm breaking down mentally?"

"I don't think you're heading for a nervous breakdown, no. However, your mother and I think a change of scenery would do you a world of good."

Kelly laughed softly. "As in minarets, whirling dervishes, and shish kebab?"

There was a chuckle from the other end. "I don't know about whirling dervishes, but shish kebab sure sounds great. Seriously, honey, it wouldn't hurt to broaden your horizons, or to offer your sister emotional support." His tone was nonjudgmental but the thrust of his message was clear. She should be with her sister, for both their sakes.

She assured Steve she would give the matter serious consideration.

A lot depends on Rick, she thought, as she put her groceries away. She didn't want to jeopardize her position at the Playhouse. It was all she had.

And Vanessa is the only sister I have, her nagging inner voice reminded her.

The man she locked eyes with in the audience was either the

132

tourist from Acapulco, a look-alike, or a figment of her imagination. Whatever the explanation, thank God it no longer was an all-consuming matter for speculation; the episode hardly seemed worth pondering any more.

It was Vanessa—only Vanessa—who filled her thoughts.

Chapter Thirteen

"I'm sorry for bursting in on you like this." Kelly was breathless as Jason ushered her into his office.

"It's quite all right. I had a cancellation this afternoon and I, uh—" He appeared to have lost his train of thought. But not his manners. "Please, won't you sit down?" He waited until she was seated before he took his place, all the while whistling something tuneless under his breath.

It wasn't all right, Kelly thought as she watched Jason's fingers tap the surface of his desk. She should have called, scheduled an appointment.

"Believe me, I don't usually barge in on people," Kelly said, rushing her words. "It's simply a matter of expediency. I thought you should know I'm going to be out of the country for a while."

"Oh?" The tapping stopped.

"Yes, I'm off to visit my sister in Ankara, Turkey."

"A trip to Turkey!" Jason had sprung to life. "What an exciting idea. You know, my dear, I'm convinced that travel, a change of scene, sets the blood racing. I can see it in your face, in your posture."

"Actually, playing tourist is only part of the plan. My sister is expecting, and we thought Vanessa would appreciate a little TLC from a family member. Also, if I'm going to be away from the theater, now is probably the best time."

"Mr. O'Hara approves?"

"Approves? He practically pushed me out the door."

A small chuckle escaped from back of the attorney's throat. "I'd say you've earned a respite. Remember, I saw your performance, and Kelly, you are, in my opinion, incredibly gifted. But what a demanding role. Surely it must have taken so much out of you. At any rate, you certainly deserve this break, and I'm sure Rick O'Hara concurs."

Oh, yes. Give Kelly this break before _she_ breaks. She smiled. "I'll remember your kind words when I'm wallowing in frustration over my next role."

He raised his hand in a gesture of dismissal. "In any case, a very interesting world awaits you."

"My sister mentioned Istanbul."

Jason nodded. "It's a lavishly exotic city, stylishly European. Now Ankara, as a part of Asia Minor, presents a different picture altogether."

She waited, wondering if he intended to elaborate, and then broke into the silence. "I wish I knew more about the Middle East, but I haven't had time to read up, I've been so rushed." She touched her arm where it was tender, the result of a barrage of shots.

"When do you leave?"

"Would you believe only two days from now, on Friday?" When he didn't respond, she moistened her lips. "Let me say it's been wild. But I'll make it. I've got to." Jason's fingers had reclaimed his desk, spread this time to strike a chord, a triad, Kelly observed. It was obvious he'd dried up on the topic of world travel.

Time to come to the point: That she was authorizing the attorney to act in her behalf in the matter of business transactions for the duration of her absence. When they'd reached agreement on the particulars, Kelly pushed back her chair, once again uttering her apologies.

"No need to hurry away," Jason said, but already he moved swiftly to see Kelly out, wishing her Godspeed as he did so.

When he was alone, Jason braced himself against the closed door, his breathing ragged, as if he'd taken a blow to the solar plexus. He wondered if Kelly could hear the thumping in his chest or read his state of shock in his expression.

He remained stationary a few moments, and then approached his desk. With trembling hands, he unlocked the middle drawer. He stared at what lay before him. It was no dream; the letter, sent by registered mail—the letter he had opened just minutes before Kelly's arrival—existed, had form and texture. It also couldn't remain in his desk.

A simple decision, but a decision nevertheless, restored calm and validated his position of being in command. His movements deliberate, he placed the letter into a locked compartment within his briefcase. Next, he set his briefs aside and jotted a couple of notes to himself as he prepared for departure. He was half out of his chair when his secretary rang in. Would Mr. Underwood accept a call from Detective Robert Cherney?

He almost said no, and then instructed his secretary to put the call through, instantly regretting his decision. His plate was full; he didn't fancy being badgered into heartburn by a determined detective. He assumed his no-nonsense voice. "Mr. Cherney, what can I do for you?"

"I promised to get back to you if anything new turned up."

Jason waited, but the detective, who sounded pleased with himself, also waited. Apparently, it was Jason's cue to prod him on. "You've come up with something, have you?"

"It's almost embarrassing how easy it was, but it seems our Mr. Scully has had some domestic skirmishes with his ex-wife. A complaint filed by Maxine Schultz alleges harassment by Myron Schultz, also known as Max Scully, in the form of breaking and entering to vandalize her apartment. Sound familiar? She also accuses him of tailing her at night and making obscene phone calls. All this, she says, in retaliation for hounding him over past due alimony payments."

"Considering his background, I'm amazed she's chosen to stand up to him."

"Maybe he forgot to let her in on some of his extracurricular activities. In any case, she's not afraid to take some action. Too bad we can't haul him in, but he didn't leave his calling card on the premises. Also, he has an alibi, thanks to his sister. In fact, this is where it gets interesting. Scully's sister Rose told Maxine her brother couldn't possibly have entered her apartment because he was in Mexico on the date of the break-in."

Jason's heart once again hammered in his chest. "The date of the break-in?"

"February seventeenth."

"Of course, he could have orchestrated the whole thing without actually taking part, but that's beside the point. Did she mention Acapulco?"

"Maxine didn't, but I also managed to have a talk with Rose. I found out that Scully is a rep for a clothing manufacturer, and that his job often takes him out of the country. She says he was in Mexico City and Acapulco for about ten days, and that he called her from Acapulco to wish her a happy birthday on February eighteenth, which pretty much substantiates his story. Unless she's lying."

"Where is he now? Does she know?"

"If she knows, she's being cagey. What she had to say was pretty vague. He'd been back in L.A. for a period of time, but it had been a while since she'd heard from him. I let it go at that because she started to act nervous, uptight, and I didn't want to arouse her suspicions and have her run to her brother."

"It wouldn't do to alert him, no. What actually do we have?"

"Not much. We don't know if he broke into his ex-wife's apartment or had anything to do with the other break-ins. We do know he followed Larry Townsend in L.A., and then presumably showed up in Acapulco in the same time frame as the Townsends; still, that doesn't explain his connection with Larry Townsend."

Jason stared at the phone, and then cleared his throat. "Unfortunately, Larry can't help us now." During the pause at the other end, Jason could picture the furrowed brow, lips pursed in concentration.

"I may want to pay Mrs. Townsend a visit," the detective said, "describe Scully to her. If she can place him in Acapulco, we'd have a definite tie-in."

"In what way? Do you suspect foul play?"

"I find it helps to explore all angles."

Noncommittal as hell, was Jason's thought. "Mr. Cherney, I must caution you that Kelly Townsend is still quite fragile. I hope you'll keep your suspicions, whatever they may be, to yourself."

"I'll be careful, I promise."

The conversation at an end, it took Jason two attempts to place the receiver in its cradle. As he reached for a handkerchief to press against his hands, he could feel the dampness in his armpits as well as the beginning of a cramp in his belly.

He was exhausted, played out, and mentally taking himself to task for allowing his emotions to corrode his thinking, to alter his physical state. He wanted to be home where he could relax and take pleasure in his surroundings; but he couldn't afford the luxury of procrastination. What lay before him demanded prompt consideration, decisiveness, and—he sighed at the thought—perhaps even prayer.

In Phoenix, Audrey Townsend refilled her coffee cup, spilling a little of the liquid into the saucer as she watched Fern dawdle over dessert. Her daughter's impromptu visit and her willingness to stay on for dinner should have sparked much pleasure. Instead, Audrey was unable to shrug off flutterings of anxiety and uncertainty. Not that Fern's appearance wasn't stylishly perfect, but the hollows under her eyes and her preoccupation as she stared vacantly into space didn't bode well.

The two women sat at the kitchen table, and as Audrey stirred sugar into her coffee, she noted Fern's half-filled cup.

"A little warm-up?" Audrey started to rise.

"Mother, sit still. And don't take offense, but I can't eat another bite." She pushed her plate aside, the slice of apple crumb pie barely touched.

"No wonder you stay so slim." Audrey said it lightly, but privately she thought Fern was much too thin, that her face had taken on a gauntness that was unattractive.

Earlier, they had spoken of the grandchildren, of Audrey's impending trip to Los Angeles. Now, Audrey wanted to talk about Fern, but she was unsure how to broach her concerns in a tactful manner.

Fern led the way. Pushing her chair back, looking relaxed for the first time since her arrival, she favored her mother with a smile. "I've been watching you watching me," she said.

"Well, yes." Flustered, Audrey hesitated, and then, deciding she had to get at the truth, plunged ahead. "Fern, I can't hold back another second. What's wrong? What is making you so dreadfully unhappy? Is it Tom?"

She shrugged. "What can I say? It's certainly no secret my husband and I are no longer close."

"Fern, I know all that. I'm certainly aware your marriage has been less than ideal. But honey, this is different. You seem so troubled."

"Could be a mild case of depression."

"Is that what you think? Have you seen a doctor?" In the silence that followed, Audrey studied her daughter, and then looked away as tears formed.

"Mother"—Fern reached over to take Audrey's hand—"there's no need to be upset. I'm fine. Really."

"You're fine?" Audrey felt the heat rise in her cheeks and disengaged her hand. "You're not fine. We both know that, and Lord forgive me, it's not natural for you to be so distant. Fern, for once, will you level with me? Don't look away. I want an answer!"

"I'm . . . I'm not used to hearing you raise your voice, Mom."

Audrey gave her daughter a long, hard look. "I've never interfered in your life. You know that. But if there's anyone in this entire world who loves you unconditionally, that you can trust, it's me. Fern, you need to talk to someone, and I'm here for you. I promise I won't judge you, or lecture you or even offer advice. Unless you ask me for it."

This time Fern blinked away tears. "I know, I know." She took a deep breath. "I suppose I should confide in someone; you're right, there is a problem."

"You're not ill?"

"Oh, no. It's nothing like that." She stared at her mother for a long moment. "I would have to swear you to secrecy," she said.

Audrey nodded, relieved Fern didn't have cancer or something equally as horrible. "Like I said, you have my complete trust." She leaned forward, receptive, waiting, only to recoil as the ringing of the phone splintered the silence. "Damn!" She started to get up, and then stopped herself. "Ignore that," she said, making an emphatic palms-down gesture.

But Fern was on her feet. "Go ahead and answer it," she said, "I have to use the bathroom anyway." Before Audrey could protest, Fern left the kitchen.

Audrey answered on the seventh ring, her agitation lessening when she recognized Kelly's voice.

"Have I called at a bad time? You sound as if you're in the middle of something."

"It's always a delight to hear from you, dear, though I do have company. Fern's here."

"Why don't I call you back?"

"No, that's all right. I may be going out later," she lied, fearing another interruption.

"I'll make this very fast." Audrey listened as Kelly informed her of her impending trip to Turkey, expressing regrets over having to cancel Audrey's stay with her in L.A.

"We'll make up for it another time," Audrey said. "What's important is for you to be with your sister."

"Thanks for being so understanding, and again, my apologies. Oh, before we hang up, how is Fern?"

"Oh, she's fine." Audrey stretched the phone cord to peer out the kitchen door. *Fern's taking a long time in the bathroom,* she thought

"Give her my best," Kelly said.

"Oh, I will. I'd put her on, but she's in the bathroom. Anyway, I know how thrilled and excited she'll be when I tell her about your trip. Now you take care, and give Vanessa my love."

With the call completed, Fern magically reappeared. However the moment of intimacy, of mother-daughter closeness, was lost, Audrey realized dispiritedly, as she watched Fern gather up her jacket and reach for her purse. "I wish you'd stay a bit longer," Audrey said. "I don't mean to press you, but I admit you've piqued my curiosity. It's not often I'm about to be sworn to secrecy, you know." She tried to keep her tone light.

Fern raised her gaze from her bag where she'd been searching for her car keys to give her mother a thoughtful look. "We'll talk later, I promise."

Why not now? Why not this very minute? It was a cry deep from within that Audrey stifled by sheer forbearance on her part. "I'll hold you to that," she said, and gathered her daughter to her in a fierce hug.

When Kelly was off the phone with Audrey, she let out a deep sigh. Fern, thrilled and excited? She couldn't picture it, and besides, Audrey's expansive remarks rang falsely in her ears, as did her vague 'oh, she's fine.' Something was off, Kelly decided, but with Fern, something always seemed to be off.

Despite Fern's display of solicitude and concern for both Audrey and herself after Larry's death, the woman Kelly had observed in Phoenix had appeared apathetic and listless, a mannequin draped in designer apparel deemed appropriate for a funeral.

She felt sorry for Fern, and then reversed her stand. Why feel pity for the Ferns of the world? If they were locked into loveless marriages, they could readily compensate with visits to expensive salons and high fashion boutiques. If their husbands chose to ignore them, they could always draw consolation from the deference accorded them by the maître d's about town. And if they defined themselves through the acquisition of luxury items, so be it.

Because that lifestyle was repugnant to Kelly, she thought it unlikely she and Fern were destined to form a lasting friendship. In fact, she concluded, they probably wouldn't meet again.

Though a little late in the season for a fire, the three B's—as in brandy, Brahms, and a roaring blaze—had mellowed Jason, putting him in an expansive mood.

He settled himself more comfortably against plump, soft pillows, a munificence of jade green and turquoise, their jewel-like clarity setting off the velvety, creamy tones of the sofa. White on white, he mused, as the edge of his slipper indented the deep pile of the carpeting. The effect, however monochromatic, didn't, in his judgment, suggest starkness or sterility, not even in concert with art objects of contemporary design. His art deco paintings and porcelain, with their sleek, clean lines, were far from austere, instead imparting the grace and flow of balletic motion. In addition, his Oriental pieces—graceful figurines, an intricately carved Chinese chest, a Japanese screen depicting a mistily romantic landscape—lent richness and definition to this room with its high ceiling and airy openness. He took special pride in showing off his treasures, enjoying the wealth of compliments on his taste, the looks of admiration or envy.

He raised his glass, made ruby red in the firelight, in a toast to absent friends and as the measured, majestic chords of Brahms' *Second Piano Concerto* swept over him, he gave way to the moment, relishing this feast of the senses.

It wasn't to last. When the music stopped, so did his flight from reality. In the absence of sound, a montage of images flashed before him: He was opening a letter, receiving Kelly into his office, speaking with Cherney, and falling apart in the process.

However. Replenishment of body and soul had worked to alleviate his stress and fatigue. Now he was ready to deal with the facts.

He took a final sip of his brandy and set it down on the cocktail table in front of his sofa. Next to his empty glass lay the letter. He would place it in his safe shortly, but first he meant to re-examine the postmark. He held the envelope close to the light. 'Mexico' was clear. Somewhere in Mexico. He squinted, straining to make out the rest, but it was too smudged to read, except perhaps, for the letter Z.

A word starting with the letter Z. He held on to the envelope for a minute, his mind traveling the coastline and interior of Mexico. Then brushing aside speculation, he decided the maps could wait until morning.

He pulled out the sheet of paper, and as he spread it open, his eyes began to tear. How many times had he scanned this piece of paper, his gaze riveted on every word, every mark of punctuation? Larry was alive! To read his words was to make it so.

Larry alive. The word *alive* seemed to echo in his consciousness like the spectral chant of some other-worldly creature. But the reality was that Larry hadn't drowned; he had planned his disappearance in order to save his life and to protect Kelly. It was a simple enough statement but with chilling implications, and as Jason reached for his cigarettes, his expression grave as he lit up, he pondered the seriousness of Larry's situation. *Lord knows, it's serious.* Money laundering. Good God, to be involved in the laundering of drug profits created a worst-case scenario. Or could be. Larry hadn't supplied details and explanations other than to relate that in the beginning, he hadn't known about the drug money, but when he'd learned the truth, he'd become determined to break away at any cost. That, at least, offered a glimmer of hope.

Jason settled back to digest, once again, the contents of the letter. Central to his message was that Larry was coming home, and that he intended to turn state's evidence in order to expose the people with whom he had been involved. Indeed, Jason could only applaud Larry for his courage in undertaking such a mission.

Then he was struck with an appalling thought. What if Larry weren't alive? What if the letter had been sent as a ruse to smoke him out in order to determine the scope of his knowledge regarding Larry's affairs?

He considered this hypothesis, and then shook his head. Not only was the handwriting Larry's, the words mirrored Larry's style of expression. He took a few more puffs before extinguishing his cigarette and turned once again to the letter, picking up from where he'd left off, concentrating on the words, hearing Larry's voice.

This hasn't been an easy decision, but if I dwell on the ramifications, it will shoot to hell my resolve. That said, there could be a glitch—I'll have to lay low for a while. Someone, a woman, I'm told, has been asking questions about me. Could be innocent curiosity or that she's on the make—I hate to think it's something more sinister—but I do need to check this out.

Meanwhile, no one is to know I'm alive, not even my darling Kelly, as I would fear for her safety. Also, when (and if) the time comes, I want to communicate with her directly.

As for my whereabouts, I've relocated in a fishing village, which isn't too remote but away from the popular tourist stops. I'll write again when I've worked out the arrangements to return home. My plan is to slip quietly into L.A. and check into a motel, at which time I'll reach you at home.

It's with a sense of relief that I write these words, but honest to God, Jason, I'm also scared shitless. All I know is that I'm doing the right thing, that whatever the outcome, I'm determined to make it home.

You said once that you would never presume to judge me. I wonder if that statement still holds true. I wonder what you would say to me now.

Jason stared into the dwindling flames, reflecting on the question Larry had posed. The answer didn't require a good deal of thought. He would say to Larry he was elated over his return from the dead, but also frightened for him and fearful over the repercussions of his actions. Then again, on the bright side, the thought of Larry's return was so incredibly exciting, so extraordinary beyond belief.

His glee dissipated as his thoughts turned to Kelly. The bereaved widow would eventually be reunited with her husband. Or would she? *God knows, it will be difficult for them both, perhaps unthinkable for Kelly, at least, to reestablish any sort of relationship with Larry.*

Mind boggling was what it was, and at this point he didn't even want to consider the outcome. On a positive note, Kelly, in Turkey, would be out of harm's way—and, he hoped, unavailable to Detective Cherney. If she could pinpoint Max Scully's presence in Acapulco, it might complicate matters for Larry. How, he really didn't know, except this wasn't the time for Cherney to raise a ruckus, or to suggest foul play to Kelly.

Jason abandoned his place on the sofa to attend to his fire, and as he poked at the dying embers, the thought occurred that soon they'd be drowning in revelations and accusations. To put it simply, all hell would break loose. If Larry survived to make it back. If Detective Cherney didn't turn into Captain Marvel. Pray God, he kept to his methodical, plodding ways. Cliché or not, this was no time to upset the apple cart.

When Kelly picked up the phone to Detective Cherney, she felt, as always, the quiver of anticipation, edged with unease. She wondered if the news of her impending departure for Turkey might shake him up a bit. She wasn't disappointed. The relief she could hear in his voice at having reached her turned to surprise at her news. Then it was on to business.

"I promise I'll be brief," he said. "I'm calling to let you know we may have a break in our case."

"You have a suspect?"

"Ah, maybe. There's a man I want to describe, someone you may have noticed hanging around where you live, or at work. It's also possible he might have shown up at your wedding or even when you were on your honeymoon."

"On our honeymoon?" She took in her breath.

"Someone in Acapulco?"

"Oh, yes. This man turned up wherever we were, more times than we were comfortable with. In fact, Larry seemed upset by his presence."

"Have you seen this man since you arrived home?"

"Yes! That is, I think so. I recognized him in the audience on our closing night. Well, I'm not completely sure," she finished lamely.

"Are you talking about a short, stout man with prominent ears, wears dark glasses?"

"No. That's not right. I don't recall anyone fitting that description. The man I'm talking about is tall and thin with straight dark hair." There was a silence. "So much for your lead," Kelly guessed.

"Not necessarily. Let me grab my note pad." After a pause, he said, "Okay. I'd like to hear more about the man you described. What can you tell me about his behavior, his personality? Also can you give me a more detailed physical description?"

Oh God, she thought, *do I have to do this: bring this man back into my life? Why dredge up images that would evoke feelings of anguish or a sense of confusion and self-doubt?*

Only for now, she assured herself, only for now. Tomorrow she would be oceans away from all these concerns. Besides, if Cherney were on to something, he deserved all the help she could give. Plus, another thought occurred: that if ever there were a way to rid herself of the memories of the thin man, it would be to unload on the pragmatic Cherney.

Kelly took a deep breath and began.

Chapter Fourteen

Ankara, Turkey

> The Assistant Air Attaché
> of the United States of America
> and Mrs. James R. Lovejoy
> request the pleasure of your company

The wording of the invitation struck Kelly as imposing, unaccustomed as she was to the parlance of diplomacy. But the function—a cocktail-buffet in the home of Vanessa's and Gordon's good friends, Major Jim Lovejoy and his wife, Barbara—turned out to be a terrific party, despite the formality of hovering waiters and a maid to attend to their wraps.

Most of the attendees were attachés to the various embassies. Kelly had enjoyed conversations with people from Spain, France, and Israel, as well as with Turks, Germans, and Englishmen, most of whom were youngish, single, and decidedly flirtatious.

It had been a stimulating, even challenging evening, Kelly declared to Vanessa later on, as they sat in their robes in the Stuarts' small living room, Kelly curled up on the sofa, Vanessa occupying a wing chair with ottoman.

"Stimulating, as opposed to what?" Vanessa questioned, green eyes narrowing slightly.

Kelly met Vanessa's gaze. "How many days have I been in Ankara? Nine? Ten? How many functions have I attended? Let's see; we can count a promotion party, a tea for an incoming commander's wife, an Officers' Wives' Club luncheon, a dinner-dance at the club, and a what-do-you-call-it, a Hail and Farewell?"

"Kelly, where is all this leading? Are you saying you would classify tonight's function under 'worthwhile'"—she brought thumbs and index fingers together to indicate quotes—"but lump everything else under 'frivolous'?"

"I think I've said enough."

"So you're going to sit there with that silly grin on your face? Kelly, you've had a burr up your rear end, if you'll forgive my bluntness, for the last several days."

"You can read me that well? *Moi,* the actress?" The attempt at levity was a washout. Kelly could see her sister was not amused. "Okay, I'll stop being a smartass and tell you what's been eating at me." She looked about the room, taking in the brass brazier the Stuarts used as a planter, the free-standing brass candle holder, and the corner hutch, displaying vases and plates depicting scenes from the thirteenth century Hittite culture. "I look at your life, and when I compare it to the way the Turks live, it affects me. I'm not talking about doctors, lawyers, and others who excel in their professions."

"But you're saying most of the people have so little."

"Yes." She straightened herself, feet now planted firmly on the floor. "For instance, your maid. The woman finishes pressing your clothes, and then hauls out her husband's work clothes to iron because they live without electricity. And in town. You know those horse drawn carts filled with produce or jugs of water? The horse looks as if it's going to expire any minute, and the man up there flogging the poor beast onward is either glowering at everyone in sight or looks as if he lost his mother, father, and best friend, all in one day. Or what about those men all bunched together in open trucks? Have you looked at the way they dress—the baggy trousers, long jackets, everyone wearing a cap? Vanessa, they look like immigrants getting off the boat."

Vanessa nodded. "Villagers coming into town to work in the outdoor markets or in construction. In the city, at least, you don't see too many peasant women."

"They dress more colorfully than their westernized counterparts, but I don't know how they can stand to be swaddled from head to toe in that bulky material when it turns hot."

Vanessa shrugged. "These women have refused to give up the old ways. As for the so-called modern woman, the majority cover up with coats and headscarves, so it's not exactly a style show out there." She thought for moment. "I'll add to your study in contrasts. You've seen Ataturk Boulevard with the shops and outdoor restaurants, so pretty at night with their colored lights? I daresay if we walked around the corner we'd find men in rags and bedraggled little beggar children."

"So we agree."

"Up to a point, yes. Of course, we have it better. Far better. The contrast can be stark, even heartbreaking. Yes, we socialize a lot. We shop. We even have TVs that work most of the time. We don't have potable water, a Sears, or fashion boutiques. I guess we're lucky to have a washing machine, even if it has to be hooked up in the bathroom. Don't you think I long for the land of closets, cupboards, and kitchen conveniences? Not to mention a dishwasher."

"All right. I'd say you've made your point."

"Oh, honey, it's a trade-off. Despite the frustrations—and you haven't been treated to cold bath water and reading by candlelight—Turkey is a fascinating country and a great jumping-off place for travel to Greece and other parts of the Middle East. As for the people, don't be put off by what you perceive as a mean or sullen expression on some of the men. The Turks are a warm and hospitable society, with one of the best cuisines in the world."

"I'll certainly go along with that part."

"I'm intrigued by the very foreignness of this place. I look out there"—she pointed to the picture window at the end of the room—"and I see a herd of goats or sheep trotting down the street, or a band of Gypsies with a dancing bear. I hear 'madam', and look over to see a man at the window displaying brass and copper works. Or it's the egg boy or the water jug man or someone washing our car. Not that we asked."

"So who needs TV?"

"Didn't I say it was a trade-off?"

"Call it what you like. I can see you've made a great adjustment. As for you and Gordon"—she had mouthed his name, nodding in the direction of the bedroom where he'd retired—"you two are back on track, praise God. Or should I say Allah, since we're in Turkey?"

The remark, though flippant, came from the heart. Kelly had agonized over her sister's domestic problems, furious with her brother-in-law, as empathetically she shared in Vanessa's hurt and betrayal. The emotional upheaval itself could adversely affect her sister's pregnancy, she feared.

When Kelly had arrived in Ankara, she questioned how she should conduct herself toward the man who had two-timed her sister. He didn't deserve even a gesture of civility. On the other hand, she couldn't ignore the man from whom she was accepting room and board. She decided to take her cue from Vanessa.

To Kelly's surprise, all had gone amazingly well, from Gordon's smiling reception and brotherly embrace to Vanessa's gleeful greetings, replete with kisses and hugs. Clearly, they were elated to welcome her to Ankara. Moreover, whether it was for show or genuine, the Stuarts' behavior toward one another appeared natural, even affectionate, with no hint of repressed hostility.

Later, when she and her sister had talked in private, Vanessa had seemed reluctant to discuss her marital problems in depth, other than to assure Kelly that the couple had reached a state of détente. That after the sound and fury, a maelstrom of emotional high drama, punctuated by ultimatums and pleas for forgiveness, they agreed to work at salvaging their marriage.

"On track, huh?" Vanessa had moved from the wing chair to join Kelly on the sofa. Now keeping her voice low, she continued, "Maybe it's the hormones or the change in my body chemistry, but sometimes I feel so bitter toward Gordon. At other times, I'm ecstatic simply to be with him—so grateful we could patch things up that I feel like ringing bells or doing handstands."

"Forget handstands," Kelly said, giving her sister an affectionate poke.

"Yeah, right." Vanessa's smile faded as she turned pensive. "I don't know, Kelly. If it weren't for the baby, I'd probably be perched on your doorstep."

"And Gordon would be on the flight ahead of you. It's obvious he adores you."

"You think so? One thing for certain, he's thrilled about the baby." Her hand strayed to her stomach, fingers performing a gentle stroking motion.

"Maybe he's changed."

"Maybe." Vanessa raised her hand to fiddle with the lace-trimmed collar of her robe. "He's promised to remain faithful for the rest of our lives. And throughout all eternity." She looked sideways at her sister. "You want the honest-to-gosh truth?"

"I can guess what's coming, but I'll let you say it."

"I hope it will never come to this, but if Gordon were to cheat on me again, I'm not sure I could leave him."

"I doubt I could be so forgiving if Larry were unfaithful to me. Though I'll certainly never know the answer to that one, will I?"

Vanessa gave Kelly's hand a squeeze.

Kelly let out a small sigh. Then, focusing on thoughts that had formulated during their discussion, she said, "Look, you and Gordon have a good life here. You enjoy your friends, your activities, the culture."

"Exotic, though it may be?"

"Okay. But you're happy, you're busy, and you've told me you feel great now that you're in your fourth month. Vanessa, you know I love you and miss you when you're so far away, but there's really no compelling reason for me to stay on. Frankly, I feel out of place, like a visiting ornament. Besides, I'm lost without my work."

(Then again, she was becoming a little sick of the trappings of wedded bliss, the devoted looks, the sounds at night from the next room—all this, despite Vanessa's inner conflicts.)

She continued, "Vanessa, if you were unhappy, sick, or needy in any way at all, I'd stay. But I can't even offer to do the ironing or vacuuming. Not with Fatima coming every other day."

150

"Sweetie, it's okay. I really, really understand what you're saying, but since you've come this far, you can't miss Istanbul. Also I'd like to take you to a couple of places here in Ankara. Why not plan to stay on for at least another week? I promise. No more coffees, no more Hail and Farewells."

"Except my own?"

"Except your own. My husband," she said, with just a hint of smugness, "will see to it we give you an evening to remember. In fact"— and now her expression had turned impish—"maybe we can even round up some of those attachés. Make the evening truly worthwhile?"

Whatever Gordon Stuart might devise as a grand finale to his sister-in-law's visit, he had decided on a more ordinary interim activity, an evening outing at Genclik Parki—Young People's Park—an oasis not far from the center of downtown Ankara.

As a leisurely stroll at dusk brought the three of them within minutes of their destination, Kelly had to admit that Gordon was a knowledgeable and entertaining escort who knew a lot about Turkish life and customs. The easy charm, the ready smile, not to mention his curly dark hair and Paul Newman blue eyes enhanced his appeal. Kelly thought it couldn't hurt him career-wise, either; in fact, his looks and personality had undoubtedly facilitated his advancement in the military. At thirty-five, her brother-in-law was in charge of flight operations for ODC-T—the Office of Defense Cooperation Turkey—and he was known as a 'fast burner', possibly in line for promotion to Lt. Colonel before his time, or so Vanessa had implied.

They had reached the entrance to the park, and now Gordon protectively took each of them by the arm, in charge.

Or is he asserting himself more than was necessary? was Kelly's uncharitable thought. Not that her sister objected. Vanessa, Kelly observed, behaved more like a honeymooner than a cheated-upon wife, beaming at her husband and hanging on to his every word.

As they moved beyond the park entrance, Kelly took in the immensity of the place and the crowds. Gordon, as protector, was now essential she decided, noticing the stares generated by their presence.

Foreigners were in the minority.

Drawn by the sound of splashing water, they started for the lake and came upon fountains that changed color, creating water ripples of crimson, saffron, and aquamarine in the lake. As a backdrop, trees festooned with tiny, brilliant, blinking lights added a touch of enchantment. Vanessa, however, had spied something beyond the lake. "Oh, don't tell me," she said. "Look, there's an amusement park. We've got to ride the Ferris wheel."

"Hon, do you think you should?" Gordon's display of solicitude was marked by his caring expression, by the proprietary hand placed on Vanessa's arm.

"It's a Ferris wheel, darling, not a loop-the-loop. Come on, let's check it out."

They wound their way through the grounds, passing several packed outdoor restaurants, where the popular drink, Kelly observed, appeared to be a light brown liquid, served in a small round glass.

"Hot tea," Gordon explained when she asked. "What the Turks call *chi*. It's a damn sight more popular than Turkish coffee."

"I can understand why." Kelly made a face. "Their coffee makes our rehearsal-break brew taste like a gourmet blend."

"Wait 'til you try a liqueur called raki," Gordon said, steering them past three men in Arab dress who, seemingly oblivious to their surroundings, blocked the path as they engaged in a loud discussion.

Now it was Vanessa's turn to make a face. "Tastes like mouthwash," she said.

"Not if you drink it straight. It's really not bad, except raki's pretty potent."

They had reached the amusement park, and Kelly let out a small sigh as she studied the various attractions.

"I'll get in line for the tickets," Gordon said.

"Wait." Kelly had placed a restraining hand on his arm. "I don't think even Vanessa knows this, but I get queasy merely looking at a Ferris wheel."

"You don't remember we used to go down to the Pike at Long

Beach?" Vanessa's expression mirrored her bewilderment.

"I think I went with you once," Kelly said, "and because I wanted to be a good sport, I toughed it out. To be honest, I was miserable."

"Kelly, I'm sorry." Gordon was frowning. "You should have said something."

"And spoil your fun? No way. Besides, I'm having a great time, taking in the sights. You two go on ahead, and I'll people-watch for a while. Maybe I can even snag us a table over there." She pointed to a restaurant closest to the attractions.

In truth, she was enjoying herself, caught up in the carnival-like atmosphere. It was good to see people smiling, having fun, and as she began to take pleasure in their pleasure, she felt a sense of buoyancy, of light-heartedness. It was about time she lightened up; she felt a bit foolish now over how she'd ranted on about lifestyles and excessive social activities. Vanessa didn't need to be judged or censured by her know-it-all sister.

Kelly studied the queue for the Ferris wheel and spotted the Stuarts as they prepared to board. She decided not to roam, but instead to check out the restaurant for an available table.

In an effort to avoid attention, she selected a table farthest from the central part of the cafe, mentally imploring all waiters to stay away. After all, what could she order? Oh, there was something. Tea—*chi*. Good thing she remembered the word, because the sibilant sounds that flowed within earshot bore no resemblance to any language she'd ever spoken or studied. Nor did the music she heard in the background correspond to a western tonality. As it was, the rhythmic, wailing, minor key gradations provided a fitting backdrop for a man she had sighted at a nearby table. Swaying to the music, his eyes at half mast, he smoked a huge contraption. A water pipe? She tried not to stare, but couldn't help herself, enjoying the spectacle—until, that is, she caught something out of her peripheral vision. When she turned to check, she discovered she was no longer alone. A bearded man in Arab garb stood over her, pointing to one of the chairs.

"I'm sorry, these are taken," Kelly said, wondering if he was one of the trio they'd passed in the park.

He stared at her, obviously not comprehending, and as Kelly searched for a way to communicate, the man continued his solemn gaze. She began to mime her response, pointing off in the distance, and then to the empty spaces at the table to indicate she expected company. Apparently, she'd made her point because he raised his hand in a show of acceptance. Only to remain in place. Now it was her turn to stare. She wondered what he intended to do next.

What he did was to draw closer, to incline his head in a slight bow. Then, before turning away, he winked at her.

It was a slow wink, not unlike that of the thin man.

Kelly let out a soft cry of fear and half-rose. In her haste, she bumped against the table, knocking her purse to the ground. By the time she was upright, there was no sign of a retreating, robed figure. Clearly, he'd made a swift exit, melting into the stream of people parading past the restaurant.

She thought back to Sunday, when Vanessa and Gordon had taken her to see Ataturk's Tomb. Kemal Ataturk, the great benefactor of the Turkish people—the man who banished the fez, created a modern alphabet, and who, in 1923 as Turkey's first president, brought the country out of the dark ages—had earned an impressive monument. The pyramid-shaped tomb at the top of a grand staircase was situated in a courtyard at the end of a long promenade bordered by statues and Hittite lions.

The beauty of the day and the location, high on a hill, afforded a view of both the old and new cities, and it had inspired in them a desire to linger. They decided to take a leisurely look at the museum that housed Ataturk's personal effects.

They had stayed together as they meandered from one exhibit to the next, until Vanessa and Gordon moved on, leaving Kelly to examine a set of silver cufflinks etched with a free form geometric design. The pattern was so similar to the cufflinks she'd picked out for Larry in Mexico that she was entranced, gazing at them.

When, reluctantly, she turned from the case, Gordon was back at her side.

"Take your time," he said. "We'll be over there." He pointed in the direction of an enclosure that housed Ataturk's cars.

Rather than join them, Kelly decided she'd take another look at Ataturk's wardrobe, now that the exhibit site was less crowded.

She had taken only a few steps, when she paused to glance over her shoulder, instinctively aware of a person dogging her. Whether intentional or not, someone was breathing down her neck. She recognized the man who had stayed close to them on the promenade, following in their footsteps, standing next to them at the tomb. He'd stood out from the crowd because of his flamboyant good looks, the longish, wavy dark hair, a full mustache, and strong masculine features. Though he looked Turkish, he stood a head taller than the average Turk. He stared at her now, not bothering to lower his gaze as they made eye contact.

He'd been eyeing her at the tomb, as well—ogling her, really, his manner so blatant she didn't know whether to laugh or become angry. She no longer felt an urge to laugh. She wasn't flattered by his attention; in fact, his manner was more menacing than flirtatious. Abruptly, she turned away, drawing her cardigan together, hugging the material to her chest. Hurriedly, now, she made her way toward the exit.

Somehow he'd managed to speed ahead of her and waited at the door, holding it open for her. She started to pass through, muttering "thank you" as she looked up at him. For a second or two, they had locked eyes; then he bowed, closing one eye in a slow wink.

She hadn't seen him again and soon dismissed him from her thoughts. It was different this time; a second time.

There was no sign of the Arab. Clutching at the sides of the table, Kelly slid down into her chair, and for a moment, the sights and sounds of the park dimmed, fading into a dulled glaze, a muffled rumble.

Vanessa and Gordon brought her back, creating an aura of normality as they approached the table arm-in-arm, and then were upon her. Vanessa was bubbling away, ". . . and for a moment, I thought we'd be stuck up there at the top. I could hear the machinery creaking and groaning, and thought, uh-oh." Vanessa paused, eyebrows raised. "Hey, sweetie, are you okay? You're not angry because we deserted you?"

"Of course not. I'm fine. Why don't we all have a drink?" *A drink*, she thought, *would hit the spot*. But forget tea. What was the liqueur Gordon had mentioned? Raki? That was what she wanted. "Raki.

Straight, if you please."

Zihuantanejo, Mexico

The bar and lounge at Playa del Mar restaurant were jammed in the late evening. The din and the smoke created an atmosphere of low visibility among the patrons, a comforting aspect for one man seated at the bar. The restaurant, a thatched-roof structure that fronted the only hotel on La Ropa beach, drew the locals—fishermen, mainly—which was good. Tourists, he could do without.

Larry Townsend glanced about him, making a casual inspection of the room. Illumination from red bulbs set into wall sconces rendered an eerie, cave-like ambience, made less sinister by the softening effect of individual table lamps. Someone's idea of giving the customers atmosphere, Larry supposed, as he sipped his beer. Frankly, he would have preferred lounging by the light of day on the sun-baked patio within sound of the surf and within sight of bougainvillea-covered trellises. But to go public could invite the wrong kind of attention. *Better to remain a night person,* was his wry thought.

He turned his back to the room, and as he gazed into the bar mirror, he became momentarily disoriented as he viewed his image. The dark brown hair, combed straight back, the neatly trimmed mustache, skin coarsened by the sun, were features common to many in the bar. What he couldn't disguise were his build and height; he slouched over his drink, in an effort to make himself smaller.

Maybe it had been a dumb idea to come out tonight; on the other hand, no further reports had surfaced of incidents to set off alarms, no more talk of anyone, man or woman, making inquiries about him. Besides, he needed a break, a change in routine from most nights when, after a day on the construction site, he retreated to the room he had rented in a modest hillside house located off a cobblestone street.

His home away from home wasn't unique; it was a clone of other houses in the area, with its laundry-draped balcony. The neighborhood was full of kids shouting and dogs yelping as they chased through the weeds. He would always remember the pungent smells of garlicky fish soup and the taste of tortillas. He would also remember the sun glinting off of red tiled roofs, with hibiscus hugging the whitewashed façades.

He began to relax. Already he was thinking in terms of remembrance, and that was a good feeling. He signaled for another beer.

It was in the works, his return home. Jose, his working buddy, would drive him to Morelia, a ten-hour trip at the outside. From there, he would fly to Mexico City and then board a plane to Los Angeles. He had the money—he had, on the day of his disappearance, stashed it, along with purchases from various beach vendors, in a locker at a hotel comfortably distanced from the Palacio.

He had worked it all out, cramming shorts, shirt, and towel into a small canvas bag he'd found in a sports shop on the beach. Into one pocket of his swim trunks, he had zipped a waterproof pouch containing dark glasses, and into the other pocket, a soft floppy beach hat, wrapped in plastic. That was the easy part.

The swim had been lengthy, a harrowing exercise in survival; however, the sea had been as calm as bath water, and he had avoided the hot rays of the afternoon sun by starting back to Caleta Beach from Roquetta Island as soon as he determined he'd not been followed.

In the early part of the swim, he had rid himself of the diving equipment, except for the spear gun. Later, he decided, when he was close to shore, he would dispose of his only means of protection. To preserve his strength, he alternated swimming with floating, and for the last leg of his journey, he had the extraordinary luck to come upon a discarded inner tube that he used to help paddle his way east of the ferry dock and past the kiosks to a point where he could come ashore without fear of being recognized. The hat and dark glasses helped to conceal his identity.

Once on land, he allowed himself only a brief rest before he made his way to the hotel to claim his bag and money. In a restroom off the lobby, he found an empty stall where he could dry himself and dress. He then hailed a cab to take him to a *supermercado* where he made various purchases, including brown hair dye. Another cab transported him beyond the airport to the fishing village of Puerto Margues, where he secured lodging in a rustic inn on the side of the road opposite the beach.

The inn was a good choice, for it was there that he became acquainted with Jose Martinez. A sometime-fisherman and part- time construction worker from Zihuantanejo, Martinez made the trip to

Acapulco whenever possible, either by bus or fishing boat, to be with his girlfriend, who was a maid at one of the resort hotels. He had wanted to find a job in Acapulco, he explained to Larry, which is why he'd learned some English, but found the living easier and cheaper in his home village. Besides, he was helping to build a new hotel there, a project that would provide a paycheck for months to come, a statement Larry readily could accept. The workers in Mexico moved at a certain pace. Speedy, it was not.

As if Jose had read his thoughts, he'd stepped back from Larry, assuming the stance of the fisherman appraising his catch, his small black eyes darting from Larry's biceps to his torso, and then down to his hands. "Señor," he said, his smile softening the angular planes of his face, "you come to my town and I put you to work. We finish *muy pronto*, yes?"

In a sudden burst of clarity, a light flashed on in Larry's mind to diffuse the fog, to clearly delineate his next move. The question of options—whether to stay put, to go deeper into the tropics, or try the interior—had bugged him for hours. The answer, he now determined, lay in the remote fishing village of Zihuantanejo. Providence had brought him Jose Martinez, and he could have hugged the man. Keeping his tone casual, Larry said, "You know, I might take you up on that offer."

Jose stared at him, started to snicker, and then apparently thought better of it. "You don' like it here? Too big, maybe?"

"Too big, too superficial, too crazy."

Martinez mulled that for a moment, and then shrugged. "Okay, I take you with me. But I don' know, amigo. It is very simple, my home."

"Well, that makes it perfect." Larry had hit upon an idea. "I'm a writer, you see, and if I'm going to write about your country, I've got to live and breathe the true Mexico. Soak up the culture, you know? Which means I need to vamoose outta this place." He explained that if he could join Jose on the job and rent a room in one of the homes, it would place him closer to the people, lend insight to his writing.

There was no further cause for discussion.

The pay was lousy—he expected that—but he needed the physical activity. It enabled him to sleep at night, to keep at bay his rage at himself and at his persecutors. It also preserved his sanity. Because if he dwelled on what he had done to Kelly and his family, and to what lay before him at home, he would walk out into the ocean and keep walking.

All that aside, he was ready for the next move, for the journey home. It was time.

At the bartender's inquiring look, he shook his head and made a scribbling motion to indicate he was ready for his check. He was reaching for his wallet when he heard the sound of laughter. High-pitched, strident, it rose above the hubbub of the bar like a misdirected soprano soloist seeking dominance over an all-male chorus.

Larry kept his eyes on the bar mirror, watching as the offender— a woman dressed in a windbreaker and slacks, her hair tied up in a scarf—made her way through the room, accompanied by one of the locals. He knew the guy. It was Antonio, the hotshot who'd been on the construction crew for about a week. The man was really full of himself, and now he'd be bragging about his hot date. *Some date,* Larry thought, keeping track of them as they settled into the far end of the bar, opposite where Larry was seated.

The laughter again. It cut through the smoke, the slap of dice on wooden tables, and the staccato cadence of the Spanish tongue. Just seconds ago he'd brushed aside a fleeting thought. Now it became a force invading his mind to take shape in the image of a blond woman with an irritating laugh. In Acapulco.

What of it? It could be any woman, anywhere in the world, whose laughter was out of control. He strained to catch her reflection in the mirror, mentally exhorting the bartender to get out of his line of sight. When finally he moved away, Larry saw the woman remove her head scarf and fluff out blond curls. In the murky light, he couldn't make out her features.

All right. It could be bad. Though he hadn't heard of any further sightings of the woman who'd asked about him, it didn't mean she wasn't lurking behind some goddamned tree. But if this woman was the party girl from Acapulco—

Oh, Jesus, she was coming his way. He hunched over his glass and lowered his head, but he kept his gaze focused on the mirror. If she stopped . . . But no, she continued on, toward the john. Frantically, he pulled pesos from his billfold. He had to get out, and fast, before she returned.

Larry didn't wait for his change, and he didn't look back. What he had seen was enough—the face, the features that went with the laugh. In Acapulco.

She hadn't needed Antonio's help. She'd spotted him the minute she entered the bar. The bad dye job notwithstanding, there was no mistaking his height, the slope of one shoulder when he was seated, the way his hair grew at the nape of the neck. As Margaret Padilla scanned the room from the archway that separated the restrooms from the bar and lounge, she congratulated herself, taking pride in her powers of observation. They made a good team, she and Joe, even if he was a little quirky, playing peek-a-boo games with little wifey bitch. One thing for sure: Larry Townsend was alive, and that meant Joe needed to get his ass down here, pronto. They had to move on this fast.

She whirled around to make her way back to the restroom area, and as she searched in her purse for change, she prayed to St. Jude that the payphone was alive and kicking.

Chapter Fifteen

*D*id I catch you before bedtime?" Kelly asked into the phone.

"Kelly! For heaven's sake! Steve, its Kelly! Quick, get on the other line." Contralto tones had soared into soprano range. When Nadine caught her breath, she said, "We're still up, but what time is it in Ankara?"

"Eight o'clock—in the morning, that is."

"Well, good morning." Steve had picked up their bedroom phone. "How are you, honey?"

"Hi, Steve. I'm fine. Having a wonderful visit here."

"Vanessa?" Nadine asked, worry creeping into her tone.

"Great, Mom, but I'll let her tell you herself in a minute. Mainly I'm calling to let you know I'll be home in about a week. I wasn't sure a letter would get to you in time."

"We received your card," Nadine said. "Now if I remember correctly, you expected to be in Istanbul at this time."

"Oh, we're still going. Vanessa and I are off to Istanbul this very evening on the night train. Picture in your mind the Orient Express!"

"That should be interesting," Steve said. "Calls to mind intrigue à la Agatha Christie. Not to mention incredibly good food?"

"Kelly," Nadine broke in, "you said you and Vanessa are going on this trip. What about Gordon?"

"Gordon's TDY in Germany again. We're not even sure he'll make it back to Ankara before I leave."

It was Steve who broke the silence. "I'd say you've saved the best for last, Kelly. You're going to enjoy Istanbul. Incidentally, can we do anything for you at this end? Do you want us to call Jason or your Mr. O'Hara to alert them when you'll be home?"

"No, that won't be necessary."

"Oh, Kelly, I almost forgot." Nadine had come alive again. "Someone from your theater called a couple of days ago. He thought I might know when you planned to return."

"Rick?"

"He gave me his name, but it didn't sound like Rick. More like Jim or Tim—we had a terrible connection. Anyway, I said I didn't know when you'd be back, but certainly not immediately because you planned to be in Istanbul about now."

"We have a Jim on stage crew, but he wouldn't be the one to call. You don't think it was Gene, our stage manager?"

"Now that I think about it, I believe he did introduce himself as your stage manager. As I said, the connection was about as bad as it can get."

"In that case, you'd better give Rick a call. With the musical in full swing, he's probably into pre-production planning for the next show. I wouldn't want him to think I'm taking a powder on that one. Not if I want to keep my job."

That said, they moved on to other topics, and then it was Vanessa's turn. No further mention was made of Gordon Stuart.

Nor did Kelly and Vanessa have much to say of a personal nature for the remainder of the day. Once they boarded the train, their surroundings absorbed them. The narrow corridors and the tiny, cozy compartment could have found a home in a James Bond movie. Missing, however, were double agents, voluptuous villainesses, and dead bodies.

Kelly, for one, would have welcomed a little intrigue. Let some winking, bowing creep get within seeing distance and she would demand answers, even if she had to chase him through every compartment on the train. No easy task, Kelly had to concede, as she and Vanessa side-stepped one another in an effort to avoid a collision in the crowded, swaying room. Enough close misses. They decided to go to dinner.

If the food rated an eight on the scale of one-to-ten, the ambience, the women decided, rated about a three. Far from the fabled Orient Express dining room with its velvety drapes, spotless napery, and gleaming silver cutlery, their dining car ranked more utilitarian than opulent, the waiters curtly efficient rather than ingratiating.

Their meal consisted of salad, tender roast beef and rice, plus eggplant which Kelly left untouched. That it was commandeered by her sister was no surprise. Vanessa viewed the eating-for-two syndrome as one of the perks of pregnancy.

Now, her expression hopeful, Vanessa eyed Kelly's plate. "You're not eating your rice," she said.

"Neither are you. Gorge now, pay later. Besides, dessert's on its way."

"That's a happy thought." Vanessa sipped her tea, and then gave Kelly a thoughtful look.

"What?" Kelly asked, catching something in Vanessa's expression.

"You wouldn't happen to be gathering material for a spy novel, would you?"

Kelly laughed. "Why on earth would you think that?"

"The way you seem to be memorizing the people on this train. I'd swear you've been scrutinizing every person who's entered this car." When Kelly didn't respond, Vanessa quirked an eyebrow. "Is something going on that I don't know about?"

Kelly picked up her fork and nudged her rice toward the center of the plate, making a mound of it. "Are all mommies-to-be so perceptive?" she asked, not looking up.

"Are all aunts-in-waiting so evasive?"

Maybe it was the cloistered setting, the lateness of the hour, and the fact that she'd downed a couple glasses of wine, but Kelly felt an overwhelming urge to confide in her sister. "Okay," she said, "if I don't get this off my chest, I think I'll burst. But first"—she took a deep breath—"if I'm going to fill you in, I'd better start at the beginning."

She began with their honeymoon, recounting the antics of the

163

thin man, his change in personality, and the curtain call episode at the Hollywood Playhouse, and concluded by revealing her experiences at the museum and at Genclik Park. "So you can see I'm sensitive as to who might be skulking in the corridors."

Vanessa had stopped eating. "Let's go back to the two men who pulled the wink-and-nod routine on you in Ankara. You're certain you've never seen them before? That it couldn't be your thin man in disguise?"

"I can't be sure about the Arab, but the man in the museum was entirely different in build, height, bone structure—the works."

"Wow," Vanessa said softly, "I have to think about this." She fell silent, not even protesting when the waiter arrived to remove their plates.

"You say," she said finally, "you've confided in the folks and in Rick. What was their reaction?"

"Puzzlement. Disbelief. I suppose they think of me as neurotic, unstable, or at the very least, overly imaginative. Oh, to be fair, I'd probably respond in the same way." She gave a small laugh. "I forgot to mention my conversation with Detective Cherney before I left for Turkey."

"Cherney? He's still in the picture?"

"Yes. I told him about seeing the thin man on our honeymoon and after the curtain call. He took me seriously, wanted all the details. I think he'll be very interested in what happened in Ankara, even though others may be skeptical." Would Vanessa entertain the same doubts? She had to ask. "What do you think? Am I turning into Kelly the kook?"

"In no way. I don't think for a minute that you're overworking your imagination. Something very strange is going on, and I suspect you haven't seen the last of these incidents."

"So what's the answer? What should I do?"

"I have no idea. We could speculate all night and frankly"— Vanessa raised her hand to stifle a yawn—"my thinking is becoming a little fuzzy."

Their desserts had arrived, puddings topped with berries. With thumb and forefinger, Vanessa delicately removed a berry and brought it to her mouth, nibbling at it. When it was gone, she picked up her spoon, and then set it aside. The look she gave Kelly was sheepish. "This is hard for me to say."

"Go on. You can tell me. Whatever it is."

"I'm glad you have Robert Cherney in your corner."

The vote of confidence would have pleased the detective. With other assignments on tap, Robert Cherney didn't have the luxury of contemplation, of unlimited time to pursue ephemeral leads. By the same token, he could no more set aside the Townsend case than he could ignore a crime in progress. Or maybe it was Kelly Townsend, the tragedy of her loss that prompted him to persist. It wasn't personal. He knew better than to involve himself in emotional aspects of his work.

Still. In odd moments, she appeared to him, a study in contrasts with her large, amber eyes overwhelming her pale skin, her dark hair framing delicate features. Vulnerable, yet strong, her sadness offset by flashes of humor—it was her courage, her resiliency that moved him. Nothing more.

While his latest investigation had been productive, bringing to light yet another phase of the conundrum, he continued to deal with bits and pieces as he sank into a quagmire of increasing proportions. Oh, sure, he'd keep on it, exercise patience and perseverance. Those were his crowning virtues. Yet he longed to trade those sterling qualities for one brilliant flash of insight. All that aside, what he needed was a listener, a sounding board. If he could lay it all out, talk it out, he might gain some perspective on the situation.

He decided to call Jason Underwood.

Jason gently massaged the space between his eyebrows. It was close to quitting time, the afternoon made especially difficult by a recalcitrant client. He hadn't been overjoyed to receive the call from Cherney. Now it was with some dismay that he learned of the detective's call to Kelly, dismay turning to interest, and then apprehension as Cherney disclosed Kelly's and Larry's encounters with this strange individual on their honeymoon, as well as Kelly's alleged experience with this same man on the closing night of her play.

"So even if Kelly drew a blank on Max Scully, she gave you the particulars on this, uh, bizarre character, did she?" Jason hoped his tone conveyed only a passing interest, though in truth, he wanted every last detail.

"Since I was armed with Mrs. Townsend's description, I decided it was worth pursuing, worth putting in a call to their hotel in Acapulco. Unfortunately, the hotel personnel couldn't come up with a name."

"That's it?"

The detective chuckled. "Not by a long shot. I won't bore you with the details—how many days, how many phone calls—but here's the scenario. I got the hotel to email me their guest checkout sheet for the day the Townsends were scheduled to depart. I checked that against the passenger manifest of Mexicana's flight from Acapulco to Mexico City on that same day. Ditto for the Alaska Airlines flight from Mexico City to Los Angeles. What I came up with were several matches on all three counts—that is, male passengers traveling individually, or at least with only one listing of the same name.

"However, my follow-up in L.A. was a washout, because no one matched the description. Still, I had five names—three Mexican, two Anglo—of folks who didn't continue on after Mexico City. At least not that same night."

"So Mexico City could have been the final destination, or an extension of someone's vacation."

"That, or even a one-night layover."

"Don't tell me you followed through on each and every name."

"I didn't have to, because lucky for me, something came to mind. I remembered Mrs. Townsend mentioning a restaurant. It was very special, she said, way up in the hills with outdoor dining around a pool, awesome views, and so on. The point is, who should show up, but the man in question and his female companion? Now according to Mrs. Townsend, this couple had been carousing earlier around the hotel pool. 'Real low-lifes' was how she and her husband regarded these people, and certainly not the type to show up at a fancy, expensive restaurant. Whether that's so or not, I can be grateful to them for turning up. And for

166

making a reservation."

"Yes, I see where this is leading. You contacted the manager of the establishment, and he, in turn, provided you with the reservations list for that particular evening."

"He did, and there it was—Joseph Wilder, the only name to show up both on the hotel registry and the airlines passenger manifest."

"Well, bully for you."

"That's what I thought. Something to work with at last, but I struck out. I could find nothing on a Joseph Wilder, either in the police or FBI files."

"Nothing to link this man with Max Scully?"

"No, but I didn't stop there. It was just a hunch, but I felt there had to be something on Wilder, so I kept digging. Then, as a last resort, I contacted Interpol, figuring on an international connection. I figured right. With the information I gave them, they were able to come up with," he paused. "Now get this: one Franz Joseph Kurtwilder. Turns out he's a Viennese who has dual citizenship, both U.S. and Austrian. He's also a real piece of goods. Into counterfeiting, smuggling, and—it gets uglier—murder for hire."

"Good heavens. Why isn't this man incarcerated?"

"They nailed him for counterfeiting, but they lacked enough evidence to back up the other charges. Apparently, they've now lost track of him."

Jason let out his breath, fingers performing a tap dance on his desk top. "Franz Joseph Kurtwilder and Joseph Wilder. Close enough, I'd say."

"Could be a coincidence, but Mrs. Townsend's description jibes with Interpol's profile on Kurtwilder. I, uh, take it you've never heard of this man?"

"Never. Nor did Kelly confide in me."

"So you can't explain why Scully or Wilder should be lurking around the Townsends?"

"Certainly not. The thought of Larry or Kelly being stalked by these animals makes my blood run cold. At least I can enjoy peace of mind, knowing Kelly's in Turkey."

"She's in Istanbul, to be exact."

"You've heard from her?" He couldn't hide his astonishment.

"No, the information came to me in a roundabout way. I spoke with Rick O'Hara on the off-chance that Wilder's name might turn up on their season subscription list. No luck there. However, he wanted me to know about a telephone call from Mrs. Townsend's mother. It seems Kelly asked her to inform Mr. O'Hara that she'd be home and back to work in about a week's time, after she and her sister returned from Istanbul. Then the mother adds she was sorry she hadn't been privy to this information earlier when their stage manager had called. All she could tell him then was that her daughter planned to visit Istanbul."

Cherney paused. "Are you ready for the punch line? No record existed of any call from the Hollywood Playhouse to Mrs. Townsend's parents. The stage manager was emphatic. The rest of the staff were equally emphatic. No one had talked to Nadine Hanson."

"But someone talked with her," Jason said, leaving the questions of who and why unspoken.

It was left for each man to draw his own conclusion.

"I think we've about done Istanbul," Kelly said, uttering a small groan. "Maybe it's me, but I could use an intermission—maybe a full day of sitting, preferably with my feet up." The two women were ensconced on the balcony of their room at the Istanbul Hilton, enjoying the view of the Bosporus—the Istanbul Strait—in the distance. They had returned from a boat trip by motor launch up the European side of the Bosporus, past palaces, fortresses, summer homes, and resort areas, to the entrance of the Black Sea. The second leg of the trip brought them around to the Asiatic side, with a stop at a typical village, before crossing back into Europe.

On another day, they had explored the area where they were staying, the cosmopolitan part of Istanbul with its hotels, parks, and restaurants of ethnic diversity. This newer part of the city was divided from the ancient quarter by a small body of water, the Golden Horn. One needed only to cross over the Galata Bridge to be transported into crowded, narrow streets populated by street vendors, money changers, and people of all nationalities. Competing with the babble of many tongues were the wailing, chanting calls to prayer from Muezzins perched on balconies encircling minarets, which soared from mosques like sentinels charged with pointing the way to heaven.

Kelly had loved it all—the aromatic scent of spices and exotic flavors to tease the senses, the crowded waterways and the touristic must-sees and must-dos, which included the Suleymaniye and Blue Mosques and the Topkapi Museum with its golden thrones, dazzling display of royal jewels and collections of china and glassware, and, of course, the Covered Bazaar. Now she wondered what possibly could be next.

"I would swear," Kelly said, with a side glance at Vanessa, "being pregnant has turned you into superwoman."

"Gotta get it all in now before junior comes on the scene."

"That's going to stop you?"

Vanessa grinned. "Let's talk about tomorrow. That's all we have left, you know."

"Why don't we tackle that subject at dinner?"

"Fine with me. In fact, why don't we dine here, try the Roof Rotisserie?"

"Why, Vanessa! Does that mean you want to forego the thrill of our nightly Indy 500 taxi chase through the streets of Istanbul?"

"So they speed a bit. Doesn't bother me, but on our next outing I'm going to insist you wear a blindfold. Better yet, we could always place a paper bag over your head."

"And deprive you the pleasure of my gasps, the nail marks on your hands, the sound of gnashing teeth?"

Vanessa laughed. "Let's save that for another time." She rose, stretched, and announced it was her turn to use the shower first.

Though Vanessa had made the same pronouncement the night before, it mattered not to Kelly. She was pleased to see her sister relaxed and happy. The subject of Gordon's TDY hadn't surfaced.

"The Covered Bazaar. That's where we'll head for tomorrow.

Also there's that luncheon place I told you about down by the docks."

"Vanessa, we've already been to the Bazaar."

"I know, but you couldn't decide on a ring, and I want to look at that leather jacket again for Gordon."

Later, at the restaurant, Kelly took a sip of her cocktail, and then set the drink down, taking time out to enjoy her surroundings. The far wall, entirely of glass, granted diners a view of passing ships and other watercraft, at this hour defined solely by their lights. Brass and copper etchings covered other areas, while plants and flowers in ornate containers added zest and color to the room. The spaciousness and comfortable elegance infused in Kelly a sense of wellbeing. Her thoughts turned to Vanessa's suggestion. *A return to the Grand Bazaar? Why not?* Though she didn't share her sister's unbridled enthusiasm for shopping, the Bazaar was such a colorful madhouse, a wonderful place to study the human condition.

About to give voice to these thoughts, she was distracted by the sudden appearance at their table of the dining room hostess. At least, she thought it was the woman who had seated them.

Slight of build, her elaborate brunette 'do giving her a top-heavy appearance, she smiled broadly at both women. "Sorry to interrupt," she said, "but which of you is Mrs. Townsend?"

"I'm Kelly Townsend."

"Oh, good. We understand your husband will be joining you. We can add another place setting, or we can accommodate you at larger table."

Kelly brought her hand to her mouth. What was she talking about? Was this woman crazy?

Vanessa, after a quick glance at Kelly, spoke up. "There's some misunderstanding," she said. "My sister has been recently widowed."

The woman, whose clipped tones suggested an English accent, appeared confused. "But we received a call that Mr. Townsend would shortly be joining his wife and sister-in-law."

"My husband is dead," Kelly said, her voice barely above a whisper.

"Oh, I'm so sorry. I can't imagine how this could have happened." Now more pitying than flustered, she asked, "Are you all right, dear? Can I get you something?"

"I'm fine. Really, I'm fine."

"Again, my apologies." She started to turn away.

"Wait a minute." Vanessa was at her side, guiding her a few feet from the table. They spoke quietly, the woman nodding and casting an anxious glimpse back at Kelly.

When Vanessa returned to the table, she looked angry. "Kelly, do you want to leave?"

"No. I want to stay, have dinner and talk about this."

"Good. Because the hostess—and I have a name, Sarah Crenshaw—promised to get back to us with some answers. She said it was the maître d' who received the call, that she was only the messenger. Anyway, she's going to find out what she can." Vanessa shook her head. "If this is someone's idea of a joke, they're sick, sick, sick."

"But who? And why? For what purpose would someone pull a sadistic stunt like this?"

"Oh, any number of twisted souls out there get their kicks tormenting their fellow man."

Kelly thought for a moment. "It's possible this wasn't a random happening."

"Right. It could be you have a secret admirer. Maybe he used Sarah as a ploy to check your marital status."

"I think it's more sinister than that. I'm beginning to wonder if the phone call has any connection with those incidents in Ankara. Why would anyone be following me or think Larry is alive and joining us for dinner?" Kelly had disturbing thoughts. *Who are these people? What if Larry's death was not an accident? Then what?* She brushed aside the what ifs, not wanting to go there. Not in this setting. Not on her last night in Istanbul.

Vanessa and Kelly continued their search for plausible explanations, at the same time managing to put away an excellent dinner. While they awaited dessert, Vanessa said, "I wonder what happened to our pal, Sarah?"

"Maybe she's having a hair crisis. We could always check the ladies room." Kelly stretched her neck to peer around the tables. "I don't see her. Tell you what. I'm going up front. If I can't find Ms. Crenshaw, I'll talk to the maître d'." She was on her feet. "If dessert arrives, no fair filching any of mine."

"No promises," Vanessa muttered as Kelly made her way to the entrance of the restaurant.

A few minutes later, when Kelly arrived back at their table, dessert had been served. Vanessa, as if caught in the act, put down her fork. But her impish smile quickly faded. "Kelly, what's wrong? You look stunned."

"I couldn't find the hostess, didn't see her anywhere, so I talked to the maître d'. Sarah Crenshaw, or at least the woman I described to him, apparently doesn't exist."

"What? Of course, she exists." Vanessa was frowning. "But not as a hostess for the Roof Rotisserie?"

Kelly nodded. "As for the call, he was the only person answering the phone and has 'no recollection of forwarding a message of that nature,' to quote his exact words."

"Well, shit," Vanessa said softly.

"There's something else. You know when Cherney called? It was because he thought he had a lead in our break-ins." She went on to relate Cherney's description of his suspect, and to explain that though she couldn't place this man, their conversation had brought to light her own strange tale. "But getting back to Cherney's suspect," she continued, "I think I saw this man today. It was when we were walking through the Covered Bazaar."

"Oh, my God. But you're not sure?"

"No, it was only a glimpse. With all those bodies moving in and out of shops and eating places, one person isn't likely to stand out in the crowd. But Vanessa"—Kelly swallowed—"a few minutes ago I saw a man pass by the entrance to the restaurant. He was a short, heavyset man with prominent ears."

"Kelly, there are any number of short, stout, big-eared men in the world."

"Wearing dark glasses at ten o'clock in the evening?"

The call came at seven o'clock in the morning, Istanbul time— ten o'clock at night, Los Angeles time. It was Jason Underwood. He had learned that Kelly and her sister were in Istanbul and had assumed they'd opt for the Hilton.

Kelly had slept poorly, but she was alert enough to react with concern over the attorney's call. Was something wrong at home? Had her parents been in an accident?

"No, no, no." His tone was soothing. "I wanted to be sure all was well with you. Also I was curious as to when you might be returning."

Maybe it was the hour, or she was groggier than she realized, but at that moment, it didn't occur to Kelly that Jason's call was somewhat peculiar. If everything was all right at home, why would he call merely to ask after her health and when she expected to return home?

"I'm practically on my way back," she said. "We leave this evening on the night train, and I expect to fly out of Ankara tomorrow afternoon. With a layover in Rome," she added.

"Aren't you the lucky one! I must say, I envy you."

"I had planned to spend a few days in Rome, but now, I want to get home as soon as possible, so I'll be leaving the next morning with a direct flight to L.A. Jason, I've got to talk with you, soonest. Some very strange things have been going on. I can't go into this now except to say that I sense Larry is somehow in the picture. These incidents are being staged for a reason. What, I don't know, except, it's all so bizarre. And scary as hell."

"We'll talk when you return," Jason said. He bade her a safe journey home, adding that she need only call, and he would make time for her. As much time as was needed, he assured her.

Kelly and Vanessa did return to the Grand Bazaar, where they shopped, haggled, and eventually purchased the jacket for Gordon, embroidered goods for Nadine and Audrey, and jewelry for themselves. Their mood, however, started out subdued and became even more so by lunch.

They found the restaurant Vanessa had heard so much about. A favorite with the locals, it consisted of one long, narrow room, unadorned and lacking color, but with each table providing a view of the Bosporus. The place had a reputation for excellent fish and their meal, the women agreed, was superb. Except that Vanessa, Kelly noted, wasn't attacking her meal with her usual gusto.

Kelly gestured out the window, at the water made drab by cloud cover, at the drizzle streaking the window. "At least we had decent weather, up to today."

"It's not the weather I'm concerned about," Vanessa said, worry lines creasing her forehead. "It's you. Such a rotten thing to happen."

"You mean last night?" Kelly gave a little snort. "Something's going on, for sure."

"I don't know how you can take this so lightly."

"What choice do I have? Oh, I still have my bad days, but I gave up playing victim several weeks ago. However, I definitely intend to unload on Jason, and I also plan to call Detective Cherney. It's possible he has information on the thin man. I'm certainly going to tell him about last night," she added.

"You do seem to have everything under control." The words, though laudatory, contained a hint of resentment.

"What about you? Are you going to be okay?"

"Of course. Why shouldn't I be?"

Kelly shrugged. "No reason," she said, turning from Vanessa to the Bosporus, to follow the progress of a ferry boat in transit to the Asiatic side, to Uskudar and a waiting train. In a few hours, they would embark on a similar journey.

Vanessa sighed. "Talk about playing ostrich. I'm about as far into denial as anyone could possibly be."

"Whoa, wait a minute." Kelly had snapped to attention. "Has

something happened?"

"Not that I'm aware of, but Gordon hasn't called. He promised, said he'd call." Vanessa met her sister's gaze. "Okay. I know that look. Spit it out."

"I don't want to say something that's going to hurt. I've really enjoyed being with Gordon. He's charming, personable, and intelligent."

"But?"

"I don't think I could live with the uncertainty. Inside my head I'd constantly be concocting X-rated pictures of him with other women."

"You think I haven't done that?"

"You don't have to stay with him, you know."

"You're right. But I want to stay with him. I know he loves me, that it's no act."

"So you're willing to accept him on any terms?"

"Maybe not any terms. Not if he were abusive or flagrantly promiscuous."

"Oh, I see. It's all right, as long as he's discreet."

"I'm sure that makes me a fool in your eyes, but Kelly, I'm not you. If my behavior or attitude seems inconsistent, then so be it. I can live with this."

Once again, green eyes met hazel eyes, straight on, neither woman faltering. Kelly was the first to speak. "I'd say we both have taken control of our lives."

"I'd say so." Vanessa grinned. "But we sure as hell have our work cut out for us."

♪ Chapter Sixteen ♪

"Ninety-five degrees today! It was on the news." Kelly struggled to open the window above her dining alcove. "This late in May, it's usually all dreary drizzle out there."

"Here, let me get that for you." Jason sprang to his feet, and in seconds, he was at her side. It was no use. The window was stuck.

Kelly cast a baleful eye at the intractable window. "One more item on my reasons-to-move list," she said. And then, to Jason, she added, "You must be sweltering in that jacket. Let me hang it up for you."

He noted a trace of amusement in Kelly's expression. Too much formality for a Sunday afternoon? Good thing he hadn't worn a tie. Jason resettled on the sofa, keeping an appreciative eye on Kelly as she carried his jacket to the closet. *Not every woman could wear shorts,* he thought, his admiration blocking out more urgent concerns.

His respite, however, was short lived. With Kelly excusing herself for a detour into the kitchen, Jason pondered more pressing issues. Topping the list was the question of to whom he owed his allegiance. Larry would expect him to uphold the client-lawyer rules of confidentiality, and under those conditions, he couldn't reveal to Kelly that her husband was alive. On the other hand, he had an obligation to Kelly as well, particularly with Wilder in the picture. Surely it was time to apprise her of Larry's circumstances at the time of their marriage—omitting, however, the nature of Larry's involvement. Besides, his disclosures might prepare her for the forthcoming revelations. . if, that is, her husband made it back.

He hadn't heard from Larry, and it worried him. This woman who had been asking about him . . . Was she a part of the alliance he meant to expose? If so, and if she had spotted him, then Larry was in serious trouble.

It's all problematical at this point, and to dwell on a worst-case scenario would serve no purpose, he thought, as his hostess placed a glass of iced tea before him on the coffee table.

"Well. How nice of you."

"The least I could do," Kelly said, as she settled with her drink into the chair opposite him, watching now as he took a sip of the tea. "Is it all right? You don't think it needs more sugar?"

"Mine's just right."

She raised her glass to her lips, and then without tasting it, set her drink on the small end table next to her chair. "Are you sure I can't fix you something stronger?"

He shook his head. "It's a bit early in the day for me, and besides, I think a clear head is definitely in order, don't you?" He said this with a smile, but the message was clear. It was time to cut the chit-chat.

He'd detected a note of urgency in Kelly's statements from Istanbul, but less so in her call to him on Saturday, the day she returned. Still, she'd been receptive to the idea of getting together on Sunday, since he would be away for most of next week. Now he sensed that she was struggling over how to begin.

He decided to come to her aid. "Kelly, I know all about your experiences with the person I think you refer to as 'the thin man'."

She looked surprised. "You've talked with Detective Cherney?"

He nodded. "Thanks to his persistence, we have a name to match the description. I don't suppose you've heard of a Joseph Wilder? Or try this: Franz Joseph Kurtwilder?"

"Good heavens, no."

Kelly's eyes, it seemed to Jason, grew larger by the minute as he described the detective's painstaking efforts in her behalf, the investigative feats that resulted in the identification of Wilder. He left out, however, the murder-for-hire tie-in. When she detailed her experience with the two men in Ankara and the series of events in Istanbul, it only reinforced Jason's decision to open up about Larry.

"You won't mind," he said, when she'd finished, "if I pass on this information to our detective friend?" When she offered no objection, he fell silent, pondering his next move. Now playing for time, he said, "Kelly, would you happen to own an ashtray?"

"Sure. Bottom dresser drawer, if I remember correctly."

By the time she'd reappeared with his ashtray, he'd made the decision to lift the curtain on Scully—again with some creative editing—and take it from there.

Carefully, he did so. He stubbed out his cigarette as he finished his commentary, wishing now he'd opted for something stronger than iced tea.

She paled. "I'm trying to piece this together," she said. "Cherney's suspect in the break-ins is this Max Scully, number one scum bum, who turns up in Istanbul. Which could mean he was responsible for the phone call hoax. Which in turn"—she gripped her glass—"brings us to Larry. Am I right?"

Jason started to reach for a cigarette, and then changed his mind. No more playing for time and no more soul searching. "Kelly, I have to tell you Max Scully has been in the picture since before you and Larry married. Larry identified this man to me when we spoke at your reception as someone who had been stalking him, at times following him when he was in his car. He was even at your wedding." He paused. "Larry also hinted at other forms of harassment."

She had edged forward in her chair. "Why? I don't understand."

"Oh, Kelly, this is the hard part. Your husband was . . . Larry's troubles stemmed from his association with individuals engaged in some sort of illegal enterprise. He didn't spell out what he'd gotten himself into, but I know he tried to extricate himself from this involvement." He paused. "It would seem someone took exception to that course of action."

"Now wait a minute. He was into something illegal, you say? You have no hint, no clue as to what it was?"

It was obvious she was becoming agitated, and no wonder, but he could only shake his head and maintain his silence.

"You mentioned his association with certain individuals. Well, who? Jason, you had the inside track on his business affairs."

"Kelly, dear girl, if only I knew." His shrug, he hoped, wasn't unkind, but more a gesture of helplessness.

Her eyes traversed the room, as if the walls, the ceiling, or her plants might yield the information she sought. "Is that it?"

"Not quite. Larry was preparing a letter to place in my safekeeping. In it, he planned to name those involved and offer proof of his allegations. The letter was to be his insurance, he said, a means of exposing this operation, should the need arise."

"He meant if something should happen to him?"

"That was my question, too, but Larry denied that he was in any danger." Jason sighed. "There is no letter. Larry was supposed to hand it over to me when he returned from Acapulco. Which brings to mind the break-ins. I believe someone feared the existence of such a letter or document—something that could expose their operation."

"If only—" Kelly stopped, a catch in her voice.

"I know. It's haunted me, the thought of having that letter."

"No, you don't understand. I wasn't referring to the letter." Kelly gnawed at her lower lip. "How could I have been so obtuse, so short-sighted? I should have recognized the signs, the symptoms of distress. Like we'd be talking, with Larry looking me straight in the eye. Except he could have been off in China or on the moon, for that matter. Then the evening we went to El Mirador Hotel to watch the cliff divers. Their performance held us spellbound; we were so caught up in the spirit of it. That is . . . at first. Then everything changed."

"How so?"

"Not long into the performance, Larry became distant and self-absorbed, as if he were brooding over something. Almost despondent, I'd say."

"Did he offer any explanation as to the change in mood?"

"He thought it was insane for those divers to chance being killed, to tempt the fates. What was it he said? Something about life being so short, so why ask for trouble? I argued with him, supporting an opposite point of view." She caught her breath. "When I think of what must have been going through his mind . . ."

"Kelly, you couldn't have known, and you mustn't punish yourself." But he thought his words were lost on her; she seemed to drift away from him for a moment, and then she was back.

"I think I caught a certain look in his eyes, almost of despair. It passed so quickly I didn't attach any significance to it. I should have. I should have known something was wrong." She trailed off once again, lost in thought, and tears welled in her eyes. "Jason, would you excuse me for a minute?"

"Of course." He stood as she made her way to the bedroom and closed the door.

He found his handkerchief and blew his nose. Then he decided it was time to explore her kitchen. Since she'd made the offer, there had to be liquor on hand. He discovered vodka and scotch. Opting for the latter, he put together a scotch on the rocks. He was returning the bottle to the cupboard when he heard her step.

"I think I'll join you in a drink," Kelly said.

"Scotch? Vodka? I'll be happy to do the honors."

"Please make it a vodka and tonic with plenty of ice."

She'd shed a few tears, he guessed, but otherwise appeared composed. She held what appeared to be an album or scrapbook.

It was a photo album, she explained, as he carried their drinks into the living room. She had moved from the chair to the sofa, and he joined her, casting an inquisitive eye on the album in place on the coffee table.

When they'd sampled their drinks, she said, "I know Larry wasn't a bad person. So what happened? What would make him enter into a venture he knew was wrong?"

"Why does anyone stray? People can be coerced into criminal undertakings, or come under the influence of a strong, charismatic individual. And sometimes it's simply a matter of greed, the means to an easy buck."

"Doesn't that bring into question his character and integrity? His ability to exercise good judgment?" She let out a deep sigh. "I don't even know what I'm talking about. I loved my husband, and I can't conceive of him as an evil man, as a criminal; but what if he was involved in

180

something really terrible—drugs, prostitution, extortion, fraud . . . You fill in the blanks." She picked up her drink, her hand unsteady.

"Kelly, we don't have any answers, but I'm sure Larry would never inflict the kind of pain and degradation associated with the types of crimes you've mentioned. You know that. Go with your gut feelings and don't dwell on what-ifs. All right?" He sipped his drink.

Her answer was a shrug, but her smile was genuine. Kelly put her drink down and reached for the album, handling it as if it were a precious icon as she placed it in her lap. "You say Larry was trying to disentangle himself from this"—she raised a hand—"predicament he was in?"

"Oh, my, yes. He wanted out. There was no question about that." When she didn't respond, he continued, "I know that doesn't make it all go away, but the fact that he was determined to make a break should offer some consolation."

She gave him a brief smile. "It does. I needed to hear it from you." She tasted her drink. "Okay." She opened the album. "On to Scully and Wilder." She began leafing through the pages. "When I told Cherney about the thin—about Wilder, I mentioned he'd shown up in one of our pictures. The one taken at the docks. It's not very clear, but at least you can get an idea of what he looks like. Here we go." She removed the photo from the book and passed it to Jason. "You'll recognize Wilder's companion."

Jason examined the photo, and then brought out his glasses for a closer look. "It's Scully, all right. And the tall man is Wilder?"

She nodded and gave a little snort. "Mutt and Jeff." She glanced over at the photo. "I'm sure Larry had never seen Wilder before. He was a complete stranger to both of us. As for Max Scully, the only time I saw him was in Istanbul, but I'll bet you he saw plenty of us in Mexico." She opened to the middle section of the album, to pictures they'd taken of the Zocalo, the main plaza. "We were on our way to a band concert, along with a lot of other people, as you can see . . ." She pointed to a short, heavyset man who was part of the crowd.

"I don't know, Kelly. It's hard to tell in a rear view. But yes, it could be Scully."

"Why don't I set this aside for now?" she suggested, as Jason

181

returned the photo. "This evening, I'll take a hard look at all of our honeymoon pictures. Chances are I'll find either Mutt or Jeff lurking in the background. Which," she continued, "explains Scully's presence, because it's apparent he didn't want to lose track of Larry. But I'm stumped over Wilder."

"It's possible he and Scully had formed a partnership wherein Scully stayed out of sight while Wilder kept an eye on Larry."

She was frowning. "It doesn't make sense that Wilder should turn up at the Hollywood Playhouse after Larry's death. And what about those two episodes in Ankara? How would you explain that?"

Jason removed his glasses and gently rubbed the bridge of his nose. "I wish I could help you," he said, feeling suddenly weary. She was frowning, he noted, her brows knitted in concentration. "You've come up with something?"

She brought her drink to her lips, and then set it down. "I was thinking about Max Scully. The more I think about it, the more convinced I am that he was behind the phone call to the Roof Rotisserie. You know, it could have been a test."

"How do you mean?"

"This may be off the wall, but isn't it possible that Scully got it into his head that Larry might have survived, that he wasn't dead after all, but hiding out in some remote place? Because I show up in Istanbul, he makes the assumption Larry fled to Turkey. So he arranges to send the phony message that Larry will be joining Vanessa and me, and his cohort, Sarah Crenshaw, is assigned the job of reporting our reactions. Now if we accept the call as genuine, what was speculation becomes fact, and so he's picked up the trail."

"Oh, Kelly, I don't know. I suppose anything is possible," he said casually. *And you may be too damn smart for your own good,* he thought.

She shook her head. "I thought of something that shoots down my theory. How could this man possibly know I was in Istanbul?"

He knew because of that phone call to your mother, was Jason's silent rejoinder. Aloud, he said, "Whatever's going on, I doubt these two men are acting on their own. Someone is issuing the orders. Whoever is in charge, that is. Wouldn't it be nice if we could identify 'whoever'?"

He drained his glass, gave her hand a pat and got to his feet, Kelly rising also. "Well, I really must be on my way. We'll talk later in the week when I return. Oh. My jacket, please?"

When they were at the door, he said, "I'm so sorry to have put you through such an agonizing afternoon. Perhaps I should have withheld my information. However, in light of those strange occurrences in Turkey, I thought it only fair to level with you about Larry. But Kelly, he is—was a fine man. Flawed, perhaps, but then, who among us can rise to perfection?"

"Jason, it's all right. I know what you're trying to say, and you don't have to defend Larry. I know the man I married."

"Good, good," he said, giving her his warmest smile. He was pleased at the strength of her pronouncement, but he'd caught a flicker of doubt in her eyes. He wondered, somewhat sadly, if Larry had even the remotest chance of reestablishing his marriage when, God willing, he made it back. But that was between them.

"I have a hunch," he said in parting, "that you'll be hearing from Detective Cherney. Soon, I might add."

She thought that she wouldn't be surprised to hear from Detective Cherney tomorrow, in fact, as she closed the door after Jason. Meanwhile, she had the rest of Sunday to get through.

Two telephone calls helped to distract her, to put on hold the dreaded confrontation with facts and feelings, with having to come to terms with the unknown. That her husband had a dark side, that he had lived a lie, would haunt her forever, she supposed, and yet, she couldn't impose judgment. For what was there to judge?

The first call, from Rick, came around four-thirty. The warmth of his greeting gave her an instant lift, and she smiled in spite of herself.

"I don't doubt you're up to your ears in dirty laundry and a mound of mail," he said, "not to mention jet lag and being overwhelmed over your entry back into the western world—Dub it culture shock in reverse?—but I couldn't wait any longer. Had to call."

"Gosh, I'm glad to hear from you. Incidentally, am I still

employed?"

"You'd better believe it. God, Kelly, if I sound like I've missed you, I have, in spades."

"The feeling is mutual. And Rick, I can hardly wait to get back to work. I'll be in, first thing in the morning."

"Good. Now let's talk about this evening. I realize this is very last minute, but I'd like to take you to dinner. Make your 'welcome back' official."

"I'd love to, Rick. I mean it. Truly. But I'm afraid tonight isn't really the best time."

"Oh, sure. I understand. You've just gotten back and all that."

From the edge in his voice, it was evident he was less than ecstatic over her response. "Tell you what," she said, "if you can stand to be around me after a full day, why don't we celebrate tomorrow evening?"

"Why don't we? Now you have to promise. No frowning, no yelling, no tantrums."

"What, and invade your territory? No way."

They continued their bantering for a bit, the subject then turning to business matters, and when the call was completed, Kelly felt a sense of calm and contentedness. Theater was the core of her existence. Through her work, she drew strength and a sense of purpose, and those convictions were reinforced by Rick's call.

Then why the sudden welling of tears? Because, damn it, she knew deep down that it wasn't enough.

At nine o'clock, Kelly heard from Nadine. She had meant to call her mother in the afternoon, had postponed calling until after dinner, and then had given up on the idea.

"I wanted to give you a chance to unpack, settle in," Nadine was saying, "and then I thought I'd hear from you. At any rate, the urge to talk to you was overwhelming."

"Mom, I'm so sorry. I started to the phone several times today, but delays because of phone calls caught me up short and—well, I don't want to go into it now."

"Is something wrong? Has something happened to upset you?"

"Oh, no, I'm fine. Really. It's been a little hectic, getting settled in."

"You're sure you're all right?"

"Yes, Mom, I'm fine."

"And Vanessa. Tell me about her. Did Gordon get back to Ankara before you left?"

"Vanessa's doing beautifully, and no, Gordon wasn't back from Germany, but he was able to get through to Ankara to say goodbye to me, and to talk to Vanessa, of course. He said he'd tried to reach us at the Hilton, but apparently we missed his calls; then on top of that, his messages were never relayed to us."

"Everything seems to be all right between them?"

Kelly sighed. "I suppose so. I guess all is forgiven. Vanessa certainly acts the adoring wife, and Gordon seems equally devoted. Despite my negative feelings, I must say he's a very charming person."

"Charming, huh? I can think of another *ch*-word, and that's cheater. In my book, Vanessa is playing the fool. How she can be so trusting, so unwilling to face reality, is beyond me."

"Well, none of us is perfect." *A cliché that hardly addressed the issue* was Kelly's thought.

"Would you stay with a man like that?"

"Probably not, but how would I know? Look, let's talk about you. What have you and Steve been up to?"

"Oh, not a lot. Steve's been away so much lately."

Uh-oh, Kelly thought, reading into her mother's inflection. *Trouble in paradise?* "On fundraising ventures or bank business?"

"Some of each, I suppose."

Her mother didn't seem her usual loquacious self. "Mom, you sound a little down."

"It's nothing. Maybe I'm feeling sorry for myself because it's Sunday and I'm alone. Steve will be back tomorrow." Reacting to

Kelly's silence, she asked, "Now what? What have I said?"

It's what you haven't said, Kelly thought. Then aloud, she said, "I don't want to pry, but I hope you two aren't having problems."

"If we are, I haven't been told. That is, I haven't been informed if there's another woman."

"Oh, come on. You don't really think Steve's involved with another woman."

"I suppose not. It's simply that Steve doesn't seem as attentive as he used to be. Maybe the bloom is off the marriage. Or it could be I'm at fault. You know me. Opinionated, have to be in charge."

"I think you and Steve need to clear the air. You should tell him you feel neglected."

"Now why haven't I done that? Sage advice, my love." For her part, Nadine supposed she'd been reluctant to admit to a problem, submitting instead to vague, unsettled feelings of dissatisfaction that had left her edgy and depressed. That she had been able to voice these concerns, to talk it out with Kelly, had done her a world of good. Such was Nadine's assessment before shifting to other topics of conversation.

They had talked for almost an hour, Kelly realized, when finally her mother was off the phone. She would have to begin her preparations for tomorrow in earnest. *But first things first.*

Back in the living room, with the album spread open in front of her, Kelly began with pictures from the wedding and the reception, lingering over each photo that included the man she had wed. *For better or for worse.*

The words cut through her, and she hurried on to review pictures of their honeymoon. The flea market caught her attention, and now, taking great care, she studied the several pictures depicting that busy scene. The one with most people in the background, she removed to hold under the light.

He was in profile, cut off from the waist down, but there was no question: It was Scully.

Only fractionally aware of the dryness of her mouth, of the need to use her tongue to moisten her lips, Kelly pressed onward, intent in her search.

She found no further sign of Scully or Wilder, except in the photo taken at the docks. As she gazed once more at Scully and Wilder standing off to the side, her inner eye suddenly focused on a series of freeze frames. A hotel room in Acapulco—photos removed from a top shelf—Larry seeking the light of the bathroom, turning ashen—Larry leaving the room. It was *this* picture that had set him off; it had to be. Because he'd recognized Scully. Worse, the man next to him now represented an additional threat.

She would never forget their last night together. There had been nothing tenuous in his touch. Yet the intensity of his passion had been tempered by a sweetness and tenderness that spoke a language of its own. To be so dearly loved, to feel so cherished. *Now, the bride stands alone.* The cheerless parody of the nursery tune echoed in her mind, a reminder of when she'd returned from Larry's memorial service. She had traveled a fair distance since then, gathering strength and courage each step in the journey, but sometimes it felt good to let go, to turn to mush.

A tear rolled off her cheek, leaving a wet mark on the album. Her tears, his tears; it came flooding back, that last treasured moment of intimacy when, in a state of drowsy contentment, she had nuzzled his cheek, only to feel the dampness.

She remembered, too, how subdued he'd been the next morning at breakfast, how tired he'd looked, and she began to sob. He shouldn't have gone to Roquetta Island. What had he been looking for? Distraction? Escape into the deep, where his persecutors dared not follow?

God only knew what Larry had been subjected to at home, but the discovery of Scully in Acapulco, obviously in league with Wilder, had pushed him to the edge, until he was drained physically and emotionally, too scattered in his thinking, too slow in his reactions to cope with an underwater emergency.

Unless . . .

And the thought stopped her sobs—Oh, no. Oh, God, no. Larry wouldn't have taken his own life. He wouldn't have given up so easily.

She was convinced of that.

Kelly reached into the pocket of her shorts for a tissue to dry her eyes. *Enough of this.* She'd look a wreck tomorrow if she kept on, if she didn't get some sleep.

She placed the album back on her bedroom closet shelf and was starting toward the bathroom when she stopped short, overcome by a sudden chill that caused her to catch her breath. It was as if a frigid hand had clamped onto the back of her neck, to dispatch rivulets of ice through the nerve center of her head, the residue trickling down her spine.

Scully and Wilder. Assassins? Why not? Larry's tormentors could have taken on the role of executioners. And what if they had murdered her husband, if his body had been spirited away, the boat and the equipment left behind to suggest an accidental drowning? Jesus, where was Cherney's card? She rushed to the phone. Not there. Where? In one of the cubby holes of her desk? Yes!

Her chill had dissipated, leaving her flushed, with beads of perspiration covering her forehead and the area around her mouth. But her hand was steady as she dialed the detective's number. Despite the hour, she felt confident Robert Cherney would welcome her call.

❧ Chapter Seventeen ❧

*A*s planned, Kelly and Rick celebrated Kelly's homecoming on Monday evening, opting for a leisurely dinner at a popular dining establishment on La Cienaga's restaurant row. What they hadn't counted on, however, was a stand-off with an over solicitous waiter.

"Oh, come on now, you have to at least take a look at our dessert menu." Their waiter, probably an aspiring actor, was pulling out all the stops: the soft smile, the coaxing tone designed to showcase his boyish charms. Undoubtedly, he'd spotted this couple as show biz types, having overheard key words such as casting, production, and rehearsals. "The cheesecake is to die for," he said, zeroing in on Kelly, flashing his perfect teeth.

"Dessert after all this?" Kelly pointed to a third of her prime rib dinner, remaining untouched on her plate.

"Oh, what the heck. Bring a menu anyway," Rick said, waving his hand in a gesture of dismissal. And then to Kelly, as the waiter removed their plates, "Something gooey or disgustingly rich might cheer you up."

Kelly wrenched her gaze from the departing waiter to focus on Rick. "What are you talking about?"

"I said, something gooey—"

"No, I mean about cheering me up."

"Well, doll, it may be the company, but you've seemed a trifle distant this evening."

"Oh, Rick, I'm sorry. Believe me, it's not you." When she failed to continue, he said, "If it's not the company, and then what? Or are you going to tell me to mind my own business?"

"I should, for all the sympathy I'd get from you."

"I may not be much on sympathy, but I'm a pretty good problem solver."

The waiter, back with dessert menus, hovered over them. "Thanks," Rick said, with a short smile. "We'll let you know." The implication being to buzz off.

When they were alone again, Rick covered her hand with his. "Try me," he said, his brown eyes serious, intent.

She met his gaze, responding to the softness of his tone and the protective contact of his hand. They generated in her a sense of warmth that caused her breath to quicken. Gently, she removed her hand, feeling suddenly shy as she broke eye contact.

"Well," he said, "I guess it's time to look at the menu."

She nodded, but after a quick perusal, snapped hers shut. "I'd rather talk."

"Fine with me." He looked at her expectantly.

"You know," she said, meeting his gaze straight on, "you can be a bear at times."

"Right. I can be a pain in the ass."

"All of the above. Also, you can be very, very perceptive. Yes, I've been preoccupied, and yes, I'd like very much to unload on you. Should we order coffee?"

They decided on crème de menthes as well, and as they sipped along, Kelly related her experiences in Ankara and Istanbul, Jason's disclosures regarding Wilder and Scully, and finally, her suspicions regarding Larry's death.

Rick was frowning, his mouth carved into the truculent expression he reserved for actors who blew their lines or technicians who missed their cues. "Larry was being hounded by those guys," he said, his frown deepening, "but you don't know why?"

She had hedged in her accounting of Jason's revelations, unwilling to present Larry in a bad light. Especially to Rick. "Jason thinks," she said, the words coming slowly, "Larry had committed to something that wasn't, shall we say, above-board? He also says Larry was trying to break his ties with this involvement."

"I see. Someone didn't want to let go of him. Feared exposure, I suppose."

"But why these weird episodes involving me? How could I pose a threat to them?"

Rick sipped his coffee, considering his answer. "If they had their heads on straight," he said, "you think that they'd realize that if you knew what was going on, you'd have blown the whistle long ago." He shook his head. "I don't know, Kelly. Either they're a couple of deranged idiots having fun at your expense, or there's a logical reason behind their actions. Either way," he said, signaling for the check, "I'd watch my back, stay alert." The frown reappeared. "Let one of those sleazebags get within punching distance of me, and I'd pulverize him. With pleasure."

"Whoa, slow down. These are not your garden-variety hoods. They're probably armed and dangerous. But thanks. I feel better already."

She did feel immeasurably cheered. On the way home, she was even able to joke about their being followed, and as they reached the door of her apartment, Kelly cast exaggerated looks up and down the hallway.

She could tell Rick wasn't amused. "Okay, I'll stop this foolishness. But seriously, why not look on the bright side? I know I'm reversing myself, but possibly this whole business is over and done with. Surely by now these guys have figured out in their little twisted brains I'm of no use to them whatsoever. I'd bet you Max and Joe are already deep into some new, fiendish project." She paused. "Or am I into denial, big time?"

"Kelly, what would you think of leaving town for a while, like visiting with your folks or with Larry's family in Arizona?"

"Are you serious? I have a job, a career!"

"Don't look so hurt. You know how important you are to me, to our theater. It's simply that I'm not convinced you're out of the woods yet. Believe me, you wouldn't be jeopardizing your career."

"Rick, I'm not going anywhere. End of discussion, okay?"

"Okay." He gave her a solemn smile.

"It was a marvelous evening," she said softly.

"Hey, you grabbed my line," he said, giving her a peck on the cheek. He stepped back from her, but made no move to leave. Instead, he placed his hands on her shoulders, his look intent, conveying only the hint of a question.

Kelly didn't resist as he brought her in closer, lowering his head to place his lips gently upon hers. As their lips opened to one another, she clasped her arms around his neck, bringing their bodies into full contact.

Seconds later, she pulled away. "I should answer that."

"Answer what?"

"My phone. It's ringing."

"They'll call back," he said, reaching for her.

"Rick, I'd better go in." She placed two fingers gently over his lips.

"On second thought, yes, you'd better," he said, but he was smiling. "I'll come in with you for a minute. Since it's after midnight, this call could spell trouble."

Once inside, Kelly dashed to the phone, managing a breathless, "Hello?" as she picked up the receiver.

"Mrs. Townsend, it's Robert Cherney. Sorry to be calling so late, but I did try to reach you earlier."

"I've been out for the evening. In fact, I just walked in. Is there a problem? Has something happened?"

"No, but in view of your concerns, I thought I should touch base with you."

"Could you hold on for a minute?" Kelly turned to Rick. "It's Detective Cherney. I'm sorry, Rick, but I do need to talk to him." Her voice soft, she said, "I had a wonderful time."

"We'll do it again. Soon." He threw her a kiss, and then closed the door after him.

"I'm back," Kelly said to the detective. "Everything's okay here, except"—she sighed—"I keep thinking about the questions I raised pertaining to Larry's death. Especially the Scully-Wilder tie-in. And speaking of those two, I don't understand why they're tracking me. Surely by now they realize I'm of no use to them, that I'm completely in the dark as to what Larry was mixed up in."

"What do you mean, 'mixed up in'?"

"His involvement in something outside the law." When he didn't respond, she said, "You didn't know about that?"

There was a silence. "Do I understand," he said finally, "that you've known your husband was involved in something shady, but you have no knowledge as to what it could be?"

"I only know from Jason that Larry was in trouble, and that he was trying to pull out of the situation. Nobody, including Jason, has any idea of what he was embroiled in."

"I see." After a lengthy pause, he said, "Mrs. Townsend, not to alarm you, but I want to err on the side of caution. I suggest we stay in close touch, and that you keep your guard up. If anything—anything at all—strikes you as unusual, call me immediately."

"I will. I promise, despite what I said earlier. Oh. One more thing. Since we'll be staying in touch, I think it's time we stopped being so formal. Please call me Kelly."

"Certainly. I'd be happy to." He gave a small cough. "Do keep in mind what I said, about keeping up your guard?"

"I'll be careful."

"Good. Well. Goodnight . . . Kelly."

"Goodnight to you, Detective Cherney."

For Fern Champion, it wasn't a good night. In bed, staring into the dark, her mind in overdrive, she purposely faced away from the clock. The last time she'd looked it was two o'clock in the morning, and the time before that, one-thirty, and the time before that—she raised herself and switched on the bedside light. It might help if she read a little. At least she wouldn't be disturbing anyone. Not with Tom bedding down at the Plaza Hotel or at the Waldorf Astoria. He did say his meeting was in New York. Or was it Philadelphia? *New York,* she thought.

She shut her eyes, concentrating, trying to remember. Then she gave up and slid back down into bed, her plan to induce sleep by reading already forgotten. Except that she'd neglected to turn off the light.

Oh, nuts, she might as well get up. She had to know for sure where her husband had taken off to. *If an emergency occurred, if something happened to one of the children . . . if, for God's sake, it turned out he was off in Timbuktu,* she thought wearily, climbing out of bed, reaching for her robe.

When she entered Tom's study, she turned on the overhead light, and then shut the door behind her. No more guessing games, she decided as she approached his desk. Tom always left instructions where he could be reached on a three-by-five index card that he placed under the paperweight, a glass Lipizzaner stallion she'd purchased for him on their honeymoon trip through Europe. The irony of this memento, a constant reminder of happier days, didn't escape her.

Catching her reflection in the wall mirror, she flipped on the desk light to counteract the harshness of overhead lighting, and reached for the glass horse. Where was the card? Her gaze traveled the surface of the desk, and then dropped to the floor. Nothing. Slowly she eased into the chair, and then set about to examine the middle drawer, side drawers, the desktop. Again, nothing.

All she could recall, albeit vaguely, was some discussion about a business conference in New York. She massaged her temples as if to clear away the confusion. Or had New York been mentioned in connection with the last trip?

Away from the desk, she paced the room, clutching at her robe. For reasons unexplainable, her breathing had become shallow, her hands clammy. Good God, she was on the verge of tears. Obviously, she was overreacting to a minor problem.

Using both hands, she gripped the back of an armchair, forcing herself to remain stationary, to work at restoring calm. There was a solution, a very simple solution. She would check with Tom's office; in the unlikely event that she met with failure, she could always call the Waldorf and the Plaza, or try to remember where he'd stayed in Philadelphia. There. Problem solved, with everything under control.

She returned to the desk as it occurred to her that with all the clutter in the top drawer, she really needed to make a more thorough search.

As she unloaded the drawer, she found the set of index cards, all blank. Seated, she studied the items now strewn over the desktop—a hodgepodge of mailing paraphernalia, canceled checks, utility receipts, the usual stuff. Even a roll of breath mints, attesting to her husband's attention to personal hygiene. Not that she was privileged to experience anymore the joys of marital intimacy. In the stillness, the mints made a sharp, plopping sound as they made contact with a nearly empty wastebasket.

She was about to restore the top drawer to its cluttered state when, as an afterthought, she thrust her hand into the far corners of the now-empty drawer. She was rewarded for her thoroughness by the discovery of a set of keys, five of them on a ring.

She wondered at their purpose. Too small to be house keys, she pictured them opening a mailbox, an attaché case, or even a desk drawer. Even though none of the drawers were locked, she decided to experiment, to see if any of the keys would fit them. Nothing worked.

Mechanically, she deposited everything she'd removed back into the drawer. She held onto the keys, unable to set them aside, and as she studied their shapes, ran her fingers over their edges, the keys seemed to take on a life of their own, with increasingly sinister overtones. These keys fit into something—a desk, a file cabinet, a strongbox. Perhaps—and the thought had taken root at the moment of discovery—to reveal some terrible secret. Pandora's Box came to mind, and she closed her eyes, fighting a surge of panic. She rose as if to flee the room, but an onset of dizziness forced her back into the chair, and for a sickening instant she thought she might faint. Then, just as suddenly, the attack was over, with calm prevailing.

She switched off the lights, in no hurry now to depart, taking comfort from the dark. She had found the keys for a reason. Beyond that, she dared not speculate. However, she knew what she had to do, what she must do: pay a visit to Tom's office.

Meanwhile, something needed attending to, something that required immediate action. She reached out, searching, until her hand made contact with glass. Vienna, romance, the expectation of a lifetime of 'foreverness' . . . Out with the trash! If Tom asked about the

Lipizzaner stallion, she would shrug and refrain from commenting, but her inner voice would be singing out a jubilant *good riddance!*

Fern had taken extra pains with her appearance, using concealer cream to erase the shadows under her eyes, even checking her makeup by daylight. The dress she chose, a soft blue to compliment her blonde coloring, was casually elegant and suitable for late spring, when the south-central part of Arizona heated up. Looking her best did for Fern what a shot of Dutch courage might do for others.

The journey from Scottsdale to Tom's office in Phoenix, in an area close to the venerable Arizona Biltmore, took less than fifteen minutes, though it seemed to Fern to take forever. She didn't anticipate any difficulty in being admitted to her husband's office since, in the early morning hours, she'd worked out her story; however, she agonized over the task she'd assigned herself, of playing a role.

She almost forgot her lines when she encountered a stranger who occupied Myra Langley's desk. This woman wasn't Tom's secretary. Worse, the voice was cold, the expression unforgiving.

"I'm sorry, but you'll have to speak up. Did you say you're here to see Mr. Champion?"

"I said, I'm Mrs. Champion. Where is Mrs. Langley?" Fern, for once in command, took gratification in the woman's sudden smile, the lofty eyebrows settling into line with the frames of her glasses.

"Mrs. Champion, it's a delight to meet you. I'm Jane Bowman. I've been with the office for about five months, ever since Mrs. Langley retired."

"Oh, of course." (Nice of you to inform me, Tom.) "Well, with Tom away for his conference, it occurred to me this would be the perfect time to take an in-depth look at his office. We have an anniversary coming up, and I've decided to redecorate the inner sanctum. As a surprise."

"What a lovely idea. It's not locked." She indicated the closed door. "If I can be of help?"

"Thank you, Mrs. Bowman, but I can manage by myself." Fern was at the door, poised to enter, when she turned back to the secretary. "Incidentally, I assume my husband left a phone number where he can be reached? He usually stays at the Plaza, but he hinted at a last minute change in plans. I need to get hold of him, and I thought you might have more recent information."

"Mr. Champion hasn't called in. Let's see what I have here." She opened a small notebook, her motions precise as she turned to a page near the front of the book. "'Refer all important phone calls,'" she read, "'to George Atherton.' He's left the number," she added, looking up at Fern.

Fern nodded. "George Atherton is Tom's associate in the New York office."

"That's it. That's all I have." She gave Fern a perfunctory smile.

"Thank you. I have what I need." She entered the office.

With the door closed behind her, Fern surveyed the room. For a man of Tom's sophisticated tastes, it was surprisingly nondescript, beiges and browns predominating, the few decorative touches bland and uninspiring. She focused on Tom's desk, resting her gaze on the framed photo of husband and wife, posed with their children. She rounded the desk, wanting to ignore the faces smiling for the camera, but was nevertheless drawn to the family portrait. For a moment, a tinge of sadness and longing came over her as she studied her husband's smile, the warmth in his eyes; she then placed the photo face-down.

With a nervous glance at the closed door, Fern seated herself at the desk. The middle drawer was unlocked, its contents displaying various clerical items, with nothing out of the ordinary. The side drawers were packed with the tools of the brokerage business: reference books, accounting materials, charts and folders. What was she looking for? She'd pondered that question on the drive over. What she wanted was evidence. Answers. Anything at all to unlock the mystery of her husband's indifference—more so, to rule out or confirm certain suspicions about Tom, his work, and his associates, suspicions she had tried to verbalize to her mother.

Tom's desk yielded nothing of an incriminating nature. She started his computer, but didn't know his password and turned it off. Damn. She turned her attention to the file cabinet in the corner of the room. Wedged between two large potted plants, with ivy spilling over the top from a smaller planter, the cabinet might warrant scrutiny. *Really, the room could use some sprucing up,* she thought, as she took note of the threadbare patch of carpeting in front of the cabinet.

But the contents of the six unlabeled drawers would remain unrevealed, at least to her, Fern concluded, as she tried the last of the five keys, without success.

Another larger cabinet stood against the wall opposite Tom's desk, its gray-green drawers alphabetically labeled. *Appropriately utilitarian,* Fern thought as, with keys in hand, she reached for the top drawer. It opened easily, disclosing stacks of files, clients' names prominently displayed. She leafed through several of the folders, and then progressed to the next drawer, and then the next, and so on down the line, taking care to make as little noise as possible. Again, she found folders, each one tagged with the name of an individual or corporation.

The bottom drawers, four on each side, were locked. She tried the first key, the second, and each of the next three, but had no success with the drawers on the left. Two tries and the next-to-the-bottom drawer on the right opened, but it was empty. One more to go. She looked toward the door, and then tried her keys. The drawer opened. But it, too, appeared empty. Except this drawer had a divider, and it looked as if something might be on the other side; she had to struggle with it, uttering, "Damn," as she broke a nail, but she was able to remove the metal insert.

Ah, there's something—a folder. Under it, she discovered a box, similar to a stationery box, but thicker. She repositioned the divider and then rose from her knees, carrying her find to the desk, leaving the drawer open. A gut feeling, a premonition of something bad, caused her to hesitate, to delay her investigation. On the other hand, she told herself, it could be something entirely innocent.

The folder contained what appeared to be a two-page résumé. She glanced at it, and then, aware of stirrings in the outer office, set it aside to take home with her for a more careful perusal. She opened the box, and at first was dumbfounded. Then, as the realization of her discovery took hold, she began to experience the same sick feeling that had overtaken her in the wee hours of the morning.

She slumped back in the chair, and then jumped at the sound of a sharp knock on the door.

Mrs. Bowman didn't wait for permission to enter. "Sorry to intrude, but I need a file," she said, striding over to the cabinet Fern had just vacated. She placed her hand on the drawer labeled *Inactive,* but her gaze focused on the opened bottom drawer. "That's funny," she said, turning to Fern, "I would swear this drawer was locked."

Light, shining on Mrs. Bowman's glasses, obscured the expression in her eyes, but her lips were pressed tautly together.

Fern slid her chair in closer to the desk and casually draped her arms over the large shoulder bag that now shielded her find.

"That's exactly the way I found it," Fern said, making a show of studying the drawer with a look of puzzlement.

The secretary moved out from under the shaft of light, her eyes no longer clouded but telegraphing skepticism. Her expression of disapproval was an almost palpable substance, barring any further attempt toward amicable communication.

"Will you be staying much longer?" Mrs. Bowman's back was to Fern as she hunted for her file.

Fern, declining to answer, remained as she was, barely drawing a breath as she waited for the secretary to leave the room.

It didn't take long for Mrs. Bowman to retrieve what she was after. "Sorry for the interruption," she said at the door, her gaze sweeping from Fern to the open bottom drawer.

"I'll be leaving in a few minutes," Fern said. "If you'd be kind enough to close the door after you?"

With a brisk nod, the secretary let herself out of the room, shutting the door with a bit more force than was necessary.

Fern let out her breath. Then, with two rapid motions, she stuffed the folder and the box into her bag. She didn't stop to bring out her compact to touch up her makeup, though she imagined her face reflected her emotional state. So what if she looked pale, haggard, and yes, frightened, as well. Slivering though all the negatives was a spark of energy, coupled with a sense of purpose. Not exactly marvelous, but an awakening, enough to propel her away from Tom's desk, to fling open the door and confront Mrs. Bowman.

"I'm sure Tom will be bowled over," Fern said with a half-smile to the secretary who peered at her over the top of her glasses. She didn't wait for a reply but exited the office with her shoulder bag firmly anchored to her side.

✍ Chapter Eighteen ✍

Kelly looked up from the script that lay open on her lap to assess the condition of her living room. She had picked up after herself, vacuumed, and even set an arrangement of fresh cut flowers on the coffee table. Furthermore, should her guests accept her offer of dessert and coffee, she could whip out a carrot cake, courtesy of the corner bakery, and set the coffee pot to perking.

Having proven that domesticity wasn't totally foreign to her nature, Kelly turned her attention once again to her script, but the page she had read and was now re-reading made about as much sense as an excerpt from the Dead Sea Scrolls. She sighed and checked her watch. Audrey and Fern were due to arrive any minute, and the anticipation, rather than pleasurable, was akin to opening night stage fright.

Not that she'd felt that way initially. When Audrey had phoned last evening to say she would be flying into L.A., Kelly had jumped at the chance to offer her mother-in-law a place to stay.

Audrey, however, had demurred, explaining that as much as she would like to accept Kelly's hospitality, Fern would be with her. They'd made hotel reservations and had arranged for a car rental. What they had in mind, if Kelly didn't object, was a drop-in visit after the dinner hour. *Say sevenish or so?*

Of course she didn't object, but Kelly was thrown by what she presumed was the suddenness of this trip to Los Angeles. Audrey hadn't disclosed the purpose of their visit, other than to express relief that Kelly would be available. She'd seemed skittish, however, racing her words, speaking at a high pitch.

Kelly decided to return the script to her desk, the act of moving from one room into the other providing an outlet for her restlessness.

As she stepped back into the living room, she heard voices, followed by a soft rapping at her door. At last, show time!

With the door open to receive both women, Kelly felt a rush of love as she hugged her mother-in-law, and then a modicum of surprise as Fern, ignoring her proffered hand, moved in to brush cheeks.

Not a bad beginning, if a little unusual, Kelly thought as she ushered the women into her apartment. "Sorry I can't offer you a grand tour," she said, as she led Audrey and Fern to the sofa, taking the chair she'd occupied during Jason's visit. "Seems the wicked witch cast a spell on my castle, and turned it into a lowly, one-bedroom apartment."

"I'd choose your place anytime over a drafty, old castle," Audrey said with a chuckle.

"This reminds me of the apartment I had before Tom and I married." Fern had addressed her mother, but now she offered Kelly a tentative smile. "I was quite happy there."

Kelly, unsure of what was expected from her, returned Fern's smile, waiting for more.

It was Audrey who broke the silence. "Kelly, we're so grateful you could make time for us on such short notice."

"Are you staying long? Can we make some plans for the weekend?"

Audrey gave Fern a speculative look before answering, "Well, maybe not this time, dear."

Both women, conservatively dressed, displayed a soberness in manner that suggested they would, indeed, be attending to matters of a serious nature. The air turned thick with their silence and Kelly was about to jump out of her skin. She decided it was time to offer dessert. "I know you've had your dinner. Why don't I top it off with a serving of carrot cake? Also, I can have coffee ready in a jiffy."

"That's lovely of you, but I don't think either of us"—Audrey glanced at her daughter—"could eat a thing."

"Mother's right. Kelly, I guess I should explain this isn't a social call." She hesitated, as if about to elaborate, and then reached for her bag.

Kelly's mind was a blank as she watched Fern dig into her large handbag. *What on earth?*

Fern pulled out a folder and a plain white box. "I have something of yours," Fern said, handing Kelly the box. "I found this in my husband's office, in a locked cabinet drawer."

Kelly stared at the box, and then at the two women whose expressions conveyed the solemnity of convicted felons awaiting sentencing, or maybe the death penalty. Gingerly, she removed the cover, and then gave a little gasp. "My journal." She looked from Fern to Audrey. "But what would Tom, I mean I don't understand what Tom—"

Fern was nodding.

"Oh, no, I don't believe this. Your husband is behind the break-ins?" She looked to Audrey for confirmation, noting the older woman appeared close to tears.

"Kelly, this is going to hurt, but Fern thinks Larry and Tom were linked in connection with . . . Well, we don't know with what, except it's not good."

"Mother, let me take it from here. I think Tom must have recruited Larry to join him and others in a scheme or scam"—she raised her hands—"call it what you will, but something went on that wasn't kosher. I happened to pick up the phone one night, back in August, I believe. Anyway, I overheard a conversation between Larry and Tom. My brother referred to a check he'd received, but couldn't accept, apparently for services rendered. They didn't spell it out, but that's what I surmised." Censure was played out in Fern's blue eyes taking on frost, in the tightness at the corners of her mouth. "I don't remember everything that was said—I suppose I was jolted by what I was hearing—but what came across was two men diametrically opposed. Simply put, Larry was adamant about wanting out; Tom, on the other hand, was just as fixed in his conviction that Larry couldn't possibly be serious."

"Excuse me for interrupting." Audrey, after an apologetic glance at her daughter, turned to Kelly. "Are you all right? Is there something I can get you?"

"I'm okay, Audrey, honestly. If I look as dazed as I feel, it's that I'm still in shock. It's incredible what you're telling me about Tom."

"But not about Larry?" Fern's expression had turned quizzical.

"I found out a few days ago that Larry was in trouble." Kelly went on to relate what Larry hadn't confided to his attorney. Then she was back to the phone call. "Fern, did Tom threaten Larry when he said he wanted out?"

"I don't think directly, but he implied it could be risky for Larry if he chose to defect. Actually, Tom seemed incredulous that Larry would even contemplate such a move. There may be more, but at that point, I suppose I tuned out."

Fern lowered her head to focus on her hands, ringless today, as she clutched at the folder. Then recovering, meeting Kelly's gaze straight-on, she said, "I'm sure you're wondering why in all this time I haven't confronted Tom. I thought about it. Oh yes. Then I chose not to think about it. As for Larry, I came close to approaching him." She paused, as if reflecting upon what she had said. "In any case, when we lost Larry, it seemed the better choice to let things stand. Why should you or Mother suffer needlessly?"

Audrey shook her head. "Fern, that doesn't hold water. Kelly and I certainly don't lack backbone. Oh, honey, I don't mean to scold." Audrey grasped her daughter's hand. "I know how difficult this has been for you."

"Difficult? Well, yes." The words came out haltingly. "More so now than before, when I was content to look the other way. Because to be perfectly honest, I couldn't deal with it. Despite what I'd overheard, despite certain suspicions I'd harbored over Tom's comings and goings, and the fact that we'd become estranged . . . Well, you see, it was okay if I didn't *think* about it, because then, the problem didn't exist. Does that make any sense to you?"

"Now, Fern . . ." Audrey released her daughter's hand, giving it a little pat. "You mustn't be too hard on yourself. You've maintained a beautiful home, and you've been a good mother."

"Dutiful on both counts, yes." Her smile was derisive. "We're not talking about that. We're talking about denial, apathy. I picture a person who's gone through a tornado. She's sitting, surrounded by rubble, everything in shambles, but she simply sits there. She *cannot-deal-with-it.*"

"I'd say that day is past," Kelly said. "It seems to me you've hiked up your skirts and are putting your house in order."

"It's a start, I suppose. With the discovery of your journal and this"—her fingers made a tapping sound against the folder—"Call it an epiphany, but if Tom had something to do with my brother's death . . ." She placed her hand at her throat and swallowed, as if a sudden rawness were choking off her speech. "I'd want him to be punished, to pay, to be locked up for the rest of his life."

As if to lend credence to her statement, her cheeks had become suffused with color, her mouth thinning to an angry line. But the disillusionment and hurt that clouded her eyes, Kelly noted, were at variance with this tough new stance. Then again, as Fern had said, it was a start.

Audrey, who had been stealing anxious glances at her daughter, now turned worried eyes on Kelly. "Well," she said, "it's certainly been no picnic for any of us."

Kelly paused a beat, and then opened her mouth to respond, but what came out was a giggle. She raised her hand to her mouth in a gesture of restraint, but a second giggle followed the first one, graduating into full-blown laughter.

Fern cast a questioning glance at both Kelly and her mother, but in seconds her shoulders were shaking; then she was laughing so hard tears streamed down her cheeks.

"What on earth?" Audrey smiled, but it was apparent she questioned the propriety of their behavior.

"Oh, Mom," Fern wiped her eyes, "given the enormity of what's happened to us, what we have yet to face . . . And then you say it's been no picnic?" She looked over at Kelly and broke into laughter once again, both women now giving way to the moment.

When they were spent, Audrey said, "Let's see, I think Phoenix has a stand-up comedy club. Think I should audition?"

"What I think is I owe you an apology," Kelly said. "But Audrey, we weren't really laughing at you."

"Oh, I know that, and I'm not so thin-skinned that I can't take a little ribbing. Besides, to hear laughter from this one"—a side glance toward her daughter—"is a real treat."

"Wish I could say this was a laugh a minute," Fern said as she flipped open the folder. She handed it to Kelly.

It appeared to be a job résumé or a dossier, Kelly concluded, as she gave the two typewritten, double-spaced pages a quick glance. Page one was headed *Background Information*. She noted the words *Current Data* at the top of the second page.

Now starting at the beginning, she found a name that meant nothing to her. Who was Myron Stubbs? She started to ask Fern, and then read on, only to come upon Mickey Schultz, an alias for Myron Stubbs. Still no flash of recognition. Until she came to the next paragraph and another name change. "Oh, my God," she said, looking up at Fern. "Your husband kept a file on Max Scully?"

"You know the name?"

"Oh, yes. In fact, I know more about this man than anyone outside of the criminal justice system would want to know." Responding to each woman's look of expectancy, Kelly said, "I'll get this information to Detective Cherney as soon as possible, but first I think it's time to put the coffee on."

The renegade laughter had been a welcome distraction from a doleful outpouring, dispelling some of the awkwardness engendered by the very nature of Fern's revelations. Furthermore, with Kelly outlining her recent experiences, their stiffness eased, giving way to a more natural give-and-take as they exchanged ideas and bonded in a common effort to arrive at the truth. The women even managed to enjoy dessert.

They had not, however, addressed the question of how to proceed from this point. "We're going to need advice," Kelly was saying, "but at least I know where to start. Now that we have evidence," she indicated the journal and dossier, "I'm sure my detective friend will be able to re-open the investigation of the break-ins."

"I suppose he'll need a statement from me?" That this would be distasteful, even painful, was evidenced in Fern's tone, in the sag of her shoulders. Kelly understood. The quest for justice was one thing; having eventually to face her husband, to deal with her children's questions was quite another matter.

"I would think so," Kelly answered. "And of course they'll want to question Tom." Fern and Audrey, she observed, exchanged looks. "When did you say he gets back from New York?"

"Tom's not in New York," Fern said. "He called from Paris to say he was meeting with a client, that he might have to extend his stay in Europe because of a possible meeting in Zurich. I do have the name of the hotel where he's staying in Paris." She spread her hands. "That is, if he's telling the truth. Actually, Kelly, I haven't talked to him since he left home. His call came when I was at the hairdressers. Our housekeeper wrote down the message.

"Well." She turned to her mother. "I think we'd better be on our way." And then to Kelly, "You may as well know that tomorrow morning I'm consulting with an old school chum," she paused, "who happens to be a divorce attorney."

"Oh." Taken aback, Kelly tried to mask her surprise. "I see. Will you be staying over?"

Audrey shook her head. "We'll be flying back to Phoenix tomorrow afternoon. Another time, dear, a better time, we'll plan a good visit." She rose, Fern following, trailing her mother to the door, with Kelly alongside.

"You'll make sure the dossier gets into the right hands?" Fern asked.

"I'm going to turn the folder over to Detective Cherney as soon as possible. And Fern . . ." Impulsively Kelly took her sister-in-law's hand. "You're very courageous. I wish you all the luck in the world."

"Thanks, I'll need it." Fern's expression was grim, but she gave Kelly's hand a squeeze, before Audrey stepped between them to hold Kelly for a brief moment.

Kelly remained at the door as the two women proceeded into the hallway. They'd taken only a few steps when Fern, placing a restraining hand on her mother's arm, turned back to Kelly.

"I want you to know that before you left on your honeymoon, I told Larry you were a very classy lady. I meant it then; I mean it even more now."

"Thank you." Kelly felt the sudden onset of tears blurring, momentarily, the image of the two women. "Let's all keep in close touch, okay?" She meant this as an honest reflection of her feelings. Something good had sprung from the ashes of grief.

Though Kelly was heartened by Fern's climb out of the abyss and into sunlight, she was sickened by the recent turn of events. Her journal and a dossier on Larry's stalker (or worse) in Tom Champion's possession? To think she'd been taken in by his charm and breeding, been responsive to his expressions of concern as to her wellbeing, her plans for the future. How ironic that he had engineered the break-ins and had obviously sicced Scully on Larry. Why else would he have this detailed documentation on this menace to society? She had read between the lines, past the purposely vague wording regarding Scully's expertise in the art of persuasion, his success in taking out his marks.

Would Tom have issued the orders resulting in Larry's death? Dear God, he might have. Tom, in a final accounting, could have looked upon Larry as a major threat to his own survival, and therefore expendable. So bring on the henchmen.

These weren't the kinds of thoughts to induce a good night's sleep.

She made it to bed, standing firm in her resolve to shut out speculation regarding Tom's role in Larry's death. The next step was to blank out the entire evening, to switch off thought in tandem with pulling the switch on her bedside light.

Fat chance.

Fern was a strong presence in Kelly's thoughts, a compelling on-screen image that refused to dissolve. And why not? The woman Kelly had come to know in the last few hours had taken a monumental leap into the real world, spirit replacing lethargy. But in small measure. When it came to the crunch, would Fern be capable of fending for herself? It was a toss-up, Kelly speculated. Fern could easily fold, become the woman of her analogy who sits immobilized in the midst of devastation. Or she could best them all—use her education and her skill, to forge a new life. It was this positive image—that of a vibrant, self-sufficient Fern—that Kelly wanted to focus on, in order to shut out the larger issues of revelations and repercussions, crime and punishment.

A good try, but Fern soon had company in Kelly's dark thoughts. The faces of the principal players, as though imprisoned within a time warp of surrealistic dimensions, flashed before her in a never-ending continuum, eventually to enter her dreams. Once there, as if in obedience to subconscious directives, the faces began to lose definition, features blurring into blob-like balloon figures Kelly could will to float out of her life, the good along with the bad. Except for Larry.

She couldn't let go of his presence. If she could will the others to drift into oblivion, she could exercise this same power to hold on to Larry, to savor what time remained with him.

Carefully, so as not to rip the fragile veil of remembrance, she elevated herself to a sitting position. And waited. In seconds the tall figure appeared in her doorway. Overwhelmed, she whispered his name, and then called to him, her voice soft but intense with longing.

He started toward her, arms outstretched, and she, too, raised her arms, bending like a dancer, stretching her torso, arching her back, her desire all-consuming.

At the foot of the bed, he lowered his arms, then froze, arms pinned to his sides. "Larry, darling, come to me," she crooned, entreating him to hang on, to remain in this world for whatever precious moments were left. She inched forward, her movements sensual, provocative, but he remained oddly still. Wondering at his reticence, she strained to catch his expression.

What she saw caused her to thrust herself against the headboard, to grab the covers up over her breasts. It was Wilder! Wilder was in her bedroom, at the foot of her bed.

Crouching low, barely drawing a breath, she concentrated her energies on listening—to catch the sound of a passing car, footsteps overhead, a ticking clock. Nothing. An unnatural silence prevailed. She was trapped in a dream, and the motionless figure had become the centerpiece of this nightmare. She had to wake up, to delete his image.

Oh, God! It was no dream—he was real! His step was unfaltering as he approached her. She opened her mouth to scream, but the barely audible moan that emerged from her throat was smothered by the harshness of her breathing, and she watched in horror as Wilder lowered himself to sit next to her on the bed.

It was his eyes that held her captive; lustful, wanton, they stripped away the bedding, undressing her, his gaze penetrating her. Helplessly, she watched as he loosened his tie, his movements slow and deliberate. As he began to unbutton his shirt, her moans formed into recognizable sounds. She had found her voice, but all she could utter was the word, "No," over and over and over again.

The sudden clamor that invaded her head to wipe out all other sound—an intermittent frenzied jangle—caused Kelly to snap awake, her heart beating wildly as she grappled with the phone, managing finally to place the receiver at her ear.

She heard the click, heard the wire go dead before she could even breathe, "Hello?" The bedside lamp revealed a blessedly empty room, as well as the hour. It was four a.m. Not exactly prime-time for a hang-up call, but it brought her out of a nightmare so hellishly real—she placed her hand over her heart in an attempt to physically restrain the pounding—that she felt beholden to the unknown caller.

She debated whether or not to leave the light on, decided against it, turned off the light, and closed her eyes. So little sleep, so much to put out of her mind.

She was nodding off when the ringing startled her into consciousness. Forget gratitude, she determined, as she snapped on the light and grasped the receiver. She didn't bother with hello when a testy, "Yes?" would suffice.

"So you are now fully awake, are you?"

It was a man's voice and something about the inflection caused her to take in her breath. "Who is this?" she asked, her tone more cautious than angry.

"Can't you guess? We haven't been formally introduced; however, we have made eye contact more than once."

Wilder? Scully? No, Wilder, was Kelly's frantic guess. Oh God, what to do? She could hang up, but he'd call again. Even if she left the phone off the hook, she'd be crazy with curiosity, too wired to fall back to sleep. She decided to play along, willing herself to set aside fear, to blot out the loathsome dream image of Wilder disrobing. Keeping her voice even, she said, "If you don't identify yourself, I'm going to hang up."

"You don't need to know my name. But I can remind you we've been within arm's reach in Acapulco, that our eyes met in your theater during your curtain call, that others across the world have, at my bidding, staged a small *entr'acte* to keep me fresh in your thoughts."

"What do you want?"

"You, most assuredly. However, that can wait. It's your husband who occupies my thoughts at present. Is he there with you?"

The chill that overtook her was a finger from the grave, coursing the length of her spine, cold expanding in a ripple effect to create an icy, tingling sensation in her extremities. "You must be insane." She choked on her words, could feel the tears come in a rush. She fought for control. She couldn't allow him to break her, to beat her up emotionally. For whatever reasons, this was what it was all about. "No," she said, "my husband is not with me. He's dead, and I think you know that."

"And I think you know where he is."

"Why do you persist?" She could hear the onset of hysteria in her voice. *Don't-let-him-do-this-to-you,* she mouthed to herself through clenched teeth. Then, into the phone: "Listen to me. Larry died when we were on our honeymoon. He drowned. Or someone made him drown."

"Is that what you think? Truly? Kelly," he drew out the final syllable in a lingering caress, "you are very convincing, yes. But then, you are an actress, consummate in your art. If you are telling the truth, if your husband has not come to you, he will, and it's important to understand that a matter between us must be resolved."

A coldness crept into his tone, and Kelly raised her eyes to the ceiling, mentally imploring the higher being with whom she communed to give her the strength to use her intelligence to help her keep her wits and to keep emotion at bay. "I don't know what you're talking about. What business would you have had with Larry?"

"I see you continue to speak of him in the past tense. Apparently, we have reached an impasse. What is that cute expression? A Mexican stand-off? I think enough has been said, for now."

"Wait. Don't hang up! You haven't answered my question. What is your connection with Larry? Why are you after him?"

"I haven't said I'm 'after' him. But I'm sure that when you speak with him, he can provide some answers."

Jesus, didn't this man ever give up? "You've confused me," she said, fighting to keep the anger out of her voice, to sound humble. "How can you possibly believe my husband is alive? Because his body was never found? Is that it?"

"He was spotted in Mexico."

"You have to be mistaken. That can't be." She waited, but he didn't respond, and his silence frightened her. "Look," she said, "I think I understand what you want with me. You believe that through me, you can get to Larry. But you're wrong. I haven't heard from my husband, and I never will. My husband *is* dead. Can't you accept that?" Her question ended with a sob.

"I don't want to hurt you, Kelly. You are very desirable, a delicious young woman. But perhaps we need to talk in person. With a woman, I can be, shall we say, persuasive? Then again, I can be very tender. It all depends, you see. I suggest you take some time to reflect upon my words."

The pause that followed seemed to Kelly almost as sinister as the thrust of his message. She couldn't respond, could do nothing but wait for the line to go dead.

There was yet the formality of terminating their pre-dawn chat. "*Au revoir,* Kelly," Wilder said, his voice disarmingly pleasant. "Sweet dreams."

Later she would ponder the erotic tenor of her dream, a sixth-sense ability to foretell events. Something called prescience. Had the dream been precursor to the phone call?

The phone call. Wilder's voice echoed in her head in a range of colorations—polite, cold, menacing . . . and seductive. She thought about that as she sat upright against the headboard, hugging her pillow, a protective numbness settling in. The dream brought Wilder to her in the role of vanquisher, empowered to expunge the image of her husband, to invade her subconscious and play out his triumph at her bedside. But as what? Lover, seducer, or rapist? Her gaze rested on the spot he had occupied in the dream, lingered there, and then shifted to the phone. Illusion and reality were in contradistinction, but blurred at the edges.

She tightened her hold on the pillow and thought about the implied threat in his message, and wondered if he were close by, watching her building. She thought it likely he knew where she shopped, banked, took her cleaning. Thought it possible he'd observed her departure time in the morning, her return in the evening. Would she find him in her apartment, waiting for her? If so, what would he do to her? What had he meant by . . . persuasive?

Oh, God, she didn't want to think about it. She was so tired, had to lie down, close her eyes. She slid under the covers, still clutching the pillow to her chest, only to raise herself to a sitting position. If she called 911 to insist that someone come out, it would be a futile gesture. Surely Wilder wouldn't be lurking on the premises. At least not yet. When he made his move, it would be after she reflected --- his pronouncement --- on his implied threats, when her fears had become all consuming. She shuddered. God knows what would come next.

She glanced at the clock, wanting to fast forward the hours, to race toward the light of day. She yearned for the sanctity of rational responses and behavior from a caring and committed Detective Cherney.

She would add Jason to that list.

Chapter Nineteen

Kelly could have been on stage, Jason reflected, as she recounted Fern's disclosures, her tone hushed or indignant, her expression mirroring puzzlement or disbelief—except this time, her theater was defined by the four walls of his office, her audience made up of himself and Robert Cherney. Major props—her journal and the résumé on Max Scully—lay side-by-side on Jason's desk.

It was Cherney who asked for clarification on several points, jotting notes as Kelly complied, but her answers, it seemed to Jason, were hurried, her manner uncharacteristically impatient. He decided to intervene.

"Kelly, excuse me, but I sense more revelations?"

She smiled. "Only the best part. I had a call in the middle of the night." She paused a beat. "From Joseph Wilder."

An attention-getter for sure, Jason thought, startled, as Kelly, once again in the spotlight, related the gist of their conversation.

"He wouldn't back off," Kelly was saying. "He insisted that Larry was alive, and that I knew he was alive."

Cherney looked up from his notepad. "Why would he be insistent about that?"

"Wilder said Larry was spotted in Mexico. As impossible as that may seem, it came to me that he could be right. Suppose Larry did survive? It would explain the phone call hoax in Istanbul and the fact that these men have been on my trail." She fell silent, and then shook her head. "But it can't be. Even if Larry were on the run, he would never, ever let me go on believing he was dead."

Jason tugged at his collar, fighting a choking sensation. What did she expect from him, corroboration? A nod of agreement? He'd been reticent throughout much of their discussion, and he knew she would

213

think it odd if he continued his silence, but what could he say? As he debated his next move, she stirred restlessly, shifting her purse from her lap to her side.

"You seem pensive," Kelly said to Jason, her smile uncertain. "Are you going to share your thoughts?"

"I guess I'd better, hadn't I." The words, so innocuous, belied his mood. This wasn't a good moment, and God help him through this. *No, God help Kelly,* he amended. "This will come as a shock to both of you," he looked over at Cherney, and then reached to cover Kelly's hand with his, "but Larry may very well be alive."

Cherney sucked in his breath, and then let it out in a soft whistle; Kelly didn't respond. She could have been carved in stone, her skin ashen, her gaze unwavering.

As if mesmerized, she held on to his gaze, and then suddenly lowered her head, as if she were about to faint.

"Kelly, can I get you something? A glass of water?" he offered.

"I'm all right. Please." She stopped to clear her throat. "Please, go on."

He released her hand and reached for his briefcase, bringing out a sheet of notebook paper.

"I'll start at the beginning," he said. "When you were last here, Kelly—in fact moments before your arrival—my secretary placed a registered letter on my desk."

"From Larry."

"Yes, my dear, from your husband. The letter is in my safe, where it must remain for now, but"—he indicated the sheet of paper—"I've hand-copied a good portion of what he wrote." *Deleting,* he added silently, *any reference to money laundering or the drug connection.*

"Let me give you a brief accounting of the letter. Now Larry doesn't spell out the details of his involvement with the enterprise he was trying to break away from, other than to say *he* wanted out, but his associates would not accept his defection. So he set up his disappearance and presumed drowning.

"He also feared for your safety, Kelly. All told, he reasoned that his apparent death would put an end to the pursuit and that with him out of the picture, you would be out of harm's way."

"But at what cost?"Kelly asked.

Jason sighed. "At any rate, Larry's message was that he was determined to return home and turn state's evidence to expose the people he'd been involved with."

"Return from where?" Cherney asked.

"I'm not sure. Only that his starting point would be from a fishing village north of Acapulco where he was holed up."

Jason raised his hands. "That's it for now. I've heard nothing more from Larry, which concerns me. But we'll hope for the best.

"Of course, I've breached the lawyer-client rule of confidentiality, but I felt I had no other choice."

Cherney was frowning. "Kelly mentioned that Larry was in some kind of trouble."

Jason nodded. "Sorry to have kept you in the dark, Robert, but that information was privileged." He regarded Kelly, noting her composure, admiring her strength, her pluck. "I'm sure you'd like to look this over," he said, handing her the copy.

"Thank you. I would have insisted."

Jason turned to Cherney. "So now you can re-open your investigation?"

Cherney placed pen and pad in his case. "I'll want to run a check on Tom Champion, talk to the FBI, as well." On his feet now, he eyed the dossier. "Mind if I take this with me?"

"Please do."

There was a sureness in the manner in which Cherney swooped up the dossier, a spring in his step as he advanced to the door. "You think you're on to something?" Jason asked.

"Possibly." He started to say something, and then shifted his attention from Jason to Kelly.

She looked up at that moment to give him a questioning frown.

He stared at her for a moment; then, his expression rueful, he said, "I don't have your gift with words, Kelly, but I care about your feelings. I hope you're going to be all right."

"I want Larry to be all right, to come out of this alive." She gave him a brief smile, and then returned to her reading.

"Go on, now, get to work," Jason said, feeling upbeat as he waved Cherney out of the office. He'd been pleased by Kelly's response.

Now, with only the two of them present, Jason leaned back in his chair and rotated his shoulders, wishing he could light up. It was a stupid rule that he had imposed on himself about not smoking on the job.

Kelly seemed transfixed on Larry's letter, just as he had been, reading over and under and between the lines for meaning and nuances. Finally she handed the paper back to him.

He regarded her thoughtfully. On stage, she could project the innermost feelings of the characters she portrayed; in real life, she played it close to the vest. *What the hell? He would opt for positive over negative.* "Kelly, about your comments to Cherney about Larry. I hope this means you have it in your heart to forgive him."

For a moment, she looked half again her age. "I don't know, Jason. I really can't say."

"Your feelings have changed?"

"No." She fell silent, as if struggling to articulate what it was she felt. "I love Larry. I'll always love him."

"How can you love and not forgive?"

"I don't believe this! I can't believe what I'm hearing. Is that the question you pose to women stuck in marriages with bastards who cheat on them or knock them around?"

"Kelly, you're not being fair."

"I know. It's not the same thing, and I'm sorry for acting the bitch. But dammit, he put us through so much anguish. In all this time, not a word to me, not a word to his family." She looked away. "I can't even begin to describe my feelings."

"He had his reasons. He was protecting you and fighting for his own survival."

"Why? Just tell me why this all had to happen in the first place. We were on our honeymoon, for God's sake."

Jason opened his mouth and then closed it, willing himself to mask his impatience. "I don't have to tell you that people make mistakes. Serious mistakes." The look she threw him was akin to despair, and he felt his irritation melt away. "I do understand your frustration and anger."

"Jason, could we talk about something else? What about Wilder and his threats?"

"Good heavens, yes. It's imperative we move you into safe territory. Immediately."

Her grin was a bit smug. "It just so happens I'm booked on an evening flight to San Francisco."

"Smart move." He nodded approvingly. "I was about to suggest that same course of action."

"Rick thinks it's for the best, too; he's even offered to drive me to the airport." She thought for a moment. "Jason, where do we go from here? What do I say to my family, to Larry's family?"

"I wouldn't discuss Larry's possible survival with his mother or sister. Let Cherney take care of that. As for your family, I'd say it's up to you."

"Play it by ear? Is that what you're saying?" She managed a smile. "Have you ever tried to keep something from Nadine?"

He inclined his head. "I haven't had the pleasure."

Her smile vanished as she turned pensive. "Where do you suppose Larry is?"

"Well, the 'Z' I could make out on the envelope is probably for Zihuantanejo. It's a coastal fishing village, north of Acapulco. However, I very much doubt he's still there. Something went awry, is my guess, and he had to move on. I say that because he's made no further attempt to get in touch with me."

"You'll let me know if you hear from him?"

"Of course."

"One more thing. He mentioned turning state's evidence. Will

217

that exonerate him, or would he have to serve a prison sentence?"

"I suppose that would depend on the extent of his culpability and the degree of his cooperation."

She rose, and Jason stood, too, poised to see her out. But she remained in place, her expression thoughtful. "I'd questioned how these people kept track of my whereabouts. I suppose it was through Audrey. I'd stayed in touch with her through an occasional phone call and postcards from Turkey. She must have passed on those nuggets of information to Fern . . . Though I can't imagine Fern in a cozy chat with her husband, sharing all the news about me."

"But Champion knew he could keep tabs on you through his wife. I can picture him pretending concern over Larry's poor little widow, asking where is she now, what is she doing with her life, and so on. Incidentally, Scully would have known you were in Istanbul." He went on to explain about the phone call to her mother from the bogus stage manager, and his own subsequent alarm as to her safety.

"I did wonder about your call, but now it's all starting to come together. Except—" Her face suddenly crumpled, and she turned away.

He came to her side and held her close, patting her gently, as he would a distressed child. "I know, I know. There's so much that hasn't been resolved. We'll get there."

"If you say so." She smiled at him through her tears. "Well." She stepped away from him to reach for her purse. "I'd better get over to the Playhouse. After I've put in a few hours, Rick will follow me home." At the door, she paused. "At least we've found out the identity of 'whoever.' I would never have guessed Tom Champion. The person I had second thoughts about was Ben Forbes."

Jason chuckled. "Don't feel bad, dear. If I were a betting man, I would have given you five-to-one odds on Ben Forbes."

As Kelly and Jason completed their conversation, another, more heated discussion was in progress, via transatlantic telephone.

"Sorry if I've tried your patience, Tom, but when someone screws up, it gets to me."

"Now wait one damned minute. I've accomplished a hell of a lot for you."

"That's not in dispute."

"Well, good. We agree on something."

"Tom, for God's sake—"

"I thought we decided no names." Exasperation colored his tone.

"If you insist. No, you're right." Then, choking on anger and frustration, he said, "Damn, if you had just left him alone."

"We couldn't take that chance. Besides, I thought he was in the bag."

"That he wouldn't defect, you mean."

"Why should he? He had everything, a fantastic future, everything."

"It backfired. Your little games, I'm talking about. And bringing in the goon from Austria was a really stupid move. If only I'd known what you were up to. Jesus, didn't I make it clear I didn't want him hurt? For Christ's sake, he was like a son to me."

"All right. Things got out of hand." There was a pause. "Look, we've turned the corner. It's time to move on." Another pause. "For God's sake, lighten up. It's all going to work out."

"Convince me."

"Let's start with the situation from this end."

"I'm listening."

"I've met with our Paris contact and can report mission accomplished. So tomorrow, I leave for Athens."

"Athens! You're taking a vacation? What the hell is going on? I thought we had a problem to resolve."

"Actually, I'm staying in a suburb south of Athens. Vouliagmeni. I'll be with Nikos Parisis. I think I've mentioned him. He has a villa by the water and operates several fishing boats. He's also willing to transport cargo without asking questions."

"Okay, I know where I can reach you. But what about your family?"

"My wife knows I'm in Paris. I explained a last-minute change in plans that brought me here from New York. Also, when I called home, I mentioned the possibility of having to go on to Zurich."

"At least your wife won't be listing you as a missing person."

"Not yet, anyway."

"What does that mean?"

"My family mustn't know about Greece—or anyone else, for that matter, except you."

"Why is that?"

"Our unresolved problem. Good God, it's my neck if he gets to the authorities."

"If he does?"

"I would have to disappear."

"I suppose that makes sense."

"Not that I relish the idea. Far better if we can pick up from where we left off."

"I'd have to think about that."

"Really." There was a pause. "In any case, *you're* home free."

"And you're not. Are you telling me this late in the game you have regrets?"

"What I regret is that you have so little faith in me."

"I've never lacked faith in you. That's not the point! What you fail to see is that by ignoring my wishes, you've courted disaster, brought down the house of cards."

"Oh, come on. We don't know that."

"As for the fact that I can't be linked with the operation, you knew the set-up from the very beginning. Look, I think we'd better cut this short."

"Okay. And stop worrying. It's not likely I'll be staying in Greece for long. My gut feeling is that soon, very soon, it will be business as usual. Trust me."

Trust you? No. And as for business as usual, never again 'as usual'. Trust me.

Later in that same day anxieties of a different nature surfaced as Nadine, having arrived at the United Airlines terminal, waited outside for her daughter. She checked her watch and figured she had just enough time for a cigarette.

Lighting up, however, was another matter. She tried her lighter again, but the damn thing wouldn't cooperate. Or maybe it was the unexpected tremor in her hands. She noticed a man standing a few feet away staring at her. He probably thought she needed a drink, a fix, or both.

Oh well, to hell with it, she decided, stuffing the cigarette case and lighter back into her bag. Blame it on nerves or, more likely, rampant anxiety over Kelly. Something was very wrong.

Not that she'd sensed trouble at the onset of Kelly's call. She'd been delighted over what she assumed was to be a weekend visit, its spur-of-the-minute nature notwithstanding. She could hear her own voice, bright with expectation. "Can you cheat a bit and stay over on Monday?" she'd asked. "We could attend an art gallery showing and reception that's been hyped as a can't-miss event."

"Mom, I'm really not sure how long I'll be staying. It could be for a while."

"Kelly, what's happened?"

Kelly's tone had been noncommittal. "We'll talk when I see you. I don't want to go into it right now."

She'd let it go at that. But Kelly away from her precious theater? An ominous sign, for sure.

Nadine began to pace, then heard "Mom!" Kelly had come out from an exit farther down and was waving and smiling. Then they were in each other's arms.

"How are you, darling? Was it a good flight?"

"A bit bumpy at times, but not enough to kill my appetite. Actually, I haven't eaten since breakfast."

"And you're famished. We'll make a stop on the way home."

"Where's Steve?"

"He really wanted to be here, but tonight's the big fundraiser for the symphony, and since he's on the Board, he had no choice but to attend."

"So instead of sweeping onto the dance floor, looking ravishing in some designer creation, you've had to come all the way down here to pick up your bedraggled daughter."

Not at all bedraggled, was Nadine's assessment, *but pale and pinched around the eyes, and for God-knows-what reason.* For once, though, she didn't verbalize her findings. "Frankly," she said, "I'm beginning to find fundraisers a bore. Same faces, same orchestras, and the same inferior champagne. Come on, let's go for some real food."

Nadine's conception of 'real food' was what the *Chronicle's* restaurant reviewer described as one of the city's favorite hangouts for politicians, sports figures, and journalists. The busy bar attested to further commentary regarding generous drinks, called 'the best in town'.

Away from the noise, in a booth near the back of the restaurant, the women studied the menu, which offered a wealth of deli selections, plus a full range of dinner entrées. Kelly looked up at her mother. "I'm glad we came here; it has character."

"Character and *characters.*"

"You're right. It doesn't strike me as your kind of place."

"Still you see your mother gliding in formal regalia under crystal chandeliers or surrounded by hovering waiters dressed in frock coats? I'm flattered, but this restaurant is a favorite of ours. Steve and I come here quite often."

"Glad to see that glimmer in your eyes, Ma. Seriously, how are you guys doing?"

"Better. Really better."

"Did you corner him for a heart-to-heart?"

"No, I didn't feel the need to. He's been very sweet, very affectionate lately. Oh, Kelly, I confess I wonder about myself sometimes. Here I am, a fif—a mature woman, upset because I don't have my husband's undivided attention. I know very well that with his responsibilities at the bank and everything else he's into, I should be concentrating on his welfare instead of making up problems where none exist. I'm simply going to have to learn to share the wealth. That said, I think we should decide on our order."

"I'm not really hungry."

"I thought you said—"

"Well, yes, I have to eat something. Maybe a salad?"

"Kelly, when are you going to tell me what's wrong?"

Kelly continued to stare at her menu, and then met her mother's gaze. "I told you about the man who followed us around in Acapulco, who showed up at the Hollywood Playhouse? He called me in the middle of the night."

"Oh, for heaven's sake. He's stalking you?"

"He insisted Larry was alive, that he was there with me."

Nadine placed a hand over her heart and took a shaky breath. "Oh my God, Kelly, this is serious. I'm so glad you left L.A. But I don't understand why he would insist Larry was alive."

"Something about unfinished business between them."

"That's all he said?"

"It's more complicated than that, but I'd rather wait until we get together with Steve before I go any further into this. Besides, I think the waiter is coming our way."

He was, and later, when their wine arrived, Nadine tried to shove her fears aside to concentrate on the here and now. Her baby was home and safe, and with Steve's able assistance, they would deal with this latest crisis.

At the breakfast table, they avoided the question of Kelly's hasty departure from L.A., sticking to topics that wouldn't interfere with digestion. Now, as Kwon brought in a fresh pot of coffee, Kelly watched as Nadine quirked an eyebrow at her husband and used her slippered foot to give him a not-so-gentle poke under the table. Because of Steve's late arrival home from a fund-raiser, they'd agreed to wait until morning to bring up the purpose of Kelly's visit.

He caught her message and cleared his throat. "Kelly, I think we should talk about something. Your mother tells me you're having a problem with this man who was hung up on you and Larry in Acapulco. That he called you in the middle of the night. Do I understand he was under the impression Larry was there with you?"

Kelly pushed back her chair. "Can we sit outside on the terrace? Take our coffee out there? It's such a crisp, sunny morning."

223

There was a breeze, as well, and as they settled into brightly colored cushioned chairs, Kelly breathed in the cool air riding in from the ocean, enjoying the openness and feeling a sense of relief from the oppression of nightmares, both real and illusory. It was as if she were being cleansed in both body and spirit to prepare her for the task ahead.

Nadine and Steve were an attentive audience, their coffees untouched, their faces mirroring her own distress as she described the phone call from Joseph Wilder. Further revelations as to Larry's troubles drew expressions of disbelief from Nadine and a gentle questioning from Steve.

It wasn't as difficult as she'd imagined to open up to the older couple. Their show of loving concern was a source of comfort. She decided to tell them everything, starting with Fern's discoveries.

That Tom Champion had presumably masterminded the break-ins momentarily stunned her listeners.

"Kelly, this is absolutely crazy." Nadine looked over at Steve, as if for confirmation.

Her stepfather, however, appeared more puzzled than shocked. "I can't help but think back to that terrible night when all of us congregated in the den. I thought it a bit strange even then that Tom questioned me about the search for a body, as if he needed to be sure Larry was really gone. In fact—and I hate to say this, Kelly—it brings up the question of foul play, especially with Tom's having the file on this Max Scully character."

"Foul play?" Nadine was beside herself. "My God, what's next? To think the Tom Champion I met could turn out to be this . . . this monster."

Steve's expression had hardened as he turned to his wife. "Rest assured, we'll get to the bottom of this." And then to Kelly, his smile softening his words, he said, "Dare I ask if there's more?"

"Oh yes, there's more." They were waiting, but her lips suddenly felt stuck, as if her saliva had turned into glue.

"Kelly, whatever it is, honey, we're here for you. You know that, don't you?" Steve asked.

She did know and flashed a grateful look at her stepfather, not only for his supportive words but for the hand placed firmly on Nadine's arm, the gesture plainly calling for restraint. Kelly parted her lips, hesitated, and then decided to get it out and over with. "Before I left for Turkey, Jason received a registered letter. It was from Larry."

There was a shocked silence. Steve leaned forward, head tilted, as if in doubt as to what he had heard. "Kelly, what are you saying?"

"From Larry? But how—" Nadine had paled and grabbed on to Steve's arm.

"Mom, Steve, Larry didn't drown. He faked his own death, and the letter was written from his hideout somewhere in Mexico."

If it wasn't total recall, she came close as she recited the contents of Larry's letter, performing like a reporter on the six o'clock news: objective, poised, and ever so careful not to fall apart on camera.

The mind games helped, and in the careful questioning that ensued, Steve, with Nadine following his lead, declined to voice either condemnation or support for Larry's actions. Nor did they try to discern Kelly's personal feelings.

Steve took Kelly's hand. "This is huge sweetheart. But personal issues aside, we need to focus on how we can help Larry out of this mess. We also need a plan of action to get to the bottom of Tom Champion's criminal acts. But most importantly, Kelly, your mother and I are here to give you unconditional support."

"Amen to that." Nadine said, giving her chair's arm a thump.

Later in the day, Nadine debated whether or not to cancel the dinner party they had scheduled for this Saturday evening. As she explained to Steve, she hated to ruin everyone's plans, but she wasn't sure she could pull off the role of gracious hostess. Not tonight. However, before she could get to the phone to cancel, she had second thoughts. Eight guests were entirely manageable, and besides, one could only endure so much in one day. They needed relief, distraction from weighty moments, catastrophic situations, and crises in the making. The party was on.

Kelly offered no argument. She insisted they proceed with the dinner, offering to serve, clear, to be the life of the party—anything to take her mind off what Kelly mockingly referred to as the four D's, as in dirty deeds, deception, and disappearing husbands.

The life of the party, she's not, was Nadine's observation, but

Kelly had always been reserved around strangers. At least she looked better than when she'd arrived in San Francisco. Whether it was makeup or the afternoon call from Rick O'Hara that brought color to her cheeks, a softer look about the eyes, Nadine didn't care to speculate. What counted was that Kelly appeared to be enjoying herself; at least she held up her end of the conversation with those seated next to her, which was more than she could say for herself. She barely acknowledged George Van Valen on her right. True, the man was a bore, with his monotone delivery, the endless details in his endless stories. However, his wife was a good friend, and Nadine finally decided to set aside her concerns over Kelly and give her undivided attention to her guests.

A minute or two later, Nadine became aware in her peripheral vision of Kwon entering the dining room. About to break into her guest's discourse in order to excuse herself, she saw the houseboy wasn't headed her way, but to where Kelly was seated. In deference to those engaged in conversation, he stood quietly at Kelly's chair. Apparently sensing his presence, Kelly looked up. Nadine watched as Kwon spoke briefly and then departed.

"Excuse me," Nadine said to George as Kelly left the table. Outside the doors to the dining room, Nadine confronted her daughter.

"It's only a phone call, Mom."

"Well, you looked disturbed. Did Kwon say who was calling?"

"Honestly, I'm not upset, just curious. And no, Kwon didn't offer a clue. But I promise to reveal all."

"Kelly, the last thing I want to do is pry into your affairs."

"I know, and I'm sorry if I sounded snippy, but I'd better get to the phone before they hang up on me."

"You're right. And I'd better return to our guests. Talk to you later."

Back at the dinner table, Nadine was aware of Steve's inquiring look, but she could only shrug and smile. Dessert and coffee would be served in a few minutes, and then they would retire to the living room for after-dinner drinks. Meanwhile, she turned over in her mind a possible roster of callers. It could be anyone: a friend, Rick O'Hara again—the thought didn't exactly enthrall her—even Vanessa. Or, God forbid the pervert or whatever he was who had frightened Kelly.

The answer wasn't immediately forthcoming. Kelly hadn't

returned for dessert, and as the Hansons and their guests made their way to the main room, made cozy for this smaller group by the strategic placement of ornamental screens, Nadine managed to take Steve aside for a hurried consultation.

He responded that probably there was no cause for concern. However, they both agreed if Kelly hadn't joined them by the time he'd served the drinks, he would excuse himself and go in search of her.

It didn't take long for Steve to serve the after dinner drinks, but with Kelly still a no-show and Nadine telegraphing him worried glances, he decided to look for Kelly.

Steve found Kelly on the terrace, hugging herself against the chill, a lone figure dwarfed by distant, towering hotels and office buildings made brilliant in an orgy of electrical exuberance.

"Kelly?" He moved toward her tentatively, as if she were a fragile piece of merchandise that might disintegrate at a step too hurried, at a movement too abrupt.

"This is where it started," she said. "For Larry and me."

"I remember, honey."

After a long pause, she said, "I was learning to deal with the finality of it all, that we'd never stand side by side, as we did that first night to watch the fog roll in, or to share a sunset. Or anything else, for that matter."

At her side now, Steve placed an arm around her shoulders to bestow a comforting pat. "And now you have to prepare for the possibility that Larry could step back into your life. Not knowing, the uncertainty is rough duty, for sure."

Kelly took a step back so she could look her stepfather full in the face. "Steve, that was Jason Underwood on the phone. He made it back. Larry's back!"

Chapter Twenty

orry about the way I look." Larry indicated his patched work jeans and the plaid shirt opened down the front to reveal a stained white T-shirt. "I have a change of clothes in my suitcase, and I'll get rid of this," he said, fingering his beard.

Jason grinned. "It got you here, so the disguise worked."

Larry grinned back. "Yeah, it worked great. Seems I had a bus seat to myself all the way from downtown L.A. It was a hell of a long ride, but I figured renting a car was chancy, considering who might be skulking around the rental agencies. Anyway I'm here."

They were seated across from each other, Jason in his wing chair and Larry on the sofa. "Yes, and I'm so damn happy to see you, Larry." Jason pulled a handkerchief from his pocket and dabbed at his eyes. Then regaining his composure, he said, "What can I get you? Coffee? A beer, something stronger?"

"Sit still, please. Maybe a beer later. Right now I'm feeling all . . . stirred up." He shook his head and stared down at the carpet.

"It might help to talk. We have all afternoon, all evening as well."

"Plenty of time for me to spill my guts, huh?"

"Why don't we start at the end of your odyssey? You mentioned on the phone you had to get out of Zihuantanejo in a hurry. What happened there?"

"I'll get to that in a minute. First, I have to know. Have you talked to Kelly?"

"I called her last night, right after I heard from you. As I said yesterday, I debated forever whether to open up to Kelly about you." He raised his hands apologetically.

"Jason, it's okay. You did what you had to do. Now, about Kelly?"

"When I told her you'd made it back, she said, 'Oh God, I'm so glad.'"

"Why, that's wonderful." Larry had brightened, and then his slow smile gave way to a tightness around his mouth. "You still think she has reservations about us getting back together?"

"Now, I didn't say that, although I suppose I implied as much yesterday. Kelly hasn't voiced her intentions either way. However, and this is going to hurt, she has questioned your . . . your integrity."

He was nodding. "I'm not surprised."

"And of course you can imagine her pain over your 'death'."

"She didn't mention my letter to her?"

"Your letter? You wrote to Kelly?"

"Oh shit, don't tell me she never received it. Jason, I couldn't let her go on believing I was dead. I poured my heart out, I—Oh, Jesus, what must she think of me? You're sure?"

"I'm absolutely sure." He would let it stand at that. Larry didn't need an accounting of Kelly's outburst, of her bitterness. "Chances are, it will arrive one of these days. Of course, you must tell her you wrote."

"It's not only Kelly I have to face. What about my mother, my sister, friends, fellow workers?" He shut his eyes for a moment, and then opened them wide, as if taking in his surroundings for the first time. "I was so wired when I walked in here. Now, all of a sudden, I feel about a hundred years old, like it would be nice to find a dark room and go to sleep. Maybe sleep forever."

"Larry, come on. You had your reasons for what you did. Compelling reasons, I'm sure. You know very well your family will be overjoyed to have you back."

"But not my wife?"

"She loves you. She told me that. The rest will work itself out. You'll find a way. Incidentally, I didn't tell her you'd be staying with me. She thinks you're still at the motel."

"What matters is that I talk to Kelly." He glanced at the phone.

"Don't call her. Talk to her in person. In fact, she wants to meet with you here in Los Angeles."

"She does? When?" Once again he brightened.

"I would guess in a few days. Kelly indicated she needed time to, uh, assess the situation."

"Oh. I see."

"Have faith, my friend."

"True love will out? Ha! Only in fairy tales."

Jason snorted. "I couldn't have said it better, given my track record. But enough of that. Tell me what happened in Zihuantanejo."

"Okay. You remember I wrote you about a woman who was asking questions about me? Well, since there was no follow-up, nothing at all to further my suspicions, I began to relax, to think I was home-free. Then, out of the blue, I was discovered. Got spotted in a bar." He described the events of that evening, culminating with his hurried exit from the hotel premises and the frantic aftermath. "I knew I had to get out of Zihuantanejo. That night, if possible. However, I began having second thoughts about Morelia. The folks I rented from knew I was headed there, and with Antonio in the picture, I figured he'd ask around and eventually point the way to my pursuers.

"Also there was another problem. Jose's car. With the shape it was in, I was skeptical about even making it out to the highway. So I hatched another little plot and gave Jose a starring role. He knew by then that some bad guys were after me. And since he'd turned out to be a hell of a good buddy, I had no choice but to go on trusting him. I had him drive me to the bus station, supposedly to board an early a.m. bus to Morelia. I took the bus, all right, but it was to Acapulco."

"Aha! Good thinking."

"Then, later in the morning, Jose was to spread the word that he'd put me on a bus for Morelia, that his amigo looked scared, was acting a little crazy."

"But all this time, you were in Acapulco."

"Actually, I stayed in Puerto Margues, outside the resort area. I'd picked up some Spanish, and being able-bodied, finding work was no problem. And then"—he spread his hands—"I decided I'd had it with being on the run, with looking over my shoulder. It was time to come home and face the consequences." He looked thoughtful, once again fingering his beard. "I don't want to shock my family, particularly my mother."

"Let's start with your sister. She can prepare your mother. In fact, Fern may already be alerted to the possibility of your survival." Jason rose. "I think it's time we played catch-up. But first, I'm going to fetch us those beers."

It was Jason's turn in the arena of tell-all, starting with the break-ins, continuing with the investigation, the Scully-Wilder stories, along with Kelly's unwitting involvement, and the dramatic finale, in which he detailed Fern's and Audrey's visit to Kelly with evidence of Tom Champion's probable misdeeds.

Throughout Jason's narration, Larry barely tasted his drink, raptly attentive as each event unfolded. Now as Jason paused, Larry reached for his beer and drank deeply. When he set the glass down, his expression reflected a mixture of puzzlement and pride. "I can't believe what I'm hearing about my sister. I confess I'm flabbergasted." Then he darkened. "As for what those bastards did to Kelly, you don't want to hear what I'd lay on them."

"They'll get theirs, I'm sure. And so will Tom Champion."

"He doesn't know that Fern found the journal and the dossier?"

"She says she hasn't talked to him since he left home, that they've been communicating through messages. Whatever their method of communication, I'm sure Detective Cherney has advised her not to say anything."

Larry nodded. "Tom might keep going. Or, he might decide to take off anyway. Once he learned I didn't die, that I was on the loose, he had to gamble on his people getting to me. It was me or him. That simple."

"And if word should get to him that you're set to testify?"

"It's goodbye, Mr. Champion."

"Apparently, he harbored doubts as to your demise all along."

"I know how his mind works, how he leaves nothing to chance. The way I figure it, when no body turned up, he had to make sure I hadn't pulled a caper on him. Consequently, he set up the hunt. Of course, I hoped he would accept my drowning at face value."

"That's all in the past. Our goal now is to decide what you'll tell the police and the FBI."

Larry let out his breath in a deep sigh. "I don't know how it could be much worse, the trouble I'm in."

"It could be serious, but maybe not as bad as you think. All right, let's focus in on the core of this situation. I assume we're talking about the laundering of drug profits?"

"Yes, through overseas banks, stock purchases, government bond purchases, and God knows what else. Like I said, in the beginning, I didn't know it was drug money. I thought Tom was involved in a stock manipulation scheme. Something about profiting by a corporation's failure?"

"Nasty business, but people get away with it. I remember a case where a brokerage house was sued by a corporation that went bust. Had to do with selling short the corporation's stock, and then spreading damaging rumors about the corporation and its directors. Which in turn caused the price of the stock to fall."

"Yeah. Well, I knew it was wrong, but he led me to believe its common practice in the brokerage business to wheel and deal. At any rate, I was the pick-up man for cash, documents, whatever, as well as the delivery boy. I also acted as their overseas courier on a couple of occasions. That's when I caught on to the fact I was making contacts with drug dealers. And that's when I knew I'd made one huge, horrendous mistake by getting involved." He shook his head. "Then I made a second mistake. By confronting Tom. If I'd played dumb, not brought up the drugs issue, they might have let me go."

"Aside from being able to identify Scully and Wilder, is there anyone else you could finger besides Champion?"

"Not really. Mostly I dealt with go-betweens, errand boys like myself."

Jason started to reach for his drink, and then left it untouched, bowing to more cerebral concerns. "You know, we might be able to arrange for you to be granted immunity from prosecution. You have proof of your allegations?"

"I have documentation of my services—bank receipts, airline ticket stubs, copies of bank account numbers, signatures, all stashed away in a safe deposit box under an assumed name."

"What about Champion's office? Fern told Kelly she'd discovered a number of locked files."

He nodded. "Remember at our reception I said my data was incomplete? I'd hoped to find a way to gain access to those files. At this point, however, Tom might have destroyed anything he considered incriminating."

"Though if he's planning to disappear, it wouldn't matter one way or the other." Jason looked at his watch. "Tell you what. Let's save the rest of this for after dinner. If you don't mind leftovers, I have a chicken in wine sauce, rice pilaf, and beans almandine."

Larry shook his head. "Sorry, if it's not refried beans and tamales, it's no go." He laughed. "Kidding. Only kidding. It sounds marvelous. But, seriously, Jason, as grateful as I am for your hospitality, I'm not sure I should be staying with you." He shot a glance at the door. "The last thing I want is to place you in jeopardy."

"I think we'll be all right. No one knows you're here, and even if I became suspect as the person you'd come to, this building is secure."

"When do we talk to the authorities?"

"Not quite yet. I think we should sit tight for a few days, see what materializes with Champion's situation and with Detective Cherney's investigation. Then we'll—Uh, Larry, have I lost you? Hello." He snapped his fingers.

Larry focused his blue eyes on the attorney, his expression sheepish. "Sorry, Jason, I was miles away."

"In San Francisco?"

"With Kelly, yes."

For most of Sunday, Kelly wrapped herself in thoughts of Larry.

After devoting the day to exploring possible outcomes of their situation (outcomes characterized by treacherous byways), her thinking and feelings were as scrambled as when she'd attempted to seek answers throughout a troubled night.

Now, at bedtime once again, Kelly sat on the edge of the bed, contemplating the novel that lay within reach. Chances were she'd have to start reading at the beginning again, her concentration had been so shot the night before. And then her gaze fastened on the clock. It would be morning in Ankara, Turkey. Earlier, she'd toyed with the idea of making the call; suddenly, the urge to talk to Vanessa was overpowering.

The response from overseas offered Kelly a respite from her own concerns as her sister bubbled on about the joys of impending motherhood, the precious layette Gordon's parents had sent, the boxes of maternity clothes—from Bloomingdales, no less, compliments of Nadine. And finally . . . Vanessa wound down with an apology.

"You know by now what a rotten correspondent I am, so I love you for calling. Things couldn't be better, Sis. Gordon is so excited about the baby."

"That's fantastic. I'll be sure to tell Mom. In fact, I'm calling from the Victorian."

"On a visit, are you?"

"You might call it that. Now I want you to know I'm okay, and that everyone here is fine. But a lot has happened; I have some rather . . . interesting news."

"What? Tell me!"

"Let me lead into this. We wouldn't want you going into premature labor." With that attention-getter, Kelly launched into the series of events that had transpired since her homecoming, working up to Friday's meeting with Jason and Cherney and the presentation of the letter from Larry.

"I'm stunned! Flat, knocked-out, stunned. You must be off the wall. Kelly, think of it! There's a chance Larry will make it back to you."

"He *is* back. Jason called last night, saying that Larry is back in L.A."

"Oh, my God, that's wonderful." She waited. "Well, isn't it?"

More silence. "Kelly, have you talked to Larry?"

"No, not yet."

"Sweetie, what's going on?"

"Vanessa, for all this time, he let us go on believing he was dead. Can you remember what I went through? What he put everyone through? And what about the trouble he's in? Does coming back mean doing time in prison?"

"Oh, sweetie, I wasn't thinking. I guess it's all pretty scary and complicated. But Kelly, you have to talk to him sometime."

"I'm going back to L.A. in a couple of days, and we'll meet then."

"Maybe you should postpone a decision. Take a timeout. If you need to examine your feelings in neutral territory, you can always come back to us."

"Thanks, Sis, but I think I'd better fight this battle on home turf. Also, whatever happens, I do have a job to return to. Any more absences and Rick might give up on me."

"I hope he's not giving you a hard time."

"Far from it. He's been in my corner all the way, going out of his way to be kind and understanding."

"Hmm. Sounds to me as if he's waiting in the wings."

"Vanessa!"

"Well, so what? It's nice to have a man around, to offer support."

"I can't think in those terms right now."

"Kelly, whatever you decide—to go back to Larry, take up with Rick, or start with a fresh slate—I want so much for you to be happy."

"That's exactly how I feel about you."

"Then you have to understand that staying with Gordon was the right choice for me."

"You're saying I should forgive and forget?"

"Not necessarily. I know it's a tough call. But give it a lot of thought. And could you try to bend a little, put yourself in Larry's place? You tend to be . . . stiff-necked, at times, and while I applaud your strong sense of morality, the human condition ain't always what it should be. We all mess up. Even thee and me. Now I'm going to shut up about this, unless there's something more?"

There was more: promises from both to keep in better touch, plus Vanessa's heartfelt good wishes for smooth sailing ahead, coupled with a pep talk as to Kelly's strength, courage, good sense, and compassion.

A real upper, was Kelly's thought as she got off the phone. She gave a little snort. Kelly, compassionate? How did that tie in with stiff-necked?

She stared at the phone, her thoughts switching from Vanessa to Larry. Soon they would be reunited. Oh, God, was she ready for this?

She shut her eyes briefly, and then reached for her book. It would be a very long night.

✣ *Chapter Twenty-One* ✣

Vouliagmini, Greece
Monday, 11:30 p.m.

*T*om Champion looked at his watch and yawned. Finally he was beginning to relax, to shake off feelings of unease, a nameless anxiety that dogged him throughout the day. He raised his glass to Nikos. "Excellent brandy."

The Greek smiled back, his chin settling into comfortable folds. "A fitting nightcap," he said, swirling the liquid before taking a sip.

The two men were seated at the back of the house in a glassed-in sun room through which one could exit into the garden. The opened door provided cooling breezes, bringing nighttime relief from the June heat, along with the scent of citrus, a mingling of lemon and orange from trees and shrubbery.

Nikos had set his glass down to retrieve his cigar from the ashtray. Now, eyes slightly narrowed against the rising stream of smoke, he gave Tom his full attention. "So, my friend, you're feeling better now?"

"I was that transparent?"

"Perhaps only to me."

They had dined at a taverna in the seaside town of Glyfada north of Vouliagmeni. Despite bountiful food and drink, along with rousing singing from accordion-playing waiters, Tom had been uptight for most of the evening, unable to shake his tension.

"The waiting," Nikos said. "I know it's difficult."

"I try not to think about what it would be like, not to go back."

"Your family?"

"My wife and I are no longer close, but I have children. Not to see them grow up, never to see them again is unthinkable."

"You don't know that will happen."

"Tomorrow, the next day, I should hear something. I'm bound to hear something soon." He thought for a moment. "If the news is bad, believe me, I'll be out of here, and I don't intend to leave a forwarding address."

"For that matter, no one would even have known you were here, except—" Nikos stopped and listened. "The phone? At this hour?" His eyes became hooded, a sudden wariness now muting affability. He was on his feet and out of the room.

When he returned, his look of expectancy redefined the broad jowls, promoting an instant face lift. "It's for you," he said, gesturing in the direction of the phone. "I'll wait for you here."

Tom jumped up, towering over Nikos as he sidestepped the Greek to reach the other room.

He was aware of accelerated pounding in his chest as he grabbed the phone. "Hello," he said, keeping his voice down.

"Are you alone?"

"Yes. Who is this?"

"You'll recognize my voice soon enough. I'm not sure about Nikos' phone, that it's safe. Word is out that he has enemies. We don't want them to become interested in us."

"I understand." Blackmail had come to mind, as well as the identity of his caller. "I know who you are," he said, his heart once again slamming in his chest. "Do you have news for me?"

"Yes, and I think you'll be pleased, but there are conditions. We have to talk. Tonight."

"Then you're here. Where? In Athens?"

"Much closer. Do you know how to find the Vouliagmini Marina?"

Good God, the man was practically in Nikos' backyard.

They spoke only briefly to settle on a meeting place and then to agree that he should come alone.

"I don't have a car," Tom said, "but perhaps if Nikos is willing . . ."

He inquired about a car after the call. The Greek was entirely sympathetic. "Of course, you'll take my car," he said, a glitter in his eyes. "That was your contact?"

Tom nodded. "He said he thought I'd be pleased with his news, but that there were conditions." He frowned, but kept silent. Nikos didn't need to know that the word *conditions* prompted ambivalent feelings. But maybe it was time to get out of the drug business, time to turn to projects that, though less lucrative, were safer, less volatile by their very nature.

The Greek's eyes still glittered, bordering on rapaciousness, as if he were about to set upon his prey. But his smile was warm, his handshake firm. "Good luck, my friend. I will eagerly await your news." He handed Tom his car keys. "It's out in back, past the garden."

"Thanks. I really appreciate this." He glanced in the direction of the opened door. "Do you suppose we could have breakfast out here?" The thought of something so mundane eased his tensions.

"I don't know why not. It should be most pleasant in the morning. We'll even have champagne. To celebrate!"

Tom smiled back at the beaming Nikos. "I'd like that. Well, see you in a while," Tom said, his wave jaunty as he stepped through the door and into the garden.

He found the entrance to the marina and slowly cruised the parking lot, looking for a spot as far away from the entrance as possible. As per instructions. When he'd parked, he blinked his lights twice and waited. It wasn't long before he heard three taps on the passenger side window. He reached to unlock the door, expecting the shadowy figure to slide in next to him; instead, he remained in place.

"I think we can talk better on the boat," the man said, gesturing in the direction of several yachts ablaze with lights. There are a number of things we have to discuss."

So the partnership was over. Too much damage has been done, he thought regretfully as he joined Joseph Wilder.

The men shook hands, and then Tom indicated that his companion should lead the way. Wilder seemed cheerful, upbeat, so maybe Tom was mistaken in his analysis. Why not business as usual? As they made their way to the marina, Tom took in the beauty of the marina and gazed at the lights showcasing the grounds and edifice of the Aster Palace Hotel, the famous international resort that overlooked the bay.

He thought about life in Greece. Here, days were carved into civilized segments of work and play, every day a celebration, with long, lazy meals taken in outdoor cafés, with aperitifs sipped in the waning light before a sea drenched in saffron colors. It would be a simple life graced by small pleasures; or, more to his style, a life of ease and gratuitous indulgence.

It could go either way. Whatever the outcome of this night, he might approach Nikos about forging a partnership, tell him he was ready for a career change. Perhaps in the morning over breakfast?

It was merely a concept in rough draft, in need of refinement. He smiled. It was an idea that merited serious consideration.

Chapter Twenty-Two

*O*n Monday, Robert Cherney put in a call to Fern Champion to arrange for a time to meet with her. He also had a request: that she withhold from her husband her discovery of Kelly's journal and the dossier on Scully. Her response pleased him. Not only did she pledge her cooperation; she agreed to meet with him at his convenience.

They chose two o'clock on Wednesday afternoon, a time when the children would be at day camp. Now as he waited for her to appear— the housekeeper who let him in explained that Mrs. Champion was on the phone—he wondered if the lady was a match for the elegance of his surroundings. He expected the inside of the house to equal the exterior in attractiveness, but was unprepared for the luxuriance of the living room, the furniture covered in a silky fabric, pristine white, the carpeting a plush deep blue. Naively, or perhaps guided by a magazine depiction of Southwestern living, he had anticipated clay-toned colors, desert russets, and couches draped in blankets of Indian design. Wrong. Also missing: pottery and wall hangings of coarsely textured material. This room was a showcase for abstract paintings, what he supposed would be termed modern art. Obviously Mrs. Champion liked blues and golds, since those colors were predominant in the rest of the décor. Except for the paintings, he liked the effect, but would bet his badge that children, pets, and anything that could track dirt were ruled off-limits.

He was inspecting his shoes when he heard a rustle and looked up. Fern Champion had entered the room, and he immediately rose.

"Detective Cherney, I'm sorry to have kept you waiting. Please sit down."

She crossed over to him—light hair, blue eyes, graceful stride— to sit with him on the sofa, but at a circumspect distance. As they exchanged small talk, hitting on the searing Arizona heat and the miracle of air conditioning, he studied her with his detective's eye. What he could ascertain was that tension and anxiety, marked by her constantly shifting gaze, the too-frequent blinking, hands held rigidly together, were only barely hidden behind the polite attentiveness and the lady-like demeanor.

He reached for his case and removed his notepad. "Mrs. Champion, I'd like to start with some background information on your husband. Tell me about his work, his associates, business trips, and the like." Pen poised, it suddenly occurred to him he had failed to ask the one question that took precedence over all others. Had she heard from Mr. Champion?

She started as if she'd been slapped. "There's been no word from him at all." She hadn't broken eye contact but ran her tongue over her lips, as if her mouth had gone dry.

"Is something wrong?" he asked.

"Yes, I'm afraid so. I was going to tell you at the first opportunity," she said, again moistening her lips, "that my husband has been reported missing in Greece. The authorities there notified our police."

"Wait a minute. Your husband is in Greece?"

"Believe me, I had no idea. I thought Tom was in Zurich. He said nothing about going on to Greece."

"I'm sorry. This must be very distressing for you." He considered what he'd said. Actually, she seemed more disconcerted than upset. "If you wouldn't mind filling me in?"

"I'll have to get my notes. They're by the phone," she said, rising and excusing herself.

When she returned, she showed him the name, Nikos Parisis, and the place, Vouliagmeni, which he took down.

"According to the police, it was Nikos Parisis who reported my husband missing. It seems Tom had come to this resort town, which I can't even pronounce, to stay with this man at his villa." She went on to relate what she'd been told: That Tom received a late-night phone call to meet someone at the marina and that he'd borrowed his host's car, but he hadn't returned to the villa.

"The car?"

"It was found in the parking lot at the marina."

"And the party who called?"

"They don't know. Tom didn't identify his caller. As for this Nikos person, I gather they're checking into his background."

He nodded. "Standard procedure." *And for good reason,* he thought, but he had no intention of elaborating. She'd find out soon enough about her husband's illicit activities. "Anything's possible," he said. "This meeting at the marina could have been prearranged. For all we know, your husband may now be sailing the Aegean, bound for a place where he can't be traced." He made a notation.

"Or he could be dead."

Startled, he glanced up from his notes, put off by the coldness of her statement. "I'll use my contacts and check this out. Again, I'm sorry."

"Mr. Cherney, there's no need to be apologetic. I think you should know I recently filed for divorce. Which isn't to say I'd want my husband to come to a violent end." Her hands were twisting. "However, I haven't ruled out prison, especially if Tom had anything to do with my brother's death."

"Your brother is not dead."

"I beg your pardon?"

"Sorry. I didn't mean to blurt it out like that."

"What are you talking about?"

He told her then about Larry faking his death, hiding out, the long journey back home.

"This is all so incredible. Where is he now? Can I talk to him? Is he all right?"

"Mrs. Champion, he's fine. Really. He's in Los Angeles, but he's keeping a low profile. With Wilder and Scully still on the loose, we can't be too careful."

"He's in danger?"

"There's some risk. But I have a lead on Scully and feel certain we'll be able to bring him in. Wilder is the big question mark."

She had reached for her handkerchief and was dabbing at her eyes. "I still can't fathom Larry being alive. I can imagine how this will affect my mother." She gave him a faint smile. "My second shock for today. What next?"

"I'm sure you're eager to talk with your mother, so I'll be as brief as possible. Let's go back to the beginning. Tell me about your husband's work, his friends, his business associates, and his travels --- whatever comes to mind."

When he finished his questioning, his notes secured in his case, they walked together to the door.

"I'll call Larry's attorney," she said, "and find out how I can reach him. To think, Kelly and Larry will soon be together!" Her smile faded as she turned pensive. "Then again, who can say?"

Showtime. Once again showtime, Kelly thought as she paced her living room on this Thursday, waiting for Larry to arrive. Except now, her emotions transcended first-night jitters. Much more was at stake; like the rest of her life.

In defiance of parental advice, she'd been back home for two days. Wilder be damned. She had to get on with her life and her work. She'd promised Rick she would vacate her place to move into an upstairs apartment, and in the meantime, she'd bowed to his demands that he see her safely home each night. She was grateful for his protection and also for understanding her desire to maintain a comfortable distance.

Before she left for San Francisco, she'd confided to him Jason's revelations concerning Larry, swearing him to secrecy. What Rick didn't know was that Larry had returned, and they would be meeting this very evening.

Kelly pushed her hair back from her face, struggling against the temptation to check her reflection in the mirror once again, and then her hand froze. Footfalls sounded in the corridor, followed by a soft rapping. She hesitated . . . and then, her heart racing, she opened the door.

He was thinner than she remembered, eyes intensely blue against the tan, his hair a darker blond. Later, she would recall how he had dressed for the occasion, perfectly groomed, attired like an applicant on a job interview in a conservative coat and tie. Now, though blurred in remembrance, she was in his arms, and then gently pulling away to lead him into her living room.

It seemed a formal occasion, despite the spontaneity of their greeting, calling for a prescribed protocol, starting with preliminary comments on how well each looked. She took the chair, indicating he should be seated on the sofa. At seven-thirty, he'd undoubtedly had dinner, but she offered him coffee or a drink.

Larry managed a wry smile. "I doubt I'd be capable of lifting a cup or a glass as far as my mouth. Probably make a mess and ruin your furniture." He bowed his head for an instant, and then looked her in the eye. "I want so badly to make everything right between us." His voice turned husky. "I even had a speech prepared, but the words came out hollow, or corny or lacking in eloquence." He gave her a helpless look. "We have to start somewhere."

"Maybe at the beginning?"

He nodded. "Yes, how all this started." He paused. "Kelly, I need to say something. You have to know I love you with all my heart— that if it helped, I would get down on my knees to beg your forgiveness."

She stared at him, weighing his words, at the same time attuned to his pain. And her pain. "Larry, I don't know what to say."

"Then don't try. Hear me out. Let me try to get through this." At her nod, he said, "Okay, from the top."

"Starting up a business is never easy – you move forward, you stumble, you sweat it out. In any case Tom Champion knew through the family my financial struggles. He approached me with a proposal that I join with him in a venture that would bring in big bucks, bring my dreams to fruition.

"I could tell my family was disappointed with my meager accomplishments, especially in comparison to my sister's lavish lifestyle, so I accepted my brother-in-law's proposition." He shook his head. "Eventually, I opened my eyes to the appalling truth of what I had committed to."

He repeated what he had revealed to Jason.

"You're telling me you didn't know you were involved with

drug dealers, money laundering?" She wanted to believe him; she had to believe him.

"Not at first. It was never spelled out, but when I realized what I was into . . . well, Jesus, I was frantic. I knew I had to get out."

"And when you expressed that intention, the harassment began."

"And got worse. Kelly, when I saw Scully and Wilder together in that photo in Acapulco, I figured they'd be closing in for the kill. I finally decided that with me out of the way, you'd be safe, and maybe, just maybe, I'd make it back." He looked down, his expression bleak, as if reliving that last harrowing day. When he met her gaze, his manner was contrite. "Maybe I overreacted—or call me paranoid, but when we took that last taxi ride into town, I made sure we were with others. With only the two of us, I could picture a setup, being joined along the way by someone with a gun and a mission."

"Wilder or Scully?"

At the mention of the names, he looked sick. "I could kill when I think of that kind of garbage touching your life."

She shrugged. "I've survived." *Barely,* she thought. "Speaking of Wilder, the man's not only a menace, but a weirdo, as well. Can you believe he showed up at the theater?"

He listened as she related the curtain call episode. "Good grief, Kelly. What he put you through. If I could get my hands on him ..." He'd tightened his fists, his mouth taunt.

The phone call came to mind, but she didn't want to get into that now. "To go back to Acapulco, I saw Wilder on that last day when he was on his way out of the hotel. He gave me the strangest look, as if he were trying to tell me something."

"As if he knew I wouldn't be coming back? Maybe he'd been out to the island and saw the abandoned boat? Or more likely, he kept tabs on us through his woman companion. I assume you were making inquiries at the desk?"

"Oh, yes."

"She might have overheard you asking if I'd called in, or she could have called from somewhere in the hotel, pretending to be you, asking if there'd been any messages."

"Yes, and she could have spotted me down by the pool where I was having lunch . . . alone. Or followed us into town when I was looking for you, or seen me on the street when I was practically hysterical. I was certainly too distracted to give a damn who was dogging my footsteps. The population could have been pea-green space midgets, for all I knew."

"When I think of what I put you through, it absolutely destroys me." There were tears in his eyes.

"You had your reasons. That's what Jason said. He's the voice of reason. But I was the abandoned bride." She clutched at the cushion of her chair, knuckles white. "That day—the day you disappeared, Larry—was pure hell for me, and the days that followed were agonizing beyond description." She had ended on a sob, unable to continue.

He sat there, head bowed. Finally, he said, "What are we going to do about us?"

"Oh, shit, I don't know. One part of me sees the logic in your actions because you were trapped, because you felt you had to do something to save us both. But another part of me, the part that is so angry, questions your values. Even your character. I know that sounds harsh."

"No. Of my own free will I chose to enter into something illegal and immoral. Worse, I rationalized my actions by deceiving myself that the end justified the means. It's easy to spout off about immaturity and lack of judgment, but greed and instant gratification were certainly a part of it. I can't deny that. Ben Forbes caught on to the fact that something wasn't kosher, and I'm sure he suspected I was obtaining funds illegally. When he wanted to talk, I was always on my way out, and when he finally managed to buttonhole me, I as much as told him to butt out. It was a serious falling out, and I can only hope to make amends."

He leaned in toward her. "But that can wait. Kelly, you haven't expressed your feelings, aside from your anger and disappointment. I wonder. Can you still love me?"

She detected nothing glib in his tone. His question was straightforward, his eyes conveying the depth of his concern. She sat for a moment, deep in thought, and then left her chair to sit next to him. "Larry, I haven't stopped loving you. If I haven't said it, I should have:

Thank God you're alive, that you coming back to us is a miracle, an incredible gift." She fell silent, struggling to maintain perspective, to disallow her emotions to override reason. When she was ready to continue, she avoided his eyes. "It's not that simple, about us, I mean; not that cut and dried."

"I can't blame you." He stared at her for a long moment, and then patted her hand. "I'd better go. I have a place not too far from here." He paused. "As I think about it, it might be a good idea to trade apartments."

"Because of Wilder? I don't think that's necessary." She explained her arrangement with Rick, her plan to move.

She'd caught something in his expression akin to distaste at the mention of Rick, but he signaled his approval, adding that for now it might be better if she didn't know his address. "But here's my phone number," he said.

She was placing his card on the coffee table when the phone rang. Kelly jumped up, hoping it wasn't her mother or Rick. Not at this moment.

It was Jason, sounding apologetic, wondering if by any chance Larry was there. He'd called him at home and didn't know where else to try. Again, he gave his apologies, but it was essential he speak with Larry.

"You're in luck," she said to Jason, bewildered, as she motioned Larry to the phone.

As they spoke, it was obvious to Kelly something major had occurred, and she watched, wide-eyed, as Larry responded in exclamations of shock and disbelief.

When he was off the phone, he took the chair Kelly had vacated, his expression grim.

"Larry, what is going on?"

"This detective I've been hearing about?"

"Cherney?"

"Yes, Cherney. It seems he met with Fern in Scottsdale to question her about Tom."

"He's still in Europe?"

"It turns out he was in Greece. Now Fern didn't know that, but on the morning of the detective's visit, she'd been notified that Tom had been reported missing." He paused and stared down at his hands.

"They found him?"

"They found his body—fished him out of the bay of this resort town where he'd been staying. It wasn't an accidental drowning. For one thing, he was called out to meet someone late at night at the marina, and not for a midnight swim. There's a clincher. Cherney has information that a police informant was an eyewitness to what occurred that night. It seems Tom, and—get this—Joseph Wilder boarded a yacht where this man was part of the crew. He says he saw Wilder slip a mickey into his mark's drink, and when the man was out of it, they left the marina, sailed out onto the bay, and dumped the victim overboard."

She shuddered. "That's awful! How grisly, even for Tom. But thank God for the police informant. His testimony could put Wilder away. And Larry, with Tom dead, you're off the hook about having to testify."

"That's entirely possible, though I am puzzled about something. The detective told Jason the FBI has had an interest in Tom for some time. In fact, the client Tom met with in Paris was an undercover agent."

"I'm surprised they hadn't made a move on him."

"I know. I don't understand. Unless they didn't have a strong enough case?" He shrugged and got to his feet. "Well, it appears Wilder's been arrested which puts you out of harm's way, thank God. It also means I can concentrate on getting back to work after I see my mother. And my sister. Fern will need all the support she can get."

"Good lord, yes. I feel so sorry for Fern and particularly for those children." She walked him to the door. "You'll be in Phoenix for how long?"

"A few days. Maybe a week." His hand on the doorknob, he paused. "I understand from Jason that you know I tried to communicate with you."

She forced a smile. "You should have picked a country with better mail service. Your letter never reached me."

"I agonized over that letter, for obvious reasons. On the other hand, with Scully and Wilder in the picture, maybe it was for the best that the letter was lost."

She nodded, her mood turning somber. "But to go all this time believing you were dead . . ."

He closed his eyes briefly, and then met her look straight-on. "The fact remains there shouldn't have been the need for a letter, for any of this. Oh, Kelly—" He looked away, and then focused on her once again, his expression a mixture of sadness and regret. "Well. I'll be on my way." He paused, but only for a moment, and then let himself out.

Kelly stood in the doorway until he was out of sight. Then, slowly, she closed her door and locked up.

The apartment retained the echo of their voices, but grayness settled over the room, like a dense fog blotting out the sun, rendering her aimless, adrift, and devoid of feeling. She knew she would replay, "I said, he said," over and over, but to what avail? The script was set; the actors had spoken of love, remorse, anger, and hurt, but they had failed, however, to produce a final act, the denouement.

As her thoughts turned to the uncertainties ahead, Kelly felt her lethargy lift, only to be replaced by a pervading sense of loss.

For the next few days Kelly spent her evenings reading scripts, writing in her journal . . . and waiting for the phone to ring.

When she'd finally told Rick about Larry's return, he'd stood glowering at her, before his scowl finally dissolved into an impish grin. "Well, babe," he'd said, "the next move is yours." Then he'd added, seriously, "Kelly, I think you know I care about you one hell of a lot, and I think it's safe to venture that you were warming up to me." At her solemn nod, he continued, "I'm hardly thrilled about where this leaves me, or either of us. It's frustrating as hell." Then, as his exasperation faded, his look became tender, and he took her hand. "It's up to you." He said it softly. "Only you can decide."

Only you can decide. The words tracked through her mind, ever-present, making her crazy. Especially tonight. In the five days since Larry had been here in the apartment, there'd been no word from him.

Not that she expected to hear from him while he was in Phoenix, or so she told herself.

But she had. She had expected Larry to call.

Since it was too early for bed, Kelly sat in front of the TV, her mind inattentive to the sitcom she viewed. She shut off the TV, but the silence made her more fidgety.

In her bedroom she examined her music library and decided she was in the mood for Debussy, something soft but not too lyrical. *Music to think by. No, to feel by,* she amended.

As the strings gave way to woodwinds, the oboe passage dreamy and reflective, she yielded to stillness within her, akin to serenity. The music evoked images of silvers and muted grays, swirling mists parting to reveal patches of pink—a wintery twilight at sea, a ship riding the swells, ghostly in the half-light. She could hear Larry's voice: "We'll sail off someday, maybe book passage on a freighter." And she could hear Vanessa: "I want so much for you to be happy."

Kelly bounded from her bed where she'd been half-reclining to grab her address book. With Audrey's number in hand—*please let him be there*—she was at her phone. At this moment, Larry could have been Attila the Hun or Jack the Ripper. All that mattered was to hear his voice.

"Kelly, it's good to hear from you." Larry sounded surprised, pleased.

She didn't mince words. "Larry, I miss you." At his silence she waited, her free hand clenched, fingers flexing, closing. "I want to be with you. Larry, I want us to be together."

"You're saying we can get back together?" It was as if her words finally registered.

"Yes. If that's what you want."

"My God, Kelly, of course that's what I want! I confess I'm stunned. I can't believe what I'm hearing."

"I can't believe what I've put us through. I was so engrossed in my own feelings, spinning around in circles, tripping over my emotions, that I developed myopia of the brain. I couldn't see beyond my own hurt."

"Oh, honey, you had every right." He paused. "I have to bring up something else, something very important to me."

His voice faded, and he seemed to withdraw from her; she strained to hear him, waiting, afraid of what might come next.

"How do I win back your respect?"

"You have my respect! You placed the blame squarely on your own shoulders. You didn't make excuses. And that takes courage. When I think of what you've been through, I want to bawl. Another confession: When you walked out of my apartment, a part of me went with you. I felt so alone, as if I were in mourning all over again."

"Kelly, honey, I wanted to call you, got as far as grabbing my cell phone, and then I thought, what do I say? And now, I can't even find the words to express my happiness. I'm beyond words. I'm simply overcome."

"I wish I could see you, touch you."

"You keep this up, and I'm going to melt into one big blob of elation."

"And you said you couldn't find the words?"

"I can find these words: I love you, Kelly. I will love you and cherish you forever."

"Now who's overwhelmed?" She wiped away a tear. Then, at his silence, she managed a shaky laugh. "You want to retract that last statement?"

"Hell, no, but I would certainly understand if you felt we should—uh, how can I put this—wait awhile?"

"You must be joking," she said, her voice a caress.

He laughed. "Race you to the airport? Seriously, my love, I'll try to arrive back in L.A. tomorrow."

"I can't wait!"

After they said their goodbyes, she wanted to submerge herself in music all over again. Only this time jubilant, soaring, celebratory music like the "Hallelujah Chorus," "Ode to Joy." Make it Christmas in June. Christmas! It was with a sense of awe that she realized she would celebrate the season with Larry. All the seasons, all the holidays for all the days of their lives. *The bride would never stand alone again.*

An hour later, when the phone rang, Kelly's lips still were carved into a smile. Was it Larry, calling to say goodnight?

It was Nadine.

"Well, you sound almost lyrical," her mother said.

"You can tell that much from 'hello'?"

"I can tell something is different about you."

"Mom, if I were a whirling dervish, I'd be levitating at this very moment." She went on to deliver a condensed version of what had transpired between herself and Larry, and to describe her joy at their impending reunion.

"I always liked Larry," Nadine said, "and deep down I hoped you two would get back together. I'm happy for you, truly thrilled."

She didn't sound thrilled. Plus, a late night call from Nadine usually signaled an outpouring of angst, along with expressions of self-reproach.

"Mom, I don't doubt that you're happy for Larry and me, but frankly I sense something's wrong."

"It does seem to be my practice to unload on you. This time I'm not calling about real or imagined slights or to indulge in neurotic fancies. Kelly, I'm worried about Steve. About two hours ago, when we were in the family room watching television, he received a phone call. He took it in the den, and after about forty minutes had gone by, I went to see what was going on. The door was closed, so I knocked and said, 'Steve, are you coming back to watch TV?' and he said, 'I'll be a few minutes. I want to finish something here.' So I went traipsing back to the family room. I waited, and I waited.

"Call it a gut feeling, but I knew something wasn't right. I went back to the den. The door was open, the lights out, and the room empty. I decided he'd gone up to our room. I couldn't find him there, nor in the bathroom and, to make a long story short, not in any other part of the house. So I checked the garage. Kelly, the car is gone. He's never just up and left without letting me know his plans."

"Did you look for a note?"

"Of course. And I questioned Kwon, but he was no help."

"It does seem strange."

"Oh, I know Steve could walk in any minute with a perfectly plausible explanation, except I can't think what it could possibly be."

"I don't blame you for being worried, but it's not as if he's missing." She thought about Tom Champion, but this wasn't the time to unfold that ugly tale. "No clues as to what might have led up to his taking off?"

"No, though come to think of it, he has seemed preoccupied. Even a bit moody. I wonder if someone demanded a meeting. It could be a matter of urgency, something that called for immediate attention."

"If Steve had been upset or angry, it's possible he didn't want to consult with you and get into an argument about leaving at that hour."

"Now that makes sense." Nadine was silent for a moment. "Well, dear one, we could spend the rest of the night second-guessing this situation, but I'm going to hang up so you can get some rest. Maybe I'll fix myself a good, stiff drink to calm my nerves. You know, Kelly, I always feel better after talking with you. And honey, I'm truly delighted that you and Larry are getting back together."

"Thanks, Mom. I wish things were happier for you. Call me if you need me. Any time. I don't care if it's during the night, at work, whenever."

When the phone rang at seven in the morning, Kelly answered with a sense of dread. Justifiably so, as it turned out. Steve was dead, a suicide. He'd been found in a downtown motel room, where he'd shot himself in the head using a .38 caliber revolver, registered in his name.

After a hurried telephone conversation with Larry, Kelly focused on making arrangements for a flight to San Francisco. Keeping her emotions in check, she packed an overnight bag and called for a taxi. Falling apart was not an option; nor could she dwell on the horror of Steve's suicide. All that mattered was getting to her mother.

When Kelly arrived at the Victorian, she was greeted by a woman she recognized from the dinner party, Jessica something. Others milled about. Police? Press? Undoubtedly business associates, as well. Kelly wanted to see her mother, and this woman seemed to understand, whisking Kelly down a back hall, as she explained that Nadine was sedated, that the doctor had just left.

Nadine in bed, eyes closed, looked drawn and gray. The chair next to the bed indicated that someone had maintained a vigil. Now it was Kelly's turn, and she was determined to sit all day, if necessary, to be there when her mother awoke.

Either Nadine had sensed someone's presence or the sedative hadn't fully taken effect, because seconds after Kelly was seated, her eyes fluttered open, focusing on her daughter. *Beautiful, violet eyes, now hauntingly sad,* Kelly thought.

"I'm glad you're here." The words came out thickly, but her voice was strong.

Kelly reached for her mother's hand, her cheeks wet with tears. "Mom, I love you very much. I want you to know I'll be here for as long as you need me. Larry, too. He'll be arriving later."

"There's a letter." Nadine gestured toward her desk.

"Please, don't try to talk. Get some rest."

"No, I want you to read it. You have to call someone. Turns out to be one hell of a mess. But I'll survive." Her voice was now a whisper. "Always have." She moistened her lips, but her eyelids were drooping . . . and then, it seemed too much of an effort to stay awake. She was out.

Kelly waited a moment, making sure her mother was asleep, and then, with a deep sigh, moved to her mother's desk. The letter, she supposed, would explain why her stepfather had taken his own life. She could only infer from Nadine's comment that Steve had been in big trouble. She wondered if business dealings had soured, leaving him financially ruined. Or worse, if he'd committed a crime, like embezzling funds from his bank. Hands shaking, she reached for the envelope.

It took her two readings to grasp fully the implications of the letter. She felt limp, as exhausted as if she had run the marathon, and for a moment she was almost envious of her mother who, at least for a while, had been granted a reprieve. She closed her eyes, conjuring up a likeness of her husband. *Larry, get here. I need you, I need you.*

With another deep sigh, she moved from the desk to stand by the bed. *And my mother needs me.* As Steve requested in his letter, she would make the phone call to John Livingston, Tom Champions's attorney.

A friend of Nadine's had described to Kelly her mother's ordeal; that Nadine had been up all night, had somehow made it through the morning hours, bolstered by friends rallying around her. But then as shock gave way to grief, she had deteriorated emotionally, the doctor had been called and, as Kelly related to Larry minutes after his arrival, her mother had been out all day and would probably sleep through the night, as well.

It was the dinner hour, and the doorbell had stopped ringing, the phones at last silent.

Kelly brought Larry into the family room, shutting the door after him. Finally, it was just the two of them, and they fell into each other's arms, holding on tightly to one another. But the moment was solemn rather than joyful.

"This wasn't how I pictured our reunion," Kelly said with a rueful smile as she led Larry to the couch.

"God, no, honey." They sat in silence and then Larry threw up his hands. "Why'd he do it? Does anyone know what in the hell made Steve take his life?"

Kelly fought tears as she thought about her mother. "Steve left something for Nadine: a letter I had to turn over to the police. In it, he expressed his love for my mother, for Vanessa and me, and said his years with Nadine were the happiest of his life." She paused.

"So then why—"

"Larry, he had a separate life. A criminal life. Does this sound familiar? Cash from drug proceeds laundered through various transactions both in the US and abroad? Steve and Tom Champion were partners in crime. Except that Steve called the shots."

"Oh, shit. Kelly, I had no idea."

"You weren't supposed to know. No one knew that Steve was the mastermind behind the operation. Only Tom knew. When I told Steve about Fern's discoveries, and then told him that you'd made it back and were prepared to go to the authorities, Tom Champion was as good as cooked. He might have succeeded in evading capture for a time, but if eventually he was to be apprehended . . . then what? Would he remain loyal to Steve or bring him down as well? In addition, Steve was furious with Tom for putting Scully and Wilder onto you. In the first place, he didn't want you hurt, and secondly, the whole scheme backfired, leading you to construct a plan that, if successful, would expose the operation. So for all of these reasons, he paid Wilder to eliminate Tom."

"Steve, a murderer?" Larry looked stricken, his expression registering disbelief.

"Maybe he looked upon it as good riddance?"

"Kelly, was all this in the letter? Did he simply up and decide he couldn't live with himself any longer?"

"No, to both questions. Some of the information came from another source: Tom's attorney in Phoenix, John Livingston. Steve said in his letter that it was urgent someone contact this man. Which I did. Talk about ironic, but it turns out Tom had given his attorney a letter, with instructions that it be opened only if something should happen to him, as in 'an untimely demise,' to quote the attorney."

"A confession?"

"And then some. Mr. Livingston told me Tom spelled out, chapter and verse, a detailed accounting of the money laundering operation, naming Steve Hanson as the man in charge. The envelope also contained a key to a safe deposit box that, according to Tom, would offer documented proof of Steve's involvement, including tapes of conversations between the two men. You get the picture. Mr. Livingston said he wanted the family to know about this before he went to the police with the information."

Larry said, "I told Jason that Tom left nothing to chance. I sure had that right. So the phone call Steve received before leaving the house was from the attorney?"

"Yes." She thought about Steve: the man she had loved and

admired. "I can imagine what a shock it was to Steve to have his whole world blow up, just like that. At any rate, John Livingston told Steve he'd checked out Tom's allegations, and that he had proof of Steve's criminal activities. He also told him he'd learned the FBI was on his case and was ready to pounce. Given all the evidence, Steve would undoubtedly be charged with conspiracy to commit murder. He was calling Steve before alerting the police because he wanted him to know that there was no need to bring harm upon anyone else, since it was over for him. He would give Steve twenty-four hours to put his affairs in order, and so on."

"Sounds as if he was giving him a choice: Break the news to his family and face the music, or bow out." Larry thought for a moment. "Honey, with a man of Steve's prominence, you can figure on wide newspaper coverage. Also, because of the letter, they'll want to question me." He took her hand. "There may or may not be big trouble ahead, but the notoriety—"

"Isn't going to make any difference."

"Aren't you being naive?"

"All right. So our theater attendance will soar. We'll be packing 'em in. Oh, sweetheart, I don't mean to make light of what's ahead. I realize you're implicated because of the letter; we have to accept that. But I'm sure the authorities will welcome your cooperation, and with Jason to see us through this, we have to hope for the best." She waited for his response, proud of her upbeat analysis, but Larry appeared locked in thought. "Larry, have you heard one word?"

"I was thinking about Steve, what he said about not wanting me hurt."

"He says he loved you like a son. Damn! What a waste. How can a man with his talents, who was so loving, become so warped?"

"Greed . . . the need to feel powerful. And you said it yourself. Some people like to live on the edge. It's in their blood."

She smiled. "You remember that?"

"Oh, baby, I remember every moment we were together." He raised her hand to his lips.

"I think," Kelly said, drawing him up with her, "the time has come to create some significant new moments. Starting with a drink on the terrace?"

It was balmy in the early evening, the sun hopscotching from building to building, bestowing pools of light that quickly evaporated into shadow.

They stood holding their drinks, looking at the Golden Gate Bridge in the distance, a still-vibrant entity against the fading light, a landmark of strength. And hope. Larry slipped his arm around her. "I owe you a honeymoon," he said.

"You did mention sailing off together."

"I did? Well, all right. We can do that."

"Someday," she said softly. But she was thinking of her mother, of what lay ahead for Nadine, of what she and Larry had yet to face. All the imponderables. She snuggled in closer to him. "I wouldn't change this moment for a gazillion bucks. Too bad we can't remain like this, suspended in time."

"You mean before the next storm strikes?"

"Oh, yes. On the other hand, we've already weathered a monster of a typhoon, so what are a few more squalls down the line?"

He smiled. "That's the spirit. When we're able to, like now, we seize the moment."

"Yes, we seize the moment, we grab on to the good parts, allow ourselves to be happy." She smiled up at Larry but in her heart she was saying, *Thank you, Vanessa!*

✐ *Epilogue* ✐

Los Angeles
February 15, 2006

*I*t was with a sense of satisfaction that Jason monitored the progress of his cocktail party. People mingled, drinks in hand. Conversation flowed, and the caterers soon would be laying out a spread, both lavish and costly.

The guests of honor hadn't yet arrived, but at some point in the evening, champagne would be served and glasses raised to toast Kelly and Larry in celebration of one year of marriage.

True, it had been a punishing year, but it was Jason's contention that if the couple could survive all that had befallen them, plus the trauma of a police and FBI investigation, they would undoubtedly remain bonded forever. At least Larry had avoided prosecution, and for that Jason could take some of the credit. Then, too, Larry had aided in his own defense, cooperating fully with the authorities who, when they heard his story, could only agree that he had seen the error of his ways. Also, it hadn't hurt Larry's case that he'd been the target of professional killers.

Thankfully, Wilder was out of commission, languishing in a Greek prison, awaiting trial. As for Scully, if anyone knew the scoop on that character, it would be Robert Cherney. Like it or not, the detective was about to be cornered at the hors d'oeuvre table.

He started over to him, pausing along the way to chat with several people, at the same time observing the detective out of the corner of his eye. He'd brought a date, a pretty little thing which, Jason decided, was all to the good. It wouldn't do, especially on this evening, to have Robert making goo-goo eyes at Kelly. Though to be fair, Cherney might not have acknowledged his crush on Kelly, even to himself.

"Jason, hello!" Cherney smiled broadly. "Great party. And what a place you have. Carol and I think your home is really spectacular."

They're a team, Jason thought as he responded in an appropriate manner. "Uh, Carol," he said, giving her a warm smile, "would you forgive me if a brought up a small matter of business?" He didn't wait for her response but came right to the point. "Robert, I haven't heard a word about Max Scully. Did he crawl under a rock for the duration of the winter, or is he expanding his already ample waistline on macaroni and cheese à la San Quentin?"

"We haven't put him away yet, but we're almost ready to haul him in. Remember that dossier on him that you let me take? I'd noticed a name, Dawn Wilcox, on the personal data page. It rang a bell. Turns out she was his first wife. It also turns out, and this is where I'd heard the name, before she married Scully she was part of a high-class call-girl ring that caters to underworld figures and even some millionaire executives. Only now, Dawn Wilcox runs this ring."

"The Madame?" Jason asked, noting that Carol was clinging to Cherney's every word in wide-eyed fascination.

Cherney nodded. "Here's where it gets interesting. She's provided information to the police that led to the prosecution of a number of high profile criminal cases. Information garnered through 'pillow talk', shall we say? In any case, we asked her to contact Scully and arrange to meet for old time's sake. He took the bait, shot off his mouth, but declined to get specific. That came later, after she'd fixed him up with one of the girls. So we do have a case. Granted, the way we're going about it is admittedly unorthodox but—"

"Excuse me. I'd like to hear more," Jason looked back at his door, "but I think some people are arriving. In fact, it's our guests of honor. *" Good,* was his happy thought. *They've brought Nadine.*

Smiles, hugs, and handshakes abounded, with Kelly and Larry emphatic in their thanks and appreciation of Jason's efforts, and Nadine voicing her admiration as she took in her surroundings.

When coats were doffed and closeted, Jason led the threesome to the bar to place their orders. While they waited for their drinks, several guests, including Ben Forbes, approached the anniversary couple to exchange greetings and offer congratulations.

Jason could have purred at how well his party was progressing. In particular, he was pleased to witness the camaraderie between Ben and Larry, a sure sign the reconciliation had taken.

As the guests moved away from the bar, Jason decided it was time to check with the kitchen. Before he could move in that direction, however, he felt a tug at his arm. It was Kelly.

"Jason, I'm so sorry we were late. Problems cropped up at the Playhouse—glitches with the lighting and costuming—and with the show opening next week, everyone's in a panic."

"I understand you're directing this one."

"My first professional attempt, and do I miss Rick! I guess I didn't tell you, he's in New York. Remember the play I was in last April, the original that everyone was excited about? Sure enough, Broadway did beckon, and Rick is currently huddling with a New York producer." She showed him her crossed fingers.

"So everybody's happy."

"Most of us, yes." She grew thoughtful. "Nadine has had it pretty rough; the complications regarding the estate are mind-boggling, as well as emotional issues. But she's toughing it out. It's Fern I'm concerned about. After being so strong for the children, she fell apart, emotionally and physically. However, she's on medication for depression, and with Audrey's help, she's doing better in every way. We're trying to get Fern to put her talents to use, maybe take some courses in interior design or check out merchandising as a career. She'd make a terrific buyer. We've even got Nadine on her case."

"Speaking of your mother, I must say she's looking well, if somewhat thinner."

"With all the anguish she's had to endure, there's been one bright spot. Vanessa delivered a healthy, beautiful grandchild: a baby girl."

"I must congratulate Nadine."

Kelly smiled. "She'd like that, but please don't emphasize the 'grandmother' part, okay?"

He looked up at that moment to focus on the lady in question. She'd been saying something to her son-in-law, and then turned her head in his direction. Their eyes met. He nodded slightly, maintaining eye contact.

Nadine was the first to lower her eyes, but he caught the faint smile before she presented her profile.

He excused himself to Kelly and started in Nadine's direction. Grandmother? He smiled. Banish the thought.

The End.

About the Author

A native Californian, Jackie Ullerich was born in Los Angeles, grew up in San Diego and graduated with honors from UCLA, earning a secondary teaching credential in theater arts and English. She also attained Master Teacher status, qualifying her to train and supervise student teachers at the high school level.

Jackie left the classroom for the world stage to travel and live in a variety of places, both in the U.S. and overseas, with her Air Force husband. Her years of living in Turkey and Greece coincided with changes in government, including tanks in the streets. But hostile environments were offset by exploration of ancient cultures and the colorful tapestries of contemporary life.

Of her many experiences, teaching English as a foreign language at the Turkish War College in Ankara, was an adventure in itself. While her novels reflect first-hand knowledge of exotic and historic locals, California provides a backdrop for most of her writing.

Presently, Jackie and her retired Air Force JAG husband reside in Palm Desert, California, where her husband golfs while Jackie writes.

CPSIA information can be obtained at www.ICGtesting.com
Printed in the USA
LVOW100021070313

323097LV00009B/220/P

9 781936 587698